SOMEONE KNOWS

Valerie was closing her purse when her cell phone rang. She flipped the lid open to check the caller ID, but didn't recognize the number. She pressed talk.

"This is Valerie."

"And this is . . . guess who-ooo?" The reply came in a singsong voice that Valerie didn't recognize.

"What? Who are you calling?"

"I'm calling you, Caroline."

Caroline! Pure shock sliced through Valerie with the speed of a laser. "Who is this?"

"Someone who knows . . . Caroline."

Panic swirled inside her. "You have the wrong number."

The caller gave a low chuckle. "I don't think so."

"What do you want?" she demanded, sounding desperate even to herself.

"All in good time, Caroline." A tiny pause, then slyly, "I love your place. So . . . sophisticated."

Valerie's heart stopped. "How did you get inside? How?"

"Piece o'cake." Another pause, then the caller's voice hardened, the playfulness dropped. "Now it's time to remind you again, Caroline, that I'm still out here . . . and I'm not leaving."

"What do you want from me?"

"What do I want, Caroline? I guess we can just call it . . . payback."

Mae Richter
183 McKnight Rd. N Apt. 209
Saint Paul, MN 55119-6641

Books by Karen Young

KISS AND KILL

SOMEONE KNOWS

Published by Kensington Publishing Corp.

SOMEONE KNOWS

KAREN YOUNG

ZEBRA BOOKS
KENSINGTON PUBLISHING CORP.
http://www.kensingtonbooks.com

ZEBRA BOOKS are published by

Kensington Publishing Corp.
850 Third Avenue
New York, NY 10022

All Kensington titles, imprints and distributed lines are available at special quantity discounts for bulk purchases for sales promotion, premiums, fund-raising, educational or institutional use.

Special book excerpts or customized printings can also be created to fit specific needs. For details, write or phone the office of the Kensington Special Sales Manager: Kensington Publishing Corp., 850 Third Avenue, New York, NY 10022. Attn. Special Sales Department. Phone: 1-800-221-2647.

Zebra and the Z logo Reg. U.S. Pat. & TM Off.

First Printing: March 2002
10 9 8 7 6 5 4 3 2 1

Printed in the United States of America

CHAPTER ONE

Valerie Olivier-Long accepted a glass of wine, avoided the eye of a recently unemployed art director angling for a job, and headed directly across the ballroom floor of the Four Seasons Hotel. Around her, cameras flashed, celebrities laughed, posed, preened. The event was the National Magazine Award ceremony. *Vanity Fair* had won, not *Panache*. No surprise, considering the inner chaos at the magazine, but she'd come tonight with a scrap of hope that *Panache* might, just might, defy the odds.

Being a bit superstitious, Valerie thought she probably shouldn't have worn the cat pin. Forget how perfect it looked perched on the shoulder of her black dress, its diamond eyes twinkling—black cats meant bad luck.

She smiled as she approached her friend, Roxanne Fielding, former supermodel turned photographer. "Having fun yet?" she asked.

"About as much as you," Roxanne replied, arching

one elegant eyebrow. She raised the camera in her hands and focused on Valerie. "Smile."

Flash. "Don't waste film on me, Rox. Publishing's heavy hitters are here tonight as well as a ton of celebrities. I saw Gwyneth Paltrow and Nic Cage a few minutes ago."

"Together?"

"No, silly. Although I suppose that would be news. Get shots of them and anybody else who's somebody and we'll do a feature on this event in the next issue. That'll show we're not sore losers."

With the camera still focused on Valerie's face, Roxanne smiled. "Do you ever quit working?"

"Do you?" A couple of years ago as Roxanne's modeling career declined, she'd picked up a camera and found her true calling. Her photographs could be riveting, although an event such as this hardly posed much of a challenge. Still, it was the kind of thing the public gobbled up. And the stuff that sold copies of *Panache*.

"I've shot at least a dozen rolls and there's some good stuff. I swear I'll offer them to *Talk* if Liz doesn't pay me decently."

"Over my dead body."

Roxanne lowered the Nikon and began removing a film cartridge. "Speaking of the dead, wasn't that Wayne Coulter I saw breathing hard on you a few minutes ago?"

Valerie laughed softly without taking offense. Dr. Wayne Coulter was the cardiovascular surgeon she'd been seeing fairly often lately, but in spite of Wayne's increasing insistence, she was reluctant to take the relationship to the next level. She wasn't sure why she was holding out. He was attractive, well mannered, extremely eligible, and didn't seem to have any obvious objectionable habits. "He invited me to a house party at his place in the Hamptons, but I think I'll pass. I'm just not interested in a sexual relationship right now."

"Or at any other time since your divorce."

Valerie's smile was wry. "And who is your date tonight, Rox?" Roxanne was even less inclined to a serious commitment than Valerie.

"I've got one, which is more than you can say." The reloading done, Roxanne tucked the cartridge in a shoulder bag. "I'm with a friend of Eric's."

"Oh? Anyone interesting?"

"Actually, yes. Very interesting." Roxanne scanned the crowd, searching for her date. "I'd introduce you, but it's impossible to keep track of anybody in this crowd."

Roxanne's sexual partners seemed to change almost daily, so it was impossible to keep her current love life straight. If one of Roxanne's relationships developed, Valerie was sure to hear about it from Eric Johns, her personal assistant.

"Maybe later you can join us," Roxanne said. "We're planning to—"

"Valerie!" A petite redhead swerved close and quickly air-kissed Valerie's cheek. She made a little moue of sympathy. "That award should be yours. Next time, darling . . ." Waving cheerily, she plowed on toward the bar.

"Speaking of the crowd, have you seen Liz?" Roxanne asked as a photographer from another of *Panache*'s arch rivals, *Talk*, took a shot of Valerie, then gave a casual high-five and moved on to Rox.

"No, I haven't, have you?"

"She's not here."

"I can't imagine why." Liz Chopin was *Panache*'s editor-in-chief. She micromanaged every facet of the magazine's operation, so it was extremely unusual for her to miss an event as important as the NMA ceremony. "It must be something personal, otherwise, she'd be here."

Roxanne lifted the camera to get a shot of Tina Brown talking with an executive of Miramax. "Liz not being here is more than odd, it's positively fateful. I thought you might have some scoop."

"I haven't a clue." Which was true. She and Liz were friends, but she wasn't blind to the problems at the magazine stemming from Liz's management style. Valerie, as senior features editor, was careful to say nothing, but lately, there were troubling internal signs. More and more decisions were delayed, features were sidelined awaiting approval, missed opportunities were piling up. More maddening to Valerie was Liz's tendency to avoid controversial topics, thus earning for *Panache* a reputation for mediocrity. It was especially frustrating since Valerie was brimming over with ideas that never saw the light of day. So far, however, Hal Kurtz, chairman and CEO of the Kurtz-Whitman media empire, showed no sign of recognizing Liz's shortcomings.

"My money says our editor and friend is living on borrowed time," Roxanne continued as she focused the lens on Christopher Hitchins and Dominick Dunne chatting beside a potted palm. She took the shot, then lowered the camera to fiddle with an attachment. "I know you like her, Val, but she's a drag on the magazine. Hal Kurtz needs to find the balls to fire her before it's too late to breathe new life into the magazine. Then the door would be open to someone new—such as yourself—to change its image."

"Thanks, Rox, but I don't see that happening anytime soon," Valerie said dryly. She'd like to capture the top spot at the magazine, but she didn't want to see Liz terminated.

"Then you'll be the only one surprised when it does."

"And I do have a date tonight," Valerie said, eager to change the subject.

"Attending the awards event with the boss isn't a date." Roxanne looked beyond her where Hal Kurtz stood with a couple of publishing's heavy hitters. "But I suppose that explains why he's been craning his neck in this direction for the past few minutes. He looks like a pro sports referee waving at you like that."

Valerie gave her wineglass to a passing waiter. "He must be ready to leave. He said something about dinner at Le Cirque later."

"Without Liz?"

"Maybe she'll meet us there." Valerie leaned forward and kissed Roxanne on the cheek. "See you Monday."

Valerie made her way through the glitzy crowd toward Hal. Meeting her gaze, he signaled with a nod of his head that he was indeed ready to leave. Now that it was time to go, she realized she was hungry, not having eaten anything all day except an apple and a yogurt Eric had plunked in front of her during a conference call at two o'clock in the afternoon. Dinner at Le Cirque would be nice.

"Let's get out of here," Hal said as she approached. Then he turned to his companion, a tall man with broad shoulders and cool gray eyes who looked as if he'd been born to wear a tux. "You've met Jordan Case, haven't you?"

Valerie's heart skipped a beat. Any appetite she had died. Jordan Case. Even with losing out to *Vanity Fair*, Valerie had managed to find some pleasure in this event until now.

Not waiting for her reply, Hal nudged her through the crowd. "My limo's out front. I've invited Jordan to join us."

Worse yet. *Why?* For Hal's benefit, Valerie and Jordan exchanged smiles, hers tight, his bland.

"He mentioned the feature in last month's *Panache* about the rise of investment scams on the Internet," Hal said. "I told him the feature was your idea. There's Franklin," he said, spotting his chauffeur, and still clutching her elbow, he guided her through the hotel's entrance to the car. Once the three of them were inside, Valerie avoided looking directly at Jordan.

"How've you been, Valerie?" He was coolly polite.

"Very well. Thanks." Much better than the last time she'd seen him. "You?"

"Great. Fine."

Seated opposite them, Hal crossed his legs and surveyed them, his fingers linked around one knee. "You two aren't still sulking over that business with the special projects editor, are you? What was her name? Jennifer? Jocelyn?"

"Jacquelyn," Valerie said shortly.

"I never sulk," said Jordan, his tone faintly mocking.

Suggesting that she did? Valerie struggled to speak without revealing an intense desire to knock the smile off his face and into next week. "Why would you sulk? It was no inconvenience to you having Jackie walk off the job in the middle of a deadline." Jordan had scoured New York publishing to find the best special projects editor to add to the staff of his fledgling magazine, *Access*, settling finally on Jacquelyn Pearson. Then he'd coolly offered her obscenely more than what she was making at *Panache*. It had been hellish trying to finish that issue without her. In fact, it had been Valerie who'd stepped into the breach, doing her job and Jackie's.

"Still expecting loyalty from your employees in this business, are you?" Jordan taunted.

She stared at him then in profound distaste, wishing her boss weren't watching and listening so avidly. Of course, Hal couldn't know that the incident with Jacquelyn was only the final encounter Valerie had had with

Jordan. By the time he had gotten around to stealing Jackie, she'd already personally experienced his ruthlessness. But thankfully no one knew anything about that except Jordan and her, and she intended it to stay that way.

"I hope the level of hostility I'm feeling doesn't set a tone for the future," Hal said, and gazed out the window as the limo crawled up Madison. "It won't make the jobs I've got in mind for either of you easy."

Valerie looked at Jordan, but found nothing in his expression to explain Hal's statement. Hal still stared out the window, silent now. She'd have to wait until they got inside the restaurant to find out what was going on.

Her bewilderment increased when Hal ordered champagne as soon as they were seated. What was going on? If Jordan weren't present, she would have asked Hal outright. And where was Liz?

There was a muted pop as the bottle of champagne was uncorked. "Liz has tendered her resignation," Hal said, as if reading her thoughts.

Valerie blinked. She looked at Jordan, who sat relaxed, watching her and toying with the stem of his glass. Hal waited until the waiter left them, then added, "She feels her usefulness to the magazine has ended. She'll be pursuing other interests."

Valerie had argued with Liz over a feature only moments before leaving the office that day. Liz hadn't acted like an editor who was quitting.

"You seem surprised," Hal said.

"Yes." And chilled. Liz would never have walked away willingly. She was blind to her shortcomings as an editor. Valerie had tried every way she knew to persuade Liz to move away from the stuffy issues that characterized her work. She'd longed to broaden the appeal of the magazine, but Liz had stubbornly refused anything hint-

ing at innovation or risk. Still, to get the ax out of the
blue was . . . devastating. Valerie could only imagine
how shattering it would be. And humiliating. Poor Liz.

"I wish her well," she said quietly.

"Of course. Now . . ." Hal lifted his glass. "How would
you feel taking over as editor of *Panache?*"

Her mouth dropped. How would she feel? Stunned.
Flattered. Thrilled. Almost dizzy with delight. Only an
hour ago, she'd been thinking what she would do in
Liz's place. Now she was being offered a chance to try
out her ideas. It was a dream come true.

"It's yours if you want it," Hal said.

She glanced at Jordan and wondered why he was here.
He was certainly no friend of hers. A closer look told
her the offer was not news to him. What did he have to
do with *Panache?* With Kurtz-Whitman, for that matter?
Access magazine hadn't been a K-W enterprise.

"I think Hal's waiting for a yes or a no," Jordan said
in that low, I-know-everything tone.

Valerie quickly turned back to Hal. "I'm just taken
by surprise, Hal. I had no idea that Liz was leaving. And
of course I'd feel honored to take over."

"Then you've got the job." Hal smiled benevolently
and clinked his glass against hers.

"You probably have some ideas about changing
things," Jordan said when they'd finished their toast.

"Is that so unusual?" She wondered again why it was
any of his business what she'd do at the magazine.

"Not unusual at all. Maybe you'd care to share a few
of those ideas with us."

"Perhaps I should explain Jordan's interest," Hal
said. "I've done some reorganization across the board.
Not only will there be some changes at *Panache,* but I've
done the same thing at Kurtz-Whitman. I believe new
ideas and new approaches at the top will strengthen my

whole publishing organization. With that in mind, I've hired Jordan to help make that happen. He'll be associate publisher and will answer directly to me. I hope you two will work well together."

"We'll be fine, Hal," Jordan said, not looking at Valerie.

"Yes, well . . ." Hal shifted to the left to allow the waiter to place a salad in front of him. "I didn't get that impression in the car, but I'm going to give you both the benefit of the doubt and see how it goes."

"Exactly what form will Jordan's authority take in relation to my authority at *Panache*?" Valerie asked carefully, not looking at Jordan. She suspected he was enjoying her dismay.

"I don't think he'll cramp your style, Valerie." Hal spread herb butter liberally on a crust of bread. "But he'll have final say on all publications under the K-W umbrella, *Panache* included. This includes—if he chooses to get involved—content, layout, hiring and firing, even article assignments."

She felt her heart sink. It was worse than she thought. "Do you realize what that means, Hal? He's essentially the editor, not me."

"Only if he believes you're taking *Panache* in a questionable direction." He chewed the crusty bread while she fumed. "Do you find the terms of the job unacceptable?"

"I find the terms uncomfortable," she said, proceeding with caution. Everything she'd worked for was almost in her grasp. A knee-jerk reaction to Jordan would jeopardize everything. "I would be less than honest to say otherwise. But we're both professionals, and as Jordan says, we'll be fine."

"Good, good." Hal motioned for more champagne. "Now, let's drink to a smooth transition, both at K-W and at *Panache,* and to a friendly relationship developing between the both of you."

Valerie only pretended to drink.

It was difficult not to pick up the phone and call Sara the minute Valerie got home and tell her the news. But it was after midnight and nobody welcomed a call at that hour, no matter what the occasion, not even a daughter. Still, she was tempted. It was such a delicious thing. Editor of *Panache.*

Success, however, had come at a high price. She'd spent eight long years at the magazine, working her way through a variety of jobs, neglecting her marriage, shortchanging Sara when her workdays sometimes lasted ten, twelve hours, even more at times of crucial deadlines. No surprise, then, that her marriage had been a casualty of her ambition, ending after only four years. Andrew Long had finally walked out complaining that she had only two passions in life—her daughter, Sara, and *Panache.* It was one thing, he told her, to play second fiddle to a daughter, but no man should be expected to tolerate coming in third after a magazine. Once he was gone, she focused even more passionately on getting to the top in the publishing world.

Now she was editor of *Panache.*

The only other person in her life who would under-stand what that meant was Janine Livaudais. But her old friend was now lost in the fog of Alzheimer's. Janine no longer recognized her or Sara after devoting over twenty years of her life to them. She had been Valerie's mainstay, capable of doing everything—driving, market-ing, shopping, managing their home—and then her brain had simply shut down. Valerie still had difficulty accepting the injustice of it. Janine, who'd once been a nun, was Valerie's mother, not in blood, but in every other sense of the word; she was the only grandmother Sara had ever known. The hole she left in their lives would never be filled, and tonight that loss was especially bitter.

With a sigh, she undressed and went to get her nightgown in the bathroom. She would have to save her news until tomorrow. She hoped Sara would be free for lunch. Her nightgown, usually behind the door, wasn't there. She stood looking about wondering if she, too, was getting forgetful. Stress, she decided with a shrug, thinking she must have tossed it in the laundry. Too many deadlines and too little down time.

Then she spotted the gown draped over the back of the chaise near her bed. Picking it up, she saw the delicate lace bodice was torn. How on earth had that happened without her knowing it? Had she torn it in her sleep last night? But surely she would have noticed. Or maybe Maria, who cleaned for her, had done it. But usually, if Maria damaged something, she left an apologetic note. However it had happened, it was ruined now, although how she could have missed seeing it as she took it off this morning was a mystery.

At the armoire, she chose another nightgown, her head buzzing with plans to make *Panache* the talk of the publishing world. Given half a chance, she believed she could breathe new life into the magazine and change its stodgy image. It remained yet to be seen whether Jordan Case would be a problem.

In bed finally, she fell asleep and dreamed . . . not of *Panache*, but of Jordan Case.

CHAPTER TWO

From the moment Janine had awakened that morning, she'd known it was going to be one of those days when nothing made sense. When she wouldn't be able to hold on to a thought. Or retrieve a memory. Or speak a name even though it danced somewhere out there, a scant hair's breadth beyond her reach. This vicious brain disease, how she loathed it. She, who'd memorized vast amounts of the Bible, whose mental acuity had enthralled students and colleagues alike in those years when she'd been a teacher, could no longer recall what day it was. She, who'd devoured the classics in her early teens, could not even read now. She could, however, still remember her own name.

"Sister Janine Livaudais." She whispered it softly.

Her name was Sister Janine Livaudais. Yes. Oh, but wait. She touched her forehead, her fingers trembling with age and Alzheimer's. She had rejected her calling. She wasn't a nun anymore, was she? Valerie reminded her of that every time she came to visit.

Valerie! A name. See, she could still remember the important things and people . . . sometimes. She turned in her wheelchair to study the collection of photographs on a table nearby. The pictures served as prompts to her failing memory. Valerie, yes. But who was that young woman standing beside her? She was supposed to know. She struggled to find a name. And wasn't there a baby? Oh, God. Closing her eyes, she tried conjuring up a firm memory, but it was like grasping at smoke. Her brain seemed smothered, covered with a veil of confusion.

Now the fear came. She was old, addled, useless, so much trouble that she worried they would tire of driving out to see her. Valerie was so busy. Sara, too. Oh, another name. Her precious Sara. But how long before the effort of visiting became too much for both of them?

"Sister Janine?"

Janine turned to see a visitor entering her room. Did she know this person? She managed a smile, hoping to hide her confusion until recognition came to her.

"I brought you something." Her visitor placed a box of chocolates in her hands before taking a seat in the small settee. "And how are you getting along here at Rose Haven?"

"Very well, thank you." She stared intently at her guest, willing her diseased brain to work. Blue eyes. A nice smile. Clothes that looked quite expensive. The chocolates certainly were of the highest quality. Who? Who? Who? Giving herself time, she gestured to the small bedside table. "I have fresh coffee in that . . ." Oh, lord, what did one call that thing?

"The thermos?" Her guest rose, reached for the jug and poured coffee into two cups, then carefully set Janine's within easy reach of her wheelchair before settling back, still smiling. "Hmm, you people from New

Orleans really know how to brew coffee. How did you manage to train the staff here?"

Janine frowned. "I think Valerie—"

"Valerie." Her guest's smile changed. "She would have connections in New Orleans, wouldn't she?"

Janine's gaze went to the window, where the branches of an elm spread naked and icy against a gray sky. "This isn't New Orleans, is it?"

"You're in New York now, Sister."

"Yes, yes. New York."

"Speaking of Valerie . . ." Her guest withdrew a large manila envelope from a briefcase. "This is for her. I'll just leave it with you until her next visit." That smile again as the envelope was laid on the table. "She comes faithfully, doesn't she?"

"She's very good to me."

"Well, she definitely should be. After all you've done for her. And Sara."

"Yes, Sara, too."

"Payback?"

"Pardon?"

A short laugh. "Give them both my best, will you?" At the door, her guest turned back. "Have a nice day, Sister."

Janine sat feeling oddly unsettled. Usually she was cheered by a visit, but somehow . . . She took a pen and small yellow tablet from the table. With the pen in her hand, she stared blankly at the notepad, forgetting what it was she had planned to write down. Things got away from her so quickly now.

The door opened abruptly and an aide came into the room rolling a cart bearing an array of medications. "And how's the Sister this morning?" She cheerfully plucked a pill from the tray, filled a glass with water from the sink, then waited while Janine obediently took the pill and drank a little to wash it down.

"What's this?" Spotting the box of Godiva, the aide made a little sound of disapproval, then turned and wagged a finger at Janine. "I don't know how this candy got here, Sister, but you know the rules. No sweets before meals."

"I'm sorry," Janine whispered, watching as the aide placed the Godiva on the lower shelf of the medications cart. Rules. There were so many she couldn't remember them all. No sweets before meals. She'd write it down. But writing was so difficult now. Her fingers could barely manage the letters even if she recalled what she needed to write.

"My word, where did this package come from?" With the manila envelope in her hands, the aide gave Janine a stern look. "It's addressed to Valerie. Has she been here this morning? Did she forget and leave it behind?" Looking around, she discovered the used coffee cups. Making more fussy noises, she took them to the sink and rinsed them, then placed them with a thump on a paper towel. "Really, your visitors should show more consideration, Janine. I'm surprised, you being an ex-nun. How much effort does it take to rinse a coffee cup? Isn't it enough that we make a thermos available for guests?"

Drying her hands on a fresh towel, the aide went again to her cart and started toward the door. "I'll just take this and hold it for Ms. Olivier-Long until her next visit. And I'll remind her then that she really must respect the rules. Guests should sign in and out, no matter who they are."

Janine was unaware of the aide leaving, having lapsed into a dreamy state, which her ravaged brain still thankfully managed to conjure up . . . sometimes. In that state, her body wasn't quite so old, her mind was razor-sharp, and she and her life had value and meaning. In that state Valerie appeared. And Sara. Happy memories.

Resist the dark ones.

Folding thin, blue-veined hands in her lap, she held fast to the images until the disease crept in again, ever greedy like the aide confiscating her chocolates, and stole even her memories.

CHAPTER THREE

Valerie met Sara at Sassafras for brunch the next day. She wanted to pick her up at her apartment, but Sara insisted on meeting her at the tea room instead. "My roommate likes to sleep in on Sunday, Mom," she said, slipping breathlessly into a chair after being shown to Valerie's table by the waiter. She was fifteen minutes late. "You know how it is."

Valerie asked the waiter to pour Sara a mimosa and sparkling water for herself. "I hope your roommate isn't having men in overnight," she said after he'd walked away.

"Is this a special occasion?" Sara asked, eyeing the mimosa.

Sara's evasion probably meant the roommate was involved with someone. Valerie decided not to press her for an answer about the young woman, whom she'd never met and whose morals she had no inclination to criticize. These days, she did nothing to further strain her relationship with Sara. Thankfully, the one thing she didn't have to worry about was Sara succumbing to the temptation to behave irresponsibly with a man, not after Charlie. She lifted her glass, allowing her smile to bloom. "Actually, I am celebrating."

Sara's face lit up with interest as she picked up her glass. "What's up? Tell me."

"You're speaking to the new editor of *Panache* magazine."

"Mom! You're kidding! Are you serious?" Her blue eyes widened. "What happened to Liz?"

"Can we toast my success before we discuss Liz?"

"Oops, sorry." Smiling, Sara clinked her glass to her mother's. "Congratulations, Mom. You'll be great in the job. You'll knock 'em dead." She took a tiny sip of her drink. "And *Panache* will win that award next year, wait and see."

"Whoa, I'll need a little more time than that." But she was grinning as much from pleasure in the telling as from seeing Sara smiling and happy.

"Okay, two years. But that award's gonna hang in your office then, count on it."

"Thank you, darling," Valerie said softly, enjoying Sara's joy. Not too long ago, her smile had been a rarity. Three years ago, her daughter had slipped into a deep depression brought on by a miscarriage and a broken relationship. Now she seemed to have her life back on track again. Valerie hoped Sara's joy wasn't an act just to please her. Maybe Sara was at last getting beyond the pain and loss that had nearly overwhelmed her.

Sara leaned forward. "So, tell me everything. What happened to Liz?"

"I'm not sure. Hal just said she'd resigned as of yesterday. It was sudden, I know that, because Liz and I were discussing a feature scheduled for the May issue just before quitting time. I thought it odd when she wasn't at the awards dinner, but to say I was stunned to learn she was gone is an understatement."

Sara shook her head in wonder. "It'll be a challenge just to survive in a job like that, Mom. Are you sure you're up for it?"

Valerie smiled. "No, but it never occurred to me to refuse."

Sara lifted her glass again. "Then go for it!"

The waiter appeared with their chicken salads. Valerie fiddled with her silver until they were alone again. She picked up her fork, then changed her mind and set it down again. Sara looked at her questioningly. "They say that nothing's perfect," Valerie said, "and it certainly applies here. There's a major fly in the ointment, Sara."

"What, you're not getting a huge raise?"

"No, I am getting a huge raise, but I don't have complete authority at the magazine. *Panache* falls under the Kurtz-Whitman umbrella, you know. It seems that Hal Kurtz doesn't quite trust me to turn things around on my own. Someone from the corporate office will be breathing down my neck. He could step in, if he's so inclined, and override my decisions."

"Uh-oh."

"Right. You'll never guess who it is."

"I won't?"

"It's Jordan Case."

Sara's face went completely blank. She glanced down at her plate. Then she reached for her glass, but missed and it tipped over, flooding her plate with mimosa. With a sharp cry, she jerked backward. "Shit, look what I've done!" With her napkin, she quickly mopped some of the liquid before it dripped into her lap. She managed a smile. "Haven't done that in a long time, huh, Mom?"

"I knew you'd be upset." Valerie waited while the waiter deftly removed Sara's plate and glass. "So was I.

Hal saw my reaction and made it clear Jordan was part of the deal. I could refuse the job if I didn't like it.''

"Mr. Case is okay, Mom. It's Charlie you hate."

"You think I'm unreasonable to object to working with Jordan Case?"

"Just because Mr. Case is Charlie's father is no reason for you to feel . . . uncomfortable if you have to work with him."

"I don't hate Charlie."

Sara simply looked at her.

Valerie sipped water. "It's just that I find it hard to forgive him for hurting you. And I've always felt that if Jordan had stayed out of it, things might have been different. Have you forgotten how he said the two of you would get married over his dead body?"

"I don't think he really meant that, Mom."

Valerie set her glass down hard. "You were pregnant, Sara," she said, her tone low, angry. "I know the two of you weren't married, but it takes two and I still find it unforgivable that Jordan assumed such a pigheaded attitude when the situation called for some understanding, some tolerance. He behaved as if his precious son was a victim of a scheming little hussy. How can you say he didn't mean it?"

"He was quoting statistics, Mom. He was worried about Charlie's future. I was only eighteen and Charlie was twenty-one. He had another year to finish college. I'd only finished my freshman year. Mr. Case's reaction was understandable. It would have been hard. Most marriages begun under those circumstances do fail. I think he would have come around eventually."

"Well, we'll never know, will we?" Sara's tolerance toward Jordan puzzled Valerie. She remembered only too well Sara's devastation over her potential father-in-law's disapproval. In fact, he'd been so intimidating that Valerie was convinced the stress had contributed to Sara's miscarriage. The doctor had dismissed that notion, but she still had her opinion.

The waiter returned with a fresh salad and drink for Sara. "Here you are, miss."

"Thank you." Sara picked up her fork. "Sorry about that, Mom. I guess I was just surprised to hear that Mr. Case, of all people, is back in your life. But don't worry, you're both professionals."

"Maybe so . . ." Valerie pointed her fork at Sara. "But he's still an arrogant, overbearing ass. We'll never see eye to eye."

"Never say never, Mom." With a tiny smile, Sara took a sip of her drink. "You two might find you have more in common than you ever dreamed."

Valerie actually breathed a bit easier as she reached midweek in her new position at the magazine and there had been no sign of Jordan Case. Maybe he wasn't going to be a problem after all, she thought, sifting through the stack of pink phone messages that Eric Johns had placed in front of her. On Monday morning, she'd quickly tackled the problem of a personal staff and Eric had been her first appointment. He'd been her personal assistant for two years and she openly admitted relying on him to handle administrative matters and the niggling details that could drive a manager crazy. She did not micromanage and had watched other talented executives' careers tank for lack of a good assistant like Eric. Now he stood waiting for her to listen while he ran through her appointments for the day. "Okay, what've I got, Eric?"

He consulted his yellow notepad. "A ten o'clock with Suzy Klein in Layout Design, an eleven o'clock with Peter Farrell in Art, lunch with Raymond Keller, that writer you like who wants to pitch an idea for a piece about aging yuppies worrying about getting senile.''

"Lovely."

Eric pressed his pen against his lips, suppressing a smile. "He said he'd cleared it with Jordan Case."

"Really." Okay. Just because Jordan didn't come around didn't mean he wasn't meddling. "Call him back and reschedule it. I can't waste a business lunch discussing a fluff piece." She'd handle Jordan's ire when and if he had any.

"Done." Eric scribbled. "And Roxanne needs you to look over the photos she took of Prince William when she was in London."

"Okay, buzz her and tell her I'll go to the photo lab first chance I get. Have you seen them?"

Eric pressed his heart. "I have and they're simply fantastic. The kid's a natural, gets his looks from his mama, no doubt about it."

Valerie picked up the phone. "You're drooling, Eric. Go do something useful."

"Yes, ma'am." He gathered up a stack of letters she'd signed. "Oh, just one more thing."

She looked up, the receiver in her hand. "Denise Grantham was seen having dinner with Hal Kurtz at the Guggenheim Sunday afternoon."

"And your point is . . ."

"She's sleeping with him. I've suspected it for weeks." He lifted perfectly arched eyebrows. "Watch your back, lady. She's no friend of yours."

He didn't have to tell her that. Denise was ten years younger than Valerie and openly envious of her. She was also one of the most ambitious women Valerie had ever known. On Monday morning, Hal had called a staff meeting at the magazine to inform them of Liz's resignation and Valerie's promotion. Except for Denise, there had been general goodwill among *Panache*'s editorial staff. She'd been brought onboard by Hal six months ago as an editorial coordinator with the clear intent of using the job as a stepping-stone to bigger and better things. If Eric's gossip was true, she was using a time-honored method of accelerating her career.

"What on earth is Hal thinking?" she muttered as she punched in the number on the phone message.

"I think we all know what he's thinking with," Jordan quipped.

Valerie dropped the receiver back on the hook and stood up. "I didn't hear Eric announce you, Jordan."

"I told him he didn't need to bother."

"Would you tolerate an assistant who allowed just anybody to walk into your office at will?"

"Depends on who it was walking in. Hal Kurtz can drop in any time unannounced. And does."

"Meaning you're going to pull rank on me."

He closed her door. "No. I meant that Hal can and does feel comfortable dropping in on me and I have no problem with it. Now that I see you plan to stand on ceremony, I won't offend you by doing the same. Next time, I'll observe all the formalities." He sat down. "How far in advance will I need to make an appointment?"

Gritting her teeth, she settled back in her chair. "What's on your mind, Jordan?"

"It's personal. I came to discuss the fiasco with Charlie and Sara that set us off on the wrong track. It's time we cleared the air."

"It happened three years ago," Valerie said coldly. "It's ancient history. What's to discuss?"

"It may have happened three years ago, but I think you're as angry now as you were then, so there's a lot to discuss, considering."

"Considering what?"

"Considering that I don't want your hostility about that affecting our relationship now."

"We have no relationship, then or now."

"Ah, but we do, Valerie. Which is why this talk is necessary. You know as well as I that you were infuriated by my interference in that little passion the kids had going. I don't want old resentments about that coloring your judgment when I make suggestions here at *Panache.*"

"Little passion?" Blood rushed to her head. "You call the affair those kids were involved in a little passion? They were dating a whole year before you ever knew anything about it, Jordan. Sara's pregnancy had progressed to the twelfth week when your son finally had the courage to tell you about it. And then it took only two weeks of your heavy-handed browbeating to bring on a miscarriage."

"I did not bring on Sara's miscarriage," he said, rising abruptly and beginning to pace. "And you know it. There was no reason the doctor could pinpoint to explain it. Spontaneous abortion is the term, I believe. It happens."

"Saving you from pressing Charlie to demand that Sara have a real abortion, right?"

"You overestimate my influence on Charlie," he said dryly. "He's as stubborn as I am, in some ways. Look, Valerie . . ." He stopped and faced her. "They were too young. Marriage would have been a disaster for those kids, don't you see that? Charlie had a hard year ahead of him academically and Sara's education would probably have ended once she had a baby to care for. Think about it. If you're honest, you'll admit I was right. Hell, doesn't it tell you something that they got over it pretty fast?"

Charlie might have, but Sara certainly hadn't. She'd entered a dark world and the bright, laughing girl she had once been had gone away, never to return. Oh, she was beyond it now, but it had changed her. Sara was less spontaneous, more cautious, simply . . . older and wiser. And nothing Valerie had been able to do or say would ever bring that Sara back again.

Not that she was about to tell this coldhearted, unfeeling man that. Sara didn't need sympathy from Jordan Case. She didn't need anything from Jordan Case. And neither did Valerie.

At the window now, he asked quietly, "How is Sara, by the way?"

"She's fine. She finished school at the end of the fall semester. She has a job at a fashion house on Eighth Avenue. She's a designer."

"Living at home?"

"No. She has an apartment, shares it with a friend."

"You must miss her."

"Yes."

"Charlie's doing great, too. He's working at a high-tech firm doing highly sensitive stuff that would probably baffle me if he ever tried to explain it to me."

"Have you ever asked him?"

Jordan gave her a sideways look, smiling wryly. "In a roundabout way. But I'm working on the communication thing."

Valerie clasped her hands and rested them on top of her desk. "And now that we've discussed Charlie and Sara, you can get to the real reason why you came today. I've got a packed calendar. What's really on your mind?"

"I told you. I made a mistake in coming on too strong with Charlie and Sara, I admit that. I knew it was necessary to clear the air between us on that before we start trying to work together."

"You didn't sound as if you thought you'd made any mistakes a moment ago. You defended everything you did."

"And because you're still holding a grudge about it, you didn't even want to hear me out. Which proves my point." He held up a hand as she prepared to lambast him again. "Now, damn it, just hold on a minute. I want to clear this up between us once and for all, Valerie. I know you resent my attitude over Charlie and Sara's—"

"Little passion?"

"Their relationship back then. I handled it badly. I said some things I regret. I went too far. I insulted you personally."

"By suggesting that because I wasn't married when Sara was born that my daughter must be a slut, too?"

"I didn't call Sara a slut. Or you. I didn't even think anything like that."

"Oh, please, Jordan. You assumed 'like mother, like daughter,' but you meant no disrespect. Is that what you're trying to say? Because that isn't the way I remember it."

"Damn it all, Valerie—"

"The way I remember it, you said some pretty nasty things. And no matter what the circumstances of my daughter's birth, she was an innocent." Valerie felt a catch in her throat, but vowed she'd show no emotion. Unlike the night Jordan had appeared at her apartment and subjected her to a blistering and humiliating tirade in a clumsy effort to protect his only son. She gave him a fierce look. "Sara was a lovely, laughing young woman when she met your precious Charlie, and when he walked out on her after the miscarriage, something died inside her. Just think what would have been the result if she'd heard the ugly things you said."

"I'm admitting I was wrong, Valerie," he said quietly. "I was over the line that night. I apologize."

She barely heard him. On her feet again now, her eyes still flashed fire. "I'm just glad that Sara wasn't

there when you came to my apartment to unload that
garbage. It was bad enough that Janine— No, it was
good that Janine heard everything, because after you
left, she was able to put everything in perspective for
me, thank heaven. She was wise enough to point out
that we're a lot better off not having someone like you
connected to our family, even by marriage. She
reminded me that people who jump to conclusions
often make fools of themselves."

Jordan studied her a moment in silence, then headed
for the door. "I can see you're not ready yet to put the
whole sorry episode behind us."

"I can put it behind me," Valerie said bitterly. "But
I can never forget it. I'm sorry if that's not what you
want. We don't always get what we want in this world."

He gave a fleeting half-smile. "Quoting Mick Jagger
now?"

"No, quoting Sister Janine Livaudais."

He frowned. "Sister Janine? Your mother is a nun?"

"Janine isn't my mother. But she is my oldest and
dearest friend."

"Charlie mentioned her frequently. She must be well
into her eighties. How is she?"

"She has Alzheimer's. We've had to put her in a full-
care facility. Rose Haven."

"I'm sorry." He had the door open now, ready to
leave. "So both Sara and Janine are gone. You have an
empty nest."

"I don't have time to be lonely." She picked up the
phone to make the call he'd interrupted. After a
moment, he left.

She spent the next hour returning calls, assuming
that Jordan had left the premises. The last thing she'd
expected from him was an apology, but the more she

thought about it, the more she was convinced that it was a very clever ploy. If she believed him, she'd be less guarded, then she'd accept his presence at *Panache,* which would allow him the freedom to walk in and out at will, interfering in her decisions, in effect relegating her to a subordinate role. *Panache* wouldn't be her magazine at all. She might as well be features editor again. She'd been forced to stand firm, she told herself, pushing the tiny suspicion that she might have been a tad too harsh in rejecting his olive branch. But if she began as a pushover to Jordan's every suggestion, she wouldn't last three months in this job. She intended to be *Panache*'s editor for the foreseeable future, to mold the magazine into something really exciting. There was a void in the magazine market in this category and she intended to fill it.

Eric buzzed her as she was finishing up. "Yes?"

"If you break away now, you have about ten minutes to look over the Prince William photos in the lab. Say the word and Roxanne will meet you there."

Valerie glanced at her watch. Ten minutes for the photos and then Suzy Klein. If she could make the meeting with Peter brief, she'd have time to lunch with Jon Palmer, one of the magazine's contributing reporters. He was doing a dynamite piece on the death ten years ago of the wife of a famous TV star. It was originally ruled as an accident, but Palmer's research indicated otherwise. Running a feature like that would be risky, but if Palmer convinced her—and the magazine's lawyers—that the material he planned to base the story on was factual, it would be a terrific scoop.

"I'm on my way, Eric." Since Jordan was so keen on the aging yuppie piece, he could have lunch with Ray Keller. "Buzz Rox and tell her to give me a couple of minutes, and then meet me in the photo lab."

She ducked into her small powder room for a

moment, the first opportunity she'd had since arriving before eight. As she washed her hands, she caught sight of her face. She was flushed, her lip gloss eaten away. Her eyes were too bright. Damn Jordan Case. With a muttered curse, she tossed the paper towel in the trash.

Eric was waiting with a cup of fresh coffee as she hurried past his desk. He knew her partiality for good coffee and kept a pot on the ready all morning long. She made a mental note to reorder from New Orleans. Sometime soon she was going to try and decaffeinate herself, but not today.

The photo lab was located at the rear of a large room in the art department. She almost turned and left when she spotted Jordan chatting with Peter Farrell, but before she could duck into the photo lab, he broke off his conversation and followed her inside the small, dimly lit room.

"There's something I want to run by you," he said, closing the door softly.

"Can't it wait, Jordan? I need to check this layout and then I'm scheduled to meet with Suzy Klein." She stepped closer to study the drying photos Roxanne had pinned to a line at eye level. At a glance, they were stunning. It would be no problem to find a cover shot.

"This won't take but a minute. I'll run it by you while you look."

She sighed, pulled a photo from the lot, and imagined it on the cover of *Panache*.

"Great cover." Jordan moved closer, studying the photo. "He's got a killer smile, hasn't he, just like his mother's."

"Yes. And he's just as irresistible to the public as Diana was. The world can't get enough of him." Using her hands, she framed the photo in a square. "With this one on the cover, *Panache* will fly off the stands."

"I had an idea for a feature." He stood leaning against

the waist-high counter. "I've been talking to Donald Derrick. He's interested in doing a piece about powerful figures in the legal profession who have ties with organized crime."

She pinned the photo back on the line and resumed scrutiny of the others. "Don't you think that's a bit hard-edged for our readership?"

"I thought you wanted to take the magazine into new and different directions."

"Not if it means losing the readers we've already got." She jerked a second photo from the line with an exasperated sound. "Look, Jordan, you're well aware that you can strike a deal with Donald Derrick without getting approval from me, but I have several ideas already in work. They've been carefully thought out. I'm asking you to let me have a few months to try and reinvent *Panache*'s image. Is that too much to ask?"

He crossed his arms over his chest. "Are we going to war over every suggestion I make?"

"Hardly. I'm a realist. I know how foolish that would be." She replaced the photo and began moving down the line, studying them. Roxanne's eye for drama was evident in nearly every shot. Suddenly Valerie frowned, spotting a small black-and-white picture pinned between two large glossies of the young prince playing cricket. It was clearly old. The snapshot was stained, as if someone had used it as a coaster. Four scruffy teenage girls in skintight jeans and skimpy T-shirts looked straight-on at the camera. No one smiled. In the background was a narrow street made of ancient brick and lined with seedy shops. A couple of the buildings had elaborate cast-iron balconies at the second level where lush greenery cascaded from pots. In the foreground was a street sign, the name only partially visible. "Rue Royale," Valerie murmured, then caught herself up short. "My God—"

Seeing her reaction, Jordan reached for the snapshot even as Valerie lunged for it. He took it down and moved to the light to get a better look. "I don't think Roxanne meant to include this one," he said dryly, trying to make out the faces of the four teenagers. "These kids look like they've been around the block a time or two."

Moving instinctively, Valerie snatched the picture from him and stuffed it into the pocket of her blazer. Even so, touching it was like handling a live snake. How? Who? Oh, God, after all these years . . .

"This is apparently somebody's idea of a sick joke." She hoped her voice didn't sound as shaken as she felt.

He was studying her intently. "I don't know that it's that bad."

She looked nervously at the door. "Where on earth is Roxanne? She was supposed to meet me here."

"You look as if you've just seen a ghost, Valerie. Can I get you some water?"

A ghost. She closed her eyes. "Yes, please."

Thinking to find a glass and water in the lab, he started toward the sink at the back of the room, but Valerie stopped him. "There's a snack room just down the hall from the art department. I'd like some orange juice, if it wouldn't be too much trouble."

"Not a problem." He walked back to her, grabbed a stool, and before she could stop him, he had his hands on her waist and had lifted her easily onto the seat. "Stay put, don't faint. I'll be right back."

The moment the door closed, she slid from the stool and waited while thirty interminable seconds crawled by and the rushing sound in her head subsided. Cautiously, she opened the door, checking to see that

Jordan was nowhere in sight. Then, she slipped out of the lab and escaped.

It was Roxanne, not Valerie, waiting in the photo lab when Jordan returned with orange juice. She was unpinning the photos of Prince William, arranging them on a tilted table to get maximum effect for viewing. "Where did she go?" he asked, setting the bottle on the counter.

"Who?" Roxanne paused, looking at him.

"Valerie. She was just here. We were talking. She saw an old snapshot and—" He stopped and set the orange juice on the counter. "I guess something else came up."

Roxanne looked at the juice and then at him. "I could have misunderstood Eric's message."

"It's possible." Jordan smiled wryly. The request for orange juice had been an excuse to get rid of him. He should have guessed she wouldn't hang around and give him a chance to ask questions. "She looked at your layout. In fact, she spotted a possible cover shot."

"Damn!" Roxanne touched the shot of Prince William that Valerie had picked for the cover. "I wanted to be with her when she saw the layout, but I was delayed when a friend dropped in and I couldn't get away. I bet it was this one."

"That's it. We were both impressed. Keep on turning out photos like these and you can write your own ticket anywhere."

"Thanks. I'll remember that when I ask for a raise." Her smile faded. "What was that about an old snapshot?"

"We were studying the Prince William glossies and someone had tucked a picture of a group of teenage girls in the mix. When Valerie saw it, she seemed startled. Do you have any idea how it got there? I think she'd like to know."

Roxanne shrugged. "Not a clue. And I'd like to know how it got mixed up in my stuff, too. I'll find out."

"It could have been a prank."

"Not funny. No one's supposed to be fooling around in the darkroom. But why was she interested in a picture of a bunch of kids taken years ago?"

Jordan's gaze was thoughtful. "Because she was one of them."

CHAPTER FOUR

Valerie collapsed in the taxi, eyes closed, her heart racing, barely aware of the curious look from the driver through the rearview mirror as he plunged into traffic. She must have seemed demented as she'd given her address and told him to get her there as fast as possible. She would definitely have some explaining to do to Eric. He'd jumped up from his chair as she'd rushed past him to get her purse from her office. He'd followed her anxiously, wanting to know what was wrong. She'd mumbled something . . . she didn't remember what. "I have to go home," was all she recalled saying before rushing blindly past him to the elevator.

Oh, God. Someone knew her secret.

How had the snapshot gotten there? Who had found it? How had they found it? Clearly, she'd been meant to see it and be shocked, but for what purpose? And Jordan. What was he thinking? Had he recognized her face in that scruffy group? And what would he think if

he did? How many people came close to fainting when
they saw a picture of themselves as a teenager?

She took the picture out of her pocket and stared at
it, fighting the memories that threatened to spill out
and destroy her. Oh, God, oh, God, after all these years,
she had thought that part of her life was behind her.
Dead. Buried. Her mouth twisted as she stuffed it back
into her pocket. What a fool she was. The past could
never be escaped.

Chicago, 1976

Valerie was born Caroline Weston, only child of Wilson and Hannah Weston. And until she was nine years
old and her father had died suddenly of a heart attack,
life had been happy and uncomplicated. Although Hannah Weston was not an impoverished widow, the income
from Wilson's estate wasn't enough to keep her in the
style she preferred. Still young and beautiful, she'd set
out to find a man who offered more. Edward Martindale
was a hugely successful defense attorney who had
already made a name for himself in a couple of high-
profile cases in Chicago. He didn't have Wilson Weston's polish—or Wilson's pedigree—but he had ten
times Wilson's ambition and his career was on a fast
track. He wanted a young and beautiful wife and one
with the right background. Hannah was perfect. He
grudgingly accepted the fact that she came with a nine-
year-old daughter. They married barely one year after
Wilson's death.

It took only a few weeks as Edward's stepdaughter for
Caroline to realize that he would never be the father
substitute she longed for. He pampered Hannah, but
he largely ignored Caroline. Not surprisingly, the onset
of adolescence was difficult. She was moody, irritable,
and rebellious. Edward was impatient, cold, and insensi-

tive. Hannah devoted herself to keeping Edward happy, which meant separating him and Caroline whenever possible. When they did clash, Edward was verbally abusive, and bitter confrontations were more and more frequent as she entered her teens. If she challenged him and he was in a particularly black mood, he didn't hesitate to backhand her. More than once, he made her head ring with a vicious slap. At those times, she begged her mother to leave him. Hannah's response was to remind her to think of the positives in their lifestyle. "We have Edward to thank for that," she said brightly. "Really, Caroline, you bring a lot of this on yourself. Don't sass him."

She was fourteen when she realized that some of the very exclusive clients who comprised Edward's law practice were significant players in organized crime in the Midwest. She tried to talk to Hannah about it. "You're too young to understand these things, Caroline," her mother told her. "And I don't want you talking to anyone else about this. Edward's reputation is above reproach in the legal community. His name is on a short list for an important judgeship. Won't it be nice to tell everyone that your stepfather is a federal judge?" Clearly, her mother liked the prospect of being the wife of a federal judge. Just as Hannah chose to ignore Edward's abuse of Caroline, she chose to ignore anything that jeopardized that future.

But for Caroline, the future was changed irrevocably one night about a month before her fifteenth birthday. She had missed her curfew after seeing a late movie with a friend and knew she was in for trouble unless she managed to slip inside the house without her mother or Edward spotting her. Once inside, she still had to get upstairs unseen before she'd be home free. But as she slipped past Edward's study, the door was ajar and she heard angry voices. Something about the ferocity of the argument stopped her. Edward had a visitor, a distraught businessman who was angrily accusing him of colluding with another client in a plot to swindle him out of his business and the prime piece of property where it was situated. Caroline heard him claim that Edward's client was known to be "connected" to the Chicago crime family. If such an accusation ever came to light, it would put an end to Edward's chance for the judgeship. Caroline knew what she was hearing was explosive stuff.

Why had she stayed and listened? Why hadn't she seized her chance to get upstairs to her room instead of standing rooted to the spot, hearing much of her own suspicions about Edward confirmed? Was the curiosity that compelled her to choose a career in journalism a part of her character even then? Did she sense that something really bad was happening?

The argument escalated, but Edward's arrogance soon had the man in a blind rage. Then Caroline saw to her horror that the man had a gun in his hand. Frustrated and desperate, he told Edward he had nothing to lose if he just pulled the trigger and killed him. Edward laughed. Caroline blinked in disbelief as Edward coolly crossed the room until he stood in front of the man. "So do it."

The man was no killer. Caroline could see the indecision in him. Edward sprang, intent on seizing the weapon. They struggled, and in the next moment, the gun was in Edward's hand. Heart in her throat, Caroline realized a disaster had been narrowly averted. He would call the police now, she thought. The man would be arrested even though she believed he was telling the truth. Or maybe Edward would just tell him to go home and cool off. Her stepfather did none of those things. As the businessman sat hunched and miserable on the floor, Edward lifted the gun and shot him pointblank in the back of his head.

Caroline screamed then. Edward gave her a startled look, then ordered her curtly out of the room.

"I saw what you did!" she cried. "You shot him. He wasn't doing anything. He didn't have the gun anymore. He was just sitting there on the floor and crying! What you did was cold-blooded murder! You're horrible!"

"And you're a pain in the ass, Caroline," he said with disgust. "Get the hell out of here while I clean up this mess. And on your way up, tell your mother I need her. Now, move!"

"Are you going to call 911? Maybe he's still alive."

"And maybe pigs fly," he replied in a sarcastic tone. "Do as I say. Get out of here and find your mother!"

"What on earth is going on down here?" Hannah appeared in the door of the study. "What was that sound? I thought it—" She clapped a hand over her mouth. "Oh, my God!"

"Get me a blanket," Edward told her, ignoring her shock. "I'll need something big enough to wrap him up good. I'll have to haul him off in the Land Rover. I don't think I can get him in the trunk of the Mercedes." As he talked, he reached for the knitted throw on the leather sofa beneath the window and roughly wiped up some blood, then stuffed it beneath the man's head. "Blood's soaking this damn rug and it cost me over five thousand dollars!" he muttered.

"What happened?" Hannah managed, still rooted to the spot.

"He shot that man!" Caroline cried. "He put the gun to the back of his head and just pulled the trigger, Mom! Now do you see what a monster he is?"

"Get her out of here, Hannah!" Edward roared.

"And bring me that blanket! I haven't got all night to do this."

"Did you kill him, Edward?" Hannah was pale, her blue eyes wide with horror. "Is what Caroline says true?"

"Hell, no! He came in here throwing around crazy accusations about a piece of land he lost in a tax sale and next thing I knew he was waving a gun at me. He was mental, Hannah. I was wrestling him for the gun and it went off."

Caroline stared at him. "That is so bogus! That's a lie, everything you said." She turned to her mother. "Don't believe him, Mom. He shot that man in cold blood. Look at where the bullet went in . . . the back of the head. How could that happen?"

"Anything can happen when a gun goes off," Edward stated flatly. "Now are you going to believe me, Hannah, or this kid? She's been trying to poison your mind against me from day one."

Hannah stood looking at them both. After a moment, she said, "I . . . I know you wouldn't shoot somebody in cold blood, Edward. But shouldn't we call the police?"

He lifted his eyebrows. "And have this plastered all over the media? If we do that, you can say goodbye to the judgeship."

She wrung her hands. "Well . . ."

Caroline knew then that her mother was going to go along with whatever Edward decided. Their cushy life and the prospect of the federal judgeship meant more to Hannah than doing the right thing. More than a man's life. More than her own integrity and her daughter's perception of her character. Well, if she wouldn't do the right thing, Caroline would just have to. She turned on her heel, heading for the telephone. "I'm telling. I'm calling the police and telling them exactly what I saw." She reached for the receiver. "You can tell whatever story you want, but—"

She cried out when Edward swung hard and swept
the telephone off the table where it clattered against
the wall. Then he caught her by the shoulders and shook
her with such force that she saw stars. "I guess you didn't
hear me, little girl," he said in a menacing whisper. "I
told you to get upstairs and I'm telling you now to keep
your mouth shut about this. Do you understand me?"

She looked at him sullenly. "I know what I saw."

The blow came so fast that she didn't even see it. His
hand connected with one side of her face, then the
other. She bit her tongue painfully, and for a second
or two everything went dark. He struck her again. And
again. Now her head was truly ringing. He wore a large
gold ring and she felt it graze the bone near her eye.
She tried to lift up her hands to ward off more blows.
Then he caught her hair in his fist and brought her face
up close to his. "Do you understand me now, missy?"

"Y-yes," she managed. Her scalp hurt from the merci-
less hold he had on her hair. "Mom . . ." she whimpered. "Help me . . ."

"Edward, please . . ." It was Hannah begging. But at
one look from him, she shrank back.

Edward released her then and shoved her aside
viciously. She landed on a small table, sending a lamp
crashing to the floor along with a collection of framed
photographs. One of them showed Hannah and Caroline smiling brightly. It had been taken the year her
father died. Edward's office was set up to suggest to the
world that he was a respectable man, a loving husband
and stepfather who was definitely made of the right stuff
to be a federal judge. If they only knew.

"Get her out of my sight," Edward ordered, tucking
his shirttails that had become untidy in the tussle. "And
see that she keeps her silly trap shut. Or else."

"Yes, right." Hurriedly, Hannah helped Caroline to
her feet and almost dragged her to the door. "Let me

take her to her room and I'll be right down with that blanket.''

"About time, too," he growled without looking at them. He was busy emptying the pockets of the man he'd just murdered.

Minutes later, Caroline stood at the mirror in her bathroom and stared at her bruised and swollen face. Blood trickled from a small cut made by Edward's pinkie ring on the bone near her left eyebrow. She used a butterfly bandage to close it up, but it would definitely leave a scar. No use in asking to go to the emergency room and have it stitched by a real doctor. They'd have to explain how it got there along with all the other lumps and bruises.

See that she keeps her silly trap shut. Or else.

Edward didn't make empty threats. He meant that he would kill her. And Caroline believed him. The fact that she was his stepdaughter was no guarantee that he wouldn't do so again, especially now that she'd shown how she felt about what he'd done. She realized that the only way for Edward to know for certain that she stayed silent was to get rid of her. She was—and always would be—a threat. There were a thousand ways a man like Edward could get rid of someone who posed a risk to his political ambitions. "Accidents" came in many shapes and sizes. If she wanted to stay alive, she would have to leave.

And no time was better than right now when Edward was gone in the Land Rover to dispose of the murdered man. He'd left Hannah behind to make certain that Caroline stayed put and made no phone calls. It hurt that her mother was too weak to stand up to evil. And Edward Martindale was an evil man. Caroline knew that with every cell in her body. As she threw together a survival kit, her heart ached. She might never see her mother again. Hannah had helped her clean up and apply a little antiseptic on her cuts and bruises, all the while making distressing little sounds, but mostly she chastised Caroline for being so rash. It disgusted Caroline that Hannah would even try to spin Edward's behavior in a more tolerable light.

"We have a good life," she'd said in a pleading tone. "Can't you just put all that happened tonight out of your mind?"

"I can't forget murder, Mom. And I don't understand how you can either."

"It was self-defense, baby! Edward explained—"

"Edward lies."

Her mother sighed. "The judgeship would be lost forever if you told."

She looked at Hannah. "And what is lost if we don't tell, Mom?"

Hannah shook her head sadly. "You're too judgmental, Caroline. Someday you may find yourself in a situation where you make a wrong choice. Everyone does, sooner or later. Maybe then you'll understand."

"I will never understand murder!" she cried.

"Here's the address, lady. We're here."

Valerie blinked, realizing that the taxi had stopped. She'd been caught up in the past for a few minutes, but now all her anxiety came rushing back. She threw a bill at the driver, got out, and hurried up the steps of her apartment building. Inside, her heels sounded loud on the glossy tile on the way to the elevator. She stopped, punched the up button with a shaky finger, then paced restlessly until it finally came. It opened—slowly, slowly as she literally danced with impatience—then she dashed inside only to fumble trying to select her floor. And once again she was left to wait, feeling as if hell itself was opening at her feet.

How? How? How? Nobody knew any of this, nobody but Janine. And even Janine knew nothing about the pictures. And the box.

Ping! At last. She dashed from the elevator, her key already out. But inserting it with panicked fingers seemed beyond her at first. Pausing, she forced herself to draw in a deep breath. There! Key in, the lock turned and she flung the door open. Inside, she dropped her purse on the floor and went straight for her bedroom. The walk-in closet was packed to capacity with her wardrobe, her luggage and a variety of ordinary other things that people hid away from view. She ignored everything, going directly to the back of the closet where access to the attic was located via a small, narrow door. She jerked it open and gave an involuntary cry that the box was still there.

Dropping to her knees, she reached for it and tore the lid off, knowing if anybody saw her now, she'd seem crazed. She felt crazed. She began wildly sorting through the contents. She tossed aside a wallet, several scarves folded neatly, a tube of lipstick, a compact with initials on it, a St. Christopher medal, a rose that she'd carefully preserved in a plastic bag, and finally photographs bound with a rubber band. It was the photos she was most concerned about. Ripping away the rubber band, she spread them out on the floor. They were all black and whites, all worn from repeated handling, all old, all dated. She studied them, her eyes moving frantically, the same group of scruffy teens as were in the snapshot planted in the photo lab. She counted them. Eleven. There should have been twelve. And when she took the crumpled snapshot from her pocket and added it, there was an even dozen.

She sank back on her heels, closing her eyes. Somebody had been in her apartment! Somebody had found this box and removed one of the snapshots, then pinned it up in the photo lab where she, Valerie, and no one else would find it. The implications were staggering. Who? How? Or more importantly, why?

CHAPTER FIVE

New Orleans

Angela LeBlanc rose suddenly from her chair, took off her shoe, and used it to crush a cockroach crawling up the wall. If she didn't owe two months back rent on this rathole, she thought, scooping up the dead bug with paper from her trash can, she'd force her scummy landlord to exterminate the place. But under the circumstances, she couldn't take a chance on pissing him off.

She sat down again and shook out the *Times Picayune*. With nothing else to do, she settled back to scan the headlines. She was no news junkie, but with business nearly nonexistent, she had plenty of time on her hands. What she needed, she thought, paging through the first section, was a really good case. With her connections at NOPD, you'd think somebody would have put her on to something. But it'd been more than a month since she'd had a paying client.

Bored and restless, her gaze fell on an article featured in the front of the Metro section. *"Disappearance of Runaway Teen Remains an Unsolved Mystery."* Then the subheading: *"Trent Family Still Hoping After 25 years."* Hunching forward in her chair, she reached for her coffee cup and began reading with more interest.

Angela remembered the case. She'd been a rookie on the force at NOPD when the Trents had appeared from somewhere up north—she scanned down a few lines—Connecticut, yeah. They'd traced their daughter, Amy, a runaway teenager, to New Orleans. The kid had been into drugs and prostitution, as Angela recalled. Of course, her folks had refused to believe that, but word on the street was that she'd been hooking for a known pimp. Angela rubbed her temple, trying to remember his name.

"Perez . . . Sanchez . . . something Hispanic," she muttered, trying to dredge it up from her mental files. "Diaz! That was it. Oscar Diaz." In spite of an extensive search, NOPD never turned up a trace of Amy Trent. Personally, Angela had always believed Diaz killed her, but with no body—or even a witness who connected him—he'd managed to weasel out of an arrest in the case. Actually, murder wasn't his style, she had to admit that. But his rap sheet was a yard long and he was known to be ruthless with his "girls." Angela suspected he'd pushed Amy into prostitution after hooking her on drugs. Maybe she'd overdosed. He was too greedy to murder outright a girl who was generating income.

Angela lowered the paper and looked thoughtfully at the window where another roach sat with antennae waving waiting to dart inside. There were a lot of ways to dispose of a body in the remote bayous of a Louisiana swamp. As for Diaz today, Angela bet he'd met an untimely end, but she didn't know for sure. It was about that time she'd stepped into her own pile of shit and her career as a cop had ended.

She took a sip of strong, black coffee. What she wouldn't give to live that phase of her life over again. Like a fool, she'd gotten mixed up with some crooked cops who were on the take from local drug dealers. And for a while the money had been good. Too good. To keep from going to jail, she'd plea-bargained, but her career as a cop had been over almost before it began. Life goes on. She'd put her training to good use by going into business as a private detective. Problem today was, she was past her prime and potential clients knew it. She looked it, too. Time was, she'd been attractive. Booze, cigarettes, and mileage aged a woman. Today, most of her income came from suspicious wives looking to find their husbands sleeping around. Or vice versa. But she was good. She had an uncanny knack for following a lead to its right end.

Amy Trent. Angela scanned the article again. The Trents had been wealthy, with ties to politics, finance, and industry in the Northeast. Seemed the father had recently passed away. Angela remembered the mother well. She'd been the one keen to find her daughter . . . or if she was really dead, to bring her killer to justice. According to the reporter who'd dredged up the old mystery, the mother was still out there hoping somebody, somewhere might tell her something.

"Hmmm." Angela drummed chipped nails on the scarred desktop. She still had contacts at NOPD. Maybe she could come up with a few details the *Picayune*'s reporter had missed. Maybe she'd get in touch with Mama Trent and try to persuade her to spring for a retainer. There was money to be made when emotions were involved.

Hell, it was worth a try.

* * *

Rose Haven was a forty-minute ride by taxi from Valerie's apartment. She'd planned to make her weekly visit to Janine on Saturday, but finding the photo changed that. Janine was the only person who knew her secret, so she needed to talk to her now. She was the only person Valerie could think of who might have a clue to explain how the snapshot could have been removed from Valerie's apartment, although how it got into the lab was another mystery. She was not optimistic. Lately, Janine had been going downhill rapidly. It had been many visits since her old friend had truly recognized her. If Janine proved unreachable, what next? There was no escaping the fact that someone had taken the snapshot from the box. Was it a guest, someone whom she'd invited into her home? They would have had to go into her bedroom—perhaps to use the bathroom?—then slip into her closet, snoop high and low before somehow noticing the attic door. But the box was always pushed out of sight. Her intruder would have had to know it was there. And nobody knew. Besides, she couldn't think of anyone—anyone!—who would do such a thing. The other explanation was more sinister. Someone—a stranger, someone who wished her harm—had broken into her apartment.

She lifted her cell phone and dialed Roxanne, who answered after several rings. There was boisterous noise and laughter in the background. "It's Valerie. Sorry to bother you, Rox, but—"

"Where are you, Val?" Roxanne asked sharply.

"On my way to see Janine. Rox—"

"Janine? I thought you only did that on weekends. Is she sick? Is there some emergency?"

"No, not really." She faltered for a moment. "I just wanted to see her."

"Oh." Clearly puzzled, Roxanne paused, then said, "Eric was really freaked out. He said you dashed into your office looking as if you'd seen a ghost, then you left with several appointments on your calendar. Is everything okay, Val?"

"Yeah, really. I'm fine. Listen, Rox—"

"Jordan Case was concerned, too. He said you saw a snapshot or something and he thought you were going to faint! What's going on, Val?"

"Do you know anything about that snapshot, Roxanne?"

"I didn't even see it. Jordan said he didn't know why you'd be upset. He said you were in it, but there was nothing that he could see to explain why you seemed so shocked."

Valerie gave a tired sigh. Jordan had recognized her in the picture. She had hoped he wouldn't. "It simply caught me off guard, Rox. You can say I overreacted, I guess, but wouldn't you be a little upset if a snapshot taken years ago suddenly shows up in the photo lab among a professional layout designed for the next issue of the magazine?"

"I'd be more than upset," Roxanne agreed. "And I am. The photo lab is my territory and having somebody fucking around in it without permission—*my* permission!—is something I won't tolerate. I intend to find out how this happened, Val."

She heard voices and Roxanne's soft laugh. Whoever she was dining with, she was clearly having a good time. "You have no idea who it might be?"

"What was that?" Roxanne asked over another burst of laughter. A woman? Man? She couldn't tell, and with Roxanne, you never knew. She'd chosen a bad time to ask questions.

"I just wanted to know if you had any idea who it might have been," Valerie said.

"No, but I intend to do some major league kicking of ass. Something's odd here."

"Thanks, Rox. Sorry to have interrupted your evening. 'Bye now."

She broke the connection as the taxi signaled to turn into the driveway at Rose Haven. The chances were slim that Janine would be any help. Only very rarely nowadays did she even recognize Valerie. But with so much at stake, there was nowhere else to begin.

Icy winter wind whipped her hair around her face as she climbed the stairs to the entrance. No matter how well managed or upscale Rose Haven might be, to Valerie it was still a depressing place. In spite of the conscientious efforts of the staff, it smelled of urine and antiseptic and cloyingly sweet body powder. And even though nobody wore the telltale white of doctors and nurses, it was still hospital-like. It had been a wrenching decision to place Janine here for the last years of her life. She'd rejected her life as a nun because of restrictive and repressive dogma. To live out her last years in an institution, even one as well run and sensitive to patients as Rose Haven, seemed heartlessly cruel. The only good thing about Alzheimer's was that Janine was beyond thought almost always now. Reaching her room, Valerie paused a moment at the door and watched Janine sitting in a chair gazing at the view from the single window in her room.

"Hello, love." Valerie bent down and kissed her cheek. "It's Valerie."

She felt a pang as Janine turned and looked at her with blank eyes. "Are you here to sing with the choir? It's Wednesday, isn't it?"

As a nun, she'd sung often in the choir and had often told of missing it after leaving the church. Wednesday had been the day designated for choir practice all those years ago. Valerie picked up one blue-veined hand and held it to her cheek. "I can't sing a note, Janine. Did you forget?"

Janine frowned. "That boy came."

"What boy?"

"The boy with the . . ." She stopped, seeking a noun. She often lost the ability to name things. Giving up, she turned her gaze again to the window.

Valerie straightened up and took the snapshot from her pocket. "Janine, have you ever seen this picture?"

She took it from Valerie and studied it intently. "I think she came with a nice young man."

"Who?" Maybe she did recall something.

Janine tapped the photo with one shaky finger. "This girl. This one right here in the middle."

"That's me," Valerie whispered in disappointment. "That's me, and it was taken a long time ago, even before we met, Janine."

"He had a puppy with him."

"What? Who had a puppy?"

"His name is Rusty."

Valerie took the photo from Janine. "Rusty was Sara's dog, Janine, remember? He was a birthday gift when she was four years old." The golden retriever had been a beloved member of the family, but he had been gone at least five years.

"Did he sing in the choir?"

Valerie sighed in frustration just as someone knocked and entered. "And how are we today, Sister Janine? Isn't it nice to have company?" The attendant handed a large manila envelope to Valerie, then reached to tuck the throw more snugly about the old nun's lap. "Did she tell you about the visit from the SPCA this morning? They brought several dogs and cats, mostly adult animals, you know, and it was such a big hit. Their visits are very therapeutic. Our patients just blossom when touching the animals." She tidied the table near Janine, picking up tissues, plucking a few yellow leaves from a plant, tossing a plastic cup. "Janine didn't want to let that golden retriever out of her sight, did you, sweetie? You'd be surprised how much they remember, too," she said to Valerie, lowering her voice. "Can't recall their spouse of fifty years or the names of their children, but dogs . . . cats . . ." She seemed to gather herself and laughed a little self-consciously. "I don't mean to distress you, but mentally, these Alzheimer patients are so puzzling."

Well, that explained the puppy remark, Valerie thought, but the stuff about the choir was still a mystery. She glanced at the envelope then, assuming it was more Rose Haven forms to fill out. Each patient generated an ungodly amount of paperwork, most of it unnecessary, in Valerie's opinion.

"You left that on your last visit, Ms. Olivier-Long." The attendant's smile was tight. "I don't like reminding visitors of these little things, but rules are rules. You didn't sign in that day and it's absolutely necessary to keep track of all guests." Still smiling, she shook a finger playfully. "And you really, really mustn't bring sweets to Sister Janine."

Valerie stared at her. "I haven't ever visited Janine without signing in and I didn't leave this envelope or any sweets." As she spoke, she tore the envelope open and pulled out the contents. It was a newspaper clipping. "What day was this?"

"Why, Tuesday," the nurse replied. "Both the envelope and the candy were left Tuesday. I found them myself. And if you didn't leave them, I wonder who it was."

Still unsuspecting, Valerie scanned the article, only taking it in after rereading the headline. She breathed in sharply. *"Disappearance of Runaway Teen Remains an Unsolved Mystery. Trent Family Still Hoping After 25 years."*

Trent family. The article was about Amy Trent.

Her knees were ready to buckle. With no chair handy, she sat on Janine's bed. "Where did you get this? Who gave it to you?"

The nurse was looking at her curiously. "As I said, it was left in the room here. Along with a box of Godiva chocolates. I thought ... At the nurse's station, we thought you'd made a quick visit and failed to sign in."

"No." Valerie looked at Janine. "Janine, who came to see you? Who left this?" She realized her voice was too sharp and tried to calm herself. "Who brought you those nice chocolates, love?"

Janine smiled as a light came on in her brain. "I remember now. The choir director is Father Patrick O'Malley."

First the snapshot and an intruder in her apartment, now this. Valerie sat in her car, stunned and shaken. The heater was turned on high, but she was still cold. So cold. She clenched her teeth against fear and a sense of violation. What was happening? Who was deliberately baiting her with these mementos of her past? How many other sick surprises were in store for her? And for what purpose? Was someone going to ask for money? Was this the preliminary to a blackmail demand? If not that, who would benefit by unmasking her? There were only three people in the world who knew what she'd done all those years ago: herself, Janine, and Oscar Diaz. With her head resting on the cold steering wheel, she felt the terrible memories come rushing back.

New Orleans, 1976

Caroline discovered within the first two days that life as a runaway was frightening, dangerous, and lonely.

Before she'd become one herself, she'd noticed kids
on the street in Chicago and had wondered at their
stupidity. She was far more tolerant now. She also understood why they tended to band together in motley
groups. It was necessary for survival.

Which is how she got mixed up with Oscar Diaz. It
took about two months of living on the money she'd
scraped together the night she'd run away—about three
hundred dollars—before she realized she couldn't
make it alone. In the two months it took to get to New
Orleans, she'd taken some dangerous chances. She'd
hitchhiked with truckers, she'd panhandled for food,
she'd slept under shelters made of cardboard, under
bridges, in parks. She'd nearly been raped by a gang in
St. Louis before jumping a moving train headed for
New Orleans. There, a fat inspector had routed her out
of a boxcar, but she'd easily outrun him. It was as good
a place as any to stay. The climate was mild almost year-
round. Winter cold in Northern states had been a major
problem from day one, which probably explained why
New Orleans appealed to a lot of runaways.

She was spotted by Oscar Diaz within a day of scoping
out the place. He was a handsome Latino, overtly sexy
with his dark eyes and sleek body. He offered her a
place to stay and she settled in with his ragtag crew
before she realized he was a pimp. In his stable were
others like herself, desperate kids willing to do what he
asked in exchange for a place to stay and food to eat.
She told herself she would never hook for him on the
street, like his other girls. She wasn't so immune to his
other sideline. He was a drug dealer with a ready supply
of products, from designer stuff to cocaine, ecstasy, and
heroin. It didn't take long for her to discover that the
fear lurking inside her disappeared when she was high.
Her mother's shortcomings were forgotten, the horri-
fying sight of Edward murdering that man receded into

the mists, even the dark ache of having no home and of being so desperately lonely were bearable when she was high. Although she held out firmly against Oscar's attempts to push her into prostituting herself, she was easily seduced by his vast array of drugs. Later, it dawned on her that he offered something else to troubled kids— a sense of belonging. He represented family, filling the void in their lives that all the runaways shared. And in that sense, she was no different from the others.

Friendships tended to be fleeting on the street. Kids came and went constantly, but Caroline bonded with one girl, a pregnant sixteen-year-old. Amy was delicate and blond, a soft-spoken and rather dreamy girl who didn't seem tough enough for the life she'd chosen. She never revealed her last name, but it wasn't unusual for street kids to conceal their identity. It was actually necessary for some. Caroline had certainly kept all pertinent facts about her history to herself, but in Amy she sensed a kindred soul and one night she told her about Edward and her reason for running away. Amy then confided her story. She'd been an abused foster child, she claimed, and had finally managed to escape, only to land in the clutches of Oscar Diaz. He'd plied her with drugs until she was addicted, then pushed her into prostitution. She and Amy had one other thing in common besides their mutual bondage to Oscar—both had nowhere else to go.

Inevitably, Caroline began selling drugs for Oscar to pay him for a place to crash and more narcotics. So far, she was still holding out and refusing to turn tricks for him. She knew he thought she'd come around eventually and she hated him. She hated how he preyed on confused and scared runaways. It was despicable. But she considered herself just as despicable for the mess she'd gotten herself into and every morning she woke up vowing to break away, to start a new life. To stop using.

So, for the next few weeks, she helped Amy cope with her pregnancy, which consisted mostly of shielding her from Oscar's cruelty. Both rejected the help of the nuns of St. Francis, who frequently approached homeless runaways in the French Quarter. Several times, Caroline was tempted just to talk to them, to see what they might suggest, but the first thing they always wanted to do was to persuade kids to call home. She'd have to tell them who she was and the reason she'd run away. That effectively nixed getting help from the nuns.

Meanwhile, Amy grew more vulnerable to Oscar's temper. Her baby may or may not have been Oscar's, but he considered Amy his property and was enraged when she refused to get the abortion he demanded. Sometimes, his temper exploded into violence. It infuriated Caroline that he was so cruel and insensitive to Amy. She overheard them arguing one day about the expense he was incurring because Amy wasn't pulling tricks anymore. Rushing over, she was too late to stop him from shoving Amy hard against a stack of boxes, which tumbled down painfully on top of her. She could have been hurt seriously, but Oscar had simply shrugged and walked out. Caroline wondered what he might have done if she hadn't been there.

"You've got to promise to help me," Amy tearfully begged that day. "He's going to hurt the baby if I don't get away. He *wants* to cause a miscarriage."

"Don't worry, I'll think of something," Caroline promised, having already scouted out an abandoned warehouse where they could stay temporarily. But finding a place and actually being able to manage was another problem. They were so utterly dependent on Oscar. He furnished what small income they needed to survive. Until the baby's birth, how would they eat?

Then, how would they take care of a baby? What about diapers, formula? She chose not to think about her own lifestyle. When the time came, she'd get clean and sober.

That was not the way it happened the night Amy went into labor. Caroline was in a narcotic stupor and more or less oblivious as yet another commotion began between Oscar and Amy. Forever after, the memory of that night was a hazy mix of Oscar's enraged curses, strange bright colors and sounds, Amy moaning in pain. And then screaming in pain. Caroline imagined herself getting up and helping Amy as she'd promised. But she was too stoned to force her drugged senses to respond.

Amy's pleas that night still haunted her. "I need a doctor . . . please, Oscar, please. The baby's coming."

"So get help from your junkie friend." Through a haze, Caroline saw Oscar standing over Amy, sneering. "You wanted this brat, now you deal with it." The walls literally shook as he slammed the door and left.

Amy lay curled in a fetal position. Did their eyes meet? Did Amy beg for help? Did Caroline, in a euphoric cloud, really turn away? Was her ecstatic state too sweet to surrender? Those answers would remain buried in guilty mist in her mind.

She was never sure how much later it was that she roused and realized to her horror that Amy was clearly in the final stages of labor. Caroline had no time to get help even as she rushed to Amy's side and yelled for somebody. Anybody. The baby was coming. And did— so fast and in a wild gush of blood and agony. Caroline frantically tied off the cord as she'd learned from a book she'd taken from the library even though she'd never dreamed she'd be called on to actually do it. But there was too much blood. Something was wrong, terribly wrong. Too late she wished for the nuns of St. Francis. The reasons for rejecting their help had once seemed so important, but now an adult would have been pro-

foundly welcome, especially someone with a straight
line to God. She was wrapping the baby, pink and squall-
ing, in her last clean T-shirt when she turned back to
check on Amy, and with that one look her heart stopped.

Amy was so white and still. Too still!

Oscar appeared then. Caroline screamed at him to get
the paramedics while she desperately—and futilely—
wiped at the blood hemorrhaging from Amy's uterus.
With tears pouring down her cheeks, Caroline took
Amy's cold hand and begged her not to die. But it was
too late. Amy had no pulse. Her body that had been
writhing in pain only moments before was now lax and
utterly still. She was dead white. Caroline dashed frantically to the door and discovered that Oscar hadn't gone
for help at all. He was leaning against the wall, noncha-
lantly smoking a joint.

Caroline flew at him in a rage. "Damn you, Oscar,
you better call 911 right now. Amy's dying, don't you
understand! She's dying."

"So, she's dying." He sucked at the cigarette, filling
his lungs to capacity, savoring the sensation. "I told her
I didn't want to fool with no kid." He shrugged. "It
was her choice. So she pays. As for the little bastard, if
he ain't dead now, he soon will be." Tossing the butt,
he started back inside toward Amy. Caroline screamed
with rage and terror and lunged at him with bared nails.
He recoiled to avoid her, but she caught him beneath
one eye and dug her nails in viciously, drawing blood.
Bellowing with rage, he drew back and backhanded her
with all his might. She went hurtling backward and
slammed into the brick wall. A shower of stars burst in
her vision, blinding her to Oscar standing over her,
yelling. "No uppity female hits Oscar Diaz, bitch. You
ever try that again, I'll kill you, too!" he roared. "I told
both of you I don't intend to wet-nurse no baby! I'm
runnin' a stable of whores, not a fuckin' nursery!"

Shaking her head to clear it, she realized his intent, but it was a few moments before she could walk. When she went inside, she found him standing over Amy's body. "She's dead," he said, balling up the bloody towel and tossing it aside in disgust. "Shit! Just what I need to explain to the cops, a dead body."

Trembling and still dazed, Caroline scooped up the baby, now squawling with all her might. Tears poured down her face and she wiped at them with a corner of the T-shirt. Inside, she was a mix of terrible emotions: grief, guilt, fear, pain. "We've got to call the p—police."

Oscar turned and gave her a hard look. "What the hell for? She's dead. We get rid of the kid, nobody'll know she ever existed."

She stared. "You mean—"

He rolled his eyes. "It happens all the time. Grow up. We toss him in a dumpster, our problem's solved."

"Her," Caroline murmured, holding the infant closer to her chest. "The baby's a girl."

"Should have known by the racket she's makin'. Even more reason to toss it." He jerked his head toward Amy's still body. "This bitch was always more trouble than she was worth."

His callousness appalled Caroline. She thought she probably should be less shocked by the lack of human decency in men like Oscar. It was eerily like the experience she'd had with her stepfather, but she knew she would never grow accustomed to sheer evil in any human being.

"First things first," Oscar said. "I gotta go borrow a car to get rid of this bitch's body and I'll dump the kid on the way. Hand her over." He started to take the baby.

"No!" Caroline backed up, then calmed herself, knowing the baby's life depended on how she handled the next few minutes. She couldn't save Amy, but maybe she could save Amy's child. "No, Oscar. You—you can handle A—Amy and—and all that, but I'll do the baby, okay?"

He gave her a hard look. "I don't want to find that kid stashed away somewhere when I get back, you got that, bitch?"

"You won't have to see this baby ever again, Oscar," she said in a suddenly firm voice. "I swear it."

Valerie was distracted for the next few days wondering when another sick attempt would be made by her tormentor. She jumped at every unexpected noise and she asked Eric to screen her calls carefully. She knew he wondered at her sudden paranoia, but he was too tactful to mention it. To prevent a second break-in at her apartment, she called a security service and had her locks changed. But when a week passed and nothing else happened, she began to breathe a little easier, although she knew better than to assume she'd heard the last of the person stalking her. It was bitter knowledge that whoever it was had chosen this moment in time to expose her. She'd finally reached the goal of all her hard work. She was at last heading up a major magazine. She was painfully aware how easily everything could be snatched away.

Even so, she worked doggedly at assembling her new staff and at choosing just the right material for the first few issues with her name on the masthead as editor. For the current one, Roxanne's cover photo and the article on Prince William would serve nicely to hook the consumer. Most of the material inside had been in the works while Liz was in charge, but for subsequent issues, Valerie wanted much stronger stuff. Roxanne, Eric, and her new production editor—a thin, intense workaholic named Greg Parker—formed the nucleus of her "dream team." Greg had been recommended by Hal Kurtz and had so far proved invaluable. The four of them frequently brainstormed ideas.

"If we had the photo layout on the Lily Carpenter feature," Greg said as he handed over the text of the article to Valerie, "it could go into production for the July issue."

"I want to go to Aspen and take some shots of the crime scene," Roxanne said.

"No one's proved it to be a crime scene," Valerie cautioned, "so we should be careful suggesting that, even privately around here. Lily Carpenter's death was ruled an accident by the coroner. Ted Carpenter has powerful friends in New York and Hollywood. He knows Jon Palmer is working on an article for us and digging into the evidence on the case and I have it on good authority that he's furious."

"We're not dropping the article, are we?" Greg asked, clearly ready to argue why they shouldn't.

"No, of course not. I'm simply warning everyone that we're bound to stir up controversy when we hint, however delicately, that a mega TV star like Ted Carpenter might have murdered his wife on the ski slopes. Just keep in mind that we don't want to be sued for libel. In fact, I've sent a draft of Jon Palmer's text to our lawyers. We want to be sure we're on solid ground."

"Liz would never have approved the article in the first place," Roxanne said as she tucked a sheaf of photographs back into a huge folder.

"So what? She never approved anything that had even a slight hint of risk," Eric said. "Thank God she's gone."

"Thank God I wasn't here when she was in charge," Greg said.

Valerie held up a hand, holding back a laugh. "Okay, gang. Enough." She stood up as the team moved toward the door. "Thanks for your input this morning. And,

Roxanne—'' She broke off as somebody knocked on
the door. "Eric, see who that is, will you?"

Before Eric reached it, the door opened abruptly.
Jordan Case spread his hands with an innocent look.
"Nobody manning the front desk," he explained.

Valerie gave him a cool nod before saying to Roxanne,
"Have somebody in Travel set up your flight to Aspen,
Rox."

"I'll keep you posted," Roxanne replied. "And there
was another idea for a feature I wanted to discuss with
you."

"I'll buzz you in a few minutes."

"Hi, Jordan." Rox smiled at him on her way out.
She'd known Jordan from her days on the circuit as
a supermodel. She'd also been a sympathetic listener
during the sorry saga of Sara and Charlie. But like Sara,
she'd been more tolerant of Jordan's reaction than Valerie. Tolerance came easier, Valerie had decided then,
when there was some emotional distance between yourself and the victim.

Greg also greeted Jordan cordially before saying to
Valerie, "I'm scheduling the Carpenter piece tentatively
for July, what do you think?"

"Fine, if all goes well," she replied.

Only Eric remained. "Coffee, boss?" he asked after
giving Jordan an admiring look.

"Would you like some coffee?" she said politely to
Jordan.

"I'll pass."

"So will I, Eric. Thanks." She waited until he'd closed
the door before sitting down and lacing her fingers in
front of her. "What can I do for you today, Jordan?"

Taking a seat, he crossed an ankle on one knee. "I
wanted to discuss an idea I had for an article, but first,
what's this about Ted Carpenter?"

"Are you familiar with Jon Palmer's work?"

"The investigative reporter who did that dynamite exposé in *Talk* magazine?" At her nod, he said, "Yeah, I've heard of him."

"He's been researching Lily Carpenter's death in Aspen ten years ago. The police ruled it an accident, but he's uncovered compelling evidence that points to Ted. Their marriage was on the rocks, he was drinking heavily. The accident occurred late in the evening when the slopes are relatively deserted. She'd recently miscarried, a fact that was never uncovered by the police. And here's the interesting part. Carpenter ordered DNA tests to see if the baby was his, and it turned out, it wasn't."

"Palmer's documented all this?" Jordan asked.

"And much more."

"Hal won't be pleased if you open us up to a lawsuit."

"Don't worry, our lawyers are studying the draft of Jon's work as we speak."

"Hmm." He held her gaze for a long moment before nodding slowly. "Okay, looks like you've got your ducks all lined up. However ... you claimed my idea for a feature about politicos with ties to organized crime was too hard-edged. Correct me if I'm wrong, but isn't the Carpenter thing pretty hard-edged, too? We've got high-profile celebrities, murder, infidelity, and scandal, all in one big story. What makes you think your readers will want that, but they won't want to read about a senator who's owned by the mob?"

"Politics is boring. Murder and infidelity aren't."

"Well, it's your decision."

She sat back, staring. "Just like that? You're giving up?"

He grinned. "Don't get too cocky. Besides, I think you're probably right. If we do anything with a political slant, it should have some redeeming element in it, something that makes it interesting to women. Tie it in with . . . say, kids. Or an issue dear to the feminists of the world.''

With growing suspicion, she nodded slowly. ''Uh-huh.''

''So, I was thinking . . .''

Valerie knew how lethal his charm could be and braced inwardly for battle. He reached into his breast pocket and took out an envelope, leaning forward as he pulled the contents out so that he could slide it across to her.

''I got this tip on my e-mail from someone on your staff who was surfing the Internet looking for ideas. I don't know why it was posted to me instead of you. Maybe you've intimidated your staff so they'd rather come in the back door, so to speak.'' He put up a hand as she started to bluster. ''Wait, hear me out. This, I think, is right up your alley. It has everything the Carpenter story has and more—sex, drugs, the suspicious disappearance of an heiress.''

''I can hardly wait,'' she said dryly. She reached for the newspaper clipping that he pushed toward her and gave it a quick glance. ***"Disappearance of Runaway Teen Remains an Unsolved Mystery.** Trent Family Still Hoping After 25 years.''*

CHAPTER SIX

"Wait'll you hear this part," Jordan said, apparently unaware of Valerie's shocked silence. "The girl is the daughter of Arthur and Emilie Trent, Valerie. That's Arthur Trent the third, of Trent Foundation fame, right here in New York."

"Who sent this to you?" she asked in a hollow tone.

"Truth is, I don't know. When I tried to reply, my Internet server bounced it back as 'undeliverable.' "

Valerie struggled to keep her expression blank. "This happened twenty-five years ago."

"The Carpenter case is ten years old and you went for it."

Was it Jordan? Was he the one? Could he stand there looking as guileless as a puppy after having already planted the article for her to find at Rose Haven? Did he somehow get into her apartment and find the snapshot, then put it in the lab to watch her reaction when she found it? Could he be that diabolical?

"This happened in New Orleans, not New York," she said while screaming inside at the cruelty of it. Now

Jordan was scooting his chair a little closer to her desk, his attention focused on the article. She struggled to calm herself and felt some measure of reason return. If it was his intent to shock her, wouldn't he be watching her?

"Listen," he said, "this reporter has dug up some interesting facts. Amy Trent was part of a tight group of runaways. They were all messed up, into drugs and prostitution, street crime, you name it. It'll be interesting to pick up where the reporter left off. This will appeal to your readership, Valerie. A lot of families have troubled kids. Some run away."

"It's a very dark subject," she said, her lips barely moving.

"Yeah. And the worst happened here. The kid just vanished . . . and her baby. That's part of the mystery, which is part of the story's appeal. Come on, you can't deny it."

"You're assuming a lot from a few facts."

"I'm not assuming this. The Trent name is big on Wall Street, and they're connected to the cream of society in New York and Boston. I tell you, this story has everything. Your readers will eat it up like ice cream." He leaned back, convinced he'd sold her. "Hell, we might even solve a murder. Let's do it!"

"Really, Jordan, it's too sordid for *Panache,*" Valerie said, hiding her shaking hands in her lap. "It's wrong for us."

"And the Carpenter thing isn't?" Jordan demanded, exasperated. "Why? This is more compelling, I think. Seeing it's the Trents, it's close to home. And it'd be dynamite if we manage to flush out a killer."

I'm the killer.

* * *

The next day brought the only bright spot in the week. Sara called and wanted to have lunch with Valerie. Although her schedule was packed, she never passed up a chance to be with Sara. The relationship between them had never really been the same since Sara's disastrous affair with Charlie Case. She would share casual tidbits about her job and her friends with Valerie, and they'd talk about people in both their orbits, but the intimacy they'd once shared just wasn't the same. Valerie wasn't sure that Sara would ever again trust her enough to confide a new love interest.

It was so unfair, she thought now as she searched the restaurant looking for Sara. It had been Jordan Case's heavy-handed interference that had turned all their lives upside down. If she felt any guilt at all, it was that she hadn't been able to deflect Jordan's disapproval and thus save Sara the stress that brought on the miscarriage. Across the restaurant, she caught her daughter's eye and smiled, then followed the hostess to the table.

"You're looking so pretty, sweetheart," she told Sara as she slipped into a chair. "Is that one of your own designs?"

"Actually, it is." Sara wore a trendy suit with touches of leather trim on the lapels. "This design is part of a major promotion we're working on in the shop. Victor is over the moon about it."

"If you're pleasing Victor Darien, your future is assured in the fashion world," Valerie said with satisfaction. Not that she'd ever had any doubt about Sara's artistic ability. Now that her naturally upbeat personality was back in place, her talent would shine. Valerie took her reading glasses from a case and put them on. "It's nice to know he recognizes talent when he sees it."

Smiling, Sara shook out her napkin. "And you're so unbiased, too."

Valerie picked up her menu and studied it. "In my

line of work, I have a better than casual acquaintance with the fashion industry. I know talent when I see it, my darling daughter.''

"Thanks, Mom," Sara said dryly. "And now let's order. I'm starved. The lemon grass beef is great here."

"Isn't that a little ... ah, robust for lunch? I was thinking of a shrimp salad."

Sara handed her menu to a waiter. "You have the salad. I'm having red meat."

After the waiter left, Valerie settled back and waited for Sara to reveal the reason she'd wanted them to get together for lunch. But whatever it was, she seemed to have trouble getting around to it. Thinking to give her more time, Valerie said, "I'm glad we're having lunch, because I've had the locks changed at my apartment."

"You had the locks changed? Why? Is there a problem with security in your building?"

"I never thought so, but ...." She shrugged. "I think someone might have broken in."

Sara stopped in the act of buttering a roll. "Really? Was anything missing?"

Without replying, Valerie asked, "Is it possible that you could have misplaced the key I gave you? Or could someone else have taken it?"

"Mom! Even if they did, no one would have used it to go inside your apartment. But no one did. C'mon, what are you saying? What was taken? Not your jewelry?" She put her hand to her throat, looking distressed. "Those beautiful pearls!"

"The pearls are fine. Nothing was taken except a ... well, they rummaged through my closet and took a picture, a snapshot."

"Was that all?"

"I think so." Suddenly she recalled the torn lace on her nightgown. Had an intruder done that? The thought of someone pawing through her most intimate apparel filled her with revulsion.

Sara looked confused. "How on earth did you even figure it out? What kind of snapshot?"

"I had a few things in a box, and oddly enough, it turned up in the photo lab at the magazine, of all places."

"Weird, Mom." Sara began buttering the roll again. "I can see why you freaked a little and had the locks changed. What do you make of it?"

Valerie waited as their water glasses were refilled. "I wish I knew. Probably, I'm overreacting, but I took the precaution of changing the locks anyway. And I brought a new one for you." She pushed it across the table. "Just be careful with it, okay?"

"Sure."

Valerie hesitated before saying, "You don't think your roommate might have somehow—"

"No, I don't," Sara said emphatically. "My roommate is the last person who would enter someone's house without permission. Especially to steal an old snapshot! Get serious, Mom."

Valerie picked up her fork. She hadn't really thought the answer to the mystery lay with Sara, who had the only other key to her apartment, but it had been necessary to ask. She studied her daughter now, still feeling as if something was on Sara's mind. Instead of eating, she was fiddling with the silver near her plate, then rearranging her water glass. She took a second roll, buttered it, but put it down without tasting it.

"Is something wrong, Sara?"

"Wrong? No. Nothing's wrong." Her smile seemed tight. "So, how's it going at the magazine? Are you happy with the staff you've put together?"

"I am. Most of them were already in-house and I knew once I got them together that they'd make a great team.

Greg Parker was the only person recruited from outside, but that was on Hal Kurtz's recommendation and he's working out extremely well. Naturally, we've hit a few snags. It's like any new venture. No matter how well you've planned or how good the people are at their particular jobs, everything must mesh eventually. It'll happen.'' She picked up her fork after the waiter placed her salad in front of her, then added, "Provided we can keep outside interference to a minimum."

"Outside interference," Sara murmured, tucking into her lemon grass beef. "Is that a veiled description of Jordan Case?"

Valerie stabbed at a shrimp. "He's a big pain, Sara. He promised to give me a free hand. He said he wouldn't undermine my authority or try and influence my decisions. Ha." Taking a roll, she broke it apart savagely. "If his actions since I took over are any indication, he's going to be micromanaging every facet of the magazine."

"He's actually overriding your decisions?"

"Not yet. But he has a new suggestion for a feature every day."

"Every day?"

"Well, often enough to remind me that I don't really have a free hand at *Panache*. Oh, I guess what really ticks me off is that I've got the title, but they don't really trust me." She took a sip of water and conjured up a smile. "But let's not ruin our lunch talking anymore about Jordan Case, hmm? What have you been doing lately? You know I'd love to have you come over more often, Sara. It seems like ages since we've spent any time together."

"I've been really busy, Mom." Sara sliced off a piece of beef and ate it. "Umm, this is so good." She touched her mouth with a napkin. "Actually, the next collection that Victor is putting together is going to be stunning.

It's a working woman theme. In fact, one of the suits would be terrific on you."

"And when I have twenty-five hundred dollars to toss to the wind, I'll consider buying it," Valerie said. "Seriously, what else is going on in your life, Sara?"

"I've been out to visit Granny Janine a couple of times lately."

"Oh? When was that?"

"When?" Sara thought a minute. "Wednesday of last week, I think. Then the week before . . . let me see . . . Tuesday, I think."

"Tuesday. Are you sure?"

"Not really. It could have been some other day. Why?"

"Did you give her some chocolates?"

"No, she isn't allowed sweets. I know that."

"Did you see a New Orleans newspaper in her room?"

"New Orleans newspaper?" Sara looked completely baffled now. "No. She's barely able to complete a sentence, Mom. Reading a newspaper is totally beyond her. Why? What's up?"

"Last week, she had a visitor who didn't sign in."

"Someone from New Orleans?" Sara perked up. The city where she was born always held more than passing interest to her. Valerie had been vague about her brief sojourn in New Orleans, going so far as to admit it was a time she wasn't proud of. Sara didn't know the details of her birth, of course, and Valerie had never corrected her assumption that she was her biological mother and that her biological father had been another troubled teenager who had disappeared before ever knowing of her existence.

"I don't know where her visitor was from," Valerie said, "and since nobody signed in, I suppose we'll never know. I was hoping you'd seen or noticed something."

"What's this about a newspaper?"

"Not a newspaper, a clipping. From the *Times Pica-yune*." She looked at Sara. "Were you alone when you visited? Or did you go with someone?"

"Umm . . . my roommate went with me."

Valerie brushed at a few crumbs on the white table-cloth. "Sounds as if the two of you are becoming good friends. Do you realize I've never met her, Sara? Why don't we ask her to join us next time we have lunch together? Or better yet, invite her over and the two of you can spend the weekend at home. It's been ages since we've had a whole weekend together."

"Maybe we'll do that sometime," Sara said, but Valerie suspected it wouldn't be anytime soon. "I'm still wondering who could be visiting Granny Janine without telling us. Are we assuming that is the person who left the newspaper?"

"And a box of candy," Valerie added, taking the check from the waiter. "I'm not assuming anything. Maybe the staff will have figured it out by the time I make another visit."

"I'm getting this, Mom." Sara reached for the check, but Valerie was already handing her credit card to the waiter. Sara leaned forward, insistent. "Mom, I invited you. I want to pay!"

"Next time, dear." Valerie paused while their plates were removed. "Now, when would you and your room-mate like to visit? Would you like to see a show? I can get us tickets. What do you think she'd like?"

"I'd better check first, Mom. Don't count on it, okay?" Sara signaled the waiter and ordered a cup of herb tea. "I wasn't quite finished," she explained, wav-ing Valerie's apology aside. "You go ahead. I know you're busy."

Valerie pushed her chair back, looking at her watch. "I'm so sorry to have to rush away, Sara, but I've got an appointment that I just can't skip. Do you mind?"

"Of course not. Being the big cheese has a down side. I understand that. No fooling around at lunch, right?" Sara stood up and hugged Valerie, bumping her cheek and kissing the air. "But thanks for finding time for me today."

Hesitating, Valerie looked closely at Sara. "Was there something else you wanted to say, sweetheart?"

Sara sat down again, avoiding her eyes. "Nothing that can't wait. Bye, now. Thanks for buying."

"We'll talk soon, okay? Call me?"

"Sure, Mom."

Sara watched as Valerie wove a path through the tables on her way out, drawing more than a few admiring gazes from men and women alike in the restaurant. Her mother was very attractive. Beautiful and intelligent and driven. Sara guessed that she had already been replaced in Valerie's thoughts by the appointment she was rushing to keep. Long ago, Sara had realized that her mother needed success in her career in a way that she herself never would. Her work was important to her, but there were other things far more vital to her happiness than her career. Still watching, she saw that Valerie had reached the entrance of the restaurant where a few people waited to be seated. She didn't notice the tall, casually dressed young man entering as she left.

Sara, however, caught his eye, waved enthusiastically, and smiled. He murmured something to the hostess and started across the room. Just seeing him lightened her mood instantly. When he got to the table, she felt like standing up and throwing her arms around him. Instead, she allowed herself only a particularly warm and lingering hello kiss.

"You chickened out," he said, still squeezing her hand as he took the chair Valerie had just vacated.

She shrugged with chagrin. "I know. I'm such a wimp! But you'd just have to be here and listen to our absolutely inane conversation to understand. She's still mad as hell at your dad and there was no way I could say oh, never mind how much hell you're getting from Jordan Case, and by the way, my roommate isn't some female I'm working with, it's his son, Charlie."

"We have to tell her sometime, love," Charlie said quietly.

"I know." They simply looked at each other for a while, enjoying the moment. Then Sara's smile brightened. "How about dessert?"

Valerie left Sara feeling she'd somehow missed an opportunity to . . . what? She didn't have a clue, but she was sure that Sara had invited her to lunch for a reason and then changed her mind. Depressed, she was distracted at her next appointment and was glad to finally head back to her office two hours later and grab a few private moments to regroup. Indulging in soul-searching while on the job was a luxury she couldn't afford. Roxanne was leaving her office when Valerie arrived.

"Val, I was just looking for you. I tried you on your cell, but you didn't pick up."

Valerie fished it out of her briefcase, stared at the display, and made a disgusted sound. "Darn, the battery's going. It didn't ring, I guess. What's the problem? Travel didn't give you any grief about your trip, did they?"

"No, it's not that. I wanted to introduce you to this fabulous person." Rox looked flushed and excited. "We met a few weeks ago at this self-defense class I'm taking and she was just in my office. You probably saw her at the elevator. Or passed her in the lobby. She left not three minutes ago."

"I didn't notice anyone, Rox." Thinking how to manage the rest of her day, Valerie took some papers out of her briefcase and gave them to Eric, who was on the phone. "See me when you're finished," she told him softly.

Cradling the phone between ear and shoulder, Eric found her messages and handed them over. Roxanne was still talking. Listening with only half an ear, Valerie went into her office, studying her messages as she walked.

"She's blond, five-five, eyes a photogenic blue, heart-shaped face, good cheekbones." Roxanne tended to describe people as if viewing them from behind a camera. "I know that face would photograph like Kim Basinger's, but she's camera-shy. Isn't that a hoot?"

"Kim Basinger's forty-six years old, Rox." Valerie pulled one of the messages from the stack and tossed it in the trash can.

"Her kind of beauty never wanes."

"You should know."

"You didn't see her, did you?"

"Who, Kim Basinger?"

"No! A.J., beautiful blond, fabulous blue eyes—"

"Cheekbones to die for. Uh-huh. Doesn't ring a bell, Rox. I guess we missed each other."

Roxanne's face fell. "Damn. I really wanted to introduce you."

"Next time."

"Actually, I've been seeing her for a few weeks. She's really interesting, Val. There's something so ... so intense about her. I'm seriously thinking of asking her if she'd like to move in with me."

Finally, she'd captured Valerie's attention. She was aware of Roxanne's sexual preference for women, although she'd had several affairs with men during the height of her modeling career. But Rox never allowed herself to get emotionally involved. Her occasional flings usually died a quick death. It was nice to see her, for once, devoid of her usual brittle cynicism. "What's her name?"

"I told you. A.J." Roxanne suddenly looked closely at Valerie. "Hey, you look like you're having a rotten day."

"Does it show?" Valerie asked, shrugging out of her coat.

"Eric said you were having lunch with Sara." Looking concerned, Rox closed the door. She had spent many anxious hours with Valerie sharing worry over Sara after the miscarriage and the broken engagement. "Is anything wrong?"

"I'm not sure." After hanging up her coat, Valerie went to her desk and sat down. "I'm probably imagining things, but I sometimes wonder if Sara and I will ever be as close as we were before she got involved with Charlie. I suppose I should be grateful he's gone, but sometimes I think if we could just have that again, then having Charlie around would be a small price to pay."

"Sara's all grown up now, Val. I know you don't like the changes that brings to your relationship, but it's pretty natural, isn't it? She's probably just staking out her adult identity." Using her fingers, Roxanne set the last two words in quotes. "And it's not necessarily bad. The two of you can connect now as adults."

"Maybe so," Valerie said reluctantly, but she wasn't convinced. Rox had never had a child and never would. Could she truly understand the hole it had left in Valerie's life when Sara had drifted away from her? For herself, maybe it would have helped if she'd been involved in a relationship with a man where mutual affection and respect were as real as the sex they shared. But then, she'd never really felt that kind of overwhelming passion for any man, not even when she'd been married.

And her successes career-wise meant far less if there was still a disconnect between her and her daughter. Janine, who at one time would have understood and whose wise counsel she had relied on, was beyond her reach now, too.

"How's Janine?" Roxanne asked, as if picking up on Valerie's thought.

"Steadily deteriorating." Valerie gazed at the photo on her desk—Janine, Sara, and herself in a happier time. "The last three visits she hasn't recognized me at all."

Roxanne touched her hand. "I'm so sorry, Val."

"I miss her."

"Yeah, I remember when my grandfather was suffering from Alzheimer's. It was hard to keep going out there to visit when he was in some strange world of his own and didn't know me from the orderlies or nurses on the staff. I'd look in his eyes, trying to strike a spark . . . anything. We'd been really close, but he was living someplace where none of us existed anymore." She gazed a long moment at the photo on Valerie's desk. "Finally I just stopped going. I've always felt guilty about that." She raised her eyes to Valerie's. "Don't abandon her, Val."

That would never happen. Ever. Valerie picked up the photo and touched the soft, gentle features of the woman who'd literally picked her up out of the gutter and given her a new life. No matter how long Janine lingered, the debt she owed her old friend could never be repaid.

New Orleans, 1976

As Caroline headed into the sultry New Orleans night, she was almost sick with fear and guilt. Was Oscar following? If he caught up with her, would he kill the baby

as he'd said he would? What kind of friend was she that
she'd failed to protect Amy as she'd promised? Pausing
with her lungs nearly bursting, breathing hard, she
looked up into the night sky. In the light of a full moon,
the spires of the St. Louis Cathedral seemed to take on
an unearthly glow. As she stood there, the baby stirred
in her arms, and as if by divine design, a plan took shape
in her mind.

She had failed Amy, but she could save Amy's baby.
To do it, she would need to make a clean start. What
harm would come if she simply became Amy? She could
have a life free of the fear that Edward Martindale would
someday find her and kill her. To atone for her part in
Amy's death, she could care for the child. Amy had no
family. She'd been a foster child lost in the bureaucracy
of the system. A swift and deep calm came over her.
Settling the baby on her shoulder, she stepped off the
curb and started once more down the dark streets of
the Quarter.

The first complication arose as soon as she went
through Amy's backpack. She discovered to her amazement that Amy was in real life the daughter of a couple
in Connecticut. Emilie and Arthur Trent III. Amy was
an only child, not the foster child she'd claimed to be,
not a no-name runaway, and maybe not an abused kid
who'd been forced to flee a dysfunctional home life.
Amy Trent was Somebody.

Standing with Amy's baby in her arms, Caroline pon-
dered what little she knew about her friend. The girl had
described long-term sexual abuse in a way that sounded
genuine. Just because Arthur Trent was rich and powerful didn't mean he couldn't or wouldn't molest his
daughter. As Caroline knew from bitter experience, rich
and powerful men could be deadly. And Amy simply
wasn't around to question whether she'd told the truth
about being abused. Still, Caroline couldn't afford not

to believe her. She nuzzled the baby's sweet-smelling neck. If Arthur Trent had molested Amy, what was to prevent him from doing the same thing to this baby? A leopard didn't change his spots. It would be nice to think Amy's mom would protect the baby, but where had she been when Amy was getting it from that bastard? Caroline also had experience with a mother who had failed to protect her own. The other option was to turn the baby over to the police. But that was sure to provoke questions, then they'd find out who *she* really was. Next step, they'd call Edward Martindale. No way could she risk that.

She stared a long time into the face of the sleeping infant, wanting to do the right thing. Amy wouldn't have run away if there hadn't been something really wrong, she reasoned. Second thing, she owed Amy. She'd failed her. So now she just needed to figure out how to approach the nuns at St. Francis without having them pick up the phone and call the cops.

First problem: She'd have to fix the name thing screw-up while at the same time keep the nuns from knowing the baby's true identity, which meant she couldn't become Amy Trent now. No way would they let her get away with kidnaping the grandchild of Emilie and Arthur Trent III. So she couldn't share that piece of information. She'd seen people on TV who'd assumed another person's identity. They went to the cemetery, found the name of a deceased infant, and used criminal connections to get the paperwork to make it all look legal. She realized she couldn't approach the nuns yet, not until that was done. It might take a few days and meanwhile she'd need to find a place to crash with the baby until all was settled. She was thankful she'd scoped out that place for her and Amy beforehand. Oscar didn't know about it and with luck they'd be safe there for a few days. But only a few. The French Quarter was small.

She'd have to stay out of sight during the day until she got everything done. And she'd have to get formula for the baby and food to eat for herself somehow. The only way was to steal it since she had no money. But she was already desperate and the thought of ripping off a few cans of Similac and some baloney seemed a small risk for what was at stake. She'd come back to the nuns as soon as she had her shit together.

Valerie Elaine Olivier, born 1961, died 1961. With the baby tied in a makeshift sling in front of her, Caroline carefully wrote down the vital statistics of the person she intended to become from the tiny crypt. Tucking the slip of paper into her pocket, she looked around warily. Wow, it was really weird in this old cemetery. The crypts were all above ground and shone a ghostly white in the moonlight. They were a strong tourist attraction in New Orleans, but that was during the day when groups of sightseers were guided through the gravel paths and regaled with the colorful history of the deceased. Besides, Caroline thought with a shudder, you could see the sunken places in the daylight. At night, such as now, no telling what you could step into if you weren't careful. And no telling who you'd run into out here, not that a mugger would pay much attention to a person with a baby, she thought with more hope than conviction. But she had to get that name.

The baby whimpered and she dropped a kiss on its downy head. She'd named her Sara, although she'd wanted to call her Amy. She felt she owed it to Amy out of respect that her child should have some connection to her true birth mother, but the risk of having somebody make the connection was too great. Sara had been her own grandmother's name. Although that Sara had died even before Hannah married Martindale, her memories of her grandmother were happy ones. She'd often thought that if Sara had played a stronger role in her own life, maybe things would have been different. Better.

Oddly enough, it had taken only a day of caring for Sara for the baby to seem her own. She *was* Sara's mother now, and she vowed to take care of her. She'd helped her into the world, she'd rescued her from Oscar, who would, without a doubt, have disposed of her in a dumpster.

And now she herself had a new name. She tried saying it out loud, "Valerie. Valerie Elaine Olivier." Yes. She liked it. There hadn't been many choices. She'd needed an infant with a birth date in the same year as her own, or close to it. She'd found a couple of others, but somehow she liked this one. She said a quick apology to the dead infant and headed out.

In the two days since she'd been on her own, she'd managed to locate a man in the Quarter who specialized in bogus IDs. He was a connection of Oscar's, which was how she'd known about him. And that was about the only advantage she could think of for ever having known Oscar Diaz. Walking carefully and giving the baby's bottom a tender pat now and then, she made her way through the spooky place and finally emerged at the edge of the Quarter. It was unlikely that she'd be spotted by Oscar or anybody else since most of the action was on Bourbon Street several blocks over in the Quarter, but she stayed in the shadows as much as possible. Another couple of days and it would be time to call on the nuns.

Sister Janine Livaudais listened in astonishment to the scruffy, intense teenager who called herself Valerie Olivier. She'd asked for Sister Janine by name and first

ascertained if what she was going to say would be held
confidential, as confidential as if the sister were a priest
and they were in a confessional. Janine recognized her
as one of a group of teens she'd seen in the Quarter
and which she had been particularly concerned over.
She recalled the pregnant girl that Valerie said had
given birth, a thin creature with delicate features. Now,
according to Valerie, she was dead. Janine had read
nothing in the paper about the death of a runaway in
the Quarter, but that didn't surprise her. City officials
viewed the hundreds of runaways on the streets as a
nuisance at best and a health risk at worst. They were
an unwelcome burden on the system, and in reality,
there weren't enough funds in the social welfare system
to cope with the high number who found their way to
New Orleans.

Valerie argued passionately for the baby. She
impressed upon the nun the fact that Oscar had been
ready to dispose of Sara like so much trash. He'd been
unmoved by Amy's death and he would certainly not
have burdened himself with her baby. Janine, of course,
insisted that the baby belonged with the birth mother's
family, if they could find them. Not an option, Valerie
said, because Amy had been abused by her father, which
was the reason she was living as a runaway. Amy's child
was a baby girl. She flatly refused to hand Sara over and
risk history repeating itself. Besides, Valerie said, no one
knew Amy's real name. She reminded the nun that
people did get lost in the nation's foster care system.

Then, seeing that Janine was still not convinced, Valerie had no choice but to tell her own history. If they
went public, Valerie argued, her situation would come
to light. Her stepfather was connected to organized
crime. Edward Martindale would kill her if he ever
found her again. Or he would have her killed. Not even

the church was big enough to protect her from those odds.

"I know a safe place where you can stay until we get this all worked out," Sister Janine said finally, surprising herself. A former nun who was a good friend lived nearby and would be likely to help in a sticky situation. The other nuns at St. Francis would never condone Valerie's action. In fact, Janine herself was in personal crisis and on the verge of leaving the church. For months, she'd been wrestling with a decision whether or not to renounce her vows. She was disillusioned and simply burned out. Was the appearance of this young teen and the baby a sign? Janine wondered. She chose to believe it was.

"Who has the baby right now?" she asked.

"I do," Valerie said. "Wait, I'll get her." With that, she walked the short distance from the foyer to the courtyard at the side of the convent. The nun followed, then watched curiously as a small fruit crate was pulled from beneath a large hibiscus. When Valerie lifted the tiny infant from the makeshift carrier, Sister Janine made an astonished sound. Murmuring soft, loving words, Valerie peeled away the makeshift bedding to reveal the perfectly healthy, sweetly beautiful girl-child. Janine saw the tenderness on the teenager's face as she looked at the baby. She raised her eyes to the nun. "Her name's Sara," she said softly.

CHAPTER SEVEN

"Is she in?"

"Mr. Case. Hello." Valerie's boy Friday stood up, but Jordan was already at Valerie's door, his hand raised for a brief tap before going inside. Eric glanced at his watch. "She's expecting someone, sir. I believe that party is on the way up."

Jordan flashed a grin as he waved a thick report at Eric. "I promise not to delay her too long."

"But sir—" Eric cleared his throat and Jordan let his hand fall.

"Got your orders, have you?"

"I'm sure she'll see you, sir," Eric said , bravely managing to withstand the laser of Jordan's direct look. "But I'll just buzz through . . . if you don't mind."

"Go for it." Jordan settled one shoulder against the doorjamb, holding the report folded lengthwise while Eric spoke softly into the intercom. Half a minute later, Valerie herself opened the door, then stepped back to invite him into her office while looking pointedly at her watch.

"This is an unexpected surprise," she said dryly.

He followed her inside, admiring her long legs in the brief skirt of her trim black suit. She was one attractive female, he'd give her that. She stopped in front of her desk, folded her arms, and rested against it. Without inviting him to sit, she waited. "Relax," he told her, holding up the report. "I come in peace."

"I don't need to relax. I'm not tense, I'm hungry."

"Perfect. Why don't we tell your guard dog out front to reschedule your appointment and let me take you to lunch?"

"My appointment is for lunch. What was it you wanted to suggest this time?"

He smiled, enjoying the glint that showed in her eyes when she was irritated. "A plan to save your precious magazine?"

"Save it? Save it from what?" She sat on the edge of the desk, crossing her ankles. Damn good looking ankles, he noticed.

"Certain disaster." He thumbed the pages of the report. "Have you seen this?"

"How would I know until you show me what it is?"

The buzzer on her desk sounded. She picked it up just as a man appeared in the open door. "Valerie? Am I early?"

She hung up the phone. "Wayne . . . no, of course not. Hello." With a bright smile, Valerie held out both hands and accepted a quick kiss on the lips. She turned to Jordan. "Jordan Case, this is Dr. Wayne Coulter. Wayne, Jordan is associate publisher for Kurtz-Whitman."

The two men shook hands. Coulter had the soft, much-washed hands of a surgeon, but his grip was firm. He was tall, maybe an inch taller than Jordan, with sandy hair going silver at the temples. "Coulter," Jordan repeated slowly. "Cardiovascular, right?"

"Yes, have we met?"

"No. Are you the surgeon who operated on the CEO of Armstrong-Rand a few weeks ago?"

Coulter's gaze narrowed. "Yes, how did you know? The company was adamant that George's health problems remain private."

"George Hall oversees a multibillion-dollar corporation. No hospital has the kind of security to keep something like that private."

"Nevertheless," Coulter said stiffly, "I would like to know the source of your information."

A moment passed, then Coulter realized he was not going to get any more information and turned to Valerie. "Is this a bad time, Val?"

"No, I—"

"Matter of fact—"

Both Valerie and Jordan spoke at once, but with an ironic nod, he gave her the floor. With a sigh, she glanced at the report he still held in his hand. "You were saying—"

"This is an advance copy of the quarterly report," Jordan told her, noting with satisfaction the keen look she gave it. "There are some numbers in here that will interest you. I asked Accounting to hold distribution until I gave them a go-ahead at—" He shot a cuff back to look at his watch. "Three o'clock."

It was after twelve now. If she went out to lunch with Coulter, she wouldn't have time to delve into the report with any detail. He watched her face—a very expressive face—as she struggled with conflicting obligations. He saw the instant she decided and there was resentment in the look she shot at him. He hadn't quite figured out why he found himself constantly provoking her. She turned to Coulter. "Wayne—"

"You're busy, darling." Coulter took her hand and squeezed it, giving her a warm smile, but the look he turned on Jordan would have cut glass. "Don't deprive her of lunch, Case. She works too hard as it is. She needs nutrition at midday, even if she has to discuss whatever's in that blasted report while eating."

Pompous ass. "I had the same thought in mind," Jordan said dryly.

"I'm skipping lunch," Valerie snapped. "We can discuss the report right here."

Coulter was shaking his head and wagging his finger. "Now this is exactly what I was afraid would happen. I'm willing to wager that Hal Kurtz would prefer you pace yourself in this new position so that you'll produce the best magazine in publishing today. If you burn yourself to the socket almost before you've begun, nobody wins." He kissed Valerie's fingers and strode to the door. "Have lunch. Handle the problem Coulter's brought to your attention. Then I'm sure you'll tackle whatever else is on your busy schedule with your usual professionalism. I'll call you tonight, darling."

He left and Valerie drew in a deep breath, then walked briskly around her desk and took a seat. "Okay, let's have it."

" 'Burn yourself to the socket?' Is that guy for real?"

"He's a cardiovascular surgeon," she said stiffly. "He sees a lot of people who sacrifice their health while building a career."

"You and Coulter have a serious thing going?"

She looked at him coolly. "About that report . . ."

"Yeah." He tossed it onto her desk and moved around to stand at her side while she opened it to a page that showed at a glance the sales performance for *Panache* as of the past quarter. Turning the page, Valerie found a second chart tracking the past year's performance. "Not a pretty sight, is it?" Jordan said.

Her eyes zipped over the numbers. "Now I understand why Hal felt he had to replace Liz Chopin. The
magazine has been in the red substantially for at least
a year."

"Hal was more than patient with Liz," he said. To
track the numbers beyond the past year with any accu-
racy, Valerie would have to request access to the audit.
Jordan knew she'd do that. "I've directed the finance
people to have an audit on your desk by tomorrow
morning."

She glanced up at him, showing some wariness.
"Thanks, I think."

"Wouldn't that have been your first act if I hadn't
suggested it?"

"Yes."

"So, let's have some lunch while we talk about strategy
to increase sales." He crossed the room to get her coat.
"How about Il Nido? Do you like Northern Italian?"

"Of course, who doesn't. But as I said before, we can
talk here. Eric can go to the deli and pick up sandwiches.
It isn't necessary to—"

"No, it isn't necessary, but personally, if I have to
work through lunch, I don't see any virtue in denying
myself a damn good meal at the same time." He held
the coat and his smile while she reluctantly turned to
allow him to help her on with it. As he settled it on
her shoulders, he caught the scent of her perfume.
Something light and flowery. He would have pegged
her for a woman who liked exotic scent, but in the weeks
since she'd stepped into her new job, he had discovered
many of his former assumptions about Valerie Olivier-
Long were skewed.

"Any more odd snapshots turning up in the wrong
places?" he asked, holding the door for her as they left
her office.

"No."

"Did you ever figure out how it got there?"

"Why would I want to?"

"C'mon, Valerie. You nearly passed out when you saw it. It was obviously intended to shock you. You're not the type to shrug off something like that."

They'd reached the elevator now. She didn't say anything until they were going down. "I got an even more shocking surprise when I got home. That photo was tucked away in a special place in my apartment." She was watching him intently. "Someone had broken in. They'd removed it and then placed it in the photo lab where I'd be sure to find it."

"Are you serious?" He was surprised at the jolt of concern he felt knowing someone had broken into her home.

"I don't joke about that kind of violation."

"Did you call the cops? Report it?"

"No."

"Why, for God's sake? Are you asking for it to happen again?"

"I can't prove someone broke in. There was no jimmied lock, no telltale signs around any window. Besides, I'm on the eighth floor. And what would I say? That someone stole a snapshot?" She gave a harsh laugh. "So, no, I didn't call the police, but I did have the locks changed."

"You don't have any idea who might have done it? How about Sara? Or maybe when you were entertaining, someone did a little snooping."

"Sara was as shocked as you appear to be. As for a guest snooping around to that extent, I suppose it could happen, but no one comes to mind, I'm happy to say. So unless and until it happens again, I can't see there's anything I can do."

Again, he was surprised at how unsatisfactory that thought was. Valerie was no China doll. She'd forged a very successful career for herself in a very competitive and ruthless business. Why he'd feel any concern mystified him. But he did.

Thirty minutes later, they were at Il Nido. "Olivier-Long. Pretty name. French, isn't it?" He sat across from her enjoying a very good merlot while Valerie nursed Perrier with lime. "I didn't get much of a chance to study that snapshot, but I know New Orleans and I recognized the street signs. Rue Royale is in the French Quarter. Is that where you grew up?"

He could have sworn there was a flash of alarm in the look she shot him, but it was quickly gone . . . or masked as she bent to take a sip of water. "More or less. I thought you were a native New Yorker."

"Almost. I was born in New Jersey. But back to New Orleans. What part of the city do you call home?"

"Um, the French Quarter."

"Not many children there, but the eclectic lifestyles in the Quarter would tend to give a kid a unique outlook. Do you visit often?"

She was studying the menu intently. "Not really. Have you tried the sea bass here?"

"Like everything else, it's great." The journalist in him scented a mystery. Why didn't she want to talk about herself?

She gave her order to the waiter and waited while he ordered. "You've probably been to most of the interesting cities in the world," she said, settling back to wait for their meal. "Which is your favorite?"

"San Francisco."

"Not Paris? London? Rome?"

"Nope. San Francisco's got the best food, a great climate, interesting history, breathtaking scenery, and of course . . ." He lifted his wineglass. ". . . wine."

"Of course." She smiled, and he wondered what her smile looked like when it was genuine. She was barely tolerating him, and he found himself wishing they didn't have such bad history. He watched her take another sip of water as the waiter set their plates in front of them. "You don't drink?"

"Not during the day."

"Or at night either, apparently. You only pretended to taste the champagne that Hal ordered at Le Cirque to celebrate your promotion."

She shrugged. "I don't have to ingest alcohol to celebrate."

He leaned back, studying the prim set of her pretty mouth and the flash of irritation in her eyes. There were depths to Valerie Olivier-Long that he'd like to explore. Suddenly he felt real regret that she was involved with Wayne Coulter. Coulter would never ignite the fire that Jordan sensed lay banked in her.

"About the report, Jordan." She lowered her tone as a party of four was seated nearby. "How much time do you think Hal is willing to wait to see the bottom line improve?"

"Depends on how much improvement you can make. If sales are increased right away even incrementally, he'll cut you some slack. Personally, I think *Panache* has the potential to equal the success of *Vanity Fair* and *Cosmopolitan*. But you'll need to define the magazine more definitely, which Liz failed to do. You can't be either *Vanity* or *Cosmo*. You—"

"I don't want to be either one of them. I want *Panache* to emerge as the new voice of the complete contemporary woman. For me, that means offering a wide range of material from child care to politics and everything in between."

"Be careful. Today's contemporary woman could be a career gal, a stay-at-home mom, a supermom, a Lesbian, a free-spirited artist. In short, she can be any female. The wider the range, the murkier your message becomes to your readers.''

"So what do you suggest?" She leaned back, looking irritated. "I assume you do have some suggestions."

"Which you would reject as fast as I could make them. No, it's your job to define *Panache*. And I know you'll do it." Finally he saw some of her defensiveness ease.

"Then what was the point of this discussion today? You could have dropped the report on my desk and left."

"To give you a heads-up on something that's almost a done deal and to tell you I had nothing to do with it."

She went stiff and still again. "What is it?"

"Hal had a call from Ted Carpenter's lawyers. I think he's going to pull the feature."

"No!" Quick and hot.

"I know you're high on it, Valerie, but—"

"We've done our homework on that story." Her tone was low, but every bit as fierce as the look in her eyes. "Our lawyers have been over the material with a magnifying glass. We have no exposure, none. There is no need for Hal to panic."

"I'm only telling you what he said to me. He's—"

Her eyes narrowed with suspicion. "Did you do this, Jordan? Do you want to clear the decks for that melodramatic . . ." She waved a hand, searching for words. ". . . farce about the Trent girl in New Orleans? Is that what this is about?"

"Would you believe me if I denied it?"

"Stop being so damn . . . cagey!"

He stared at her. "Me, cagey! You're hardly one to talk. What's the reason you don't want to do the Trent story? Is there some reason that subject is off-limits? Or is New Orleans off-limits? Before you start accusing me

of being evasive, maybe you'd better take a look at yourself."

"Oh, this is too much!" As she fumbled with her
napkin, she accidentally upset her untouched plate. It
made a clatter, tipping over the edge of the table in a
cascade of Caesar-tossed greens. With a soft cry, she
scooted back in her chair, but not quick enough to avoid
getting some of it in her lap. She stood up, brushing
fastidiously at the sticky Romaine.

"Damn!" Jordan, too, was on his feet, but when he
put out a hand to help, she stopped him with a killing
look.

The waiter materialized at her side, murmuring with
sympathy and offering fresh linen. "If Madame would
like to use the powder room, there's club soda on hand
that will minimize the stain until it can be professionally
removed."

"Yes, thank you," Valerie said faintly. She looked
around with distraction. "Where is it?"

"Just through there, madame, then turn left."

Cheeks burning, she reached blindly for the purse
that Jordan held out to her and quickly disappeared.

In the lounge, Valerie dabbed at the greasy spots on
her skirt with a soda-soaked napkin while muttering
with disgust at her idiotic overreaction. What an embar-
rassing moment! She'd like to blame Jordan, but all
he'd done was deliver the bad news. She'd dumped the
salad into her lap without help from anyone. Actually,
except for grilling her on her personal life, he'd done
her a favor. She paused for a moment wishing she could
recall her angry reaction. By letting her know what Hal
intended to do, she at least had a chance to muster her
arguments in favor of keeping the Carpenter feature
alive. And there was no benefit to Jordan to share the

figures for the magazine with her—at least none that she could see.

Finishing up, she stood in front of the mirror and studied the damage. Thankfully, her suit was black. She wouldn't have to go home and change. After washing her hands, she retouched her lipstick and was closing her purse when her cell phone rang. She flipped the lid open to check the caller ID, but didn't recognize the number. A beat or two passed while she decided against letting the call go to her voice mail. She liked to be immediately accessible if someone on her staff needed her. She pressed talk.

"This is Valerie."

"And this is . . . guess who-ooo?" The reply came in a singsong voice that Valerie didn't recognize.

"What? Who are you calling?"

"I'm calling you, Caroline."

Caroline! Pure shock sliced through Valerie with the speed of a laser. "Who is this?"

"Someone who knows . . . Caroline."

Panic swirled inside her. "You have the wrong number."

The caller gave a low chuckle. "I don't think so."

"What do you want?" she demanded, sounding desperate even to herself.

"All in good time, Caroline." A tiny pause, then slyly, "I love your place. So . . . sophisticated."

Valerie's heart stopped. "How did you get inside? How?"

"Piece o' cake." The sound of a commuter train came over the cell and Valerie missed the next few words. "—been a few days. Did you think I was gone? Uh-uh, I have a life, too." Another pause, then the caller's tone hardened, the playfulness dropped. "Now it's time to remind you again, Caroline, that I'm still out here . . . and I'm not leaving."

Valerie's own reflection in the mirror blurred in her gaze. The voice was hoarse, like a person who smoked too much. Man or woman? She couldn't tell. Struggling to keep fear and revulsion from her tone, she asked, "What do you want from me?"

"What do I want, Caroline?" There was a sound, as if the person drew deeply on a cigarette. "Hmm, I guess we can just call it . . . payback."

New Orleans

Angela LeBlanc hit pay dirt at the NOPD, courtesy of an old acquaintance. She'd only had to buy Pete Benoit three drinks at a seedy bar on Esplanade before he agreed to let her come to the station and take a look at the case file on Amy Trent. It was stored in a cardboard box marked COLD CASES, and Benoit had to shift a couple of the boxes around to get to the *T*'s. Huffing and puffing, he hitched his pants up over a bulging belly before waddling back to the counter where Angela waited, wishing for a cigarette.

"I got my ass in trouble over giving that reporter from the *Picayune* access to this file," Benoit claimed. "So anybody asks, you ain't seen it, right?"

"Right. Was that the guy who wrote the article that came out in the paper a few weeks ago?"

"Yeah. And since you ain't no reporter, what you planning on doing with the information in that file?" Benoit had been a sleazy rookie twenty years ago. For the past ten, he'd been relegated to a desk job and he was still sleazy. It puzzled Angela how some cops played fast and loose with the rules and never even came close to getting nailed, while she'd messed up just that once and bam! But cops like Pete Benoit had their uses.

There was a slew of photos in the file jacket. The girl's disappearance had happened at a time of public awareness of the number of homeless kids roaming the French Quarter, so there had been several spreads about them in the paper. It hadn't been from any sense of social awareness that folks wanted the kids rounded up and put out of sight. No, panhandling and teenage prostitutes were bad for tourism, the lifeblood of the city at that time, considering that the bottom had fallen out of the oil industry.

"Who the hell are these kids?" she muttered, squinting at a photo. She recognized the rundown building as an abandoned grocery distributorship on Magazine Street. The place was still there, still derelict. What was gone now were the half-dozen teens sprawled willy-nilly on the floor zonked out on drugs.

Benoit leaned over to see. "Check the backs of the photos. Some of them have names. Others are in the statements that we took."

"We?" She looked at him.

He shrugged. "I remember the case."

"Uh-huh. Did he take anything out of the file?"

"Who, the reporter?"

No, Santa Claus, you idiot. "Yeah, Pete, the reporter. From the *Picayune*. What did he take?"

"Coupla photographs. You saw 'em in the article."

"Was there anything else that belonged to her?" She riffled through the file looking for the evidence list.

"To who?"

"Amy Trent, Pete. Who the hell are we talking about here?"

"What d'you mean, anything else? Like what?"

"Personal items. Clothes. A purse." She should be so lucky. "Keepsakes."

"Keepsakes?"

Angela drew in a long-suffering breath. "Teenagers like to keep stuff, like teddy bears or hair clips . . . diaries. Did Amy have a diary?"

"If it ain't on the evidence list, I guess she didn't have no diary."

She deftly palmed a couple of photos that looked promising. "There is no evidence list."

"Huh?" Pete took the file and, licking his fingers, began turning the pages. After a futile search, he finally slapped the file closed. "I remember now. We never found the place where she lived before she disappeared, which is why we never could get a lead on her murder. Those kids squatted anywhere they could, and in the Quarter there had to be dozens of possibilities. So there ain't no evidence list."

"Wait, I'm not finished." Angela took the file back. "I see somebody took statements from 'known acquaintances.' Can I copy these, Pete?"

"Hell, no! I already—" Behind him, the phone rang. "Shee-it! I gotta get that." Keeping an eye on Angela, he lifted the receiver and began talking. Then, with a curse, still trying to watch her, he edged around his desk to get a pad and pen to take a message. In the instant that he bent to jot down a number, Angela pulled two of the printed statements from the file and slipped them into an inside pocket of her blazer. Then, without waiting for Benoit to hang up the phone, she lifted her hand in a wave, mouthed a thank-you to him, and left.

She was proud of the quality of her detective work when, two days later, she had managed to locate one of the girls in the group that Amy had run with. It hadn't been easy. Using the photos with a few IDs scribbled on the backs, then comparing the statements, picking up on a few details inadvertently revealed by the kids, she'd found Kelly Lott.

Kelly Lott was now Mrs. Perry Fontenot. She lived across the river from the city, or on the "west bank" as it was known to locals. She was married to a building inspector who worked for the city. They had two children, a boy and a girl, ages ten and twelve. She did not have a job, unless doing part-time work in the church counted. She was the almost stereotypical personification of a middle-class housewife and mother.

Angela stood outside studying the house for a few minutes before making an attempt to get inside and persuade the woman to talk to her. It was an attractive house, well maintained with nice curb appeal. Somebody liked gardening and was good at it, Angela thought, admiring several varieties of camellias in full bloom. In another month, those azaleas all along the front would burst out in a profusion of color. She'd always liked flowers. Maybe if her plans worked out, she'd be able to get another place, something with a small New Orleans–style courtyard. Maybe have a fountain in it, tinkling and gurgling while she had her morning coffee. Turn one of the bedrooms into a study with a computer and work right out of her house. She'd kiss goodbye to that rathole she lived in now. Dropping her cigarette on the sidewalk out front, she ground it out with the toe of her shoe and headed for the front door.

Kelly Lott opened up on the first ding of the doorbell after checking through the peephole. What, had this woman forgotten life on the dark side, Angela wondered with an odd spurt of irritation. She peeped out and saw an old broad with a face that looked honest? Maybe those drugs all those years ago had damaged some brain cells.

"Yes?" Soft voice. Only a little curiosity. No fear.

"Hello, Ms. Fontenot. I'm Angela LeBlanc." Luckily, she still had a few business cards left over from the initial printing at least seven years ago. She handed one over. "I've been retained by a client to try and find a relative. I wonder if you'd be willing to answer a few questions."

Kelly Lott Fontenot looked momentarily puzzled.
"Who are you trying to find?"

"Could I come inside for just a few minutes?"

"Well . . ."

Angela gave her arms a brisk rub and smiled ruefully.
"Whooo, it's chilly out today, huh? I can't believe I left
my coat in the office."

Just as Angela hoped, the woman stepped back and
let her inside the house. "I was just going out," she
said, looking slightly uncertain.

"This won't take five minutes." She made a quick
survey of the house. Kelly had come a long way, baby.
Her present digs were as different from that dingy grocery warehouse as Angela's dreams were from reality.
She smiled. "What can you tell me about Amy Trent?"

CHAPTER EIGHT

Jordan rose with a concerned look as Valerie approached the table. "What's wrong? You're as pale as a ghost."

"I'm fine." Her first thought had been that the caller could have been Jordan, although his look of concern now made that seem ridiculous. Besides, unlike the caller's slimy voice, Jordan's deep, strong tone could never be disguised into something so . . . so creepy. So sick.

She glanced around the restaurant, not sure what she was looking for. The tables were filled with busy people intent on eating or on the business at hand. No one was watching her. No one seemed especially sinister. Besides, there had been nothing in the call to make her think it had originated here. The caller could have been in another state.

"I must get back to my office, Jordan."

"You didn't touch your lunch. Are you sure you're okay?" He was watching her shrewdly.

"It's just a headache. Stay and finish," she told him. "I'll catch a cab."

He ignored that and caught the waiter's eye. "You didn't have a headache five minutes ago."

"I have one now," she said evenly.

Not waiting for the check, he tossed his napkin on the table along with a few bills, then guided her through the tables and on out the door. "You're going to catch hell from Coulter. Be sure and tell him it wasn't my fault."

"That I didn't eat?" A taxi rolled to the curb and she grabbed the handle, yanked it open before he could, and got inside. "I'll get a candy bar out of the machine," she said as they pulled into New York traffic.

"Oh, he'll really approve of that."

"No one dictates my diet or anything else about my life, Jordan. Certainly not Wayne." She turned to see if anybody was following them.

"What are you looking for?"

"Nothing."

He muttered something profane. "Something happened when you left the table, Valerie. What the hell's going on?"

Was it risky to tell him? Not the whole truth, of course, as that would be the end of her career. He knew about the snapshot and he'd made the connection to New Orleans on his own. Telling him something would give her a chance to watch his reaction, if nothing else. "I had a phone call while I was in the lounge. Apparently, I've joined the ranks of celebrities who are harassed by their fans. But it's a little weird."

He shifted to get a better look at her. "Does it have anything to do with the snapshot and the break-in?"

She gave a short laugh. "I guess it does. The caller admitted breaking into my apartment." She shuddered. "I'm feeling a bit spooked."

"What did he say?"

She couldn't tell him, although for a quick, almost irresistible moment, she found herself wanting to. Sighing, she pressed a spot between her eyes with two fingers. Old lies were coming back to haunt her as well as old mistakes and bad choices. She was definitely caught in a tangled web now, just as Janine had often warned her she would be someday.

Payback.

What did that mean?

"Valerie?"

"I don't know that it was a man," she said, avoiding a direct reply. "It could have been either since I had a feeling something was being used to distort the voice. I think whoever it was just wanted me to know that he or she could find me anytime, talk to me anytime. Could even access my home . . . at will."

"We need to call the police." There was real concern in his voice. He reached into a breast pocket and pulled out his cell phone.

"No."

He gave her an astonished look. "No? You're going to let this guy get away with harassing you this way? Don't be foolish, Valerie. There's a law against stalking in New York. And before you tell me you don't know who it is and can't file a complaint against an unknown person, it is also against the law when someone's home is burglarized. At least let the cops come and take a statement. If you're being watched as closely as it appears, that might scare him off."

And under ordinary circumstances, that's exactly what she would do. How to explain to him why she wasn't going to do the logical, safe thing without sounding like a blindly stubborn idiot? Or a fool? "I hear you, Jordan, but actually, no one's threatened me in so many words. I'm just being . . . harassed. And I have already changed the locks at my apartment. I'll call today and make arrangements for a security system ... and I'll alert the apartment security people. This whole thing isn't dangerous, at least I don't think so. It's ... well, it's an irritant that I don't need just now."

"An irritant." He was looking at her as if he couldn't believe what he heard. "You didn't look irritated when you came out of the restroom. You looked pale and shaken. Hell, you looked scared."

"Anyone would be. I was caught off guard." The cab had reached her office building. Again, before Jordan did so, she opened the door. "Thanks for the heads-up on the Carpenter thing, and I owe you for the advance look at the numbers for the quarter."

"Valerie." She was halfway out of the cab when he stopped her with a hand on her arm. "I don't know what's going on here with you and this thing, but you could be making a big mistake by ignoring this guy. Sometimes these creeps are harmless, but sometimes they're not. I wish you'd let me call the cops."

"As I said, I couldn't tell if it was a man as the voice was distorted."

"All the more reason why he could be dangerous. Why would he go to so much trouble? He wants to rattle you, to keep you off guard. He wants to scare you and I hope to God he doesn't plan to hurt you. But it could happen." He gave her arm a little shake. "Get your security people on this right away. Promise me you'll at least do that."

"I'll think about it." She got out of the cab. "Thanks."

"And eat something."

Her thoughts when she left him were not on getting something to eat. She was thinking how to flush out whoever it was who threatened to destroy her and it couldn't be as Jordan suggested. There would be no phone call to Security. She sensed her tormentor was too smart to be unmasked that way. Nor was she going to sit idly by and let herself be victimized again. She was no longer that vulnerable, frightened, and homeless teenager who had been without the means to survive except under the control of a drug dealer and pimp. She'd come too far to see it all vanish in a firestorm of scandal after working so hard to turn her life around. Oh, she'd done things she was ashamed of, yes. But she'd tried to atone for that. She'd worked like a Trojan to become the woman she was today, and no sick tormentor was going to steal everything and dictate the terms of this game. For that was what it felt like to Valerie. A sick and manipulative game.

She didn't take the time to remove her coat upon entering her office. Instead, she went right to her phone and picked it up, muttering grimly, "Two can play this game."

New Orleans

"I told you I didn't want to talk to you again, Ms. LeBlanc. I'm going to call the police if you don't go away."

"I understand exactly how you feel, ma'am." Angela smiled her best smile and gave Kelly Lott Fontenot a shrug that she hoped looked believably apologetic. "But if you could just help me out once more, I swear to God you won't ever see me again."

Kelly wasn't nearly as gullible now as she'd been when Angela first approached her. This time the woman didn't allow her inside. "I wouldn't have helped you the first time if you'd been honest about the reason you wanted to see me. Amy Trent should be left to rest in peace. It's been twenty years, for heaven's sake!"

Shifting slightly, Angela managed to wedge the toe

of her shoe in the door. "If your little girl was missing,
Mrs. Fontenot, and no trace of her was ever found,
don't you think you'd still want to know what happened
even after twenty years?" During that first visit, Angela
had seen the pictures of a blue-eyed child on the wall.
She watched slyly as her words reached a place where
the woman was most vulnerable. "I think you would."

Kelly sighed. "Maybe, but it hardly matters because
I can't help you anyway. I don't know anything about
Amy's disappearance. Can't you understand that I just
want to forget that period in my life? Dragging up the
past isn't always a good thing. I . . . I'm different now.
What I did then . . . what I went through . . . well, people
think that kind of free lifestyle is fun and exciting, but
they're wrong. It was hell. You're hungry most of the
time. And cold. And lonely. And confused. I would die
if I thought my Lindy and Michael would ever wind up
like that."

"But you were one of the lucky ones," Angela said,
producing a photo she'd stolen from Amy Trent's case
file. Five girls faced the camera—Anna Swenson, Becky
Barfield, Amy Trent, and one still unidentified. Angela
had managed to trace Anna and Becky, but there was
no information to be gained there. She held the photo
up for Kelly to see. "Do you know if the people in this
photo with you were as lucky?"

Reluctantly, as if she couldn't quite help herself, Kelly
looked at the picture. "Becky died of AIDS a few years
ago. I read it in the paper. As for Anna . . ." She touched
the face of a lost-looking, dark-haired girl. "She overdosed and sustained brain damage. The last I heard she
was institutionalized."

Anna Swenson had been in and out of the state mental
hospital at Mandeville. At the present time, she was
inside and had been unable to furnish Angela anything
useful about the past she'd shared with the group. "I

was able to locate her at Mandeville," Angela said. "She's paid a high price for those years she spent on the street."

"Thanks to Oscar." Kelly made a disgusted sound. "He had all of us under his thumb and we were all dumb enough to allow it. If anybody got in trouble, it was always one of his girls, not Oscar."

"And Amy was one of them?"

"We all were, don't you understand? It makes me sick now, just thinking about it." She took the picture. "That's Amy, but I guess you know that. There's Anna and this is Becky. This one . . . her name was Caroline. She and Amy were close friends, but they were really into using. Amy was pregnant and Caroline was always trying to keep Oscar away from her. He wanted her to have an abortion and maybe it was a good thing since she couldn't seem to function without getting high and who knows how that would have affected her baby. But then one night they just disappeared."

"Who, Amy?"

"Amy and Caroline. Together. Poof, they were gone."

"What about the baby?"

"Who knows? But I bet Oscar forced her to get the abortion. He wasn't about to allow a little kid inside his playhouse."

"This would be Oscar Diaz, right?"

"I'm not telling anything you didn't read in that article last month. That reporter had it right. He just didn't have the rest of the story."

"The rest of the story . . ." Angela's hand was inside her carryall praying the recorder was getting all this. "And that would be—"

"Whether Amy had the abortion, whether she died, what happened to Caroline . . ." She sighed again. "Of course, Caroline was a nobody like the rest of us, so there was no one around asking about her when the whole thing blew up."

"Quite a few unanswered questions," Angela observed.

"Yes, and I think they should all just die a natural death. Some things are better left in the past."

Back in her car, Angela took out her recorder and spoke into it. "Three things: Check for rap sheet on Oscar Diaz. What about Amy's baby? And who is Caroline?"

CHAPTER NINE

"There's no excuse for this." Valerie shoved back in her chair and eyed her staff as if expecting one of them to stand and admit to the screwup. "I spent two hours today with Hal Kurtz persuading him that this feature is good journalism, that we were fully protected from every legal angle, and that our readers will love it. I practically had to promise that Ted Carpenter would be indicted for murder as a result of this feature, and as the publisher of *Panache*, Hal would be nominated for a Pulitzer." She paused, pushing hair behind one ear to say, "And now you tell me Jon Palmer wants to pull the feature from us."

Greg Parker slouched in his chair, twisting his coffee mug with his left hand. "I had a call from someone at *Talk* who told me he plans to offer it to them."

"Which means he got wind that Hal was thinking of backing off." Valerie gave each of the four people sitting around the table a direct look. "Does anybody know how Palmer might have heard that?"

Roxanne gazed at a painting on the opposite wall. Greg stared into his coffee. Suzy Klein met Valerie's eyes straight on. Eric was scribbling notes in case Valerie wanted to refer later to someone's remarks. No one appeared inclined to answer. She stood up with impatience and began pacing. "There's no place in this organization for disloyalty, folks. I'm not accusing anybody here, but I want you to go back to your people and find out where the leak could have originated. Meanwhile, I'll call Jon and try to repair the damage."

"That's not all, Val." Roxanne tapped a fresh cigarette on the back of her hand as if to light up. She'd quit smoking months ago, but still missed handling the things. "I've been in the process of choosing the photo layout on the Carpenter feature from the pictures I took in Aspen. When I went into the lab this morning, I found a container of fluid tipped over. Several negatives were damaged. It'll take me a couple of days to do the project over again. We're in a time crunch since we're trying for the April issue on this feature, right, Greg?" He nodded, still slowly turning the mug round and round. Roxanne looked directly at Valerie. "I don't think it was an accident."

"You think—"

"It was no accident."

Valerie's gaze narrowed. "You're saying someone deliberately damaged the pictures for the Carpenter feature?"

"I don't leave chemicals sitting around where they can spill over and ruin my work."

"Why these particular photos?" Valerie asked, puzzled.

Roxanne shrugged. "Because they were mine?"

"You think it was personal?" Nothing in Roxanne's life meant more than her career. Her name on the photographs that accompanied the Carpenter feature

was sure to boost her stock as a professional. Did somebody hate Roxanne enough to want to sabotage her
career?

"Maybe it's not Roxanne who's the target here," Eric
said, looking up from his notepad. "Maybe you're the
target, Val."

"Me?" She put her hand on her chest. "How do you
figure that?"

"It'll mean a delay, right? And another headache for
you. Just one more thing to complicate your life. Think
of it like this." Eric hitched his chair forward to make
his point. "Someone's messing around in Rox's lab obviously up to no good and someone had to tell Jon Palmer
about Mr. Kurtz getting cold feet, knowing it would
have some negative effect. Maybe it's one and the same
person doing this shit."

Valerie stopped behind Eric's chair, thinking he
could be right. If he knew about the endless list of weird
things that had happened to her lately, beginning with
the snapshot planted in the photo lab, the break-in at
her apartment, the cell phone call, and the newspaper
article in Janine's room, he would definitely think it was
all about Valerie. She herself was beginning to think it
was about her. But who? Why?

"Isn't it routine to lock the photo lab over the lunch
hour, Roxanne?" Valerie asked.

"Yes, and I locked it."

"Who else has a key?" Standing behind Eric, Valerie
studied the faces around the table.

Roxanne sighed. "Several people, Val. It's a magazine
we're running here. That means photographs and tons
of them. We've got several photographers on the staff.
You can't keep people out of the photo lab."

"So it could have been any one of several people. Or
a stranger." Valerie went back to her place at the end
of the table and picked up her briefcase. "I'll leave it

to all of you to make a good effort to get to the bottom of this. I want names. That goes for the leak to Jon Palmer, too."

"You're going to call him?" Roxanne asked, crushing her unlit cigarette.

"It's either that or scrap the project, and damn it, that was going to be the article featured on the cover next month." She snapped the lock and turned to go. "Pulling it is not an option."

Jon Palmer was embarrassed that word had gotten back to Valerie that he was considering reneging on a contract. He had good reason, he told her. According to his agent, Hal Kurtz was getting ready to pull the plug on *Panache* magazine. If he wanted the Ted Carpenter article to get the attention it deserved, his agent advised trying to place it elsewhere. After a lunch where neither ate very much, Valerie finally convinced him that he'd been misinformed. She swore that *Panache* was in solid financial shape. Hal Kurtz—and thus Kurtz-Whitman— was behind her a hundred percent. Palmer may have had some lingering doubt, but by the time the check came, he'd agreed to honor his contract. With conditions.

"How'd you manage it?" Jordan asked later that day when he called. Apparently, Hal had informed him that the Carpenter feature was okay for printing and that she'd dodged a second bullet with the author.

"Three guesses." Valerie removed an earring and cradled the receiver between chin and shoulder. With both hands free, she began signing the correspondence Eric spread in front of her. "He promised to stay the course if we'd sign him for another piece he's researching. A walk in the park," she added dryly.

"An expensive outing," Jordan said just as dryly. "And unethical."

"I had no choice."

"You're probably right." He waited a beat. "Don't do business with him again."

Valerie scribbled her signature on a letter. "I think I now know what kind of man Jon Palmer is, Jordan." It surprised her not to get an argument on her decision even though he must be as concerned as she was over the magazine's bottom line. Since he kept a close eye on costs, he also knew that the Carpenter story had already made a sizable hole in her budget. Scrapping it would have spilled a lot of red ink. "And when he submits the new article, you can believe I will not be easy to please. He should have let his agent handle this."

"His agent probably refused."

"Whatever." She tossed her pen aside and leaned back. "Was there another reason you called?"

"Two reasons and neither is the flap with Palmer," Jordan said. "First of all, did you get a new security system installed and did you mention to your apartment manager that your place was broken into and did you demand increased surveillance to prevent it happening again?"

"Jordan . . ."

"Before you say it isn't any of my business, damn it, Val, I'll tell you straight out that I don't understand your attitude." Before she could say anything, he added, "If you won't do this for yourself, think of Sara. How would she feel if a tragedy happened?"

"All this nagging is for Sara's sake?"

He was clearly struggling to hold his temper. "It's for your sake, woman! Wake up and smell the coffee. Somebody out there is stalking you and it could be dangerous."

"Okay, okay. You can cross me off your worry list.

I've arranged for a security system, although they can't
come until next week. And you'll be happy to know that
the people who manage the apartment building were
extremely concerned that this happened. To cover
themselves, however, they told me I'd been careless in
not having my key on my person at all times, as if that
were actually possible. How many women carry a wad
of keys in their pocket?"

He made a grudging sound. "Well, it sounds as if you
came to your senses. I admit that after leaving you at
the restaurant, I had my doubts."

"Thanks."

"Second reason." She heard the squeak of his chair
and imagined him laid back with his feet propped on
his desk. The image was almost stark in its clarity. "I
was calling to suggest we go together to Hal's party
tonight. You're invited, aren't you?"

"Yes." She motioned Eric to take the signed letters.
"He mentioned it when we talked earlier today."

"You are going?"

"Yes, but—"

"Why don't I pick you up? And before you start, hear
me out. I'll be passing your place heading for the same
location. Why not just go together?"

She looked up as Roxanne tapped quietly on her
open door. "This is about my stalker, isn't it?" She
motioned Roxanne inside. "I don't need a bodyguard,
Jordan."

"And you don't need to invite danger either. Besides,
would it be so bad putting up with me for a couple of
hours? Think of it as a date."

"A date?" With Jordan Case? "Now that would be a
stretch," she said dryly.

He paused as if struck by a new thought. "You weren't
going with that stuffed shirt, were you?"

"Who? Dr. Coulter?" She realized she was smiling.

"I'm afraid he's unavailable. He's at a conference in L.A."

"Well then, good thing I called. So, I'll pick you up around eight, okay?"

"Okay, around eight." She hung up, looking bemused.

"I can't believe what I just heard," Roxanne said, taking a seat on the leather couch. "Was that Jordan Case? And the two of you are going out? It's not a command performance forced on you by Hal Kurtz and you're going without even token reluctance?"

"I know it sounds odd." Valerie got up, putting her earring back in place as she left her desk. "Actually, it's simple. He's playing bodyguard, would you believe? I got a crank call on my cell phone while I was with him at lunch a couple of days ago and he assumed the worst right away. I tried to tell him that sort of thing comes with the territory when you're in the public eye, but he didn't seem to see it that way."

"What kind of crank call?" Roxanne asked sharply.

"Oh, just someone wanting to rattle my cage a little. And erase that look, Rox. I can't allow myself to be intimidated by someone so twisted and sick that he has to get his kicks that way."

"Then I'm glad Jordan's going with you. And as for offering himself as a bodyguard, I don't suppose it's occurred to you that he might genuinely like you."

"No, it hasn't."

"Then guess again."

"We're not even friends, Rox. And I don't think we can ever be friends. There's that business between Sara and Charlie, remember?" She smiled slightly. "Which doesn't mean that we can't learn to coexist without too much open hostility. Accepting him as an escort to a business event is pretty benign." She pulled a chair near the couch and sat down. "What's up with you?"

"I'm done with the photo layout on the Carpenter feature. As for the damaged negatives, I lost the whole lot. Fortunately, I still had a few rolls of film at my condo that I hadn't gotten around to developing and I used them. Some were quite good, although not as smashing as those I originally chose."

"So all's well," Valerie said. "Isn't it?"

Roxanne stood up abruptly. "I'm not sure. I've been thinking. We have the leak to Jon Palmer concerning Hal Kurtz and the damage to the photo lab. Then I remembered you asking about an old snapshot that mysteriously turned up in the lab, which according to Jordan really spooked you." She took her long hair in one hand and pulled it back, meeting Valerie's gaze. "Did you ever find out anything about how it got there?"

"No." Valerie was very still. For some reason, she hesitated telling Roxanne about the break-in. She wanted her role as editor to be the focus of interest at the magazine, not any threat to her security.

"You didn't volunteer and I didn't ask, but even without Jordan's comment, I also had the feeling that picture freaked you out."

"It was . . . personal, Rox."

"I guessed that and I'm not prying any further into your reasons. It's none of my business." She propped one hip against Valerie's desk. "However, the magazine is my business and I've been thinking about Eric's take on the situation . . . that you could be the target. He could be right, you know? Now you say someone's threatening you over the phone. What—"

"I didn't say anything about a threat. It was a crank call."

"What if this is some kind of sick plan aimed at you?"

"In what way? Has something else happened?"

Roxanne shrugged. "It's just something I was talking

about with—'' She stopped. "Have you thought about Denise?"

"Denise Grantham? No, what about her?"

"You know how ambitious she is. How far would she go to screw things up for you, Val? Delay costs money. It also takes a toll on your efficiency. Could she have planted the idea in Mr. Kurtz's mind that the Carpenter feature was too risky? She's sleeping with him, everybody knows that. She damn sure has motive and opportunity to connive against you. She could easily sneak into the photo lab and she damn well wouldn't care if she screwed up a photo layout of mine. Could it have been her voice on the phone? Hey, I know it sounds sick and twisted, but I think Denise is capable of doing something sick and twisted.'' She watched as the suggestion took hold in Valerie's mind, then pushed away from the desk. At the door, she looked back. "Just think about it, okay?"

With Denise's name added to her list of suspects, Valerie now had so many people who might have cause to wish her harm that she felt overwhelmed. They were like mushrooms springing up in her mind. The problem was that when she tried to visualize her tormentor, nobody who was an obvious suspect seemed right. Denise Grantham? Liz, who might resent losing her position as editor to Valerie? Somehow . . . no. Jordan? Didn't fit. Ted Carpenter was a stretch, but anything was possible. Or was it someone she knew in New Orleans? But who? And why wait twenty years to appear? God, it was enough to drive her crazy!

Her thoughts were interrupted by a commotion from Eric's desk out front. She rose, but before she'd taken more than a few steps, the door of her office flew open.

"I don't give a shit whether she wants to see me or not, goddamn it! I'm going in."

Eric stood firmly blocking the doorway, but the man he was fending off was a head taller, thirty pounds heavier, and in a towering rage. "Sir, you are not going into Ms. Olivier-Long's office until you calm down."

"Get outta my way!" He grabbed a handful of Eric's shirtfront to shove him aside, but Eric spread his arms and gripped the doorjamb, standing his ground.

"Call Security, Val!" Eric managed as he was jerked up and shaken like a dog, feet dangling.

Ted Carpenter. "Omigod," Valerie muttered, rushing over to the men. She tugged on Carpenter's arm. "Take your hands off my assistant unless you want to be arrested for assault."

He glared at her, his handsome features contorted with fury. "You'd like that, wouldn't you? Drumming up a murder charge against me isn't enough, now you want to see me behind bars?" He still held Eric.

She wheeled and started toward the telephone.

"Okay, okay." He muttered an oath as he abruptly dropped Eric. He was breathing hard when he faced Valerie. "This is private between you and me. I don't want your fairy godmother in the room."

"I'm perfectly willing to talk to you privately so long as you keep your temper under control."

Eric hovered anxiously at the door. "Val, I don't think—"

"What'll it be, Mr. Carpenter?"

"I'm calm." He brought up both hands in a show of peace, but his gaze was hard and mean.

"Are you okay, Eric?" she asked before allowing Carpenter to sit down.

"Yes." With a dark look at Carpenter, Eric straightened his collar and shoved his shirttails back into his pants. "But I'll be right outside. With Security. Just scream if you need help."

Carpenter gave a disgusted snort before turning to Valerie. "Can we get on with it?"

Valerie went to her desk, but didn't sit. "What was it you wanted to discuss?"

"Cut the bullshit! You know what the hell I want to discuss. I want to know exactly what's in that filthy piece you're running about my wife's death. And before you give me a rash of lies, you need to know that I've been told what you're accusing me of, and if you don't pull it, I'm going to sue your ass! There won't be enough advertisers left for you to publish this piece of shit you call a magazine one more month."

"The article is fully documented, Mr. Carpenter. Our lawyers have gone over it meticulously. There's nothing in it that's untrue."

"Here's one for starters. It's a goddamn lie that I murdered my wife!"

"No one's saying you murdered your wife. That would be libel. Jon Palmer is simply revisiting the case, reviewing the facts that were in evidence at the time of your wife's death. Of course, if you have reason to fear that . . ." Spreading her hands, she let her words hang in the air.

"It's not fear that's got me upset," he growled, now pacing like a caged bear. "You know how people are. You print that garbage, spinning the facts this way, that way, every way but straight and folks are going to think I did it and that's all it'll take to destroy everything I've worked for." He stopped and leaned toward her, his arms braced on her desk. "I don't intend to end up like O.J. with my life in ruins. You trash my name and my reputation and I'll take you down with me." His gaze narrowed with menace. "How would you like the closet opened on your own skeletons?"

Her heart leapt with suspicion. She'd never seriously considered Ted Carpenter to be her stalker. "Exactly what skeletons would that be, Mr. Carpenter?"

"We've all got 'em, Ms. Olivier-Long. Some worse than others."

"Did you call me yesterday?"

"Hell, yes! And for days before that, trying to get in here and—"

"On my cell phone. Did you call my cell phone number? Have you been in the photo lab? Was it you who damaged the original prints?"

"Cell phone? Damage . . . I haven't damaged anything . . . yet. I don't know what the hell you're talking about. And now that I'm finally in here, I'm telling you that if you print this trash about me, I will sue your ass. And when I do, this magazine—and your career—are toast."

"I think you've made your point," Valerie said, striving to sound calm. If she'd wondered whether he was capable of violence, she no longer had any doubt. She wasn't certain whether he was the type to torment her behind the scenes. He seemed a more up-front bully. "If there's nothing else—"

But Carpenter wasn't finished. "There was a hearing when my wife died," he said, his tone going very soft. Then he hit her desk with the flat of his hand. Valerie jumped. The sound was like a shot. "It was a goddamn accident!" he yelled.

She nearly quailed in the face of his fury, but she held her ground. She hoped Eric was as good as his word and that Security was on standby. "Maybe you should review the facts, Mr. Carpenter. It was not officially ruled an accident. There was trauma to her body inconsistent with an accidental fall from the ski lift. And you can't sue *Panache* for restating the facts in a case of

unexplained death. I should think you'd want to know
what happened."

"I *know* what happened, goddamn it!"

"So you say."

He fixed her with a mean glare. "You think you've
got all the answers, don't you?"

"Not really." She met his look with one equally determined. "But we at *Panache* think there are still questions
that need answers."

Carpenter stared balefully at her. The sound of his
breathing was unnerving in the small space. She could
almost see the anger emanating from him. His hands
were fisted at his side as he strove to contain it. Another
long moment passed as he tried to stare her down.
Failing, he turned abruptly and went to the door. "See
you in court, bitch."

She winced as he slammed it going out, then sat down
shakily in her chair.

Could he be the one?

New Orleans

Angela LeBlanc was elated. She was over the moon
with glee. She had a retainer for five thousand bucks
in her purse and she was flying home higher than the
crowded 747, almost unable to believe her good luck.
Airfare to New York had pretty much wiped out the
pitiful nest egg she had, but she'd taken a chance that
Amy Trent's mother was so hungry to hear something
about her daughter after all these years that she'd ante
up with a retainer if only to have somebody tell her
once and for all that Amy was probably dead. Which
was exactly what Angela believed based on the slim to
nearly nothing traces of Amy she'd detected in the girl's
last weeks in New Orleans. She was pretty certain that
was what NOPD believed, too, which explained why

they'd let the case grow cold. But for a resourceful private investigator, there was still money to be made on the case and Angela planned to milk Emilie Trent for every dime she could get. Hence, the bold and risky move to fly to New York to make her pitch to the woman, face to face.

It had been almost too easy, but Emilie had bought the whole spin. Angela had confided to the woman with a look of sincere regret that the work of the NOPD was sometimes less than professional. Angela knew how she'd feel, if she were a mom, not actually *knowing* that her daughter was . . . gone. Then, preening a little with the boast, she'd told Emilie that she had uncovered certain facts that the cops had missed. Angela promised her an end to wondering. A chance at peace. No more agonizing what-ifs. Closure.

At the end of her pitch, Emilie had opened her check-book and written a juicy retainer! It was only as the woman was actually writing the check that Angela realized she might have left money on the table. Emilie had been so desperate for information about her daughter that she probably would have sprung for a lot more, damn it. Next time, Angela promised herself. She could drag this out for who knew how long.

Now, with the check in her purse and a checklist of things to do to get down to the serious business of prolonging the scam, her brain was working overtime. Hell, this was a legitimate contract, the deal she'd made with Emilie Trent. She was a professional, after all. She planned to give the lady her money's worth. Amy Trent was dead, but there were facts to be learned about her during her months on the street. Angela owed Emilie a full and factual account of Amy's last days and she would give it to her. First stop: Oscar Diaz.

CHAPTER TEN

The day was cold, but beautiful at Rose Haven. Bright sunlight sparkled on the surface of the lake. Birds floated on invisible currents in the almost impossibly blue sky. Janine, along with half a dozen other residents, had been wheeled in her chair after nap time to a spot overlooking the scenic grounds, then left to enjoy the sunshine and a brief exposure to fresh air. They were all lined up like so many rag dolls, the brakes on their wheelchairs firmly set for safety's sake and "seatbelts" buckled to hold them securely in their chairs. All were snugly tucked up in soft, woolly blankets. They wore knitted caps pulled low, covering their ears. In spite of the warm sunshine, it wouldn't be possible to linger outside more than a few minutes. The wintry cold penetrated their old bones far more quickly than that of the bustling staff, all of whom were healthy and at least three decades younger than the patients they tended.

Janine spotted a bright red bird feeding from a dangling tube filled with sunflower seeds and struggled to recall its name. She spent a few laborious minutes sorting through the flotsam and jetsam cluttering up the workings of her brain, then with a sigh, gave it up. How could she ever hope to identify a bird species when she couldn't even remember what day it was most of the time? Or the year. Or whether it was time for breakfast, lunch, or dinner. Often, she couldn't even remember if she'd eaten at all on a given day.

"Hello, Sister." The voice came unexpectedly from behind, soft and mocking. Startled, Janine turned to see who had spoken, but the sun was directly behind and she was able to make out only the outline of a figure. Not a regular caretaker. She knew all their voices and this one was unfamiliar.

"How about taking a little stroll with me?"

Before Janine could respond, the brake was released and her wheelchair was being pulled back from the others and then pushed rapidly along in a direction opposite from the route that had brought her to the lookout spot. In seconds, they were out of sight of any staff monitoring the line-up of elderly women.

The landscaping at Rose Haven was artfully designed with hedges and trees offering a sense of privacy for family members who might wish to stroll the winding walkways. Janine's visitor wasn't strolling. As the old nun held on to the arms of her chair with growing alarm, she was pushed at a smart pace up small rises, then down and around beds thickly planted with rhododendron and lilac on a path that led eventually to the lakeside. During spring and summer when the weather was mild, it was a charming vista. Now, however, it was a bleak, brown-toned winterscape. Absent the sunshine, the cold quickly penetrated. Small, icy gusts that formed over the lake struck with chilling effect, and she wished for a warmer wrap.

A wheel of the chair hit a crack in the stone walkway

and sent bone-jarring pain throughout Janine's arthritic body. A helpless sound escaped her and she clutched wildly at the blanket slipping from her lap while gripping the arm of the chair with the other hand.

"I don't think we should be out here," she managed in an imploring tone. She made a worried attempt to look behind her as the wheelchair rolled inexorably toward the ramp and pier jutting out over the lake.

"Don't think." Again, that mocking tone. "Let's play a little game instead. Let's imagine it's Valerie who's come to visit and the two of you are going to have one of your cozy little chats."

"I'm cold," Janine said, wincing with discomfort as the wheelchair bumped up the ramp. They were now in an area completely obscured from view of anyone at the main building. As she clutched at her cap, the blanket suddenly slipped from her lap. She made a futile grab for it, but it caught on the wheels and was rolled over and left behind as her caretaker brought the chair up on the pier. A sharp gust of icy wind stung her face. Without the blanket, her clothing was little protection against the cold and she began shivering. "I want to go back," she begged, as the wheelchair bounced over the uneven boards of the pier, jarring her aged bones.

"Think of your family," the visitor suggested in a bright tone. "Don't you get warm and fuzzy thinking of Valerie and Sara?"

Valerie and Sara. She clung to the glimmer of familiarity that came with the names.

"But they aren't really your family, are they?"

"My . . . my family—" But the brief flash of memory was gone. Struggling, she tried to concentrate, tried desperately to sort through the disjointed minutiae in her brain to make some sense of what was happening. Her ability to reason was damaged, but not enough so that she missed the presence of evil in this person. She was confused and powerless, but the primitive urge to survive gave her voice strength. "Stop, please," she ordered in the stern tone of the teacher-nun she once was. "I want you to stop."

"The two of you plotted and schemed to create a new identity for Valerie, didn't you?" her visitor said, the tone now hard and accusing. "You stole Amy's baby without a thought for the evil of it." A short, harsh laugh as she was given a vicious shake from behind. "And you a handmaiden of God, Sister Janine. You should have known better. You should have stopped her, but no. Instead, you fell in with her hellish plot. You renounced your vows and made a pact with the devil. She is the devil, Sister. You know that, don't you? And for years there have been no consequences to you for your part in this." The chair stopped abruptly at the pier's edge. "Today, Sister Janine, you must pay for your sins."

Janine looked down at the dark green surface of the lake. Deep, cold water. No mental acuity was needed to understand personal peril. Helplessness and overwhelming fear welled up in her. A whimper came from her and, with it, a flash of true mental clarity. Consequences. She knew that word. She knew its meaning. She'd always known that she would have to pay for grabbing at a chance of joy and fullness of life with Valerie and her darling Sara. She closed her eyes. That time had come.

"God have mercy," she whispered, crossing herself.

With a quick shove, the chair was heaved over the side, striking the water with a huge splash. As cold water closed over her, Janine heard the sound of maniacal laughter and prayed that Valerie and Sara would be spared this monstrous end. Then, there was only blessed oblivion.

CHAPTER ELEVEN

Jordan was late picking Valerie up for Hal's party that night and Valerie found herself in the rare situation of having nothing to do but wait. She enjoyed the social obligations that came with her job and tonight was no exception. In spite of the strange threat lurking, she'd met some challenges in her new position today and successes, even small ones, were exhilarating. By anyone's standards, she'd accomplished quite a bit. It was no small feat to turn Hal Kurtz from his decision to pull the Carpenter feature. Sticking out her neck by bribing Jon Palmer seemed puny in comparison, and by the time she found herself facing the maniacal Ted Carpenter, she'd had so much at stake that she couldn't afford to let him intimidate her. She was confident that the material in the article was based on solid fact and that Carpenter's fears of a ruined reputation were probably well founded. Once the article appeared, there was little to be gained by a lawsuit since there were already rumors that his dead wife's family was filing a civil suit against him for wrongful death. He could rail against fate and *Panache* magazine until hell froze over, but the special place he'd occupied in the heart of his fans was soon to be a thing of the past.

The television was on, and as she passed it, she heard the electronic beeps that signaled an upcoming weather bulletin. The arrival of a storm was hardly a surprise. For a day that had begun beautiful and sunny, it had taken a steep downturn by midafternoon. A cold rain had started as she left the office. Pausing to listen, she learned that rain would turn to sleet by midnight, then snow by morning. Glancing at her watch, she realized that probably explained why Jordan was late. She toyed with the idea of calling him and canceling, but he was probably already on his way and caught in traffic. Meanwhile . . .

She picked up the phone and dialed Sara's number. Having spent most of the time when they were together last venting her frustration with Jordan, it would be nice to let Sara know that she was coping better. But nobody answered as the phone went into its third ring.

As she waited for Sara's voice mail, she gazed with pleasure around the room. She was an avid collector, but only a fraction of the pieces she'd acquired over the years were displayed for lack of space in her apartment. Her eyes went to a collection of Murano glass arranged on a black chinoiserie table in front of the sofa. Something seemed different about the grouping, she decided. With the phone still ringing in her ear, she moved closer trying to decide what it was. A favorite piece, a tiny ballerina, was missing. She'd bought it years ago because it reminded her of Sara at age seven when she'd first begun taking dance lessons. Had she moved the ballerina herself and just forgotten? She scanned the room, but just then the receiver was picked up to the sound of masculine laughter and she forgot about the ballerina.

A good-natured oath followed as the phone was dropped with a clatter to a gale of feminine giggles. Muffled words were uttered in a deep tone, and finally there was Sara's breathless "This better be good, whoever you are." More giggles.

"It's your mother," Valerie said dryly. "Is that good or bad?"

"Oops. Mom." With only a trace of chagrin, Sara laughed outright. "I always wanted to say that . . . and it's not what you think. What's up?" She whispered something fierce in an aside, provoking another masculine chuckle and more shared mirth.

"Have I caught you at a bad time?"

"I . . . No, not really."

Valerie felt a stir of curiosity mixed with cautious hope. Sara had a man in her apartment? Was it a date? Or was it her roommate's guest? Whoever he was, Sara's laughter was a welcome sound. She was clearly enjoying herself. "I was just going out to a party and had a few minutes to chat. It's nothing that can't wait. Um, you and your roommate are entertaining tonight?"

"That's right, Mom. My roommate and I are entertaining tonight," Sara said with mock seriousness.

"I'm sorry. I was being nosy, wasn't I?"

"Nosy? You?" With a smile in her voice, Sara added, "But that's okay because I know you worry about me." Another pause and then she said gently, "You need to stop worrying about me, Mom. I'm okay now. I really am."

"Well—"

"So . . . where's the party tonight?"

"Hal Kurtz is having a few people over and I'm expected to show up. The guest of honor is a Pulitzer nominee."

"Oh. Cool." She gave a sigh of resignation. "I suppose you're going with Dr. Coulter?"

"No, Wayne is out of town."

"You're going alone? Mom—" Sara's tone firmed. "You need to broaden your circle of friends. Just because the dweeb is out of town, you shouldn't go to a party all by yourself. You're a beautiful woman. There are men who would jump at a chance to—"

"Hello-ooo? This can't be my reclusive daughter speaking. You haven't even been to a party in two years, but suddenly you're concerned with beefing up my social life?"

Sara giggled again. "Beefing it up is exactly what I was thinking, Mom. And not with the likes of Wayne Coulter."

"Wayne is a very nice man."

"But he's so *boring!*"

Valerie smiled. "Actually, I'm not going alone. But I'm not sure you'll approve of my escort any more than Dr. Coulter."

"Who is it? Anybody I know?"

"It's Jordan Case."

Sara gave an audible gasp. "Charlie's dad? You're going to a party with *Charlie's father?*"

"I'm not having an affair with him, Sara," she said dryly. "He's simply an escort, as we're both working for Hal."

"It's just so *weird!*"

"Well, weird or not, it's happening. And it's strictly business. Besides, I thought you liked Jordan."

"I do, I do. It's just that I'm kind of . . . surprised that you'd go anywhere with him even if you do call it business."

It was a little surprising to Valerie herself. "I'm not calling it business, Sara. It is business." She glanced at her watch. "At least I think I'm going with him. He's late, probably because of the rain. You know how terrible traffic conditions get in bad weather."

"Tell him I said hello, will you, Mom?"

Was there a wistful note there? "I'll tell him," she said, looking at the now-streaming windows. There was a virtual downpour going on outside. "If I get a chance, that is. As he hasn't shown up yet, I may have to get there on my own. I had planned on doing that originally, but Jordan talked me out of it. I'm telling you, he can—" She stopped, realizing Sara, of all people, didn't need to hear her blathering on about Jordan.

"He talked you into going with him instead?" Sara almost squeaked. "As in, he *wanted* to escort my mother to a glitzy party?"

"Whether he wanted to or not, he asked me, probably because Hal insisted." She heard the sound of her doorbell. "And he's here now." Valerie hesitated, then with a soft smile added, "And tell your roommate that she's some kind of miracle worker if she's persuaded you to mingle with her guests and enjoy it. I really want to meet this woman."

"Have a good time, Mom," Sara said demurely.

The doorbell pealed a second time before Valerie made it to the foyer. She put a hand on her waist, feeling an involuntary flutter in the pit of her stomach. Nervousness? Anticipation? She made herself take a slow, calming breath. She didn't want to open the door to Jordan Case looking flushed and breathless. It was silly enough feeling that way. And definitely unsettling. She had not succumbed to a case of nerves when she'd met the President and First Lady, for heaven's sake. Jordan Case was nobody special. She gave a cursory glance through the peephole and opened the door.

He seemed bigger and more intimidating standing on her threshold than when they met in her office or a restaurant. The collar of his overcoat was turned up and his wide shoulders were rain-spattered. He was smiling, almost as if he knew he unnerved her. She felt a spurt of irritation that brought her down to earth with a thump.

"Sorry I'm late," he said, bringing with him the scents of rain and cold, wintry air mixed with masculine energy. "It's raining like crazy out there and cold as a hooker's heart," he said as he swiped a hand over his dark hair. "This is the kind of night when you want to curl up in front of a fire."

"We can cancel if it's too—"

"Not an option. Hal wouldn't buy bad weather as an excuse for missing his tribute to Peyton Caine. You know how he feels about all things literary." Without taking his eyes off her, he closed the door with the flat of his hand. "You look great. Black is definitely your color."

He did have a way of disconcerting her, damn it. "Black is every woman's color," Valerie said dryly, knowing he probably said something like that to every halfway attractive woman he escorted on Hal's orders. But that fluttery something was back in her stomach again.

She reached for her umbrella in a tall ceramic stand. "I guess we should be going then. Hal must be wondering where we are."

"The rain's our excuse to delay for a while." He took the umbrella from her and put it back in the stand. Then, before shrugging out of his overcoat, he produced a bottle of wine. "If Hal wasn't the boss, we'd build a fire in that fireplace and do what most sensible people do on a night like this." Turning, after tossing his overcoat on an ottoman, he caught the look on her face. He laughed softly, wagging his finger at her. "Why, Ms. Olivier-Long, I'm shocked. I had in mind just kicking off our shoes, drinking a little wine, and getting to know each other a bit better. But I'm definitely open to anything you might suggest beyond that."

Her cheeks were warm with embarrassment. Damn him! Two minutes alone and she was behaving like an adolescent girl with a crush on the football captain. "Have you been drinking?" she asked.

"No, but I plan to . . . if it's allowed." He held up the bottle of wine. "I know you're a teetotaler, but it's nasty out there, and because of some late-breaking calamity I had to rush like crazy to get here, otherwise I suspected you'd take off without me. How about I pour myself something and we both relax for a minute? Nobody will notice if we're a few minutes late, and if they do notice, they won't care."

After a moment, she waved a hand. "Whatever. But just one drink and then I'd really like to get on over there."

"Just one," he agreed. With a light touch on her waist, he urged her toward the big sofa with its inviting collection of colorful pillows. "Tell me you have a cork-screw."

"Yes, I—" About to sit, she stopped, intending to head for the bar to get it, but he stopped her, and again with just a touch she found herself being gently urged down on the sofa.

"My idea, I'll do the work."

"The corkscrew is in the middle drawer of the bar."

He went around the small island that jutted out from the smaller yet kitchen, opened the middle drawer, and found the corkscrew. "How about something for yourself?" He scanned the bottles in the glass-front cabinet overhead as he worked the corkscrew. "Tonic?" She shook her head. "Cranberry juice? Tomato juice?"

"No, I'm fine." she said firmly.

"A real teetotaler." Smiling at her, he pulled the cork from the bottle with a soft pop. "I bet there's a story there."

"If so, it's my story."

He gave her a wry look as he poured himself a glass of cabernet, then came around and sat down beside her, not close enough to make her feel crowded, but she shifted into the corner of the sofa anyway. Lifting the glass, he toasted her silently, then leaned back and looked around, taking in her treasures and the warm, inviting decor. "I like your place," he said.

"Thank you."

His gaze flicked over the Murano collection in front of them on the low table, then to some pieces of African art sharing space with her books in built-in shelves covering one whole wall, before moving on to an arrangement of vases in a recessed alcove. Without getting up, he studied several original watercolors marching up the stairs to the second floor. "You have a passion for collecting. It's great. The tapestry above the fireplace is Chinese, isn't it?"

"Yes. I got it in Hong Kong."

He was still looking around. "Is everything a memento of your travels?"

"I haven't been to all the places represented by these pieces, if that's what you mean. You don't have to leave New York to travel the world." She looked around as if seeing her treasures through the eyes of a guest. Gazing at the Murano collection, she was reminded again of the missing ballerina. Had it been gone when she discovered someone had rifled her closet? She simply didn't recall, but the idea of someone slyly invading her apartment and pawing through her things was too eerie for words.

"You have exquisite taste."

"When I see something I like, I may buy it—if I can afford it—but I don't have much of a theme, as you can tell."

"Collecting just for the fun of collecting, huh?" He was watching her now, not her things.

"I suppose so."

"You'd hate my place." He took a taste of the wine, then leaned forward to place the glass on a coaster on the low table. "I don't have a theme either, and without the collecting bug, it makes for some pretty uninspiring decor."

"Let me guess," Valerie said, tucking one leg beneath her. "Leather furniture, brown or blue. Oversized, because you need it, but few extra pieces except for lamps because you hate shopping. Tables, iron and glass, which look somewhat incompatible with your favorite ratty old recliner."

He was staring at her. "Charlie told you all that, didn't he? Or he told Sara and she told you."

"This may shock you, but I wasn't curious enough about your lifestyle to discuss it with Sara and certainly not with Charlie."

"I'm that predictable?" When he smiled like that, she had to admit that he was entirely too attractive. In fact, she wished he were more predictable. Maybe then she wouldn't be so on edge when she was with him.

"How long have you been divorced?" she asked, choosing to ignore his question.

"Why?" He threw his arm over the back of the sofa. "What made you ask that?"

"You described your house as if you don't take much interest in decorating. Also, since you aren't married, you haven't had to consider anyone else who might have an opinion in furnishing it. I bet you see your house not so much as a palette to express yourself as simply a place to live. You probably spend a lot more time on your wardrobe than in choosing a couch." She wrinkled her nose. "Leather is pretty boring, whether blue or brown."

"Fifteen years."

"What?"

"I've been divorced fifteen years." He took a swallow of wine and held the glass up, squinting as the light shown through, ruby red. "Barbara and I should never have married in the first place, as it was pretty much a disaster from day one."

Valerie did the math in her head. If Charlie was twenty-three now, he'd been only eight when his parents divorced. She realized she didn't know whether he had lived with Jordan or his mother. Had they shared custody? She had been so opposed to the idea of Sara being seriously involved at such an early age that she hadn't really listened to the girlish confidences Sara might have shared with her about Charlie's background. And why was she interested now?

"Barbara was pregnant, which is one reason I was so bent out of shape when Charlie told me he'd gotten his girlfriend pregnant," Jordan said. "I knew what that meant. I was nineteen when it happened to me. History was repeating itself. I stuck it out for eight years with Barbara, but it was hell. Everybody was better off when we split."

She was frowning now and sitting up straight, not sure she heard him correctly. "You're telling me that you had to get married because your girlfriend got pregnant, and when you learned about Sara and Charlie, you attacked me"—she touched her chest—"insinuating that my daughter probably had some kind of gene for loose morals since I had had a child out of wedlock. Now you sit there and casually admit having done the same thing."

"Not exactly the same thing. I got married."

She sat for a moment staring at him, outraged. "I can't decide whether you're just naturally insensitive or whether your personal experience soured you so that you weren't willing to give our kids a chance. Which is it?"

"Maybe a little of both?"

"I'm serious, Jordan. Answer the question."

"I've already apologized for any hurt I caused. It wasn't intentional. Maybe that's the insensitive part. And yeah, I still think I was justified in expressing disapproval. Maybe that's the part of me that was soured by experience." It was plain that he didn't like anyone analyzing his behavior. He removed his arm from the back of the sofa and reached for his wineglass. "I'd been down that road, damn it. I knew that was the wrong way to start a marriage."

Valerie crossed her arms over her chest and said stonily, "Well, you'll never know whether you were right or wrong. And as for Sara and Charlie, it appears that both of them have managed to survive. Fortunately."

"So how long have you been divorced?"

"Three years."

"About the time the kids were breaking up. That really was a rough time for you."

"I survived, too."

"Meaning, I should mind my own business," he murmured, but there was understanding in the look he gave her. "Sara's really okay now?"

"Lately she has been swearing to me that she's fine, so I suppose she must be. I called a few minutes ago as I was waiting for you and she sounded as if she really was enjoying herself. If I didn't know better, I'd say she was flirting with one of her roommate's guests. That's a milestone, since she hasn't looked at another man since Charlie—" She stopped abruptly.

"If Charlie really was the guy for her," Jordan said, "neither one of us could have screwed it up."

"Maybe." She wasn't willing to admit more than that. She pulled at a loose thread on the cushion nearest her and added dryly, "Sara seems to think I need a lot of reassurance where she's concerned and apparently she's right. I'm trying to cut the apron strings, but it's hard. What constitutes apron strings and what constitutes a parent's natural desire to be there for her child?"

"I'd be the last to know the answer to that one."

She was smiling softly now, hugging the pillow. "The funny thing is that Sara worries about me almost as much as I worry about her."

"She sounds like a sweetheart of a daughter," he said. "I understand why you went on the offensive when you thought she was being hurt."

"In that sense, I'm like any other mother."

"Do you see a lot of her?"

More relaxed now, she toyed with the fringe on the plump cushion. "Not nearly as much as I'd like."

"Where does she live? What part of town?"

She told him, adding, "It's near her job, and to tell the truth, she didn't consult me because she considers herself capable of finding her own digs." Her outrage was fading. Jordan was a good listener. A trait like that made it difficult to keep her distance. How, she wondered, had they reached this semitruce?

"Charlie's place is in that neighborhood, too," he said. "I've been to see him a couple of times and, I must confess, he seems to be like Sara, bent on convincing me that he can manage his life without advice from me."

She felt a pang of envy that Charlie invited Jordan to visit while Sara always had an excuse to put Valerie off when she hinted for an invitation. "What's his choice," she asked dryly, "brown or blue leather?"

"Black and white checks with red accents. Actually, it's very sophisticated. You'd approve. He must have inherited those genes from Barbara." He finished the wine and set the glass aside. "The truth is, he didn't actually invite me, I just dropped in suddenly one night, then after the second time, he told me flat out that I should call before coming again."

Then they'd both paid a price for whatever part they'd played in the breakup. Maybe she should feel some sense of satisfaction that Jordan had not gotten off scot-free, but all she was feeling at the moment was sadness that neither of them enjoyed the kind of relationship with their only child that they'd once had. She watched as he shot back a cuff to check his watch. He stood up and extended a hand toward her with a wry smile. "I guess the message to both of us is to back off, huh?"

"I guess." A beat or two passed while she hesitated, then took his hand and allowed him to help her up from the sofa. "Well . . . if you're ready?"

He stood for a moment, just looking at her, then as she turned to get her coat, he caught her hand. "Valerie . . ." She was startled. Their conversation had stopped just short of intimacy, but there was something in his expression now that brought the flutter alive in her tummy again. She thought of pulling her hand out of his, but didn't.

"What is it?"

"I'm sorry that we got off on the wrong foot. About Charlie and Sara, I mean. I should have explained where I was coming from, my history and all that."

"I agree, in hindsight," she said. "And maybe someday, I'll tell Sara. But if it will make you feel any better, she doesn't seem to have any hard feelings about the way things happened. In fact, she asked me to say hello. She still speaks well of you."

"I wasn't thinking only of Sara, although it's a relief to know she doesn't despise me."

"No one despises you, Jordan." Now she was tugging at her hand. He let it go.

"Are you sure about that?"

"Shouldn't we be starting out?" She heard rain and the chilly sound of sleet gusting against the glass windows.

He didn't reply. He didn't even glance at the window.
Instead, to her amazement he reached out and touched
the lobe of her ear. The diamond studs with a pearl drop
had been a purchase to celebrate her recent promotion.
Thinking one might be working loose, she asked, "Am
I losing it?"

"I think we should call a truce right now." He still
toyed with her earring.

"A truce?"

"A truce," he said, cupping the nape of her neck
and drawing her nearer. She had a quick, astonished
thought as she stared into his eyes. *He was going to kiss
her!* She should back away, avoid whatever would be the
effect of a kiss from Jordan Case. But she felt almost
mesmerized by the shape of his lips so close to hers.
And tantalized by the feel of his other hand now slipping
around her. Without more thought, her own hands
found a place at his waist and then he leaned down to
close the distance between them.

"A kiss," he said softly, "to seal it."

Slow, deliberate, absolutely devastating. That's what
it was like. She stood for a timeless moment just . . .
awash in sensation. Taste. Touch. Keen, sharp pleasure.
Her pulse quickened, and for an insane moment, she
wanted to take this moment to its ultimate end. It had
been ages—maybe never—since she had responded so
to a man.

No novice at this, Jordan sensed her need. He made
a low sound and gathered her closer, deepening the
kiss, turning it more carnal. One hand went to her hips
and pressed her hard against his erection. For both,
there was heat and desire and complete disregard for
where this might lead . . . for the moment. Thoughts
half formed in Valerie's head, only to dissolve like sleet
on a warm windowpane. Somehow, her hands lifted to
his chest, spreading to push him away, but instead her

arms wound around his neck. She liked the way it felt to be held in his arms. Of all the men on the planet, how could it be Jordan Case who made her feel so alive?

It was Jordan who brought her to her senses.

"Jesus," he breathed, breaking the kiss. Gripping both her arms, he rested his forehead against hers. "Where's the bedroom?"

The bedroom? She blinked, realizing what he meant, and pushed away from him. "We aren't going to have sex, Jordan."

"Why not?"

She stared at him a full five seconds. He looked rumpled and aroused and ... extremely appealing. She turned away, wrapping her arms around herself. "Because it would be absurd. It would be beyond stupid, that's why."

"That's not the feeling I got about half a minute ago. You were with me, Valerie. You wanted it as much as I did."

"We're not going to bed, we're going to Hal's party!" She grabbed his overcoat and thrust it at him, then yanked open a closet and grabbed hers. "This was a very bad idea. I don't know what it is but every time I get involved with you, it turns into a disaster. First Sara and Charlie, then Hal forcing us into a professional ... straitjacket, now this."

She was babbling. She sounded like someone in a panic. Which was exactly how she felt. She had one arm in her coat and was struggling to find the other, but she refused to let him help. While still wrestling with it, the doorbell rang. Muttering an oath, she marched to the foyer and, after finally getting both arms into her coat, yanked the door open.

There was no one there, but a small gift bag overflowing with pink tissue had been left on the threshold. As she bent to pick it up, she looked both ways in the hall, but whoever had dropped it off was gone now. Maybe Jordan—

"What've you got there?" he asked, coming up beside her. If he was offended by the harsh words she'd hurled at him, he didn't show it. He had his coat on and was apparently taking her at her word that they should leave for Hal's party.

She held it up. "Did you send this?"

"No. Was it a special delivery?"

"I don't know. I didn't see the messenger." With a confused frown, she peered into the bag. "Usually Security gives me a call when a delivery comes for me. I order from catalogs a lot, but nothing arrives looking like this." As she talked, she reached into the stuffing of bright pink tissue and pulled out a small gift box. Setting the bag aside, she opened it. "It's odd they didn't alert me. Even when it's flowers, they—"

Now that she had the box open, she stared at the contents in shock. Lying on a square of cotton was a small silver medal on a chain. Obviously old, tarnished. Eerily familiar. The medal had been in her hands only a few days ago when, in a panic, she'd emptied the box in her closet. More panic threatened now.

"What is it?" Jordan asked, seeing her reaction. He looked in puzzlement at the box. "What's wrong?"

She dropped the box. Or did she throw it? Without thinking, she blurted, "I ... It's ... I had the locks changed." Her tone rose in confusion and fear. "How did this—"

Looking up, she found Jordan watching her narrowly. "You had the locks changed and ... ?"

"I ... They ... must have gotten in again somehow. But the locks—"

"Someone has been inside your apartment? Again?"

She managed a confused nod. "But how?"

"Locks don't present much of a challenge to a bur-

glar," Jordan said. Looking grim, he scooped up the
medal from the floor, leaving the box where it lay. "St.
Christopher," he said, letting it swing from his hand.
"You recognize this?"

"It was in a box inside my closet last time I checked."

"Which was?"

"The day the snapshot appeared in the photo lab."
She pressed a hand to her stomach, remembering the
glass ballerina. "I don't understand how someone got
inside again."

He swore softly. "For a New Yorker, you sound amaz-
ingly naive. Some folks make a living getting beyond
the locks on doors. For them, it's as easy as jumping
the ignition on a car to steal it."

"But that's criminal," she said, still shaken. "I don't
know anyone able to do that kind of thing."

He was shaking his head as if she still didn't get it.
"Maybe you don't know your stalker, Valerie. Or if you
do know him, maybe he hasn't shared all his talents
with you." He made an impatient sound and shoved
his hands deep into the pockets of his overcoat. "None
of which matters right now. What's important is that
there's clearly a threat here. He's broken into your
apartment twice now, at least twice that you know about.
You're going to file a complaint with the police, right?"

"And say what? That I've been burglarized and the
thief didn't steal anything, he just returned something?"
Pacing away from him, she decided not to mention the
Murano. Or her nightgown. Stopping at a window, she
wrapped her arms around herself. Whoever was doing
this wanted her to panic. She wouldn't give him the
satisfaction.

"Is that a no?"

"You know the police generally put the lowest priority
on things like this. The most they'd do is fill out a report
and urge me to change the locks yet again. They might

suggest I put in a private security system, but as I told you, I've already scheduled that."

"At least let me call Building Security." He waited, then added with exasperation, "Or are we going to the party and leaving it up to fate whether you'll return to find your apartment still in the condition you left it?"

"I'm calling Security." Still wearing her coat, she walked to a small desk, took out an address book. While he stood scowling, she found the number and dialed it. She reported the break-in to a bored clerk and demanded increased security on her floor, with special emphasis on her apartment. When he began listing reasons why individual surveillance was considered beyond the scope of their responsibilities, she demanded to talk to the chief of Security. She'd met the woman briefly after the first break-in. "As I told you the first time this happened, I don't have a clue who might be doing this, but at least we'd have a picture of him if a surveillance camera was installed. What's to prevent him from entering other apartments?" She paused, listening to the woman's assurances that everything would be done to ensure security for her and the other tenants. She then added apologies for any inconvenience and promised to have the camera in place "shortly."

"Tomorrow," Valerie insisted before wishing her a curt goodbye. She hung up and turned to face Jordan. "I'm ready to go now."

He was studying her intently. "Did the St. Christopher medal have some special significance?"

"All keepsakes have special significance." She began pulling on a pair of soft kidskin gloves.

"I could be wrong, but your reaction on seeing that medal reminded me of the way you acted when you saw that snapshot in the photo lab. Which reminded me of the cell phone call you got in the restaurant from the screwy fan. Was anything said in that phone call that leads you to connect the two incidents?''

"Are you in the detective business now?" They stood facing off. The passion that had flared between them only a few minutes before seemed like a figment of her imagination. How could she respond so wantonly to this man one moment and in the next want to scream at him?

He looked at her, as if trying to decide whether to back off or not. Then he shrugged, but she knew him better now. Whether she admitted having done so or not, he'd connected the incidents in his mind. He would let it go for now, but he was tenacious and smart and the journalist in him sensed a mystery. If she didn't figure out who her stalker was—and soon—Jordan just might. Once he flushed him out, he would also unearth her secrets and any attraction he felt for her he would consider an irritating complication. It would be forgotten in a heartbeat. And her career would be over.

CHAPTER TWELVE

Hal Kurtz's party was well under way when Valerie and Jordan finally arrived. The house was overflowing with guests, flush with cash and influence. Apparently bad weather was no deterrent when opportunity presented itself for New York's elite media types to get together. Valerie recognized many of them, but failed at first to spot the host.

Beside her, Jordan drew a deep breath as he surveyed the crowd. "An hour of this at the outside and then we can leave."

"You don't have to stay on my account," Valerie said, forcing a smile at an investment broker across the room she'd met in Hal's office one day. The atmosphere in the cab as she and Jordan rode to the party had been strained. He was obviously mystified over her reluctance to notify the police that an intruder was coming and going at will in her apartment. Meanwhile, she wrestled with her fear that all she'd achieved was in jeopardy. Added to that was real consternation over her abandoned response to a kiss that she was certain meant no more to Jordan than the promise of ten minutes of sexual gratification. How much more complicated could her life get? "I'll get a taxi when I'm ready to leave."

"Meaning you like this kind of thing."

"Hmm." She nodded and waved at the CEO of a major bookseller. Any enjoyment of Hal's party was wiped out by her many personal distractions. And Jordan sticking close to her side wasn't helping. She'd planned to separate herself from him as soon as she decently could, but acted as if they were actually on a date.

"Well, hello, Valerie. Jordan. We were wondering if y'all would ever show up." Denise Grantham, sleek, Southern, and feline in a pencil-thin tube of black stretch satin, materialized at Valerie's elbow. "Hal was saying only a few minutes ago that he hoped you understood the importance of his little tribute to Peyton Caine. I assured him that in light of your new position, it'd have to snow in hell as well as New York for you to miss an opportunity like this."

"To meet Peyton Caine, you mean," Jordan interjected before the fur could fly.

She smiled at him. "Well, of course, sugar. What else would I mean?"

"Yes," Valerie murmured, "what else?" She'd always found Denise's Southern accent to be exaggerated and hearing it spread like honey on a buttered biscuit grated on her nerves.

Denise plucked the olive from her martini with two blood-red fingertips. "And I told Hal that you, of all people, Val, understood absolutely every nuance of the publishing business. Just look at your meteoric rise at *Panache.*"

"I'd hardly call it meteoric," Valerie said dryly. "I've been in publishing for a few years."

"Some weather we're having," Jordan commented.

Denise gave him a lazy smile while slowly biting into the olive. "But I knew a little thing like a snowstorm wouldn't keep you away, Jordan. Valerie . . . well, she's originally from New Orleans, you know, and might be tempted to stay home and keep warm . . . although you'd never guess her Southern roots, not from her accent. Sounds more Yankee-fied to me than Southern, but"—she shrugged—"what do I know?"

She didn't only look like a cat, Valerie thought viciously, she was behaving like one. "I haven't been in New Orleans for over twenty years, Denise. That's more than enough time to lose an accent and to get acclimated to cold weather."

"Well, honey, that's all a matter of opinion, isn't it? You can still hear Texas in my voice and I guess it'll be that way 'til I die."

"I was in Dallas a few weeks ago," Jordan said, still trying valiantly to stave off disaster.

"Oh?" Denise said with a feline smile and much interest. "We'll have to find a minute to talk about it sometime."

Valerie snatched a glass of champagne from a passing server, not to drink, but to have on hand to toss into Denise's green eyes if the occasion arose. "Why don't you two find a couch and reminisce right now?"

Denise's smile became more seductive as she studied Jordan from lashes heavy with mascara. "Sounds good to me."

Jordan, deadpan, asked for Scotch from the server, then took Valerie firmly by the elbow. "I think we'll do better to circulate for a while. Talk to you later, Denise."

"Oh, wait," Denise said, detaining them with a hand on Jordan's arm. "Hal's heading this way. He'll be really happy that y'all are getting along so well. Anybody can see you two are no longer strikin' sparks off each other."

She gave an exaggerated shudder. "I can feel the electricity a mile away. Ooo, it's delicious."

Valerie made a disgusted sound. "How many martinis have you had, Denise?"

"That's some imagination you have," Jordan told her while giving Valerie's arm a warning squeeze. "You're wasted in an administrative capacity at the magazine. Have you thought about writing a book?"

"You know what? I'm considerin' it, sugar." Seeing Hal approach, she flashed him a brilliant smile. "There's definitely material enough around here to fill a book."

"Well, I see you made it." Hal kissed Valerie's cheek and clapped Jordan on the shoulder. Then, still smiling, he looked questioningly at them. "What's this about a book?"

"Party talk," Jordan told him before Denise had a chance to stir up any more mischief.

Beside him, Valerie was rigid with fury. Denise was known to have a sharp tongue, but the spite directed at Valerie tonight could only be done if she felt invulnerable. Obviously, the gossip was true. She was involved with Hal. Which didn't seem to preclude cozying up to Jordan, she thought darkly. Like many opportunistic females, Denise was probably keeping her options open in the event that things soured between her and Hal.

Jordan glanced beyond Hal to the crowded buffet table. "Where's the guest of honor? Val and I need to pay our respects."

"He's upstairs in the guest room, passed out." Hal waited until a television critic drifted out of earshot, then said with a chuckle, "Knocked back too many drinks before the party began and puked his socks up. As I poured him into bed, he told me that he's shy in a crowd. I don't know how he plans to handle the publicity if he wins."

"Maybe the money will help him cope," Jordan said, lifting a skewer of shrimp from a platter that was offered.

"So, how's it going with you two?" Hal asked as if sensing the tension in the air.

"Val and Jordan have buried the hatchet," Denise said with a sly grin. "Isn't that interesting?"

Hal's smile expanded. "Well, what do you know? I counted on a truce between the two of you because I'm convinced you make a dynamite team. Advertising rates at *Panache* are sure to increase after the first issue under Valerie's name hits the stands, then I'm expecting the quarterly report to reflect a bottom line in the black." He rubbed his hands together with glee. "I love it when a plan comes together. In fact, when it's clear that you've turned things around at *Panache,* there are other projects I have in mind for you. As a team."

"I don't suppose you'd care to share them with us, Hal," Jordan suggested, taking his fresh drink from the server.

"All in good time." Hal beamed at them. "All in good time."

"I have something I'd like to share," Denise said, sipping a fresh martini. "I have this super idea. Valerie's given us the guidelines for features, Hal, and this one passes the test, big time. Just listen. What if—"

"This is hardly the time to brainstorm feature ideas, Denise," Valerie broke in coolly. There was a protocol to be observed in the management of the magazine, and by pitching her idea directly to Hal, she was undercutting Greg and Valerie herself. "If you have something you believe is promising, Greg is the person who needs to hear it."

Hal was suddenly looking uncomfortable. "I think Denise's suggestion may have merit, Valerie. Why don't you hear her out?"

Valerie looked narrowly at the two of them before addressing Hal. "You already know about it?"

"Well . . ." Hal tugged at the collar of his shirt while Jordan gazed at his feet.

"I see," Valerie said dryly.

Denise's eyes gleamed. "Actually, in light of my new position, I thought it would save time all around to get clearance to begin working on it. That makes sense as everyone who matters is here." She spread her hands with an innocent shrug. "Doesn't it?"

Valerie again questioned Hal Kurtz. "What new position?"

Denise managed to look puzzled. "Didn't you tell her, Jordan?"

Hal spoke up finally. "I asked him not to." Then he swore softly before admitting to Valerie, "I've appointed Denise the new features editor. The slot's vacant and I know you've been looking for the right person, but she's brought some bright ideas to the table in the past and I think she can do the job."

Valerie was seething. Appointing Denise to an upper-level position on her staff without consulting her was a slap in the face of her authority. When exactly was she to be told? She flashed a look at Jordan, furious that he had known and hadn't told her. The possibility of tossing her champagne into someone's face was rapidly rising.

When she felt she could manage an even tone, she asked, "What bright ideas would that be?"

Denise traced the rim of her glass with one finger. "You remember the feature on Bob Bentley, the TV anchorman who adopted all those handicapped kids?"

"That idea came from Roxanne, Denise."

"I wrote most of the text!"

"Yes, but Roxanne met him at a photo shoot on Maui,

struck up a conversation, and got him to agree to an interview."

Denise crossed her arms, while carefully balancing her martini. "What about the story I did on gay bashing in that sleazy little town in New Hampshire?"

"You mean when Eric was arrested on a bogus speeding charge and wound up in jail overnight? He came back from his vacation loaded with material to do that story. If I recall correctly, I assigned you to research it. The idea was Eric's."

Denise waved a hand airily. "Well, I can see you're not going to give me any credit except for doing the grunt work. Fortunately, Hal's perspective is more reasonable. He's excited about my latest idea."

Valerie turned deliberately to the chief executive. "Are you, Hal?"

"You'll have the final say, of course," Hal said, glancing over his shoulder at his guests. "So, be brief, Denise, as duty calls."

"Okay, I'll make it quick." She set her martini on a table. "You're gonna love this, Val, really . . . once you get over being in a snit. It's about juveniles and judges."

"So go for it," Valerie murmured between her teeth.

"Juvenile crime is a topic women care about, right? And even though being assigned to the bench in juvenile court isn't considered the pinnacle of success among judges, doncha know, there are several who're quite innovative. Each has a different approach, with varying success. These judges aren't pansies when it comes to meting out punishment for juveniles. They're tough. In fact, one of them has implemented a program like boot camp in the military. Only ten percent of the kids repeat offenses within two years. Another judge— in Iowa, I think—forces kids to work full time in, say, the humane society or the city hall. Even the jail. They do not get paid. The third one's in Chicago. He removes all amenities from juvenile hall. No TV, no workout rooms, no computer games. Instead, they have intense schoolwork. If they can't read or do math when they get there, they damn sure can when they leave. They have no choice but to serve the time productively.''

It wasn't particularly interesting or original. It was the kind of article that Valerie might consider as filler, parked in the file and pulled out when there was space to be used and time was running out at deadline. Hal, however, apparently thought otherwise. She decided he was dazzled as much by Denise herself as her idea. She met Jordan's eyes and saw with a rush of irritation that he appeared to be positive about it.

"Well, what do you think?" Hal asked.

Denise spoke before Valerie could reply. "She won't think it's particularly interesting until she knows something about the personal lives of these judges. That's what makes it special, Val. They're really unusual. I've already made some preliminary contacts to their offices and they're all agreeable to being profiled in *Panache.* One of the judges came from the ghetto himself, in St. Louis. He's the one who adopts all those kids. One was a pro football star whose career was wrecked when he got into drugs. He uses his star power to influence kids for good. The third guy has a daughter who was kidnaped. She just disappeared and he's devoted his life to juveniles.''

"Who are these judges?" Jordan asked.

She held up a hand, ticking off names. "Judge Lawrence King, Judge Vincent Barton, and Judge Edward Martindale.''

Jordan followed Valerie out of the elevator and through the lobby. She headed in a straight line for the revolving doors, and without waiting for Jordan, asked the attendant in a curt voice to hail a taxi for her.

"I'll handle it, Valerie," he said, passing a bill to the attendant. It had started to snow and a sharp wind whipped about them as they stepped out onto the sidewalk.

"You didn't have to leave on my account," she said, huddling deeper into her coat.

"I never abandon my date, especially in a snowstorm."

He was puzzling over her abrupt decision to leave the party after the encounter with Denise. She had reason to be offended by Hal's highhandedness in promoting Denise, but her reaction when Denise outlined the particulars of her feature idea seemed out of proportion. It had been shock, not outrage, that had sent her rushing to the ladies room.

"Okay, let's have it," he said as the taxi pulled into traffic a few minutes later. "I didn't buy it for a second that you've got a family emergency. You couldn't have gotten a call since you weren't out of my sight long enough to take a call."

"I have a cell phone," she said through her teeth.

"Which you left on the coffee table at your apartment. I saw it."

She rubbed a spot between her eyes as if in pain. "What's the problem? Why do you care? You didn't want to go to the damn party in the first place."

"Call me curious. I want to know what it was about Denise's idea for that feature that freaked you out."

"I was furious over the way she engineered her promotion."

He shook his head. "Not your style. You're too professional to ever let your judgment be clouded by personal animus. On the other hand . . ." He paused, trying for a lighter note. "It did occur to me that you might hurl that glass of champagne you were nursing in her face."

"I even thought of drinking it," Valerie said darkly.

Maybe, as a teetotaler, that was the ultimate, he thought. "You'd never give her the satisfaction. No, your reaction has something to do with that feature."

"You wouldn't be offended if Hal went over your head like that?"

"It defied all good management principles," he agreed. "Hal should know better. If he wanted to promote Denise, he could have been more professional. You're right to be offended. Blindsiding you was unfair. He's created unnecessary tension at the magazine. If it's any comfort, I warned him, but he's enthralled with Denise right now. He gets like that. When he falls, he's putty in the hands of his lover."

"I'm aware of his reputation as a womanizer."

"She's the fourth woman he's been 'in love' with"— he used his fingers to make quotation marks—"in as many years."

"Then we can look forward to the fire petering out, so to speak, in a few months?" She gazed blindly through the side window at the swirling snow.

Jordan gave a bark of a laugh. "Maybe even sooner if she continues to use him so blatantly. But back to the feature. What about it set you off?"

"She didn't just pull that idea out of thin air, Jordan. Contrary to what Hal believes about her being talented and creative, she's not. I wasn't being argumentative when I contradicted her on those features she mentioned. She was on the team that got them into production. She's an adequate writer, I give her that. But she's even more valuable to the magazine as a researcher. So I know she didn't come up with the idea of the juvenile judge thing on her own. Not that she'll ever admit it," she ended tartly.

"What does it matter where it came from?"

"What does it matter?" she echoed, turning to look at him. "Hal claims to be promoting her based on her creativity and talent. That's how it matters."

"Okay, I'll concede that point, but—"

"I'm betting somebody else nudged her around to the idea."

He paused, weighing his words. "Actually, I think the idea itself was suggested in an e-mail to her."

Her eyes narrowed. "From whom?"

"She didn't say. In fact, she wouldn't have revealed that much, but I insisted on getting more information when she pitched it to Hal and me. The details were sketchy, as if her idea was still half-baked. She finally had to say she'd get back to me as she'd picked up the idea from something that came to her in an e-mail. Then when she tried to respond to the originator, she couldn't."

"Undeliverable?" When he nodded, she added, "Like the story idea you got about the Trent teenager in New Orleans."

"Yeah, I did notice the similarity," he said.

"Are you seeing a pattern here?"

"In more ways than one. You overreacted about the Trent story, too. Which brings us full circle. What is it about Denise's feature—and the Trent story—that scares you?"

"I'm not scared! That's ridiculous."

"Okay, you were upset. And don't deny it. You thought up an excuse to get the hell out of there and I'm wondering why."

"What are you now, Jordan, the thought police? I'm forced to defer to you on editorial decisions at the magazine if there's conflict, but you have no right to intrude in my personal life, thank God. Just know this. I'm within my rights as editor of *Panache* to accept or kill a feature and I'm not doing the juvenile judge feature."

"Hal may have something to say about that."

"Then you will have to put your famous skills to work and convince him otherwise," she snapped, then added bitterly, "He seems eager enough to value your judgment over mine on any other given day."

"In my judgment," he said, feeling his temper rising, "there's nothing wrong with the feature. At least, give her a chance to work something up. If the proposal stinks, then we kill it."

"And you don't have to take a chance on antagonizing Hal by suggesting his darling's idea is a no-go?"

"I'll see Hal if it's necessary," Jordan said shortly. "Not before."

The taxi pulled up in front of her building, but neither of them noticed. "You're saying you'll ignore my decision to reject the story?"

"Unless you give me a better reason than that the idea came from Denise."

He knew he was being pigheaded, but damn it, there was something else going on here and he wasn't going to be sidetracked before finding out what it was. There was as much panic as outrage in the way Valerie argued.

"We're here, folks," the driver said.

She began fumbling with the clasp on her tiny evening bag to get at her keys. Her hands were gloved, but still he could see that they were unsteady. "I knew this would happen," she muttered.

"What?"

"I'd be overruled when and if it came to a conflict between us." She snapped the clasp on the bag. "Now it's happened. What is it, Jordan? Frustration for being ousted at *Access* magazine? Are you going to use the authority Hal's given you at *Panache* to second-guess my decisions, then take credit—if there is any—when the magazine takes off? You aren't satisfied being second in command of his empire? You want to be top dog at your own publication?''

Muttering an oath, Jordan told the driver not to wait after paying him. Valerie started to object, but he had had enough. Before she could react, he took her keys and didn't give her a chance to fight him as he hustled her out of the taxi. Snow was falling steadily now and she was forced to hang on to his arm and tread carefully in her high-heeled shoes.

He was still in charge as they headed to the elevator. "I'm not getting into a pissing contest with you over this, Valerie," he said, stabbing the Up button with his finger. "For some reason I've yet to figure out, you've tap-danced all around the real issue here, which is that you've overreacted about two features now for no reason that I can see. You've clammed up when asked to defend your decisions. I'm willing to give you the benefit of the doubt, but—''

"Ms. Olivier-Long?''

Both turned as a man in an all-weather overcoat approached.

Valerie frowned, not recognizing him. She watched as he reached into an inside pocket of his suit jacket and pulled out a small leather object. "Valerie Olivier-Long?'' he repeated, extending the object in his palm.

"Yes?'' She glanced at his hand and saw an official-looking badge.

"I'm Detective Gerald McGowan, NYPD. Could I have a minute, please?''

"What's this all about?'' Jordan asked, moving a little closer to Valerie in a protective stance. Their argument was forgotten the instant he'd looked into McGowan's face.

Valerie's hand went to her throat. "What's wrong?''

"Are you a friend?'' McGowan asked, looking at Jordan.

"Yes," he replied impatiently. "What's up? What's wrong?"

"I'm afraid I have some bad news, ma'am," McGowan said, focusing again on Valerie. "There's been an accident."

"Sara . . ." she whispered, reaching blindly for Jordan's sleeve. He slipped an arm around her.

"Is it her daughter?" he demanded, holding her close.

McGowan consulted a small notebook. "I'm not . . . Is her daughter . . ."

"For God's sake, man, speak up!"

"There was an accident at Rose Haven," McGowan said, managing to sound official again. "They've been trying to reach you—"

"Janine. Is it Janine?"

McGowan glanced again at his notes. "Yes, Janine Livaudais is the name. She's had an accident, Ms. Long."

"Is she okay? Is she in the hospital?"

"No, I'm afraid it's worse than that." He shook his head. "It's . . . we're still trying to figure out how . . . I mean, nobody's near the lake this time of year. How she even got down there is a mystery. She's—"

"Is she dead?" Valerie's voice was rising.

"I'm sorry."

"Oh, my God." She clung to Jordan's arm. "How . . . what . . ."

McGowan gave her a sympathetic look as he tucked the small notebook back into his pocket. "We're trying to work all that out. All I can tell you at this point is that there are suspicious circumstances."

"What kind of suspicious circumstances?" Jordan asked.

"Well"—he was shaking his head—"it looks like she was murdered."

CHAPTER THIRTEEN

"Valerie?" Jordan called urgently from outside the door of the powder room. "Are you okay?"

Unable to speak, Valerie stood with her hands covering her face, vainly trying to stem a flood of tears. There had to be a mistake. Janine could not be dead. She was too good, too kind and gentle. She'd never made an enemy in her life. How could she be murdered? Why would she be murdered?

"Please open up, Val."

She'd fled into the privacy of her tiny powder room to escape the keen gaze of both men, the detective and Jordan. Janine was gone, not a victim of the hateful Alzheimer disease, but of a more evil human force. There would be only a few more minutes to compose herself, to deal with the reality. But how to deal with the unthinkable?

Jordan knocked softly and called again. "Valerie?" His voice was low, tense with concern. She closed her eyes and more tears rolled down her cheeks. She had to get hold of herself, but how when all she wanted to do was scream with the unfairness of it? Another wave of grief washed over her and she pressed her hand to her mouth in despair. Janine. Oh, Janine.

Jordan knocked again, softly. "Valerie?"

She grabbed some tissue and blew her nose, wiped her eyes, took a deep, shuddering breath. Swallowing, she whispered, "I'm fine." A lie. But her whole life seemed a web of lies lately. And terror. Now this. What more could happen?

"Come out, Val," Jordan coaxed. "Do you need a doctor? I can call someone."

No doctor could heal the anguish in her heart. Resting her forehead against the door, Valerie imagined that final plunge into icy cold water, the panic Janine must have felt at being trapped in a wheelchair, the certainty of her own impending death rising and breaking through the prison of her Alzheimer's as no happy moment could have done.

"Valerie."

Jordan tapped again with more urgency. "Do you want me to call Sara?"

Sara. Oh, God, she would have to be told, but not by Jordan. She would have to go over and tell Sara face to face. She wiped both eyes and opened the door. "I'm all right, really."

Detective McGowan stood at Jordan's shoulder. "I know it's difficult when something like this happens, Ms. Olivier-Long, but if you could just answer a few questions . . ."

"Yes." Clearing her throat, Valerie walked to the sofa and sat down.

"Can you think of anyone who might have reason to . . . ah, dislike Ms. Livaudais?"

"No. No one. Absolutely no person on the face of the earth. She was an angel." Her voice broke. "She didn't have an enemy in the world. She was a *nun!* Don't you understand?"

McGowan nodded, making no notes. "Did she have any friends outside your family circle? I understand she'd lived with you since leaving her order in New Orleans years ago."

Her stomach rose and fell, almost sending her lurching to the toilet. Janine's death was only a few hours old and already they knew details of her past. What if they probed deeper and began to ask questions about the circumstances that led to the renouncing of her vows? What if they learned of Valerie's role in that?

It was impossible to sit with grief and outrage and guilt roiling around inside her like snakes in a pit. She rose quickly and went to the window feeling the chill of the wind whipping against the panes. She hugged herself, remembering another time, another cold and cheerless city. And another Valerie.

Boston, 1977

She wanted a drink. She wanted drugs. She wanted *out!* Those thoughts obsessed her for the first few months after successfully persuading Sister Janine that they should keep the baby. She couldn't believe how naive she'd been. She hadn't thought through the consequences of her decision. Had she actually been stupid enough to think she could take on the responsibility of a baby and accept the sacrifice that Sister Janine made and then everything would just work itself out with no effort on her part? She loved Sara, but it was hard to change from a life of aimlessness and self-indulgence to one of responsibility and . . . rightness. Now she was stuck with the baby, with responsibilities, with the burden of staying clean and sober and with the stern expectations of a former nun of the Catholic church to whom she owed everything.

Boston is where they went. It was Janine's idea, a city that was almost as far away from New Orleans as it was possible to be. The nun had a little money, enough for them to live on if they were careful. Valerie would have to go back to school, of course. Janine would care for the baby while she finished her education. She got off to a rocky start. She'd learned much on the street—too much. She felt far older than her classmates. It was difficult to settle into a normal routine after the life she'd lived for the past eighteen months. Twice she came home late from class. High. Janine was understanding, but stern. If Valerie wished to resume that way of life, then she was on her own. She'd have to sever all ties with Sara and Janine. Of course, such a decision would make a mockery of Janine's decision to forsake her vows to the Church. It would also make a mockery of Valerie's vow to atone for having failed Amy. That was not an option. Her own guilt was as strong an incentive to stay on track as much as anything Janine might say.

But a baby was so damn *constant*. A baby was always there, always needy, always so . . . in your face. What she recalled most about that time was longing for escape in the ecstatic high that came with a cocaine hit. Or the blessed oblivion to be had from Oscar's new stuff. But Oscar was in New Orleans and she wasn't going to do drugs anymore, she kept telling herself. She had to stay clean and sober now, for Sara. Fortunately, Janine was always there as Valerie struggled to do exactly that.

Eventually, she settled into her new life. Once she got into the routine of the classroom again, she found she was actually a good student. She liked the challenge of it all. She liked looking around and imagining what others would say if they knew her story.

As time passed, she dwelled less and less on her life before Amy. And more and more on Sara, who was a delight once the demanding months of her infancy were over. Sara and Janine were her life now. They were a family, the ex-nun, Sara, and Valerie, a family complete with all the ingredients that had been missing in Valerie's other life. She wondered at times about Hannah and whether she and Martindale were still together, but not enough to risk calling. Or visiting. Besides, Chicago was a long way from Boston. When thoughts of Amy did pop up, guilt followed close behind. There was no getting around it, she was responsible for Amy's death. If she hadn't been high that night, her friend would have survived. No matter where she went or how much she made of the new life she'd snatched from her shameful past, she would have to live forever with Amy's blood on her hands.

"Are you okay, ma'am?"

Valerie turned from the window with her arms still wrapped around herself. "What?"

McGowan glanced at Jordan, then consulted his notepad again. "I was asking about friends, connections, anything about her life that might give us a clue to why somebody would want to . . . ah, do this."

"She attended church here," Valerie said, rubbing a spot on her temple. She would have a world-class headache soon. "Most of her friends are very elderly. Besides, she hasn't been able to communicate for a long time as her Alzheimer's worsened, so hardly no one visits her anymore, except me. And S-Sara, of course."

"That would be your daughter?" He jotted something in his notepad.

"Yes." Her reply was barely audible.

"Are you familiar with her estate?"

"Janine's estate?" Then the full implication of his question hit her. Her reply was as chilly as the sleet now stinging the windowpanes. "If you're searching for a motive, Detective McGowan, try again. Janine's assets didn't even cover the expense of living at Rose Haven. She was, for all practical purposes, penniless."

McGowan shuffled from one foot to the other, looking uncomfortable. "Sorry, but it's my job to ask these questions." He thumbed a few pages back in the notepad. "And you say you can't think of any reason someone might want to hurt her?"

"None. Absolutely none." It shook her very foundations that the life of a woman like Janine who expected and gave only kindness should die by an act of such unspeakable evil. She got up from the couch, snatching a tissue from a box on the table. "Have you thought that it might be simply an accident? I mean, there are several patients at Rose Haven who have Alzheimer's. Maybe someone . . . somehow thought taking a stroll on the grounds was a . . . a nice thing to do. These people get confused." She looked at him as fresh tears welled in her eyes. "They wouldn't think about the weather. Couldn't it have been just a . . . a tragic accident?"

"All the patients were accounted for when she went missing, ma'am," he said in a quiet tone. "Those that were sitting with her outside were all secured in their chairs. None was capable of getting up and pushing a wheelchair that far."

"She can't have been murdered!" Valerie cried, sitting down again and putting her face in her hands. "It's . . . it's . . . just so . . . unthinkable."

Jordan moved beside her. He put his hand on her shoulder, but looked at McGowan. "Can we wrap this up for the time being, Detective? I think she's answered enough questions for now."

McGowan nodded. "Sure, I understand. It's tough. I'm sorry, but when a death is ruled a homicide, it's different from an accidental death, you know?" He gave Valerie another sympathetic look. "I'll get out of your hair now, ma'am, but there will probably be other questions as we get deeper into the case, you understand?"

Valerie nodded numbly.

He slipped his notepad into the inside pocket of his coat and turned to go. But at the door, he stopped. "Oh, about the funeral, ma'am. I'm sorry, but you'll have to wait for the release of the body for burial purposes. Again, in a case like this, it's different than if she died of natural causes."

"I understand," Valerie said, as tears again clouded her eyes.

Jordan opened the door to see him out. "Keep us informed, okay, McGowan?"

"Sure, we'll be in touch." The detective flipped up the big collar on his overcoat, then pulled on his gloves. "Count on it."

New Orleans

It took some digging, but Angela finally located Oscar Diaz. Unlike Kelly Lott, who'd put the days of drugs and prostitution behind her, with Diaz it was business as usual. With a few glitches here and there. He'd served time twice and was currently out on parole, a fact Angela learned from Pete Benoit at NOPD, but only after considerable effort. It had been like getting money from a banker, the main obstacle being that Pete was convinced that she'd swiped those missing witness statements from Amy Trent's file. She'd worn him down eventually, but it had taken a couple of nights of heavy drinking with him in a dingy bar at the edge of the Quarter, a practice she normally liked, but couldn't afford right now. But her diligence eventually paid off. Pete had finally pulled up Diaz's rap sheet for her and produced the name of his parole officer, who had then given her Diaz's address without demanding much of anything. The right to privacy wasn't a privilege an ex-con enjoyed.

Oscar resided in a rundown section of Algiers, a community just across the river on the west bank. The New Orleans skyline was visible from almost any point in Algiers, which made it a desirable location for commuters, but Diaz's digs would never be coveted by anybody with a decent job. The grass surrounding the three-story building needed cutting, boards left over from the last hurricane warnings were still nailed over the windows in several of the apartments, junk cars rested on concrete blocks at curbside in the street, and several seemed to be the permanent residences of the homeless. It was a depressing place.

As Angela got out of her aging Toyota, she wondered if it would be there when she finished her talk with Diaz. But just then a kid of eight or nine appeared and offered to watch it for her. "It'll cost you twenty bucks," the boy told her.

"Twenty bucks!" she replied, wondering if he was armed. "Does your mommy know you're not in school?"

"Fifteen. And I'm sick today."

"With what?" She looked at him suspiciously. "I don't want to catch a virus."

"I ain't got no virus. You won't catch nothing. I broke my leg."

She looked him up and down, but he was swathed in jeans so wide in the legs and so long that they dragged the ground when he walked. She really couldn't tell if he had a broken leg, but it was highly unlikely. "Ten's my best and final offer."

"Okay." He stuck out his hand. "In advance."

She must have "sucker" written all over her, but

damn it, she'd be up a creek if her Toyota was ripped off while she was interviewing Diaz. "Don't spend it all in one place," she muttered, slapping the bill into his outstretched palm and walking off while she still had enough cash to get a cab if he proved to be conning her. She squinted at the windows on the second-floor apartment where Diaz reportedly lived. Now that the kid had her money, it would be just her luck to find that Diaz had moved.

She was breathing hard and sweating by the time she'd climbed the stairs and found his apartment. Inside, music blasted from a boom box, which encouraged her. Leaning against the wall, she caught her breath after a minute or two and then banged on his door. Instantly, a neighbor down the hall yelled at her to cut out the noise, a kid was sleeping. Diaz opened up only after she'd pounded several times and yelled his name repeatedly, prompting the irritated neighbor to threaten to call the cops.

"Yeah? Can't you take a hint, for crissake? Whatever you're peddling, I don't need any."

For a career criminal, Oscar looked pretty good, Angela thought. Drugs, alcohol, and various other vices hadn't taken the toll on his looks that she'd observed in other ex-cons. He was damn sexy. Assessing him from head to toe, she thought of an aging Ricky Martin. Darkly Latin features. Smoldering brown eyes. Nice body, even if he wasn't tall enough. And jeez, the guy had to be nearly fifty.

"I'm not selling anything," Angela said, offering her card. "I'm buying."

He ignored the card. "No drugs here. I'm outta the business." He had a faint accent. Business came out as "bis-ness."

"I'm not looking to buy drugs. It's information I'm

after." She settled her bag more comfortably on her shoulder. "Can I come in?"

He said nothing for a moment, just sized her up with those sexy night-dark eyes. "Information about what?" He made no move to let her in.

"Amy Trent."

His gaze narrowed. "I don't know any Amy Trent."

"I think you do. Or did." Angela raised her eyebrows. "How about letting me inside and I'll explain how I found out about you."

He glanced beyond her, but the only person in sight was the pissed-off neighbor. With a shrug, he stepped back and let her in.

CHAPTER FOURTEEN

Jordan closed the door behind Detective McGowan and went to Valerie's bar. "What can I fix for you, Val? No alcohol, I understand that, but how about tea? I can make—"

"I need to tell Sara." Valerie stood up abruptly and looked around in confusion. "Where . . . I must have . . ."

"What is it?"

"My coat. I need my coat. I have to go to Sara's apartment."

"Okay, I'll go with you." He dropped the box of Earl Grey and left the tiny island that served as her bar. "Your coat's on the back of that chair near the door. Just let me—"

"It's not necessary for you to go with me, Jordan. I'm all right. I—It was a shock, that's all." She rubbed her temple, frowning. "But I can manage. I'll take a taxi." She sent a vague look toward the telephone. "Maybe I should call Sara first to be sure she's home, but what would I say? I can't tell her over the phone and she'd hear in my voice that something was wrong."

"We'll take a chance she's at home." He pulled a cell phone from his jacket. "I'll get us a taxi while you change into boots. Those shoes you wore to the party are soaked. They're a hazard waiting to happen on a snowy sidewalk. Better get something more sensible. It's shaping up to be a long night."

He was right, of course. She wasn't thinking straight. Or rather, she wasn't thinking about her own comfort. She opened a hall closet and found serviceable boots. While she sat to put them on, Jordan phoned down to the concierge for a taxi. She wasn't allowing him to go with her, but she wasn't up to arguing about it. Telling Sara was going to be difficult. With an audience, especially someone like Jordan, it would be that much more difficult.

By the time he finished the call, she was bundled up and ready to go. "Thank you for offering to go with me," she said, as they headed down in the elevator, "but I'll be fine on my own now."

"You don't look fine," Jordan said flatly. "You look like a person who's just received a severe shock. And telling Sara will be more stress. Nobody will think less of you for accepting a little help at a time like this."

"I can handle it." She stepped out of the elevator. The doorman ushered them out of the building and scurried over to open the taxi. She climbed in and gave the driver Sara's address before looking up at Jordan, who seemed unfazed by snow swirling about him. With her hand on the door handle, she said, "Actually, there's something you can do for me, Jordan. Would you call Eric tomorrow morning and tell him that I'll probably be late getting to the office? Tell him I'll be in touch. And thanks again." She closed the door, leaving him standing at the curb. Another time, she would think about his surprising chivalry, even kindness. But right now, all she could think about was how to tell Sara that Janine had been murdered.

Jordan watched the yellow cab ease into traffic barely crawling in the deteriorating weather. "Get me a taxi," he told the doorman. Now that he knew the address where she was headed, he had even more reason to go with her. She had reacted stoically over the news that her old friend had been murdered, but he wondered how she would handle the other surprise awaiting her at Sara's apartment.

The building where Sara lived was almost obscured by heavy snowfall as the taxi pulled to a stop at the curb. Valerie paid the driver, who declined to get out and open the door for her. Consequently, she was gasping for breath and struggling to keep the hood of her coat on her head in gale-force wind as she stumbled up the steps to the old brownstone.

Inside the tiny entrance, she studied the addresses of the occupants in the building, but before she spoke to the intercom, the main door opened and a man came out with his dog on a leash. Valerie caught the door before it closed, explaining that she was visiting Sara Olivier. Then, behind her, the outer door opened, letting in a rush of frigid air and Jordan Case.

"I'm with her," Jordan explained to the tenant, whose dog was barking wildly and lunging at the door in anticipation of a romp in the snow. Shrugging, the man renewed his grip on the leash, turned his collar up, and ducked outside.

"What are you doing here?" Valerie demanded. "I told you I would handle this. Surely you have something more interesting to do than to insinuate yourself into something that's extremely private and difficult."

"It's going to be more difficult than you think." He took her arm and hustled her across the tiled floor to the elevator. Without waiting for her to tell him, he punched the button for the fourth floor. "Aren't you wondering how I knew the floor?"

"Have you been here before?" Her eyes narrowed. "Have you been seeing Sara behind my back?" Struck by an awful thought, she felt a rush of fury. "How dare you, Jordan? Don't you have any sense of decency? Wasn't her involvement with Charlie enough—"

He quieted her with just a lift of his eyebrow. "Calm down, Val. It's nothing like that." The elevator pinged and the doors slid open. "I know the floor because Charlie lives here, too."

"Charlie—" She stared at him in bewilderment.

"Apartment 4C, right?" he asked.

After a second or two, she nodded with growing confusion.

Jordan reached over and pushed her hood back, then brushed snow from the scarf draped around her neck. "Of course, it could be merely that they're living in the same building and occupying separate apartments. But somehow I doubt it." The last was added in a dry tone.

He took her arm again more gently now and walked with her to the door of Apartment 4C. "And before you accuse me of being in cahoots with them, I'm telling you I'm not sure what's going on either, but I think we're about to find out."

He rang the doorbell, and while they waited, Valerie's thoughts went in ten different directions. The whole evening had taken on a surreal quality. First was that kiss from Jordan that had left her more flustered than she ever would have dreamed. Then came the prospect of Edward Martindale being thrust into her life after all these years. And finally the news about Janine. Now

Charlie and Sara were living in the same building. She could only imagine what that meant.

Inside the apartment, a dog was barking excitedly while someone tried to quiet him. Still waiting, they heard the rattle of the security chain as it was removed and the lock turned with an audible click. Another second or two passed and the door finally opened.

Charlie and Sara stood side by side, his arm around her. A tiny Yorkie yapped at their feet, jumping and straining at the leash in Sara's hand. Charlie was openly protective. Sara was guarded.

"Hi," Jordan said to them both, although it was doubtful he could be heard over the Yorkie's greeting.

"Mom, Mr. Case. This is a surprise." Sara picked up the dog and he hushed only to start licking ecstatically at her face.

"Sara, what—" Valerie was stopped by Jordan's firm grip on her elbow.

"May we come in?" he asked in the same tone he'd used hours earlier when arriving at Hal Kurtz's digs. Then, however, he'd been talking to an anonymous person hired to cater a party.

Charlie did not smile. "You should have called first, Dad."

"Next time," Jordan said, equally unsmiling.

Sara suddenly stepped back, looking slightly more welcoming than Charlie. "Of course, come in. We're just . . . surprised to see you. Together. Ah . . . I mean—"

"Yeah, you're here. Come on in." Charlie still looked far from happy, but he moved aside enough to let them enter.

Jordan ushered Valerie into the apartment as Sara set the small dog on the floor and hurriedly swept cushions aside on the couch. She picked up and folded a newspaper, tucked it into a magazine rack. A bowl of popcorn was on a low table. Sara handed it to Charlie, who took it to the tiny breakfast bar before moving to the television and switching off a hockey game. As Jordan shed his heavy coat and gloves, Valerie tried to come to grips with this newest shock. Sara and Charlie were together again? Or was this only a date? Oh, lord, was Sara's roommate her ex-lover and not the nice, wholesome female coworker Valerie had assumed? And from their behavior, it appeared they could be far more than simply roommates. Valerie rubbed the aching spot between her eyes and wondered how many other shocks were in store for her tonight.

"What's going on here, Sara?" she asked, finally finding her voice. It seemed necessary to clear that up before mentioning Janine. "Are you dating each other again?"

The two young people looked at each other from across the room. Now as Valerie and Jordan stood waiting for an answer, they moved close again, their hands reaching out, joining. The little dog jumped off the couch and stood with them, his tail wagging joyfully. They looked braced to face two enemies, Valerie thought with a pang.

"Charlie's not just a date, Mom," Sara explained softly. "We aren't just watching a hockey game tonight. Charlie is—"

"We love each other," Charlie interrupted in a firm tone. "It was a mistake to break up when we still had feelings for each other."

Valerie sank down onto the nearest chair. She had not removed her coat or her scarf and gloves. "You're not . . . living together here. Are you?"

"We are, Mom. And since we're of age and capable of making our own decisions, please save the lecture." Sara left Charlie's side and went to Valerie. "Here, take off your coat. You look a little pale. Is it really that bad, us being together again?" Without waiting for permission, she slipped Valerie's coat from her shoulders and stuffed the gloves into the pockets. "Why on earth are you out on a night like this? I thought you were at Mr. Kurtz's party."

Was it only tonight when she was at Hal's party? It seemed an eternity. "The party's over," Valerie told her, still struggling to take it all in. This was a more self-possessed Sara than she had ever seen.

Sara handed Valerie's coat to Charlie. "We didn't want you to find out like this, but since you've arrived together, maybe it's the best thing. We've been seeing each other for . . . well, quite a while. I actually did have another roommate, someone I worked with. Then she was offered a job and had to leave New York. Charlie and I had gotten back together by then. It seemed meant to be." She smiled at her mother. "I wanted to tell you. It's been awful keeping it a secret. In fact, I planned to tell you that day we had lunch when I spilled the salad in my lap. But you were so fixated on your new promotion and"—she threw a quick glance in Jordan's direction—"you were a bit upset over Charlie's dad. I could just imagine your reaction if I'd said we were seeing each other again."

Valerie simply looked at her. After the way Charlie had failed her, Sara still loved him?

Charlie turned from hanging up her coat. "I told Sara that we didn't need permission from our parents to do what we wanted. We have the right to please ourselves and she agreed." He moved back to his protective stance at Sara's side. Watching him, Valerie recalled the last time she'd seen him three years ago at the hospital on the day Sara had miscarried. If Sara's self-confidence had increased since her disastrous affair with him, then Charlie's had increased tenfold.

Jordan stood with his back to the window, scowling. "Pleasing yourselves meant moving in together?"

Charlie quickly slipped a protective arm around Sara's waist. "You have a problem with that?"

"Goddamn it, Charlie! If you're so hot to be together, why sneak around?"

"Oh, sure, Dad." Charlie's gaze locked with Jordan's, as straight and unfaltering as his father's. "You'd have welcomed the idea of Sara and me being back together? Yeah, right."

"Well, you'll never know now, will you?" He might have said more, but Charlie seemed bent on driving home his and Sara's decision.

"We made mistakes three years ago. You can hold that against us forever, it's your choice. But it won't change anything."

Watching, Valerie was struck by the similarities between father and son, not so much in a physical sense, although there was that, too, but Charlie was developing Jordan's sheer male presence and something about his chivalry toward Sara reminded her of Jordan. Charlie was no longer young, vulnerable, and overwhelmed by unexpected consequences as he'd been three years ago. He was signaling openly that he would not be so easily manipulated by his father now.

"I get the message, Charlie," Jordan said dryly. "But just as a matter of interest, when did the two of you plan to share all this with Valerie and me?"

"Whenever it suited us," Charlie stated, radiating belligerence.

"Sara?" Valerie gave her daughter a bewildered look.

"It's true, Mom. It was difficult, leaving you out of something so important to us, but after everything that had happened in the past and knowing how you felt about Charlie and his father, we just didn't want the hassle. I hope you understand."

"Well, I suppose I do. Of course, I do," Valerie added quickly, feeling nothing of the kind. "But if I had known you were considering something like this and you'd shared it with me, I think I could have overcome—"

"Oh, come on, Mom, get serious." Sara gave a short laugh. "You'd have had a kitten if I'd said I was involved with Charlie Case again. You nearly had a stroke when you learned your job was going to force you into frequent contact with his dad."

"That's different!" she exclaimed. "That's business. This is . . . it's . . ." She looked at Jordan for help.

"It's unexpected, but we'll survive, " Jordan said, adding sternly to Charlie, "There's nothing else we need to know about, is there?"

"Even if there was," Charlie said, with a dangerous glint in his eye, "Sara and I would choose the time and place to tell you."

Sara quickly stepped close to Charlie and touched his jaw, which was set as stubbornly as Jordan's. "It's okay, Charlie." She looked at Jordan and smiled. "We know about birth control, Mr. Case. That last experience taught us both a lesson."

"It's none of his business," Charlie said.

"A grandchild is none of my business?" Now it was Jordan's turn to issue a challenge.

"Jordan." Valerie stood up suddenly. "I don't think the time is right for a confrontation."

"Suits me," Charlie snapped. "Bring it on."

"Charlie," Sara said again softly.

Although filled with dismay, Valerie realized this was no time to voice her doubts. She glanced at the little Yorkie, who was now standing alertly on the couch as if sensing the hostility in the air. "I wasn't aware that you'd adopted a pet, Sara."

Sara's hand went to the Yorkie, rubbing him behind his ears. "He was a present from Charlie. Isn't he cute?"

Cute, yes, but very different from the large golden retriever that she'd grown up with. "What's his name?"

"Curly."

The dog's ears perked at the sound of his name. "As in Curly, Larry, and Moe?" Jordan asked, doing his part to diffuse the situation.

Sara looked surprised. "Yes, how did you know?"

He looked at his son, who was studying his shoes, but his scowl seemed to be fading. "Charlie always had a thing for the Stooges."

Still smiling, Sara poked Charlie playfully. "I know."

"So . . ." Jordan took the only empty chair in the tiny living room. ". . . now that your secret's out, do you plan to let Val and me come and visit, provided we call first, of course?"

There was some laughter, and although it was a little strained, it worked to break the tension. It was too bad, Valerie thought, that the four of them wouldn't be able to spend more time tonight mending fences before she had to reveal the reason for this surprise visit. Thankfully, there was one good thing about Sara's renewed relationship with Charlie. She would have someone to turn to in her grief.

Drawing a deep breath, she turned to Sara and took both her hands. "I'm afraid I have some bad news, darling."

Jordan seated Valerie in the taxi, got in beside her, and closed the door. After giving the driver her address, he settled back, realizing the snow had let up a little. Beside him, Valerie seemed caught up in her own thoughts. Glancing at his watch, he saw that it was well past midnight. It had been a long day, and for Valerie, tomorrow the ordeal of arranging Janine's funeral would begin early. He could help her out there. With Charlie involved with Sara, it seemed right somehow.

The hour with the kids had been unsettling for him.

He had a heavy feeling somewhere deep inside, part disappointment, part failure. No mistaking Charlie's hostility and it hurt. Jordan knew he'd done damage to his relationship with his son by interfering when Charlie finally got up the nerve to say his girlfriend was pregnant and he wanted to marry her. Maybe if he had it all to do over again, he'd do things differently. Hell, wouldn't anybody do some things differently if they had second chances? But damn it, he was still convinced that teenage marriages were doomed for the most part, and that it had been his responsibility as a father to try and avoid the same thing happening to Charlie. Then somehow when the dust had settled, Jordan was left feeling he had been tested in Charlie's eyes and found wanting. He reached automatically to shield Valerie as the driver took a corner a little too fast. At least he wasn't having to deal with the shock of sudden death in his family.

"Are you okay?" he asked.

She looked at him. "I have to be, don't I?"

"Sara took the news like a trooper, I thought."

"She was very brave," Valerie said, turning quickly, but not before he'd seen the sheen of tears yet again.

"She seemed very concerned about you."

Valerie simply nodded, her gaze fixed to the side. Jordan had the sudden, unexpected impulse to lean close and gather her into his arms. She'd been through a hell of a lot the last few weeks. Now, twice in one night, she'd been hit with shock and surprise. Seeking to try and distract her, he said, "The kids seemed pretty determined to ignore anything we had to say about them getting together again, didn't they?"

She wiped quickly at her eyes with a tissue. "Can you blame them?"

"I guess not. I don't know about you, but I could have been knocked over by a feather when the two of them and that silly little dog finally decided to let us in."

"I think they're serious, Jordan." She gave a delicate sniff and tucked the tissue back into her purse.

"It could be plain old teenage rebellion. I wouldn't worry about it."

"Except that they aren't teenagers."

"Yeah, there is that." The taxi slowed for a pedestrian to hurry across, bent almost double in the swirling snow.

After a moment, she said almost wistfully, "Charlie was very protective of Sara, did you notice that? And her behavior was . . . wifely, don't you think?"

He turned as she rubbed a spot between her eyes. He guessed she was developing a headache. No surprise there. "You know how it is when you're living with someone without taking the vows—it'll probably pass."

"And Sara will be devastated. Again."

"Charlie suffered after they split, too, Val." The taxi pulled to a stop at the curb in front of her apartment building. "Maybe I didn't see it so much at the time, but a blind man can see that there's something going on with them now. Maybe they'll get it out of their system this time. Or maybe not. I just know that last time, Charlie blamed me."

"Then we're even because Sara blamed me." She put her hand on the door, ready to open it. "I don't know if my relationship with my daughter will ever be the same again, but I do know this. Whether they're serious or not, they're of age. This is their choice."

He looked at her as a rush of cold air entered the car. "Are you having second thoughts?"

"About our involvement the first time around? Maybe." She turned up the collar of her coat and pulled her gloves on. "I'll be there if and when Charlie walks again, but his leaving won't be over anything I do or say." She was out of the car now and bending a little to look him in the eye. "This time, I'm taking them at their word."

"I guess I'll do the same," he said.

Both of them knew they had no choice.

The coroner released Janine's body for burial after three days. It seemed a lifetime to Valerie, but everyone said it was quick considering the red tape usually associated with a homicide in New York City. Eric was in the process of trying his hand at writing a work of mystery fiction and had some knowledge about the procedures surrounding a homicide. "It's a miracle that we're able to have the funeral so soon," he told Valerie as they waited for Sara, who was in the powder room of the small chapel where the services were to be conducted. "I see the hand of the big boss in this."

"Jordan? How do you figure that?" Unable to sit still, she began examining cards on the flowers. She felt that she'd done the right thing in scheduling the service in the chapel rather than the huge sanctuary. For years, Janine had been a faithful member of the church before moving into Rose Haven, but many of her friends had died or, like Janine, were now living in rest homes.

"Sometimes a body is held for a month awaiting an autopsy," Eric explained, giving a twitch to the rose in his lapel. "You can bet that Jordan—or Hal Kurtz—dropped a hint to somebody high up the food chain at the coroner's office. Otherwise you might have found yourself waiting who knows how long for the body to be released. Whoever did it, my money's on Jordan as the force behind it. He's been an absolute doll since all this happened, Val. You've got to admit that."

She studied a tiny card without actually seeing it. Jordan had been thoughtful. In spite of her efforts to discourage him, he'd insisted that they were "family" now and he was duty-bound to offer a helping hand. And what he didn't do, Charlie did. Between the two of them, they'd relieved her and Sara of much of the burden of the funeral arrangements. For Valerie, it was a unique experience to rely on someone other than herself. Sara, of course, felt no reluctance about leaning on Charlie. It gave Valerie a pang to see her turning more naturally to her lover for comfort and support than to her mother. Watching them, it was becoming more difficult to hold on to her doubts about their relationship.

"I see Sara's back from the powder room," Eric said, watching her take a card that was attached to the lavish floral sprays sent by friends and acquaintances. "And there's Jordan at last. His son is with him. That Charlie is a dreamboat, isn't he? And there's Roxanne." He waved, keeping the gesture discreet. "I saw her earlier. She said she'll be at the service, but she'll have to leave before the interment. Something about her new friend and some event they just have to do." Eric made a little sound, a click of his tongue against his teeth. "Not to be ... indelicate at this delicate time, Val, but do you like her?"

"Roxanne?"

"No, silly. Her friend—what's her name."

"I haven't met her, Eric."

"Well, I don't see how you could miss meeting her. God knows, everybody else in the building has." Eric waved again—discreetly—at three other colleagues from *Panache*. "She's all over the place at the magazine. I mean, she's at Greg's desk one minute, then Rox's at another. When she starts to give me dictation, I'm going to have to tell her to fuck off."

"Eric—"

He put his hand to his cheek with a theatrical shrug. "Will you listen to me, for God's sake! I'm sorry, love.

I'm just carrying on because death makes me nervous, you know what I mean? And especially violent death."

"Why in the world are you trying to write crime fiction, then?" She stood up, not really hearing his reply, as Sara rushed over ahead of Charlie and Jordan. "Sara, I was getting worried. Are you okay?"

"I'm sorry, Mom. Roxanne wanted to introduce me to her friend, but she must have left early."

Valerie ignored the significant look Eric sent her way. Instead, she glanced at her watch. "We have only a few minutes before the service begins in the chapel."

"Arrangements have been made for you to ride in the limo to the cemetery," Jordan said. "There's room for the four of us."

She nodded. "That's fine. Thank you."

He gave her a narrow-eyed inspection. "Are you okay?"

Okay? With the person solely responsible for rescuing Sara and me all those years ago lying dead in that casket? Murdered! Am I okay? No. And I may never be okay again, God forgive me. But she said none of that out loud. Instead, she squared her shoulders, managing a wan smile. "I'm as well as anyone could expect to be under the circumstances." She patted Sara's hand. "I just need a little time alone. I wasn't quite finished looking over the flowers and I might not have another chance. Do you mind?"

"Mom—" Sara's expression was filled with concern.

Aware of all eyes on her, Valerie waved wordlessly and escaped to the other side of the room where more flowers were grouped. She stared unseeing at a stunning arrangement of star lilies. The shock of Janine's murder had kept her in a state of confusion for days, but her guilt could no longer be ignored. From the beginning, she'd longed to believe that Janine's death was a tragic accident. She accepted that pushing the old nun off the

end of the pier was a deliberate act, but she wanted to
believe that one of the demented patients had somehow
managed it. But nothing useful had been gained from
the patients nearby when Janine was plucked from their
group and wheeled away. Some said it was a man. Others
said it was a woman wearing slacks. And sunglasses. No,
ski goggles. A furry parka. Hair? Long. Short. Color?
Brown. Black. He/she wore a hat. The staff at Rose
Haven, who might have furnished the most useful information, were fearful of a lawsuit and consequently
claimed to have seen nothing out of the ordinary that
day. Bottom line, the police were left with a mystery.

Yes, it was a mystery, but Valerie knew something
beyond a doubt. It was about *her!* It was about that
snapshot. The article. Amy Trent. And James Martindale. Somehow, and for some reason, it was all about
her. By sitting about and passively allowing herself to
be manipulated and tormented and stalked, she had
emboldened the killer and thus paved the way for Janine
to be murdered. For the second time in her life, she
was truly responsible for the death of a friend.

"Val . . ." Coming up quietly behind her, Jordan
touched her waist. "The priest is signaling that he's
ready to start the service. Are you all right?"

She reached blindly for the card tucked in the fragrant arrangement of pink-tipped lilies. "Yes. I just—"

"We can hold off if you need another moment or
two," he said, rubbing her back. She wasn't sure he was
even aware of the sympathetic gesture. This habit he
had of touching her, of projecting strength and support,
was dangerously appealing. She'd seen it in Charlie with
Sara these last few days. These Case men were too compelling. But how long would Jordan's support hold out
if he knew her secrets?

Still holding the small card that came with the lilies,
she thought of her marriage. She had never told her

ex-husband about her past even though he had been curious. Kenneth Long, a loquacious trial lawyer, had talked openly about his family, his work, anecdotes in his past. He'd been baffled by her reluctance to share childhood experiences or teenage escapades. He often told her that without real intimacy in their relationship, their marriage was doomed. She'd thought, almost with amusement, that their marriage would definitely be doomed if she'd been foolish enough to tell of her teenage escapades.

"Valerie . . ."

On the point of answering Jordan, the words on the card she held in her hand suddenly swam into focus. She stared at them in shock, blinking frantically as if to change the message scrawled on the card.

My condolences. Like your mother, Janine had to die. You understand why, don't you?

"No," she murmured.

"What was that?" Jordan bent his head to catch the strangled sound.

"I . . . Nothing." *I can't let him see this card!* Fighting panic, she slipped it into the pocket of her suit jacket and took his arm. "I'm ready to go in now."

"Like hell you are! You're trembling like a leaf, Val. And you're pale as a ghost. You need to sit down." He signaled an attendant of the funeral home standing nearby. "Get Ms. Olivier-Long some water, would you?"

"No," Valerie repeated again with more force. With real effort, she managed to sound almost normal. Almost. "The service needs to begin. Let's go in."

He studied her intently for a long moment before nodding reluctantly. "Your call, but you look ready to collapse, Val."

She took his arm and, holding her head high, allowed him to escort her into the chapel where Sara waited with Charlie. At the door, she caught the eye of the priest, who nodded and summoned them forward. Music from an organ swelled softly. The hymn was familiar, a favorite of Janine's. How had that happened? Then she saw Sara's tears and realized her daughter must have had a hand in choosing the music. As she started down the aisle, she saw Roxanne on the back row and a few rows in front of her, Hal Kurtz. And Denise Grantham. Then Greg. Half a dozen more staff members from *Panache*. Her throat closed painfully. She would not forget her friends' thoughtfulness. As she blinked back tears, she was brought back from the edge when her gaze settled on Detective McGowan in the crowd.

Sensing her reaction, Jordan reached for her hand on his arm and squeezed it. "What's wrong?"

"Why is McGowan here?"

He guided her into a pew closest to the altar and sat down beside her. "It's part of his job. Forget him. This time is for Janine."

She stared at her hands, saw they were trembling, and clasped them tightly together. Jordan, sensing her distress, covered them with one of his. He was warm, steady, comforting. His touch helped her calm herself.

Only then did she allow herself to look at the closed casket. A spray of creamy white roses adorned it. White roses for winter, she thought. White roses to mark the end of a saintly life. Why in such a cruel way? Tears flooded her eyes once more, and again, Jordan sensed her distress and put an arm around her. With a broken sigh, Valerie allowed herself to lean into his warmth. To draw from his strength. Just this once, she told herself. What could be the harm?

While in her pocket, the note burned like the fires of hell.

CHAPTER FIFTEEN

Jordan stood at the desk of Father Alphonse in New York's archdiocese feeling his patience dwindling by the minute. It had been made clear to him by the priest, a slight, emaciated-looking man sitting hunched up at his desk in a swivel chair, that Jordan was on a wasted mission. Father Alphonse was like many low-ranking bureaucrats in a huge organization. It wasn't worth his job—priest or not—to bend the rules. He'd listened without expression while Jordan explained the purpose of his visit. He needed background information about Sister Janine Livaudais to try and uncover the motive for her death. The killer could be the same person who was stalking Valerie. And if he'd struck that close to Valerie, his next victim could be Sara or Valerie herself. It was a possibility that he wasn't going to ignore.

"Absolutely no one is allowed access to the background files of nuns or priests in the Church," the priest said, looking at Jordan as if he'd asked for the formula to construct a hydrogen bomb. "Such records are sealed to the public."

The priest's reply was not unexpected, but Jordan was determined to make the effort. "This could be a matter of life and death, Father."

Father Alphonse's bony shoulders lifted in a shrug. "Life and death are in God's hands, not ours, Mr. Case."

Jordan's breath was released in a gust of anger and frustration. He swung away and began pacing in front of the priest's desk. Years ago as a rookie reporter he'd wheedled secrets out of more hardened gatekeepers than this guy, but it had been more years than he cared to recall. Of course, his investigative skills were rusty, as he'd learned lately. In the two days since Janine's funeral, he'd reached a dead end in researching Valerie's background. He knew in his gut that the nun's death was related somehow to the mysterious harassment that was happening to Valerie, but he'd hit a blank wall beyond the meager information in her file at Kurtz-Whitman. Logically, an employee's records revealed that person's background, birthplace, parents, secondary schooling, et cetera. To his surprise, the information in Valerie's employee files was extremely limited. It was almost as if her life began in her teens. In Boston. When she herself had admitted that she'd grown up in the French Quarter in New Orleans. Stymied there, he'd refocused on Janine.

He stopped, thinking to appeal to the priest's loyalty to the Church. "Look, all I'm asking for are a few details about Sister Janine's past. The woman was murdered and no one has a clue as to why. Don't you want her killer brought to justice?"

"That is a job for the police, Mr. Case."

"What if someone's targeting other nuns?"

"Again, that is a matter for the police and we've had no hint of that from them."

How could a priest be so heartless? "Then think of others who were close to her who might be in danger. I'll keep anything I learn about her in strictest confidence, you have my word."

"I'm sorry, I can't help you."

Jordan stared into Father Alphonse's muddy brown eyes for a long minute. "You'd force me to get a court order?"

"You must do whatever you think expedient," the priest said coolly. "At this point, my hands are tied."

A court order was impossible with no evidence to back up his suspicions and the priest knew that. Jordan cast a look around the dingy room as if searching for a way to reach this sanctimonious little toad. If something happened to Valerie or Sara as a result of Father Alphonse's thickheaded bureaucratic posturing, he vowed to come back and choke him with his own collar.

Struggling to be civil, he tried again. "A woman that I care about is in danger, Father." He paused for a beat or two, realizing that he meant that. He did care about Valerie. "She and her daughter were the closest thing to family that Janine had. There must be a connection and I need to find it before another tragedy happens. Surely, as a man dedicated to the service of humanity, you can suggest something."

The priest swiveled in his chair and looked out of the window through squinty eyes. As he thought, he drummed his fingertips on the desk. Jordan waited, almost growling with frustration. It was clear to him why Father Alphonse had been placed in an administrative capacity in the priesthood. He would be a washout shepherding a congregation. It was impossible to imagine him listening to the confessions of ordinary people with any compassion.

Then, after a moment, the priest swiveled his chair back around so that he faced Jordan directly. "If what you say is true, Mr. Case, then perhaps you might uncover something of use in Louisiana."

"Louisiana?" Pulling out a notepad, Jordan uncapped his pen and prepared to write.

"Sister Janine resided at a convent there. St. Francis, I believe it was . . . before renouncing her vows." He paused a moment as if just mentioning renouncing one's vows left the scent of something unpleasant in the room. "The Order of St. Francis is, of course, a part of the archdiocese of New Orleans."

Two days after Janine's funeral, Valerie was in New Orleans. The hotel reserved for her by a travel agent was deep in the French Quarter, an old-world charmer that the agent had assured her she'd adore. She might have . . . under different circumstances. She was familiar with the hotel, although it had been more than twenty years since she'd panhandled on that very same site. And under different circumstances, she might have found some amusement in that irony, but there was little in her life to amuse her lately.

It was the note that had sealed her resolve to go. Ever since the appearance of the old photo of her and her friends in the French Quarter, she had known that the key to the identity of her stalker would be found eventually in New Orleans. Someone knew about her past, and this was the place where her life had gone off-track. The trip might prove to be a wasted effort, but she had to begin looking for answers.

Getting away hadn't been easy. She'd been forced to rely on Eric to keep her plans confidential, but she'd had to tell him in case something happened—God forbid—and Sara needed her. He'd been nearly salivating with curiosity, but like any good personal assistant, he was paid to be discreet in all things. As for Jordan, she

could only imagine his reaction when he learned she
was unavailable and Eric refused to tell him where she
was. Thankfully, no one knew why. With Janine now
gone, she alone knew her secrets. Or so it had seemed.

But someone knows . . .

She tipped the bellman and locked the door behind
him when he left. Next, she took off her jacket. She'd
forgotten how mild the weather could be in February.
Azaleas were in bloom, riotous reds, pinks, white. And
everything was so green, so lush. Upon arriving at the
hotel, she'd been keenly aware of the smells, the soft
inflection of speech, the city's age and ambiance, the
sheer decadence of it. All were vivid reminders of the
months she'd spent on the streets of "The Big Easy,"
it was now called, although that term was not known
twenty years ago. It seemed another lifetime. It was
another lifetime, she reminded herself.

She sat on the bed and opened her briefcase. She
had an appointment with the private investigator she'd
engaged after the cell phone call that day she'd had
lunch with Jordan. She had the man's report, but she
wanted to talk with him personally. He'd found nothing
that shed any light on the mystery, but she'd been careful what facts she'd revealed to the investigator. The
agency was known for its discretion, but she still needed
to safeguard as much of her past as possible. Still, she
couldn't sit like a trussed chicken and wait for another
tragedy. She'd waited too long and Janine had died.
Was she to be next? Or—horrible thought—was Sara
in danger?

Sitting on the bed, she read again the note that came
with the flowers.

*My condolences. Like your mother, she had to die. You
understand why, don't you?*

The small card was tattered from handling. She'd lost
count of the times she'd read it with horror, chilled at

the implication. The stalker was responsible for her mother's death? Though Hannah had made no effort to locate her over the years, Valerie knew of her mother's life through Janine's connections in the church parish where the Martindales resided. She'd hoped someday, somehow, they might mend their fences and had been saddened when she learned of Hannah's death in a carjacking incident.

Driven by grief and regret, she had attended the funeral. There was an enormous crowd as to be expected when the wife of a man in Edward Martindale's position died; however, she'd been careful to keep out of his sight. He'd looked distinguished and prosperous. She recalled thinking that a man's character should somehow be revealed in his face. Of course, had that been true, his expression would have shocked the mourners. She'd stayed inside the taxi at the cemetery nursing bitter memories, then as soon as the graveside rites were over, she'd ordered the driver to leave. It galled her that flowers for her mother had to be sent anonymously.

Now, with the note, the findings by the police of her mother's death were suspect. To Valerie's knowledge, there was no suspicion of foul play. The police viewed it as a simple case of a suburbanite being in the wrong place at the wrong time, a random act of violence. Was it possible that Hannah had been murdered simply to flush Valerie out of hiding?

Was this the moment when the killer had found her?

"Valerie Long?" A huge man with thick steel-gray hair stopped at Valerie's table. She set her water glass down, touched her napkin to her lips, and nodded. Her hands were a little unsteady and she tucked them out of sight in her lap. Nerves, she thought. She was going to have to get hold of herself if she didn't want to trigger unwanted curiosity in the investigator. It was his business to pry into people's lives. She wanted his attention directed elsewhere, not to herself.

"Yes, I'm Valerie Long," she said, gesturing at a chair. "Sit down, please."

"Roy Bergeron." He stuck out a huge hand, and without getting up, Valerie shook it. "Call me Roy."

"Thanks for coming, Roy. Were you able to find Oscar's present address?"

"Yes, ma'am." He pulled an envelope from inside his jacket and handed it over. "And just so you'll know, his parole officer told me I'm not the only one asking about Diaz's whereabouts these days. Another party is on his trail."

"Another party?"

"Another private eye."

The waiter appeared then, asking for their order. Valerie chose quickly, hardly glancing at the menu. Bergeron did the same. "This Oscar Diaz is not somebody you want to mess around with, Ms. Long. He's a sleaze from way back. Served time twice, once in Angola. And they only send the worse felons there. You make sure you don't let him know you're asking questions about him."

"Thank you for your advice," Valerie said, wishing she could heed it. "But about this other party, as you call him. Who is it?"

"A woman. Angela LeBlanc. I know her. She's been around for years in this business, but she's a lush and hasn't had a client worth dirt in I don't know when. I can't figure why she'd be interested in Oscar Diaz." He took a sip of water. "I'd go around to her place and ask, but not before clearing it with you. I wouldn't want to tip her off to something."

Clearly, Bergeron was curious about her reason for wanting to locate Oscar Diaz, but she planned to handle

everything from this point on her own. But it was interesting that someone else was asking about Oscar now.
The timing was too pat. And Valerie had never believed
in coincidence.

"Do you have her address?"

He glanced at the envelope. "It's in the second
report. Does that mean you're going to see her on your
own?"

Valerie waited while the waiter placed a bowl of
gumbo in front of her and a poor-boy sandwich bulging
with fried oysters in front of Roy. "I'm not sure what
I'm going to do, Roy. I don't have a plan."

"You can get in trouble here in the Big Easy if you
don't know your way around, ma'am. Begging your pardon, but just looking at you, I can see you aren't used
to dealing with characters like Oscar Diaz or Angela
LeBlanc. I'd feel a lot better if you'd let me go with you
. . . provided you've got plans to see these two."

"As I said, Roy, I have no plans." She stirred the
gumbo before taking a taste. It was delicious. She wished
Sara could have come with her. There were some won-
derful things to be seen and enjoyed in New Orleans
and they might never have the opportunity to share
them.

"Is this a private party or is there room for one more?"

"Jordan!" Valerie dropped her spoon with a clatter.
"What are you doing here?"

"I could ask you the same question." Jordan looked
at Bergeron, who rose slowly. "Jordan Case."

The investigator's gaze was steady. "Roy Bergeron."

They stood a moment eyeing each other. Then Jordan
gave a small nod, almost as if passing approval on the
man, and they shook hands. He turned to Valerie and
smiled, baring a lot of teeth. "I take it you have no
objection if I sit down."

"Actually, we were just leaving."

She didn't notice the wry look Bergeron cast at his untouched plate. "Yeah, I'm out of here. You know where to reach me, Ms. Long."

"Yes, thank you, Roy."

Nothing was said as the investigator walked away, then Jordan sat down in the chair he'd vacated. Shoving aside the untouched food, he signaled their waiter.

"I didn't know you were planning a trip to New Orleans," Valerie said.

"It's winter. It's snowing in New York. It's sixty degrees here. It seemed a swell idea." He waited until the waiter approached the table. "I'll have a martini, please. Make it a double."

She realized with a start that he was furious. As for herself, she was torn between feeling a rush of relief and gladness at seeing him and being furious that he'd defied her and chased off after her, knowing she wished it otherwise. What she said next sounded bitchy, even to her own ears. "Do you have some other reason to be here or are you just doing your usual thing, throwing your weight around and second-guessing my decisions?"

"If haring off to New Orleans when a killer could possibly be chasing your pretty butt is second-guessing your decisions, then hell yes, that's what I'm doing."

The waiter appeared with the martini. Jordan tossed off most of it in one gulp. "Are you nuts?" he demanded, leaning a little closer across the table. "Have you lost your freakin' mind? Do you realize that some nutcase is out there stalking you, killing your mother, breaking into your house whenever the hell he feels like it, and thumbing his nose at any attempt to flush him out?"

"Killing my mother?" Did he know about Hannah? Had he seen the note?

"According to you, Janine was the closest thing to a mother you had," he said, and she felt a slight lessening of the knot in her stomach. "Or is there some other deep, dark secret you haven't shared with me?"

"Why should I share anything with you?" she hissed, leaning forward to give as good as she was getting. It felt liberating to light into Jordan, the one person she could spout off to and it didn't seem to faze him. "Just because Sara and Charlie are involved, you assume some kind of patriarchal role and start trying to dictate what I do. Well, think again."

"This has nothing to do with Sara and Charlie, damn it! This has to do with common sense, woman. Why in hell did you come to New Orleans?"

"How did you even know I was here?"

"Eric blabbed it." He stared darkly into his martini. "After some persuasion."

Her eyes narrowed. "Did you threaten him?"

"Damn right I threatened him. I told him his job wasn't worth a plugged nickel if he didn't tell me where you were within the next thirty seconds and guess what? He caved . . . not because he was afraid I would actually fire him, but because he knew it was crazy for you to be down here on your own trying to solve a murder! So sue me."

She looked away. "It's still my decision, crazy or not."

"You can't stay here on some cockamamie quest to flush out a killer, Valerie. What about Sara? If something happened to you, she might be next."

"Don't you think I'm aware of that?" she asked fiercely. Then suddenly she felt tears threatening. "You don't understand, Jordan," she managed, averting her eyes. "And I can't explain it to you. I wish I could. I . . . I'm just in a bind here. I'm horrified over Janine's death. To think that it could have something to do with me is almost more than I can bear."

The anger went out of him with a sigh. Shoving his drink and the table appointments aside, he took both

her hands. "Are you suggesting that you know something that might be relevant to the investigation?"

She made a frustrated sound, but didn't try to free
her hands. His touch was comforting somehow. And
right. "I don't know what I know. That's just the
problem."

He dropped her hands. "What the hell does that
mean? Does this have anything to do with that picture
that sent you into a panic? Don't bother to deny it wasn't
here in New Orleans. I recognized the street sign. You
were raised here, you said. Are you here to try and trace
those kids? Do you have some reason to believe one of
them might be your stalker?"

"It doesn't seem likely, but it's a place to start." She
was going to have to tell him something, she thought.
At least a part of it. Her need for hiding her past wasn't
nearly as urgent now that a killer was on the loose and
Sara could be his next victim.

"Was that why you contacted an investigator?"

She frowned. "What?"

With a hitch of his chin, he indicated the envelope
on the table. The return address was plain to see. "Bergeron and Hatch Investigations. Is Bergeron someone
you've known in the past or did you find him in the
yellow pages today?"

"His agency was recommended. I called him after
the episode in the restaurant that day."

"You never told me what was said." He had one of
her hands again. "How about sharing now?"

"He called me by a name that only someone who
knew me here could have known. But it was more than
just that. There was something evil in the way he—"
She paused. "I'm not sure it was a man, but the way
I was threatened seemed so . . . evil. That's the only
word."

"He threatened you? How?"

"Something was said about payback."

"As in revenge?"

"I don't know. Just payback."

"And you can't think of anything you've done that someone would want to pay you back? Or to take revenge?"

"No, I can't." Her reply came quickly because it was an honest one. She had wronged no one. At least, no one who was still alive.

"No cheating, no lying? No stealing a boyfriend? What other stuff do teenagers get into? Drugs, maybe, but I can't see you doing anything like that. There must—" He stopped, catching the look on her face. "What? Why are you looking like that?"

"We—I—did do some drugs back then."

She'd succeeded in surprising him. She tried pulling her hand free, but he held on. "Was it occasional or were you into the drug scene seriously?"

"I don't think this has anything to do with that part of my past, Jordan."

"Don't want to go there, eh?"

"I haven't touched any illegal substance since . . . well, for many years."

Jordan studied her face. "At least now I understand why you avoid alcohol." Moving almost idly, he lifted her hand and rubbed it against his cheek. "So, what other dark secrets are you willing to share today?"

His eyes on her face now were gentle, almost caressing. "I was a runaway," she said. "Janine took me in."

"And your baby."

Her heart took a plunge. How much to admit? "Yes. And my baby."

"What about the father?" Jordan's gaze was more intent now. "Could he be the one?"

"No."

"Just 'no'? How do you know?"

"He's . . . Because he was never . . ." She frowned. No one was certain that Oscar had fathered Amy's child. But if he had, could he be resentful that Valerie had run away with Sara? Could he be experiencing some late-breaking fatherly feelings? But he never knew the baby survived. He never knew for certain that she'd taken the baby. There was never any indication over the years that Oscar had another thought about Amy's child. He'd been ready to kill the baby himself. No, it couldn't be Oscar. Could it?

"What's his name?"

She drew a deep breath. "You're never going to understand this, but I'm not sure who Sara's father is. I know who it most probably was and I was planning to see him myself." Oh, God, he would probably see that admission as proof that she was horribly promiscuous. But what other choice did she have except to tell him everything? Rampant promiscuity would pale compared to the rest of her story.

"You know where this guy is? You've been in touch with him over the years?"

She gave a dry laugh. "Hardly. But . . . again, I have to start somewhere and Oscar Diaz seems the logical choice."

He released her hand, picked up his martini and finished it, then stood up. "Okay, let's get started."

She went with him. At least he hadn't walked away in disgust.

Jordan was dealing with it. Or trying to. Struggling might be a better word. He'd done a few things in his past that he wasn't proud of—especially when he'd been young and hot and in rebellion. In that, he'd been no different from most teenagers as the sixties were winding down. Valerie had come out of the feminist freedom movement, so expecting her to hold to an old-fashioned standard of behavior was pretty . . . well, old-fashioned. He admitted, albeit reluctantly, that if men were free to rebel and experiment, then women were entitled to the same thing. But he didn't have to like it.

Their first stop was the archives of the *Times Picayune*, the daily newspaper that had run the article about Amy Trent. Jordan paid off the taxi driver, then followed Valerie up the steps of the building. "You're going to explain why we're here and not knocking on Oscar Diaz's door, right?"

"You wanted to know another of my dark secrets," she said, digging into her shoulder bag for her tattered copy of the article as they waited for the elevator. "Amy Trent is one of those teens in the picture. I knew her. More than that, we were close—or as close as runaways tend to get. Oscar didn't like it. He thought of Amy as his exclusive property."

Jordan whistled softly. "Wow, no wonder you hated the idea of a feature in *Panache*. Pretty awkward if that had come out after all these years." He frowned looking over the article. "Funny that they never found her body. I wonder if your friend Oscar knows anything about that."

"He's not my friend. He never was. And you can bet your life he knows where Amy's body is."

"You're saying he murdered her?"

"I'm saying he did nothing to save her when he could have."

The elevator pinged and Jordan followed as she ducked inside. Several people crowded back to let them in, saving her from the questions that had leaped to his mind.

The clerk manning the desk at the newspaper's archives was a gregarious sort whose pale skin reflected the hours he spent guarding the musty shelves stacked with old records. "Why does he wear sunglasses?" Jordan asked under his breath. "There's no glare. There aren't even any windows in this cave."

"I don't know, Jordan. I don't care about his quirky personality. I just want to ask him some questions." She conjured a smile and brought out the article. "I wonder if you could answer a few questions, Mr. ... ah ... Miles?"

He studied her first and then Jordan, peering at them over the round dark lenses. "That depends, you know? What was it you wanted to ask?"

"I wondered if anyone had been into your area lately asking about this article. The date it ran is on my copy."

Pushing his shades back into place, he scanned the article. "What is it about this piece? There's been a run on it lately. Had an investigations consultant—that's what they call themselves now—come in and ask about it. A woman, you believe that? I call 'em the same thing we always did years ago, man or woman. Private eyes. Still in the same business, call it whatever you will, it's still snooping into other folks' business. Prying into stuff better left buried. But no money in that." He shoved the article back at her.

"Was that Angela LeBlanc?"

"Yeah, one and the same. She's been around since God invented grass." He pulled a stenographer's tablet from under the counter and began flipping pages. "Another guy was in here, too, but I don't think I got his name. Sometimes they don't want to own up who they are. He was a big guy, lots of curly hair, gray as a possum. Six foot four if I'm any judge."

"Roy Bergeron," Valerie said softly to Jordan.

"And I think we had a phone call." Miles flipped the pages in the steno pad rapidly. "I try to keep all requests in my notebook. Yeah, here it is. Couple of days ago. Some magazine mogul from the Big Apple, and seeing as we were both in the media business, maybe I could do him a favor. Fax him something. Wanted photos, like I could just pull 'em from our files and ship 'em off. Like schmoozing me would get him what he wanted."

"And did you?" Valerie wanted to know.

"Give him what he wanted? Hell, no."

CHAPTER SIXTEEN

"That was you, wasn't it?" Back at the hotel, Valerie was assisted from the taxi by a valet while Jordan paid the driver.

"Schmoozing Miles the Mole?" He slipped a money clip back into his pocket and cupped her elbow to escort her through the entrance. "Can you see me identifying myself as a magazine mogul from the Big Apple?"

She freed her elbow. "No, but I can see you doing whatever it takes to satisfy your curiosity and you've been dying of curiosity for weeks now."

He followed her into the hotel and across the lobby to the elevator. "Only because I couldn't get a straight answer from you. I'm still baffled over how stubborn you were about reporting the break-ins at your apartment and the stalking to the cops. And the snapshot. If you'd told them—or me—that you suspected the answer might be found in New Orleans, we might have flushed this character out by now."

"And Janine might not be dead." Valerie punched

the elevator button to the fourth floor. "Is that what you think?"

He was shaking his head. "Not at all. That's assuming more facts than we have in evidence. I think whoever this is isn't going to be stopped easily. But if you'd been more up-front, maybe we'd be closer to identifying him. That doesn't mean we'd be any closer to finding him."

"Oscar may know something. I haven't given up on seeing him. He's still the best bet." They'd stopped at the address for Diaz furnished by Fontenot, but there had been no response at his door. They were finally told by a couple of young teens who'd been lounging on the front stoop smoking that Diaz had driven off an hour before and wasn't likely to be back until after midnight since his peak working time was just beginning.

"What is his line of work?" Jordan had asked.

"He a pimp," one boy had replied.

"Big-time pimp," his cohort agreed.

Without another word, Jordan had hustled Valerie back to the waiting taxi where she'd been subjected to another lecture on the folly of pursuing Oscar Diaz on her own.

I know the neighborhoods to avoid in this city, Jordan."

The sound he made said it all. "Sure you do. That's why I'm feeling so safe and secure right now."

"I'm unfamiliar with this area, but if I'd been alone when the taxi driver found the address, I would not have gotten out of the car. I'm not a fool."

"Somehow I don't see you giving up so easily."

"I would then have tried to reach him on the phone and arranged for us to meet in a safer place. Like a mall or something."

"Yeah, well, none of that will be necessary, since I plan to be with you. Night and day."

She had the key to her room in her hand as the elevator stopped and the doors opened. She stepped out and Jordan followed. "I'd like your promise that you won't see this guy unless you're with me, Val."

She took a moment to get her bearings in the hall before turning left. Jordan fell into step beside her. "We'll try again early tomorrow morning." he said.

"Where are you going?" she asked, pausing in the middle of the hall.

"I didn't hear your promise."

She sighed. "Okay, I won't make a date with Oscar without telling you first."

He squeezed her arm. "Good girl."

She rolled her eyes. He was a strange mix of New York sophisticate and old-fashioned knight. It was endearing. And dangerously appealing. "This may surprise you," she said, "but now that you're here, I'm actually glad to have you go with me. We may be wasting our time, but I'm determined to talk to Oscar. He has to be able to shed some light on this whole thing."

"Yeah and he's such a sweetheart, too. I can just see him admitting he knows who's stalking you and why. Not to mention the question that might arise if there's a suggestion of linkage with Janine's murder."

"You think I don't know what a lowlife he is? Facing him again is the last thing I want to do." They approached a window at the end of the corridor which overlooked a lush courtyard thick with tropical plants. Years ago, there had been a courtyard near the rundown building where Oscar housed his "girls." It had been a favorite place where Valerie had escaped to get high. Not a memory she allowed herself to dwell on. She didn't like recalling it now.

"Janine is dead, Jordan. I can't rest until I know I wasn't somehow to blame. I have to get some answers. I can't just do nothing."

"I understand that." They'd arrived at her room now and he reached for her key.

She held on to it. "What are you doing?"

"I'm planning to unlock the door."

"I'm a grown-up, Jordan," she said, although she found herself relinquishing the key. "I can unlock my own hotel room."

"Humor me. I'm coming inside with you. Hotels aren't the securest places in the world."

"What are you going to do, check under all the beds? Nobody knows I'm here."

"Except Eric. And Charlie. And Sara. And Roxanne, who happened to be worried sick about you, so I told her. And those two kids lounging on Oscar Diaz's stoop. And the clerk at the newspaper. Possibly even your stalker."

She put her hands on her hips. "You told everybody where I was? Damn it, Jordan, why didn't you just take out an ad in the *Times?*"

"You agree that Charlie should know that Sara could possibly be the target of a killer, don't you? He'll be able to look out for her the same as I feel obligated to look out for you. This is—"

He went silent as a couple coming out of the elevator strolled past them. She waited until they were out of earshot. "You don't have to feel obligated to look out for me," she said, stung at the thought that that was his only reason.

"It's a guy thing, don't waste energy fighting it."

What could she say to that? "You don't really think Sara is in danger, do you?" she asked.

"Hell, I don't know, Val." He unlocked the door and paused a second before going in. "I'm more baffled now than when I got here. I just think we can't afford to take any chances with a killer on the loose."

She watched as he checked out the room, opening

the closet, even going so far as pulling back the shower curtain in the bathroom. "No need to look under the bed," she told him dryly. "It's too low to the floor to conceal anybody." He looked anyway, then went to the French doors opening onto a balcony. Turning the lock, he stepped out. "Great view."

"I like it."

He came back inside and began taking off the leather bomber jacket he'd traveled in from New York, where the temperature had been in the midthirties.

"What are you doing?"

"I'm hot as hell," he said, throwing the jacket on the bed. "How did you ever get used to the humidity in this town? I remember visiting once during Mardi Gras. You'd think because it was February that it wouldn't seem so much like a steam bath, but I never stopped sweating from the time I got off the plane."

"Why didn't you change into something more comfortable when you checked in?"

"I haven't checked in." He pulled his shirttails out of his jeans, giving her a flash of tanned male middle. Not an ounce of middle-age spread. Plus there was a tantalizing arrow of dark hair that disappeared into his jeans. She felt an unexpected rush of awareness. "I spotted you and Fontenot in the dining room before I had a chance to get a room. Besides, the more I get to know you and the way you think, the less I like leaving you on your own." He headed for the phone. "Let's call down for something cold, what do you say?"

"What does that mean?"

"Beer for me and whatever you want."

"I mean what about not leaving me on my own? You're not staying here."

He picked up the receiver with a gleam in his eye. "Only if you beg me."

"Jordan—"

"Relax, Val. I'm going to order something to drink and then I'll see about getting a room. Iced tea for you, right?"

"Yes. Thank you." She sounded prissy, she knew that. But he had a way of making her react like a teenager when he looked at her like that. In spite of herself, her gaze strayed to the bed and she wondered how it would be making love to Jordan. But it would be sex, not love, she told herself. Impossible for her to fall in love with Jordan as long as she resisted telling him her secrets.

Flustered at her thoughts, she went to the thermostat to check the setting, shedding her blazer with relief. He was right. The humidity was a killer here, something she'd almost forgotten. At least, she hoped it was humidity and not the thought of Jordan and the bed that was making her uncomfortable.

"Okay, that's done. Drinks'll be here in twenty minutes." He put the phone down and stretched, rolling his shoulders. It was an utterly male movement and blatantly sexual. She looked quickly away. "What do you want to do next?" he asked.

"Take a shower," she said, without thinking, then looked up at him.

"Good choice." That wicked gleam was now dancing in his eyes.

She added hurriedly, "I mean, I'll take a shower while you wait for room service."

"Oh. Right."

She grabbed a robe and ducked into the bathroom.

Twenty minutes later, she was out of the shower, toweling off and feeling slightly more comfortable. Their drinks had arrived while she was in the bathroom. Jordan had taken his and then called to her through the door that he was leaving to go to the lobby and check

in. He said he'd be back in a few minutes and they'd
decide where to go for dinner. She'd considered telling
him that she had already made plans for dinner, but as
she was standing in the shower shampooing her hair,
it seemed more expedient to choose another time to
declare her independence. Besides, it was not fun to
dine alone in a strange city. What was strange was how
easy it seemed having Jordan around.

Tossing aside the towel, she donned a silk kimono
and began drying her hair. She thought of Sara and
wondered whether there was something in Jordan's concern that she might be a target of the killer. It seemed
logical if the stalker and Janine's killer were one and
the same. Eerily logical. But the stalker had never mentioned Sara. She, Valerie, was the stalker's target. Or
she had been up until now.

She turned off the hair dryer, and as she reached for
a brush, she heard Jordan in the next room. He must
have caught the desk clerk at just the right time. When
she'd checked in, she'd had time to take a nap waiting
for the clerk to process her registration. Stupid not to
have taken her clothes into the bathroom, but with all
this humidity, she preferred a fresh outfit to a limp and
steamy one. What the heck. He'd seen a woman in a
robe before. Still, she wished it was terrycloth and not
this clingy silk thing. She could ask him to hand her
her things, but that meant rooting through her luggage
to find her underwear. No, not an option. She opened
the door.

It was not Jordan standing at the foot of the bed
pawing through her luggage. It was a total stranger.

"Hey, babe. Jesus, you're looking good. Real good."

She stared, absolutely stunned for a beat or two. Coming alive suddenly, she scrambled backward, reaching
blindly for the handle on the bathroom door. The
stalker! Somehow he'd found her. But her foot slipped

on the wet tile and he was on her, clamping a hard hand over her mouth before she could even think to scream. The brush fell with a clatter and she clawed at his fingers trying to breathe while her legs churned and her body twisted in a desperate struggle to get away. He grunted when her heel connected with his shin, but it was a puny blow, and instead of letting her go, he caught her neck in a tight vise, choking off her breath. Only seconds and she was close to blacking out.

She was mindless with terror. She was going to die!

"Shit, Caroline, calm down or I'll have to hurt you." He spoke right in her ear, but the words took a few seconds to penetrate her panic. Caroline? She went still and he shifted his hold on her throat and she could breathe again. "Man, you're still as wild as you were twenty years ago."

"Who—" All she could manage was a croak. She cleared her bruised throat. "Who are you?" she finally said.

"I'm hurt." Still holding his hand over her mouth and keeping her body tight against his, he pushed his pelvis against her buttocks. "You recognize me now, babe?"

She'd caught only a glimpse of his face, but she knew. "Oscar?"

"Your main man, sugar." With his breath hot on her, he gave her earlobe a vicious bite. "Although we never did get it on back then. But hey, I'm game if you are. Right now."

Sick, oily nausea churned in her stomach. "I won't scream if you'll let me go, I promise."

"Still a frigid bitch, huh?" He sighed with regret, removed his hand from her face only to lower it to her breasts. She froze with dread as he slipped a hand inside her kimono and gave one nipple a hard pinch. She swallowed a gasp, determined not to give him the satisfaction of knowing how terrified she was. He was going to rape her. He was a huge man. And brutal. There was nothing to stop him no matter how hard she fought. Jordan wouldn't be back until he'd checked in. Even then he'd probably take a shower and change for dinner. She closed her eyes and fought off a wave of despair. She had only her wits to save her now.

"Are you the stalker?" she asked in a shaky voice.

"What you talkin' about?" The hand inside her kimono moved lower, stroked across her belly. Every muscle in her tightened.

"Someone has been threatening me for weeks now, Oscar. Is it you? Did you kill Janine?"

She actually felt his shock. He turned her loose and pushed her away so that he could look in her face. "I would never touch a nun, bitch. You think I'm crazy?"

"Then what are you doing here? Why did you break into my room?" she demanded, holding the edges of her kimono together at her throat with one hand while her mind raced to find a way to escape. "How did you get in here?"

"Ain't no lock can keep me out of a ho-tel room, babe. You oughta know that." He saw her glance at the door. "But turned out I didn't need to pick the lock. I just walked in off the balcony."

"Five floors from the ground?"

"Room next to yours is vacant, Caroline. Y'all share a balcony."

Still keeping her kimono tightly closed, she sat on the edge of a chair locking her knees together. "What do you want, Oscar?"

"I believe I'm the one should be askin' that. The question is . . . what you and that guy you're traveling with want from me? Hey, I'm minding my business and then some kids tell me you're nosing around my place.

Save you the trouble, I'm here to confer with you about it. And while we're at it, what's this about a stalker?''

So it wasn't him. His surprise was genuine. Her heart rate was settling a little now as panic faded. Maybe she could keep him talking until Jordan returned. "If it's not you, then I don't think I'll bore you with the details," she said, knowing if he believed she was still Caroline Weston, she wasn't about to tell him otherwise. Or to give him information that would pique his curiosity. "I don't suppose you've kept up with the girls in our group, have you?''

"My girls, you mean, don't you, babe? Sure. I owned them, I kept up with them.''

She had herself under control now. Barely. "I've got a snapshot of five of us, Anna Swenson, Becky Barfield, Kelly Lott, myself, and Amy. Do you know where they are today?''

"Well, we both know Amy's address, don't we?'' he said slyly.

"You know I was never told where she was buried, Oscar. But I'd like to pay my respects before I leave New Orleans.''

He wagged a finger at her. "Quick as ever, aren't you, Caroline? But whether I fill you in, so to speak, or not, you're still an accomplice. I tell you what, I'll put a posy on her grave next time I'm there.''

Bastard. Slimy creep. It was sad enough that Amy had died in a filthy hole-in-the-wall warehouse, but the thought that she'd never been properly laid to rest had always tormented Valerie. But since Oscar had no conscience or decency, there was no way that wrong could ever be righted.

"What about Anna?''

"O-D'd about a year after you split." He flopped down on the bed, stretched out, and lit a cigarette. "Last I heard, she was in the state loony bin.''

Valerie didn't hide her disgust. "You're all heart, aren't you, Oscar?"

He shrugged and blew smoke at the ceiling. "Hey, if you can't handle that shit, you shouldn't use. And speaking of using, how you been doin' all these years, hon? I mean, you liked coke and that crazy shit pretty good yourself, way back then. Who's your supplier now?"

"I came to my senses the day Amy died, Oscar. I just wish it had happened a day sooner. She might still be alive."

He shrugged again. "Man, I don't load up myself with that guilt shit. We all responsible for what we do and she got herself knocked up. Now, when you're using, that is a real stupid thing to do."

The man was a heartless pig. "What about Becky Barfield?" she asked evenly.

"Ol' Becky was with me longer than anyone. But AIDS got her in '84."

Valerie rubbed a place between her eyes. Becky had been funny and smart and a talented sketch-artist. "And Kelly Lott?"

Tapping ash from his cigarette, he reached for her glass of iced tea on the tray that had been delivered before Jordan left. Taking his time, he sweetened it, squeezed a lemon wedge into it, stirred it, then took a long, refreshing swallow. "Ahhh, Kelly Lott. Now that's a success story, Caroline. She's a happy housewife and mother living in Gretna. It's sad, but we aren't close now."

"Really."

"But if you want to continue this search for your stalker, I admit I have kept in touch . . . even though she's plumb unfriendly. But I gotta be honest, babe. I don't see Kelly stalkin' anybody."

She watched him set the tea aside and sit up, swing

his legs off the bed, and pick up the tiny notepad beside
the telephone. After scribbling something on it, he
stood up. Her heart flew to her mouth and she sprang
up from the chair. She could tell by his expression that
he liked seeing her fear. When he reached out to touch
her, she backed up, but could only go so far. She
bumped up against the armoire housing the television
and felt new terror when he put a hand on her throat.

She knew her face was filled with fear. "You don't
want to do this, Oscar."

"Oh, yeah, I do want to do this." He caught a piece
of her kimono in his fist. "And you owe me, don't you,
babe? Not only did we never get it on back when I was
good to you, but you're gonna see Kelly thanks to me."
With one hard jerk, he ripped the kimono off her.

She shrieked and tried to ward him off, but he had
a fistful of her hair. Holding her, he landed a heavy
blow on her cheek with the back of his hand. Pain
exploded in her head. She fell against the chair as the
room spun crazily. He pulled hard on her hair, twisting
so that her scalp was on fire, forcing a whimper from
her. With his face an inch from hers, he hissed, "And
you're not goin' to the cops either, are you, Caroline?
Too many questions and your cozy life turns to shit."

She watched in horror as his hands went to the zipper
on his pants, but he froze suddenly at the sound of a
lock turning in the door. "Shit!" Diving to the other
side of the room, he jerked the French door open and
dashed onto the balcony.

"Valerie!" Jordan slammed into the room, looking
wildly about, then spotted her on the floor. "Oh, no.
Oh, jeez, no, no . . ." Rushing to her side, he went down
on one knee.

"Balcony," she managed.

Looking up, he saw one of the French doors standing open. "Stay." He went over and looked out, then slammed and locked it. "It's okay. Nobody's there." Slipping an arm beneath her, he looked into her face. "You're hurt. Goddamn it, I shouldn't have left you."

"I'm okay, I think." She blinked, trying to clear her head.

"You're bleeding. Don't move." He propped her against the chair and rose to go to the bathroom. His hands were shaking as he turned the water on, found a washcloth, and wet it. Grabbing a towel, he rushed back, fighting down a fierce, dark fury and the dregs of desperate fear. When he heard her scream—

"It was Oscar Diaz," Valerie said, trying to get up.

"Will you stay put, for God's sake." He crouched down beside her again and pressed the wet cloth to the corner of her mouth. "A little closer and you'd have a shiner." Dropping the cloth, he felt along her jawbone, moving his fingers gently.

"You're shaking like a leaf," she said, closing her eyes.

"Don't pass out on me, lady."

She tried for a laugh. "I'm not passing out, I'm just—" Her voice broke.

With a smothered oath, he gathered her into his arms and just rocked with her on the floor, back and forth. Inside, his heart was beginning to settle back into its rightful place. For a minute, it had dropped to his feet, he'd been so terrified.

"It was Oscar," she said again, shuddering.

"I know. I heard you." He stroked her hair, while easing her head onto his shoulder. She was almost naked. The silky thing she'd been wearing was ripped and covering nothing above her waist. "Did he . . ." He swallowed hard and tried again. "Did he do anything else? Are you—"

"No." She turned her face into his neck. "He was almost . . . when he heard you at the door." She burrowed closer and his arms tightened. "Thank God you came when you did."

"It was a fluke." He pressed her head against his cheek. "I'd taken your key by mistake. I didn't want you to think . . . whatever."

"That you wanted to come and go as you pleased?" she said, beginning to sound more like herself.

"Yeah." He was still stroking her, his hand now moving gently on her bare back.

"I'm okay, Jordan. Really." She began to push back and try to sit up. It was only then that she realized the kimono was in shreds. "Oh." She grabbed at what was left and tried to cover herself. Jordan handed her the towel on the floor.

"Here, use this while I get something for you to wear. Tell me what."

She pulled the big towel up to her armpits and tried to think. "A shirt. I've got a large white shirt. It's hanging up."

He got it and helped her put it on. When he began buttoning it for her, she pushed his hands away. "I can do it. I'm really all right now, Jordan."

"Do you have a headache?"

"A little. But wouldn't anybody after—" Her voice clogged up. Her breath caught in a little hitch as she gave a shudder of disgust. "He's an animal, Jordan."

"How did he find you? How did he get in?"

"The room next door is vacant. Somehow he got in there and used the balcony entrance to simply walk in here. I was in the bathroom. I thought it was you."

"It was my fault. He walked in through the balcony because I left the freaking door unlocked." He drove

a frustrated hand through his hair. "After all that big
talk to you about caution and security, I'm the one who
invites him in."

"Don't be ridiculous. You didn't invite him in.
Besides, you saved the day when you came back." She
went to her suitcase and opened it. The oversize shirt
she wore looked like a man's dress shirt, but there was
nothing masculine about the look of her long legs and
the brief flash he had of her pretty butt as she rooted
through her things. She straightened, holding a wisp
of something—string bikinis?—in her hand and caught
him staring.

"I need to put these on," she said before scooting
past him to the bathroom.

He stood a moment trying to sort through the riot
of emotion in his chest. There'd been a couple of times
in his life when he was genuinely scared out of his skin.
Once when Charlie had fallen into the swimming pool
as a toddler and the seconds it had taken to jump in
and pluck him out had seemed a lifetime. Another time
when he'd been on a hunting trip with his father and
a friend's gun had accidentally discharged, hitting his
father and severing an artery in his leg. It had been
several harrowing minutes before the bleeding had
been under control, thanks to the presence of a doctor
in the group. Both times, people he loved were in danger, narrowly escaping death. His reaction was the same
a few minutes ago when he'd heard Valerie scream.
He'd nearly lost it when he saw her on the floor half-
naked, bruised and bleeding.

"Oh, my God," he heard from the bathroom.

Heedless of her modesty, he yanked the door open,
sharp-eyed for signs that she was about to faint. Instead,
she was standing in front of the mirror. Ready to sweep
her up, he went up close from behind and put his hands
on her arms. "What's wrong? Are you dizzy?"

"No, I'm horrified. I look like a witch!" She swept her hair back from her face and bent closer to look at the now-discoloring skin on her cheekbone. "I'm going to have a black eye tomorrow!"

Relaxing, he slipped his arms all the way around her and pressed his face to the back of her head. "I don't think so, but you'll have a nice, interesting bruise. You're still beautiful no matter what," he told her, managing a chuckle.

She turned in his arms, making no effort to get away. "You're just saying that because you're still feeling guilty. I'm a mess and I know it."

For a minute, he allowed himself the pleasure of just looking at her. She was one good-looking woman. Even with her hair in a tangle and a bruise on her cheek, she was lovely. Without thinking, he kissed the spot that would soon be black and blue. "You scared the hell out of me," he said unsteadily.

"I was pretty scared myself."

"From now on, I'm sticking as close to you as white on rice . . . as they say here."

"I'll be extra careful," she said, making no effort to get away.

"What I mean is that I'm not sleeping more than a foot away from you tonight. The hell with that room I just got. You know that, don't you?"

"No argument. He scared me, too. Thank you."

With a sigh, he gathered her even closer, burying his face in her hair. Nuzzling her neck, he trailed kisses up to her ear. She winced and he stopped, eased back to look at her. "What?"

She shuddered. "He—Oscar—he bit me."

Swearing, he lifted her hair and found a red mark on the delicate skin of her earlobe. "Bastard," he murmured as rage came alive again.

"It could have been a lot worse, but I want to take

another shower. I feel . . . contaminated." She slipped
out of his embrace and reached for soap and a clean
washcloth. "He's the same as he was years ago when he
had all of us in his power. He still enjoys inflicting pain."

"I'll be just outside," Jordan said, needing a minute
alone to handle these unfamiliar emotions. "Take your
time."

While Valerie was showering and Jordan was trying
to calm down, her stalker was in a New York apartment
fuming. Tossing things. Slamming books against the
door. Ripping apart a feature proposal stolen from the
desk of an unsuspecting employee at *Panache*. Pausing
finally, gasping for breath, snatching up a drink from
the low table by the telephone.

Bourbon helped. It always had. They'd tried medica-
tion and counseling and fucking shock treatments at
the hospital. Some of the methods that were used in
institutions today were straight out of the Middle Ages.
The staff at those places were baffled by patients whose
IQs were superior to theirs. Which made it ludicrous
when they labeled a unique person ready to function
in a supervised environment. Valerie's stalker had succeeded in earning that label with so little effort that
it had been almost no fun, then after a second visit,
pronounced socially integrated. Laughable. If they only
knew.

Valerie's stalker was not laughing at the moment.
Oscar had always been capable of stealing all the enjoyment out of a plan . . . as when he'd called a few minutes
ago.

"What the hell do you think you're doing?" he'd
yelled.

A cigarette was lit. "What are you talking about?"

"Caroline and her Yankee macho friend are down

here askin' questions. She claims she's got a stalker on her tail. What have you been up to?"

"You knew what the plan was when I left, Oscar. We agreed, remember? This is a partnership, no argument about that, but we also agreed I'd play things the way I thought best when I got here. That's exactly what I'm doing. She's coming unraveled, trust me. She's going to be so willing to do what we say when I get through with her that—"

He cut off the speech with a oath. "She didn't seem unraveled to me, you psycho! And what's this about her old nun friend? If you've killed a nun, I'm coming up there and bringing your skinny ass back home before you get me nailed for murder and I find myself back in Angola. Say you didn't have nothing to do with that and I want to hear it now!"

"I had to kill her, Oscar."

There was a moment of hot silence before Oscar began spewing profanity. "You idiot, you fuckin' *idiot!* You killed that old lady? What for? What the hell did you do that for? Don't you know that kind of loony behavior can get our asses in trouble like you ain't never seen . . . ever! Places you been in will seem like kindergarten if they can pin the murder of a nun on you. And I'm not goin' down with you on this one, you can take that to the bank!"

Smoke was calmly aimed at the ceiling. "Are you finished?"

"Get on the first plane, damn it! We'll do the scam after all this shit settles."

"And how long will that be, Oscar?"

His voice went deep, low and menacing. "I guess you didn't hear me, right? 'Cause sounds like you're trying to argue with me. And that wouldn't be wise."

A sigh. Oscar was fast becoming a pain in the ass. "Okay, Oscar. Okay. Don't freak. I'm on my way."

A quick trip to New Orleans was a minor delay, although it was irritating when things were going so well. Oscar in one of his macho-mean moods could ruin everything. He must not be allowed to interfere in the master plan. Caroline was to be destroyed.

CHAPTER
SEVENTEEN

"We don't need to do this right now, Val. We could have ordered in from room service. You could rest and take something for that headache." Jordan spoke in an undertone after Valerie punched the doorbell at Kelly Lott's house. "We don't even know that the woman lives here. Nor do we know she'll welcome a couple of strangers appearing out of the blue."

"You think we'd make a better impression tomorrow?" Valerie returned in the same low tone. "Believe me, it'll be a lot worse then because I'll look like somebody from the Addams family when Oscar's handiwork blossoms out fully."

"This isn't anything to joke about," he grumbled.

"Who's joking?"

"And another thing," Jordan said, turning to check the street both ways, "I'm not comfortable about your buddy Oscar just giving up Kelly Lott's address."

"She's Mrs. Perry Fontenot now."

"Okay, but why would he do that?"

"Because he knows it's a dead end?"

"Maybe. Or maybe not. Diaz is bad to the bone, Val. We could be blundering into something better left to folks who're accustomed to handling this stuff."

"Such as the police?"

"Or Ray Bergeron." He rang the doorbell again. "Since we know how you feel about the cops," he tacked on dryly.

"If you're regretting getting involved, you can wait for me in the car."

Jordan released a sarcastic snort. She was enough to drive a man nuts. Whether he liked it or not, he was involved up to his neck. He'd walk away when it snowed in hell. Or New Orleans. Still suffering from stifling humidity, he pulled his shirt away from his sweaty skin.

"How's your headache?"

She touched her cheek gingerly. "I'm okay."

Looking at her in the soft glow of the gas lantern nearby, he decided that she'd succeeded in masking the damage to her face. The bruises had been painfully obvious in the bathroom mirror before she'd attempted to cover them with makeup. She'd reasoned that if Kelly saw she'd had been assaulted, she might shut the door in their faces before they learned whether she knew anything that might help them. At this point, they couldn't afford losing what few slim leads they had.

Both quieted at the sound of the lock turning in the door. A woman peered out cautiously.

Valerie knew her instantly. She was older, of course, and had gained a few pounds, but her striking auburn hair was still beautiful, as was her face. As a teenager, Kelly had been shy and disinclined to talk, but there was more than simple timidity in the way she looked at them now. There was wariness. Clearly she did not recognize Valerie.

"Yes?" she said, keeping the door open just enough to see them.

"Hello, Kelly," Valerie said softly. "It's been a long time."

Her gaze narrowed, studying Valerie before moving to Jordan. "I don't believe—"

"I'm Jordan Case," he said, trying for friendly charm while watching as her eyes darted back to Valerie. "And this is—"

"Caroline?" she said in a stunned tone. "Is that you, Caroline?"

Valerie gave her a wry smile and spread her hands out, palms up. "It's me." She felt Jordan's reaction to the strange name, but now wasn't the time for explanations. "May we come in?"

But before Kelly could step back, a man appeared at her shoulder, a big, surly guy. "Who is it, Kelly? What d'they want?" Bald and paunchy, his reading glasses rode at half-mast on his nose.

"I—It's . . . This is such a surprise," she said.

"How come? Who is it?" her husband said.

"I . . . It's someone I used to know, Perry." Flustered, she put a hand to her cheek. "My goodness."

"It's so rude to barge in on you like this," Valerie said. "I do apologize. But if you could just give us a few minutes . . ."

"Well—" She glanced sideways to a room as if concerned over its appearance.

"Hold it," Perry Fontenot said, scowling at them. Showing none of Kelly's reticence, he opened the door wide. He held a folded newspaper. "Who are you? What do you want?"

"Perry—" Kelly touched his arm. "I used to know Caroline a long time ago. It's okay."

"And who's this with her?" he asked suspiciously. "Do you know him, too?"

"I'm Jordan Case, Mr. Fontenot." Jordan did not put out his hand, sensing Perry wasn't ready to shake just yet. "I'm a friend of . . . this lady's. We're visiting New Orleans and we had a little skirmish today at our hotel." He looked directly at Kelly. "Your name came up, Mrs. Fontenot."

"Kelly," she whispered. "You can call me Kelly. Come in. Please."

"What kind of skirmish?" Perry wanted to know before allowing them inside.

"Actually, Valerie was attacked. By Oscar Diaz."

"Valerie?" Kelly repeated in confusion.

"That's me. It's a long story," Valerie said with another wry shrug. "May we come inside, Kelly? I'll try to explain."

Tugging at her husband's arm, Kelly managed to move him aside to let Valerie and Jordan in. After closing the door, Perry touched a switch on the wall, flooding the small, windowless foyer with bright light. That was when Jordan saw the pistol partially concealed in the folded newspaper.

"Maybe we'd better come back another time," he said, catching Valerie's hand before she took another step. "Come on, Valerie."

"About that skirmish," Perry began, pushing his reading glasses into place and peering hard at Valerie. "Is that what happened to your face?" The pistol was in his right hand, pointed at the floor.

"Perry, please—" Kelly put out a hand as Jordan turned with Valerie to leave. "Caroline, don't go yet. Perry, for God's sake, put that gun away. You said Oscar Diaz, right?" she asked, turning again to Valerie.

"Yes," said Valerie. "He came to my room at the hotel today." She touched her cheek. "He roughed me up a little, but Jordan broke it up. I don't know what might have happened if he hadn't. He's still an animal,

Kelly. Just as he was years ago. Please tell me he hasn't intruded into your life."

"Not before a couple of weeks ago," Perry said shortly. He opened a closet in the foyer and lay the pistol on the top shelf. "But I'm ready for him the next time he comes."

"What is this all about?" Kelly asked. "But first, come into the living room and sit down. Would you like something to drink? I have iced tea and some canned drinks, I think. No alcohol, I'm afraid." She gave Valerie a brief smile. "I haven't touched anything for years."

More of Oscar's legacy, Valerie thought. She wondered how many young women he had victimized in his sleazy career.

"Nothing, thanks, Kelly," she said. "We'd just like to ask if you know anything about Oscar and his life lately. Someone has been making some threatening phone calls to me and . . . other things have happened that are disturbing."

"Someone is stalking her," Jordan said bluntly.

"You think it's Oscar?"

Jordan rubbed his chin thoughtfully. "We didn't before we came to New Orleans, but now I'm not so sure."

Perry sat down in an oversized recliner. "He's capable of anything, don't underestimate him. He roughed Kelly up, too. Waited in the carport behind some storage cartons, then attacked her—right in front of our kids."

"Were you hurt?" Valerie asked.

"We have a dog, a German Shepherd. Stays in the backyard. When he heard Kelly scream, he jumped the fence. Oscar dove inside his car, but still he told Kelly before he left that he'd hurt the kids if she was tempted to talk about stuff that happened to them back then on the street. But hell, we'd put that part of Kelly's life behind us. It was ancient history. We couldn't figure it out." He paused as Kelly came to sit on the arm of his chair. "Now you're here asking about all this. Like they say, it's getting mighty curious."

"We think Valerie's stalker knows that she was once a runaway and that she spent some time in New Orleans," Jordan explained. "We're trying to track down some of the people who knew her then. It's the only lead we have to try and flush him out."

"Have you changed your name, Caroline?" Kelly asked, still looking confused.

"I . . . yes. There were reasons."

Kelly nodded as if she understood. "Yes, if Perry hadn't come along—" She looked at him, her face gentling as she put a hand on his shoulder. "But he did and I was lucky." Then, to Valerie. "I don't know anything about your stalker, but the timing of all this strikes me. Oscar showed up after a major article came out in the newspaper about the mysterious disappearance of Amy Trent. You remember Amy, don't you?"

"Of course."

"And then after that, this private investigator named Angela LeBlanc knocked on my door. She wanted information about Amy, but none of us ever saw Amy again after the two of you left. No one ever knew whether she'd died or been kidnaped or what. The two of you were such close friends, Caroline. Did you know that she came from such a wealthy family? I certainly didn't."

"I don't think she told anyone that," Valerie murmured.

"She was pregnant," Kelly said, looking beyond them to a photo of her own children. "I've often wondered about that. I mean, that's the saddest part, isn't it? Her baby never had a chance."

* * *

Jordan's jaw was set as hard as granite. He slammed the door of the rental car after Valerie got in, then stalked around to get in on the driver's side. He'd rented a car that afternoon after it became clear that Valerie was bent on visiting Kelly Lott. He'd had questions before seeing Kelly, but his curiosity then was nothing compared to the thousand and one he'd like to ask Valerie now.

"Who's Caroline?" was the first one.

She sighed. "Do we have to go into this right now?"

He gave her an incredulous look. "No, we don't have to. But it would be nice for me to know who the hell you are since I'm down here trying to ward off a killer. Or a blackmailer. Or a loony. But since I don't have half the facts of your life, I suppose I could just keep on shadowboxing in the dark."

"It's not possible to shadowbox in the dark."

"Goddamn it, Val! Everything I learn about you triggers more questions."

She was watching the traffic as he attempted to navigate Lee Circle. "You took a wrong turn," she said.

"Yeah," he said, screeching to a stop and executing a skillful three-point turn. "I think it happened the day I told Hal Kurtz I agreed with him that you and I would make a good team."

She was looking straight ahead. "I didn't ask for your help. You're free to leave."

He stopped with his hands on the wheel. "You'd like that, wouldn't you? You'd be just fine with it if I dropped you off at the hotel, picked up my things and caught the next flight to New York. Well, it isn't going to happen, lady. That sonofabitch Oscar Diaz wants a piece of you. I don't know why, but that's the reason he gave up

Kelly's address. It was to scare you off. You'd find out how he threatened her and you'd go home."

"Then he miscalculated. I'm not going until I say I'm ready."

"Exactly. Which goes to show that he might have known you years ago, but he doesn't have a clue about the woman you've become." But now his anger had burned itself out. He took the next turn at a reasonable speed. "I might be able to suggest something if I had more than an abridged version of your past, Val. At the very least, I wouldn't be working in the dark. But no matter what, I am involved. Get used to it."

"Why?" She dropped her cool facade and turned to him hotly. "Why are you doing this, Jordan? You already know more of my past than I've ever told anyone. You know it's not . . . pretty. Even now, you could destroy all I've worked for when you get back to New York. Hal Kurtz might respect my professional achievements, but if he knew" she waved a hand—"all this, he'd dump me so fast that I'd never recover. So why are you doing this?"

"Call me crazy."

"Is that a joke?"

"Why can't I give a flippant answer when that's about all I ever get from you?"

"Why are you doing this, Jordan?" she asked, spacing out the words.

He swerved into the parking garage of the hotel and stopped the car. A valet headed toward them, but Jordan ignored him. He turned to Valerie, who'd already opened her door, bringing with it the mugginess of a New Orleans winter and the sound of the horse-drawn carriage as it clopped by. "I'm doing it because I think I'm in love with you," he said.

That silenced her. She was staring at him with shock in her eyes. She was no more shocked than he was himself, he thought. *I'm doing it because I'm in love with you.* Where had that come from? A crazy, male panic welled up in him. He hadn't said those words to a woman since two years before his divorce. He looked away, rubbing a hand against the back of his neck.

A sound came from the valet, now waiting at the window. With a grunt, Jordan started to get out, but Valerie put her hand on his arm. "Wait." She closed her door. "Turn around."

He looked at her in puzzlement.

"I want to show you something."

"What is it?"

"For once, would you just cease with the questions? If you'll do as I ask, at least one of them will be answered."

He signaled the valet that they were leaving again and put the car into gear. At the exit, he asked, "Which way?"

"Left. All the way to Basin Street. We're going to a cemetery."

He gave her a startled look. "A cemetery? Why?"

Their eyes locked in silence, but it was Valerie who turned away first. "You'll see."

Valerie had never expected to see the St. Louis Cemetery again. It was a fabled landmark in New Orleans and the burial place of several historical figures. Like all cemeteries, it had an eerie silence about it, and with the sun setting rapidly, the ghostly presence of the inhabitants was too real to her. With Jordan following, she walked between crumbling vaults, sunken paths, tangled confederate jasmine vines, and ancient crepe myrtle trees. A mockingbird trilled from a perch on a tall cross adorning a magnificent vault. Over all was the haunting fragrance of sweet olive.

"Marie Laveau is buried there," she said, pointing to a large above-ground crypt cluttered with odd flotsam.

"The voodoo lady?"

"Uh-huh. There's a constant stream of admirers through here every day, in all kinds of weather. They leave little things—mostly tokens with personal significance."

"What do they hope to get from that?"

"Who knows . . . deliverance?" She felt his quick look. He must be totally confused by now, and who could blame him? How many women would haul a man off to a cemetery after a declaration of love? Closing her eyes briefly, she allowed herself to imagine telling Jordan all her secrets without disastrous consequences.

She slowed, searching an area near the back of one quadrant. And then she saw it. Odd that she'd found it so easily as she'd never actually seen the tiny gravestone except that one time. Approaching slowly, she felt a tightness in her throat. Now she saw there were flowers entwining the marker, scrolling over and around the name and dates.

"Valerie Olivier," Jordan read slowly, frowning as he studied the dates. "Is this a relative?"

"No. It's me."

His gaze moved quickly to meet hers. She saw that he understood the implications of what she'd said. "You assumed the name of a dead baby?"

"I needed a new identity and I found it here."

"Yeah, that would work."

"It was a despicable thing to do, I know that. But there were reasons—compelling reasons, or so it seemed to me at the time. I'm sorry that I had to take advantage of someone else's tragedy. But . . . well, I can only say that I was desperate."

He was looking at her as if he'd never seen her before. Stung by the expression on his face, she stood a little straighter, but she met his gaze directly. "You asked who I am. Well, I'm Valerie Olivier-Long. I wasn't born with that name, but it's mine now." Beyond the cemetery walls, a fire engine roared by, siren screaming. Uncomfortable with his scrutiny, she pulled a tiny sprig of sweet olive from a tall shrub and inhaled the fragrance as the sound died away. It was hard to tell what he was thinking, but she could guess. "You'd have to be in my shoes at that time to understand," she told him. Did he hear the guilt? Did he sense her deep regret?

"What about this . . . this Caroline person? Wasn't there anybody who wondered about her . . . your disappearance? God knows there were tons of people looking for Amy Trent. Why not for Caroline?"

"There was someone looking for me, but luckily I was never traced to New Orleans." She bent suddenly and placed the fragrant little sprig on the child's grave, then stood up and faced him. "I know what you're thinking. Stealing a dead baby's name is an illegal act, but for me it was a necessary first step in starting a new life for myself. I vowed never to abuse her name and I think I've managed that. But it was wrong. If you have trouble understanding that kind of desperation, then you're lucky."

"So how about explaining it to me, Val?"

"I don't think so." There was too much suspicion on his face. And something else. Disappointment? "I think I'll keep the rest of my sordid past to myself."

The sun was gone now and the cemetery was settling into deep gloom. Jordan's face was grim, made even more so with the shadowy growth of a day's beard. She felt a pang for having destroyed the brief moment in time when they might have come to a deeper understanding of each other . . . and then, maybe something better than that. With an ache in her chest, she turned and started toward the main path.

"Just one more question," he said, coming up behind her.

She didn't slow down. "I don't promise to answer."

"You said you were close to Amy, so you must have had the same concerns after she disappeared that Kelly mentioned."

"What concerns?"

"Did you ever wonder, like Kelly, what might have happened to her baby?"

She did not answer.

Angela LeBlanc was in a quandary. Now that she was actually putting in an honest day's work on a regular basis and digging into the mystery of Amy Trent's disappearance, her effort had paid off in spades and she was feeling pretty proud of herself. She couldn't have done it without her connections at NOPD, she admitted that. Give 'em their due. But once she had her hands on those statements from Amy's file, she'd begun doing some really professional sleuthing and she damn sure hadn't learned how to do that at the Academy. It had been a long time since she'd felt anything but a cynical certainty that she'd been born under an unlucky star, but here she was at this late date on the brink of something that was almost as good as winning the lottery.

Leaning back in her new executive chair—genuine leather, ergonomically engineered, purchased with funds from her Trent retainer—she lit her third cigarette in an hour. She was trying to ease up on the bourbon lately. She allowed herself only three drinks daily now, never starting before four in the afternoon. It was a big change from her lifestyle pattern for the past five years or so when she'd have bourbon with her first cup of coffee in the morning. But booze screwed up the brain and the old gray cells were working for her pretty well nowadays. Time enough to enjoy life after her scheme paid off.

It had taken some digging to uncover the scandal of one Sister Janine Livaudais, formerly of the Order of St. Francis. Hell, maybe Oscar Diaz had helped, although he'd been a bastard that day she'd appeared at his apartment, but he'd revealed more than he intended as she'd questioned him about Amy Trent. Or maybe it took thinking like a woman, Angela decided as she tipped her chair back and put her feet up on the desk. Mentioning Amy Trent had really pushed his buttons. Seemed he'd been pissed for years over Amy, who'd probably been a cash cow for him before she got knocked up. Angela pulled deeply on her cigarette. Like the girl getting knocked up had been a large inconvenience to him and not her. Angela had decided that day that he was one mean dude. Then it had dawned on her. Maybe Amy'd been so scared of Oscar that she'd run away. It had seemed a possibility worth following up on. The question was, where would a scared sixteen-year-old with no money, no friends who mattered, and no family—since she was obviously estranged from the Trents—go in the Big Easy? The answer was almost too . . . well, easy. The nuns at St. Francis still patrolled the French Quarter today, maybe not with the same zeal of the seventies, but they were still around. Good place to start.

And that was where Angela had stumbled upon Sister Janine Livaudais's disgrace. Nuns were like everybody else in the world once you got past the habit. Bound to be a gossip-monger there. It was just a matter of finding her. And Angela did. Sister Frank—why did some of them have guy names?—had been more than happy to repeat the scandal. At about the same time as Amy disappeared, Sister Janine—*former* sister, that is—had become involved with a scruffy, homeless teenager who'd had an illegitimate baby. For a minute there, Angela had been ecstatic over learning this. She just knew she'd found Amy Trent. A little more high-tech investigation on Angela's part had uncovered Sister Janine's whereabouts today. A nursing home in New York City.

Duck soup from there.

It didn't turn out to be Amy Trent who'd latched on to Sister Janine. It was another runaway with only one name. Caroline. She'd run with the same bunch as Amy. But it got even more interesting then. This Caroline person was now Valerie Olivier-Long, editor-in-chief of *Panache* magazine. My God, it was almost too delicious. The kid had to be Amy Trent's baby. Caroline, according to the other runaways she'd been able to reach, hadn't been pregnant.

But the quandary. Whether to tell Emilie Trent about the possibility that she could have a live grandchild out there or not? She could first milk Emilie for as much as possible and then move to her next victim, Valerie Olivier-Long. Or she could go directly to Valerie, bypassing Emilie altogether. Valerie had a hell of a lot more to lose and therefore would probably cough up who knew how much? Rarely had Angela been faced with so delicious a decision. Actually, never.

Forgetting her resolution about drinking, she opened the bottom drawer of her desk, got out the bourbon, and poured herself a double, but she'd barely tasted it when the phone rang. "ALB Investigative Services," she said, liking the sound of her new, more sophisticated moniker.

"ALB Investigative Services." A snicker came from the caller. "My, how you've come up in the world, Angie. Has your client base improved since you nailed that cheatin' politician for his wife and drove him out of office?"

Angela set her drink down carefully. "Telephone consultations start at fifty bucks. So, who is this?"

"Someone who's not dumb enough to pay you a crying dime for your time . . . on the phone or on the job."

Angela tapped ashes into the dregs of yesterday morning's coffee. "So why are you wasting my valuable time?"

This drew a disgusted snort from the caller, who covered the mouthpiece and spoke to someone else before continuing. "What's this we hear on the street about you hittin' it big with the Trent widow up north?"

Angela dropped her feet to the floor and sat up, every nerve now on alert. "What's it to you, asshole?"

"Here's what, you used-up lush! And listen up good if you want to stay alive to enjoy your retirement. Stay away from Emilie Trent. Stay away from Valerie Olivier-Long." The caller's voice dropped to a menacing hiss. "And most of all, stay away from Amy Trent or anything that even smells like the Trent case."

"Valerie who?" she repeated as if she'd hadn't caught the name.

"You hear what I'm sayin', Angie?"

"Actually, I didn't. I—" Angela flinched as the phone line went dead, then slammed the receiver back in place. "Shit! Shit, shit, shit!" Somebody else was in the game. She bolted out of her chair and began to pace frantically. After a minute or two, she stopped and thought hard, trying to recall any familiarity in the caller's voice, but couldn't quite pull up anything. How could she deal with somebody she didn't know? She muttered another obscenity, cursing the fact that she'd failed to put a recorder on her phone line. She'd been thinking about doing it and now it was too late.

Okay, so someone else had realized the potential for profit in the Trent situation. She could deal with that.

Do a bit of reorganizing, maybe another trip to see Emilie and make sure she wasn't being hassled by this creep, whoever the hell it was. She stopped, picked up her drink, drained it, and flung herself back in her new chair. Then she lit another cigarette and, squinting through the smoke, settled back to decide what to do.

CHAPTER EIGHTEEN

Valerie stood at the French doors in her room watching the activity going on in the courtyard below. Two elderly women wearing wide-legged pants, sandals, and Hawaiian shirts flagged a passing waiter for refills of something served in half a pineapple. A man sat alone, his face obscured by a newspaper, a drink at his elbow. But his foot moved in time with the jazz combo playing softly beneath the shade cast by huge ficus and banana trees. Another couple, barely twenty years old, sat with fingers laced, faces two inches apart. Even their feet were entwined. Newlyweds, she guessed, and thought of Sara and Charlie. Thank goodness he was there to keep an eye on her, although it was Jordan she should thank. He'd been the one with the foresight to alert Charlie.

Behind her, Jordan unlocked the service bar. She heard it close and assumed he was going to make himself a drink. Dinner had been a sorry affair. He'd wanted to take her out somewhere, but she'd refused. He was hardly in a mood to enjoy anything, no matter how exceptional New Orleans cuisine was touted to be. Once they'd gotten back to the hotel, he'd insisted on ordering room service for two in her room. He wasn't convinced they'd seen the last of Oscar Diaz and he wasn't going to risk leaving her alone to be assaulted again.

"You managed to get your room changed to the one connecting with mine," she argued, "so it's not necessary to babysit me."

"You may underestimate Diaz, but I don't. He'll get to you if you're not careful. For some reason, he wants you out of here." Jordan loosened the top button of his shirt and went to the thermostat to lower it. "What time is your flight tomorrow?"

"It's an open ticket. I wasn't sure how long I'd need to stay. How about yours?"

"The same." He sat down and took a sip from his drink. "We still have to see Angela LeBlanc."

"You don't have to see anyone, Jordan. This is my problem. I—"

"Save it, Val. I don't know what's going on, but I do know that if you got hurt, I'd feel rotten telling Sara I was aware that you were in up to your pretty neck in something, but I hopped a plane and left you to handle it on your own." He tossed off half of his drink. "I know how you think. The minute you got rid of me, you'd head for her place."

"You make me sound like an ungrateful witch," she said, turning from the window. "I don't mean to be. I know I shocked you when I told you about my name. I know my drug use back then disgusts you. I know you're wondering about my . . . my morals, about how I survived on the streets as a runaway." She watched him rise abruptly from the chair and go to the balcony. He rested one hand on the iron railing while he took another taste of his drink. The band below was playing a slow, bluesy tune. From his body language, nothing registered to Jordan. His back was too rigid, he stood too still.

"Look, I understand," she said with quiet regret. "You're wishing you'd never heard of me, but because of some . . . some kind of misplaced chivalry, you feel you can't just walk away. You admitted as much a minute ago. But I'm telling you that you don't have to—" She stopped, blinking as he wheeled about and slammed the French door with a crash.

"Stop." The order came out, tight and short. "Will you . . . just . . . be quiet."

She got a look at his face then and realized that he was furious. No, not furious. Not exactly, but he was filled up with something, and whatever it was, he looked ready to explode. She put a hand to her throat. "What—"

"You don't know what the hell you're talking about." He spoke in a low, raspy voice, as if keeping it calm was an effort. "You give me just enough about yourself to keep me in a state of terror and lust combined, then you presume to tell me what I'm thinking. And then you add to that, as casually as ordering a cheeseburger, that it's okay if I just wash my hands of the whole thing."

"I—That's not exactly what I said."

"But it's what you meant."

Terror and lust? It was Valerie's turn to turn away. Whirling about, she wrapped her arms around herself and wished for a place to run to. But escape was beyond the doors of the hotel room, and contrary to what Jordan thought, she was scared to leave. And scared to stay. She didn't want him to abandon her, but wasn't it unfair to drag him deeper into this mess? He knew there was more in her past still to be revealed. Why didn't that turn him off? Which made him even more appealing, and God knows, her attraction to Jordan had been growing stronger and stronger for weeks.

"Turn around and look at me, damn it!" he ordered.

Both arms were rigid at his side, fists clenched. "You're always wimping out when things get a little sticky, Val. I'm not judging you, I'm trying like hell to figure out who you are. And I don't mean your name. Caroline or Valerie, what does it matter? What's more important is the next revelation. Hell, I want to make love to you tonight and yet I don't know who I'll wake up with in the morning. Worse than that, when I'm with you, I don't even know who the hell I am anymore. Would you be willing to start a relationship like that?"

She stood wordlessly for a long minute, fascinated and excited, filled with a kind of glorious, gleeful anticipation. Had she been trying to push him to this end? She spread her hands in a helpless shrug. "I am if you are."

His eyes narrowed. "You mean that?"

"It may be—"

But he didn't wait for her to start qualifying. He caught her by the arms, ignoring her startled little yelp, and hauled her up on her toes. Then he swooped down, crushing her mouth in one devastating kiss. For a second, she was so surprised that she simply stood there tasting his impatience. And frustration. His assault was like a dark tide, but oh, so was his passion. He was wild, just on the edge of violence, and her heart was leaping right along with the urgency she sensed in him as his mouth plundered and his hands pushed and tugged and tore. He must surely have more finesse as a lover than this, she thought dizzily, even as her arms went around his shoulders and her insides were turning into liquid heat.

He lifted his mouth a fraction, framing her face with both hands. "You'd better stop me now, Val, if you intend to, because in about half a minute it'll be too late."

It was already too late. Before she could say anything, he had his lips on hers again, his tongue in her mouth. Her heart was leaping crazily as he moved in, seeking a better fit of their bodies. Then somehow he had her clothes off and was dragging her to the bed. Lying naked and flushed and ready, she had a brief moment of respite while he rid himself of his shirt in one quick, over-the-head motion, then kicked free of his pants and underwear.

"What are we doing, Jordan? Is this crazy?"

He paused for a second, his gaze hot and hungry and assessing, then he eased down on top of her, smiling before kissing her again, lushly and deep, and grinding himself against her. "No, sweetheart, it's the most uncrazy thing that's happened since the day we met." Then he was shimmying down her body, kissing her breasts, her tummy, her belly button. And beyond.

From far away, Jordan heard her gasp his name, but he was now bombarded with his own lust and the sounds she made only fanned the flame. He knew she was beyond thought, beyond modesty, and it filled him with a sense of power and sheer male exultation.

She writhed now as pleasure and lust and need swelled and grew, turning her body into a quivering mass of wild sensation. Her first climax erupted with the force of a tidal wave. He had his arms around her while the shock slowly subsided, his head resting on her midriff. He was slick with sweat, breathing hard. Everything about him was hard, he realized, except his heart.

And then he was hovering above her, gripping strongly at her hips and lifting them. He watched her face as he pushed himself deep inside her. He saw her eyes fly open even as he felt a moment of shock. So tight. So good. But then she was wrapping her legs about him, arching into him, and the quick thought that had almost crystallized was lost. As he was. It was as if a

floodgate had been thrown wide. They tumbled head-
long into a frenzied rhythm. Riding her hard, he found
fresh and fierce pleasure in watching her as she rose to
meet him. And then she came again, crying out, sobbing
his name, steeped in her own delirium. Only then did
he band his arms about her, press his face to her throat,
and empty himself into her.

"We didn't use a condom."

"I know." He'd rolled over and was staring at the
ceiling. "My fault. I . . . Usually I have more poise. This
time, I don't know what happened. Actually, I do. I've
wanted to take you to bed for weeks now." He turned
on the pillow and looked at her. She was lying on her
side watching him, her face resting on a folded arm.
She'd pulled up the sheet to cover herself. He felt regret
at that. He'd like to see more of that lush body and her
long, long legs. A lot more. "I guess I rushed it, huh?"

She glanced at the clock radio. "It didn't take very
long."

He sighed and sat up, swinging his legs off the bed
so that she was looking at his back. "I acted like a jackass.
For what it's worth, I apologize. Please say it's not a
delicate time of the month for you."

"To tell the truth, I'm not sure. We'll just have to
wait and see."

"Christ, I'm sorry."

"It takes two, Jordan. And I was only teasing about
the time."

Oh. He began to feel a little better. "It'd be a disaster
for Charlie to find out I don't practice what I preach."

"But you probably do . . . most of the time."

He looked back at her. "Yeah." Then he swore softly.
"That sounds like I have casual sex often. I don't. I'm
forty-two years old. I haven't had a serious relationship

in a long time. Years, in fact. I'm choosy about . . . that."
He squeezed his eyes shut and swore again. "Damn, will
you listen to me! I'm going on about my sex life when
it should be you giving me hell. Or at the very least,
you should be irritated by the way I was manhandling
you. Hell, I was out of control there. That doesn't happen very often." Never happened, but it wasn't likely
she'd believe that. He was having trouble believing it
himself.

"I wanted this as much as you, Jordan."

He shifted so that he could look at her directly. "I
wouldn't have guessed it."

"Why? Was there something lacking in my response?
Is this the equivalent of, 'How was it for you?' "

"No! No. You just seemed—I mean, I had the feeling
during . . . ah, foreplay, I guess, that you were pretty
inexperienced." He added hastily, "I mean, you're
what, thirty-eight years old? You've been married before,
you've had a baby—"

"Out of wedlock," she said, lifting an ironic eyebrow.

". . . and you have this steady guy, Dr. Nerdly."

She smiled. "Dr. Coulter, Wayne Coulter."

"Yeah, that's the one." He'd like to ask a few questions about Coulter, but he'd save them for another
time. "I guess the two of you do things less . . ."

"Wild and crazy?"

"Different. I was going to say different."

"Wayne and I never got around to having sex."

"Why is that?" he asked curiously. "Is he gay?"

"Because I didn't want to."

Interesting, because she'd been extremely interested
a few minutes ago. She'd been with him all the way.
"What about Mr. Long, the ex?"

"Andrew?" She sat up, still shielding herself with
the sheet. "He didn't have much imagination beyond
investments."

He watched her trying to reach the big white shirt draped on the chair nearby. She couldn't quite make it. He enjoyed the flash of her cute little ass as she flopped back on the bed. They'd just had wickedly wild and delicious sex. He'd kissed her all over her delectable body and she'd responded in a way that had given him a rush of male pride. And yet with the passion banked— for the moment—she seemed shy of him.

"The gentlemanly thing would be to get up and hand me that shirt," she told him testily.

"Sorry. You should have asked." Still buck naked, he rose lazily, curious to see how she'd react. She cast a quick, furtive peek then looked away, but there was no hiding the rosy flush that crawled up her neck and settled on her cheeks.

"Shouldn't you put on your pants or something?"

"In a minute." He held the shirt for her, amused to see that she realized she'd have to drop the sheet to put it on. She gave in with a muttered word that he didn't quite catch and backed up, ramming her arms into the sleeves. Chuckling, he bent and kissed the nape of her neck. She made a small sound. He slipped his arms around her and pulled her back against him. She went weak and pliant as he kissed her ear. She smelled warm and sexy. She felt soft. His body responded by turning hard instantly. "I'm sorry I rushed it, sweetheart, but we have the whole night to get it right."

Lifting an arm, she curled it around his neck from behind and rubbed her cheek against his, scratchy with six o'clock shadow. Across the room, he could see them in the large mirror above the vanity. He took in a harsh breath at the sight of her, the shirt casually parted, her breasts bared, nipples prominent with arousal. His hands dark on her white, white skin.

"This is so strange, Jordan," she whispered, pressing her lips to his jaw. "I've never done anything so—"

The telephone rang. For a moment, neither of them seemed to hear it. Then Jordan swore, releasing a string of words, some of which were new to Valerie. He turned her in his arms, kissed her hard on the mouth, and gently shoved her toward the shrilling phone. "It's your room, sweetheart. It could be one of the kids."

Still slightly dazed, Valerie picked up the receiver. "Hello."

"Hi, Caroline. Enjoying the reunion?"

She knew the voice instantly. "How did you find me? What do you want?"

Jordan, in the act of pulling on his pants, looked up sharply. "Who is it?"

Valerie told him, saying "stalker" silently. He moved quickly to her and put his ear close to the receiver to listen. "Ahh, you've got company, Caroline. Who is it, Jordan Case? Not Oscar, hmm? I can't see you diddling Oscar, but who knows. Lives change, people change." The caller's voice went hard. "But some things never change, do they, Caroline?"

"What do you want from me!" Valerie cried, covering her eyes with one hand. Jordan slipped a supportive arm around her waist.

"Payback, bitch. How many times do I have to say it?"

Trying for calm, Valerie leaned into Jordan, felt the touch of his hand on her. Somehow it helped. She took a deep breath. "Can we meet? Wouldn't it be better if you tell me face to face what this is all about?"

"Stupid, stupid question, bitch. It's about Amy, who else?"

"But Amy's dead! What could I possibly do about that?"

A brief sound as if smoke from a cigarette was being exhaled. "You'll know when it's time. But not before my work is done."

"What work? What are you going to do?"

"Ah, but that would be telling, wouldn't it?" The voice was as soft as warm honey.

Valerie knew with bitter resignation that she would get nothing from a person whose whole being was dedicated to tormenting her. "Who *are* you?" she said finally.

"Amy's ghost?" A soft, evil laugh. "Yeah, that's me. You can just call me Amy's ghost."

And the connection was severed.

CHAPTER NINETEEN

Jordan and Valerie went to the airport at noon the next day and waited on standby status for two empty seats on a flight to New York. "What do you think our chances are?" Valerie asked as they stood studying the departure screen in the terminal.

"It's not a Monday or a Friday or a holiday, so we'll probably be out of here on the next scheduled flight. It might not be nonstop, but we'll be in New York in time for you to clear your desk and arrange a staff meeting for seven A.M. I'll sit in just to be sure you've got everything under control."

She was ready with instant objection until she looked at him and saw that he was teasing her. "That had better be a joke," she told him, bumping him with her shoulder. They were holding hands, had been since leaving the airport shuttle at the terminal. In fact, they'd hardly been able to keep their hands off each other in the last twenty-four hours.

They each took a seat in the waiting area at gate nine

and prepared to wait. Shoulders touching, they sat in silence, people-watching for a while. Except for Jordan, Valerie felt unconnected with the faceless crowd and sensed the same thing in him. She was aware of Jordan with every cell in her body. It was an incredible thing, this newly discovered passion for each other. She wanted to verbalize it, to tell him that she'd never felt like this before, but there were other things in her past and until—and if—she ever did, only then would she feel free to say what was in her heart. She was in love with Jordan, no doubt about that now.

With a sigh, she removed her hand from Jordan's and pulled out her cell phone to check her messages. There were several, but nothing was urgent. After hearing them out, she tucked the phone back into her carry-on. It felt odd to be away from her job for almost three days without feeling an intense urgency to return. She couldn't decide if her ambivalence was due to the stalker and the need to find him, or this incredible attraction to Jordan. For years nothing—except for Sara—had taken precedence over her career.

"Are you upset that we didn't get to talk to Angela LeBlanc?" Jordan asked, breaking into her thoughts. They'd found an address for the PI in the yellow pages, but when they got there, nobody was around except the landlord. LeBlanc's digs appeared to serve as both efficiency apartment and office.

"I'm disappointed, but not upset. I think we probably got more information from her landlord than we would have gotten from Angela herself."

They'd found the landlord standing on a stepladder in a stairwell replacing a low-wattage lightbulb into a ceiling fixture. There were sockets for two, but he left one empty. "LeBlanc's into me for two months' rent plus repairs over the last couple of years," he'd complained as he replaced the fly-specked globe. "It's her lowlife clientele. Nothing meaner than a man discovering that his wife's hired a PI to spy on him. They come around here, and next thing, they've put a fist through her door. Or kicked the glass out of the window. It costs money to have that shit fixed, and it's like pulling teeth to get her to pay up.''

"What time do you think we might catch her today?'' Jordan wanted to know, adding dryly, "If we're lucky.''

"No way today.'' He got down from the stepladder and picked up a can of Dixie Beer he'd left on a windowsill. "She's outta town. Somewhere up north. Claims she's hooked a rich client who's gonna end her financial troubles and be the key to her retirement.'' He put a hand on his chest and belched. "Buncha bullshit, you ask me.''

Seeing no reason to stay, they'd called the airlines for reservations, and less than two hours later, here they were waiting for seats.

"Do you think it could be Angela?'' Valerie asked now, watching a mother struggle with a toddler and another infant in arms.

"Your stalker?'' Jordan held his cell phone in his hand using his thumb to retrieve his messages. "It's possible, but I don't think so.''

"Why not?''

"Angela has made no effort to hide her interest in the Trent mystery, but it came about only after the newspaper story. Kelly told us that as well as the clerk at the newspaper. The rich client has to be Emilie Trent. Odds are, your stalker probably killed Janine. At least, that's the way I see it. Angela's too streetwise to get herself mixed up in murder.'' He put the phone to his ear and listened for a moment. "What would be her motive?''

"I'm the last person to know that.'' She looked thoughtful. "How about Oscar?''

"He's mean enough." Jordan punched more buttons on his cell phone. "And he's linked in some way, but he's more likely to have someone else do his dirty work."

"He certainly used a hands-on method when he assaulted me," she said.

"And I still owe him one for that." With a grim look, he tucked the phone back into his jacket pocket. "It's not over until it's over."

She gave him a quick glance. "Does that mean we're coming back to New Orleans?"

"It means it's not over until it's over." He caught the eye of the ticket agent at the counter and stood up. "Think about it, Val. The threat of this cheesy creep is now with you every minute. You can't go to work, you can't pop in somewhere and make a quick purchase, you can't have your hair done . . . in short, you can't live your life until he's out of it. And don't forget Sara. We have to assume she's at risk, too."

"What do you think we could have done in New Orleans that we didn't do?"

"We didn't question the cops. It's risky for you. They're sure to want to question you when they find out you were one of the last people to see Amy before she disappeared." He squeezed her hand before she could protest. "Don't worry, your secret's safe with me. But as a member of the media, I can ask to see the file." With a nod to the ticket agent, he held out his hand and assisted her to her feet. "Come on, looks like they might have space for two on this flight."

There was nothing in first class even though Jordan pushed for the upgrades when he spotted two unoccupied seats up front, but he was told by the flight attendant that a VIP was expected and the celebrity always flew with a companion. The two seats they were offered were deep in the tail section, but Valerie was happy to settle for anything. She hadn't been looking forward to spending hours and hours in the terminal. Jordan stood aside to let her slip into the window seat while he searched for bin space to stow her carry-on. Most of the passengers were already seated, which meant that most of the overhead space was taken. She lost sight of him as he approached an attendant to help him find space for her carry-on, which was destined, presumably, for the front of the cabin.

A second attendant paused at the aisle and motioned to her to fasten her seatbelt. At the same time, she offered Valerie a magazine. She took it, amused to see that it was the current issue of *Panache.* Jordan would get a kick out of that, too.

A few minutes later, she looked up from the magazine, realizing that Jordan had not returned. The engines on the jet were revving up, preparing to move out. She fumbled at her seatbelt to release it and rose slightly to try and see what was keeping Jordan, but the entire aisle was empty. She sank back into her seat frowning. Now the pilot was issuing the order to the attendants to make final preparations for departure.

"Your seatbelt, miss. You need to keep it fastened."

She looked at the attendant, the same one who had assisted Jordan in trying to find space for her carry-on. "What happened to my friend?" she asked.

"I'm sorry?" the attendant said with a look of confusion.

"The man you were helping to find a space for my carry-on. Where is he?" Maybe he'd slipped into the restroom. "Aren't we about to take off?"

"Yes, and you'll have to fasten your seatbelt. Please."

Valerie did as asked. "What about my friend? Is he in the restroom?"

"Oh. I remember him now." She gave a slightly rueful shrug. "He said he received an urgent call on his cell phone. He was able to get off the plane just before we secured the hatch."

"He left?" Valerie repeated in disbelief.

"I'm afraid so." She moved away in response to the final signal for takeoff.

Valerie sat back as the plane backed away from the terminal and struggled with the furious realization that she'd been had. It was almost impossible not to leap up and try to force them to let her off, but of course it was too late for that now. Just as Jordan had planned, the devil! He'd waited until the last possible moment, trumped up an excuse to delay taking his seat, and ducked out while she sat stupidly rereading an issue of *Panache* that she'd already scrutinized from page one to the end. And he was probably telling himself that he'd done it for her own good. At this very moment, he was probably renting a car with the intention of continuing his search to fill in the gaps in her past that she'd withheld. Like a fool, she'd lowered her defenses and it might cost her everything.

"That's a fabulous magazine, isn't it?"

"Pardon?" The woman seated on the aisle was looking at her, smiling.

"*Panache*. Don't you just love it?"

She managed a polite smile. "Here, take it. I'm finished."

Jordan would never be mistaken for one of the neighbors as he cruised Oscar Diaz's street, but he had no choice if he wanted to talk to him. It was several hours after leaving the airport when he finally came face to face with him, thanks to the two kids he'd met when he'd been with Valerie. They'd spotted him cruising in his rental car and volunteered to watch the apartment, then call him on his cell phone when the pimp returned.

Their services didn't come cheap. They wanted a hundred bucks, fifty in advance. Once he drove up, they added insult to injury by pitching another deal to watch his rental car while he talked to Diaz. He managed to bargain them down to twenty bucks each, thinking with amusement all the way up the sidewalk to Diaz's front door that they'd probably go far with such keen entrepreneurial skills. As he waited for Diaz, they played basketball in a parking lot across the street, all innocence.

"What you want, man?" Oscar greeted him when he finally came to the door. He wore a satin shirt, untucked, and black leather pants. A single diamond stud adorned one earlobe.

"Are you Oscar Diaz?"

"Who's asking?"

"I'm a friend of Caroline's." There was no sign of recognition on Diaz's face. Which meant that he hadn't been hanging around the hotel waiting for another chance at Valerie since she'd never been out of Jordan's sight after his assault.

Jordan watched him search the street, checking the upscale rental car, his gaze passing over the kids playing basketball, the only sign of life. Stepping out over the threshold, he propped his hands on his hips, pulling his shirttails apart to make certain Jordan saw the pistol tucked in his belt. "How you fin' me, man?"

"Your parole officer was extremely cooperative," Jordan lied, knowing the gun was a parole violation. But Diaz conducted his whole life outside the law and possessing an illegal firearm was penny-ante stuff. Mainly Jordan was interested in diverting attention from the two kids. He wouldn't be surprised at anything Diaz might do to a snitch, even two who weren't yet into their teens. He had the strength. He wasn't a tall man, but he was heavily muscled, bulked-up from body building, Jordan guessed, with a vivid image in his mind of Valerie's bruised cheek. It was obvious how he kept a stable of "girls" in line. If drugs didn't work, there was always brutality.

"Are you the dude from New York?"

"Yeah, I'm the dude from New York." *You sleazy snake.*

"You and Caroline are close, am I right?"

"We're friends."

"More than frien's, dude. I know the signs." Lifting one hand, he made a show of studying his nails. "It's my trade, this love business, know what I mean?"

"Prostitution?" The word had a vile taste.

Oscar grinned. "I guess you got a problem with our sweet Caroline's past, huh, dude? But you got to hand it to her, gettin' outta this town, inventing a family for herself . . . man, who could do something like that? Then gettin' educated so she'll have a ca-reer, then the icing on the cake, she goes and changes her name." His tone was friendly, but his black gaze was flat and ugly. "Now there's a chick with real guts. But guts is something that Caroline has always had, know what I mean, dude?"

Jordan focused on the single diamond in Diaz's ear, thinking how he'd like to rip it out and use it to carve a few choice words on his bare skin. "She showed a lot of courage by getting out of a dangerous lifestyle," he said evenly.

The pimp crossed his thick arms over his chest. "Now that's where we had a problem, me and Caroline. She never knew her place, man."

"What does that mean?"

"Hell, she was a bleedin' heart back then, all fiery-eyed and ready to rescue every lost soul on the street. She was a pain in the ass to me."

"I don't see where helping people is a problem."

"Long as it didn't interfere with my operation, man.

Which it did. Only thing, she was just like them. She liked to get high good as they did." He cut his eyes to Jordan, then back to his nails. "I hated to lose her, man. She was . . . you know . . . real profitable to me. When she split, she owed me."

Jordan pushed his palms into the pockets of his jeans to keep from grabbing this creep by the throat. "You waited a long time to remind her of that debt."

He grinned. "Ah, you mean our visit at the hotel yesterday? Is that why you're here? Want to challenge me, man?" The idea seemed to amuse him. "Yeah, it disappointed me to be interrupted at just that delicate moment, you know?"

Jordan was beginning to understand how utterly desperate a runaway would have to be to seek help from someone like this. Did he have sex with every young girl unlucky enough to fall into his clutches? No doubt that was what had happened to Amy Trent, but had it happened to Valerie, too? Had this lowlife fathered Sara? The thought was enough to make his blood boil.

"You gave her a real fright," he said through his teeth.

"Man, she don' know anything about fright. That little visit was almos' frien'ly."

"What was it you think she owed you?"

Oscar crossed his arms over his chest, his dark eyes going small and black with spite. "She was a troublemaker. She stirred up my girls. She was always tryin' to reform them, get them riled up and say no to me." He turned and spat on the steps, missing Jordan's foot by a hair. "Hell, next thing the bitch would have organized them into a union!"

"So raping her was your way of settling the score?"

"She said I raped her?"

"She said you tried."

"Yeah, well. That's like being a little bit pregnant. You do it or you don't. And I didn't."

"You're a real prince, Oscar."

"I am what I am." He paused, then added, "And both of us know what she is, dude."

Jordan looked away, knowing he was being baited. With Diaz armed, he would have to leave it to the law to deal with this garbage . . . after he was satisfied that Valerie was out of harm's way.

"Let's talk about Amy Trent," he said.

Oscar made a disgusted sound. "Ancient history, man."

"Okay, but Caroline had nothing to do with her disappearance, right?"

"Is that what she tol' you?"

"It's what I'm asking you. She and Amy were friends, she told me that, but nobody seems to know anything about Amy beyond the fact that she was there one day and gone the next."

"If she tol' you about Amy, then you know it's her fault that Amy died."

"You're accusing her of having something to do with Amy's death?"

"I'm saying all that independent soul-sister shit didn't matter when she was standing over Amy and watching her die. I bet she didn't share that little fact when y'all were talkin', did she?"

"That's a serious charge. Did you tell the police? Did you tell anybody?"

He gave a short laugh. "And get my ass in trouble? You gotta be kiddin'."

"There's one other thing that nobody wants to talk about," Jordan said as Oscar reached behind for the door, ready to cut off the conversation. "What about Amy's baby?"

Oscar moved back, studied Jordan's face for a long

time, enjoying playing out the moment. Then he gave an elaborately casual shrug.

"You two are so close, you ask Caroline."

Behind Oscar, a visitor came out of the tiny kitchen. Both stood for a few moments and watched Jordan Case walk to the expensive wheels he'd rented. "Serve the prick right if one of the little bastards in the 'hood hada slashed the tires," Oscar muttered, adding spitefully, "and mugged him to boot."

"Do you realize what just happened, Oscar?" There was disgust in the voice.

"What you talkin' about?" He removed the pistol from his belt and laid it on the breakfast bar.

"Jordan Case came here to pump you for information and you gave it up."

"So what?" Oscar gave a dismissive shrug. "Nothing he can do about anything without messing up the sweet life Caroline has invented for herself. Besides, he's sleeping with her, so he knows her."

The visitor was looking thoughtful. "I'm not so sure about that. She's a very private person. Even if she's taken him as a lover—and I haven't seen any proof of that yet—she's not likely to tell him that she's not who she says she is."

"So what?" Oscar repeated. "It's a stalemate. Neither one of them can do anything. They're stuck with her livin' a lie and him havin' the hots for her."

"He's going to keep digging, Oscar. I know him."

"And I repeat, all we have to do is lay low for a while. Back off with the stalking shit. You keep it up, it might push her into doing something that will screw up our plan." Standing face to face, he pointed a finger. "You do anything to freak her out before the money comes in, you're gonna find your ass tied to a rock and sunk in a swamp. Do you understan' me?"

"I understand you, Oscar." The visitor watched him walk to the refrigerator for a beer. "You may not understand me, but I have always understood you."

"That crap again," Oscar muttered, rolling his eyes. Swearing, he shoved food and various bottles and jars aside in the fridge, looking for beer. "Where the hell is that six-pack I put in here last night? Damn you, it pisses me off to—!"

He swung about and saw the gun pointed at him. "What the hell—"

The first bullet caught him in the throat, a clean shot through his spine that killed him instantly. But a second bullet struck him squarely between his eyes, pulverizing the back of his skull as it exited. Without a flicker of emotion, the killer calmly wiped all prints from the gun and left it on the kitchen counter before leaving by the back door.

CHAPTER TWENTY

"So, how was your trip?" Eric set a cup of coffee in front of Valerie before moving to her credenza and tweaking an arrangement of exotic anthuriums with a delicate touch. "I'm assuming Jordan managed to . . . ah, connect with you once he got to New Orleans."

She gave him a hard look as she sprinkled a few grains of sweetener in her coffee. "I'm glad you mentioned that, Eric. It was going to be the first thing on my agenda this morning."

"I thought the staff meeting was first."

"That's the second item. This is a private matter between you and me."

His blue eyes grew wary. He clutched his ever-ready yellow legal pad to his chest and sat gingerly on the edge of a chair, knees together. "Okay, I'm ready."

She sighed inwardly. It was going to be like kicking a puppy. "Eric, when I told you my destination was not to be revealed to anyone, I didn't intend that to mean everybody except Jordan. But I'm willing to give you a chance to explain why you misunderstood. Were my instructions vague?''

"Not exactly, but—''

"Incomplete?''

"No . . .''

"Distasteful then?''

"Ah . . .''

"Or did you allow yourself to be charmed out of your socks by a man who you know is capable of doing anything to get what he wants?''

"Well, you ought to know, Val.'' His shoulders rose in a helpless shrug.

"Damn it!'' The coffee cup was set down with a thump and a splash. "I don't want this to happen again, Eric. My trip was meant to be . . . private.''

He jumped up and began mopping the coffee. "I understand, Val.''

She quickly rescued her daybook. "If I can't rely on you to do as I say, then maybe I'd better look around for an assistant who will.''

"You're saying you'll fire me?''

"That's what I'm saying!''

Her desktop clean, Eric now slumped back into the chair. "That's exactly what he threatened, too.''

"And you believed him?''

"Well—'' He shot her a quick look. "About as much as I believe you.''

Her eyes narrowed. "Just what exactly does that mean?''

"This is a pointless discussion we're having, Val.'' He stood up again with an explosive sigh. "Look, you know I'd die for you. I'd go to the stake for you. I'd lie, cheat, and steal for you. I—''

"Oh, please.'' She leaned back in her chair, tap-tapping a pen on the desktop. "But would you stand up to Jordan for me?''

He grinned. "Now that's asking a lot." He laughed at her expression, adding, "Well, it's tough. Put yourself in my shoes. He's just so . . . manly, Val. I could just eat him up, you know what I mean?"

She did. Ten times over. She was still fuming over being tricked into leaving New Orleans while Jordan did . . . whatever he wanted without interference from her. Twirling in her chair, she gazed at the flowers, which had been delivered just as she was arriving this morning. The card said simply, "J." It was an apology, pure and simple, but she wasn't ready to forgive him just yet. Besides, he wasn't back in New York and hadn't had the decency to answer her calls to his cell phone so that she could tell him exactly what she thought.

"He called this morning."

She looked up, startled. "What? Here? He called you? When? What did he want?"

"My word, such passion . . ." He threw up his hands as if to ward off artillery fire. "He wanted to be sure that you were okay. He called Security at your apartment last night, demanding a special watch for your floor. He notified Security in this building to keep you under surveillance until he got back. He—"

"He told you all that, but not me?"

"I got the idea you were mad at him."

"I was. I am."

"He's thinking of your safety, Val. He's worried. And speaking of worried, that idiot Ted Carpenter was back demanding to see you."

She sighed. "I don't have anything to say to him. He's dangerous."

"You're so right." Eric shuddered delicately. "He's still muttering threats about suing us. The man's all ego on two legs."

"Let him stew. I'm convinced he murdered his wife on that ski slope."

"Maybe *Panache* will bring about new interest in the case."

"Don't count on it." She ran a finger down the appointments for the day in her date book. Packed. What did it matter? She was simply going home to an empty apartment anyway. "Did he say when he'd be back?"

"Jordan?" Eric was up and toying with the anthuriums again. "He was vague, but take heart, Val. No man who sends this particular flower to a woman will stay away from her for long."

"This particular flower?" She looked at the arrangement. It was expensive and exotic, but if there was any message other than the simple initial on the card, she didn't get it.

Eric touched the elongated spike growing from the center of the scarlet spathe and gave her a wicked grin. "It has a Latin name, of course, but the common name is sex plant."

She pressed two fingers to her forehead while he chuckled like a monkey. "Is the agenda for the staff meeting ready?" she asked faintly.

Still chuckling, he handed over a sheaf of papers. "Oh, and one more thing . . ."

She looked up.

"Something's wrong with Roxanne. Don't ask, because she won't tell me a thing. Plus she's started smoking again, foolish girl." He went to the door. "Maybe she'll talk to you."

She convened the staff meeting a few minutes past nine. The early birds, like Eric, were ready to go, but others with a nighttime inner clock still yawned and struggled to focus. Jenny Bloom, newly promoted copy editor, was looking as perky as the iced sparkling water she was drinking. Greg was staring intently at the screen of his laptop, oblivious to everything and everyone. He was a workaholic with an odd personality, but brilliant. She was reminded often how good he was at his job, but he had a way to go in refining his people skills. Denise, on the other hand, looked like a cat who'd licked all the cream. If she was going to be part of the *Panache* team, then Valerie had to accept it. God knows, Denise had given her all to get the job. But railing against Hal for forcing Denise upon her would get her no points. Hopefully, his lust would cool soon and he'd allow Valerie to run her magazine as she saw fit. If Denise wasn't measuring up when that happened, she was out.

Roxanne appeared at the last minute carrying her huge portfolio. One of the night owls, she dropped with a grimace into her chair and took a huge gulp of hot, black coffee.

With Eric's remarks in mind, Valerie looked narrowly at her. "I'm the one suffering jet lag," she said. "What's your excuse?"

"Long night."

As Valerie watched, she opened a portfolio with hands that were visibly unsteady. Eric was right. There was something wrong. There were dark circles under her eyes and she had lost weight, Valerie realized suddenly. The stylish long sweater emphasized an alarming thinness. Rox was not anorexic, she didn't dabble in drugs, not even socially. She was a very moderate drinker. Why was she looking so fragile?

Roxanne finished laying out a series of photos. Then, as she started to close the portfolio, the edge glanced her coffee mug and knocked it over. She lurched forward to rescue the shots before they got wet.

"Let me," Eric said, already dabbing at the coffee. "I'm getting really good at this today."

"Here, Rox, come into my office and let's try to blot some of the stain on your sleeve."

"I'm okay." She tucked the rescued photos back into

the portfolio. Her movements were clumsy and she looked close to tears.

Tears from Roxanne? "No, I insist." She took her arm and urged Rox toward the door. "We'll be back in a few minutes," she told her staff.

"Now, what's going on?" she said to Roxanne as soon as they were inside her office.

"I'm a fool. An idiot." Roxanne wiped tears from her eyes with a tissue from the box Valerie thrust at her. "I'm—I—It's . . . it's A.J."

"Who?"

"The woman I've been seeing," she said, sitting down in the chair Valerie pushed over. She drew her long legs up, knees together. With her toes turned in, she looked oddly vulnerable, almost tragic. Utterly unlike herself. Rox had had many relationships, as Valerie knew firsthand. She'd been propositioned, lied to, abused, treated like a queen by some men and a slave by others. And mixed in with her varied heterosexual relationships had been several affairs with other women. But they'd never seemed very intense to Valerie. Until this A.J. person. When was it that Rox had been gushing with joy about her new love interest?

Valerie sat down opposite her, their knees almost touching. "What is the problem? You seemed so happy the last time we talked."

Roxanne stared morosely at the mangled tissue in her hand. "It seems like forever in a way and now that it's . . . it's over, so *quick*, Val." Fresh tears welled up. She dabbed at them, looking miserably at the floor. "I knew she probably would walk, but I just didn't expect it so soon. Or that she'd do it this way."

"How? What happened?"

Roxanne gave a pathetic little hitch of one shoulder. "She just left. I came home a couple of days ago and she was gone. Poof. Like she'd never been."

"Had you quarreled or something?"

Roxanne gave a brief, ironic laugh. "When didn't we quarrel? We fought constantly, but when we weren't fighting, it was so . . . so . . . exhilarating, Val. It was as if my emotions were always on a roller coaster. When it was good, as they say, it was so damn good."

Valerie couldn't understand Rox's affinity for the same sex, but she could certainly understand the emotional pain her friend was suffering. "What can I do to help?" she asked.

"Nothing." Rox met her gaze with a look of misery. "Just don't fire me until I get my shit together. Please, Val."

"Why do you even say a thing like that? You know I'd never do that. Have you gotten behind in your work? Do you need to take some personal days off?"

"No. The apartment is awful without her. And the current feature . . . well, I'll have it finished by the end of the day. Tomorrow noon at the latest." She stood up, smoothing both hands down over her body. "I look like the devil, don't I?"

"You're so beautiful that awful on you is still stunning."

Roxanne tried to smile. She reached for Valerie's hand and squeezed it. "You're the best, Val. Thanks."

They were met with curious looks when they returned. Valerie took her seat and quickly convened the meeting. She glanced at the group sitting around the table. "Thanks to all of you for doing your part to mind the store while I've been gone these last few days." She gave a brief smile. "I'll try not to do that to you more than once every ten years or so. Okay, let's begin."

Using her reading glasses, she glanced over the agenda that Eric had worked up for her. She looked up, wanting to get rid of the most troublesome topic first. "Have there been any more incidents of outright sabotage at the magazine such as Roxanne's damaged photos last week?"

Murmurs around the table, generally negative. Greg was still focused on the screen of his laptop.

"Nobody has had the notes of an idea mysteriously ripped off?"

More murmurs and shaking of heads.

"So we're back on track, gang?" She looked around, her smile more genuine. Except for someone snitching to Hal Kurtz about the Ted Carpenter feature, maybe the sabotage going on at the magazine was a series of coincidental screw-ups. It was worth hoping for.

Greg cleared his throat. "This may not mean anything, but I thought I'd mention it." He pushed his laptop over for Valerie to read. It was the web page from a competitor magazine promoting an upcoming feature on death row inmates.

Valerie read it, then pushed it back to Greg. Head bent, fingers pressing her temples, she sat for a few long moments, knowing this was no coincidence. A nearly identical article was in work, but scheduled for *Panache* in two months. There were a couple of coughs, some shifting in chairs.

"Does anyone know anything about this?" she asked, eyeing the group. Her question was answered again with a chorus of denials and blank faces.

"Is anybody keeping track here?" She scanned the room as she spoke, studying the faces of each staffer. "Didn't I ask this question ten minutes ago? This is the third time in as many weeks that someone has leaked our ideas to a competitor. Or sabotaged a feature. Any thoughts, people?" Her tone rose with her anger.

Roxanne, still pale and shaky, was reading the piece on Greg's laptop in silence.

"It could be just an unfortunate coincidence, Val," said Jenny Bloom. "I can't think of a single person in-house who would resort to such a sneaky way of killing a feature."

"Unless someone wanted to kill *Panache* magazine," Valerie said bitterly.

"It sounds personal to me," Eric said, his hands folded in front of him on the table. "It's plain as day that someone wants to see you fail."

"Excuse me." Roxanne rose abruptly and dashed for the door. "Bathroom . . ."

Valerie started to follow, but Jenny stood up. "I'll go, Val."

Denise had been sitting silently. Her recent promotion had won her no friends and she was under no illusions as to what Valerie's supporters thought of her. "How about Liz Chopin?" she said. "Everybody knows she was axed without any warning. That's enough to embitter a person. And she still has connections, people who might be indiscreet, not meaning to," she added hastily. "I mean, well, could it be Liz?"

"It's not Liz," Valerie said with a troubled gaze in the direction Roxanne had fled.

"Not to impugn your judgment, Val," Greg said. "But it could be anybody. You should alert all employees that this is happening. People talk shop when they're having lunch. They chat on the phone to former colleagues who're at different magazines now. Maybe it's as innocent as that, but it's doing damage to *Panache* as we try to build a new image. So we're pretty helpless until we get some idea who it might be."

All that was true, Valerie thought, reluctantly putting her concern for Roxanne aside. Unfortunately, she couldn't afford to be worrying about her right now. But somehow she couldn't shake the feeling that something evil was closing in. That—as Eric said—it was personally directed at her. But was she allowing the stress of being stalked and Janine's death to influence her professional

judgment in managing the magazine? Maybe Jordan
would have some ideas. She could talk it over with him
when—

"I'll call a general meeting of all employees," she
said, pulling herself up short. It was dangerously easy
to fall into a habit of sharing her thoughts with Jordan,
who didn't show any signs of doing the same. "Set it
up, will you, please, Eric?"

"It's done." Eric scribbled a note on his legal pad.
"Today's Friday. Let's do it later today, say at four,
okay?"

"I may have a glimmer of good news," Denise said,
bestowing a smile around the table. She pulled a bound
proposal from her briefcase and slid it across to Valerie.
"With so many things going off-track, I know you'll
appreciate that this is one feature where everything is
just fallin' into place beautifully."

"Let's see what you've got," Valerie said, gritting her
teeth as usual over Denise's Southern accent. She
opened the slick-looking folder.

"I was sort of on my own when you left town on that
really mysterious errand," Denise explained, blinking
innocently. "So—no offense, Val, but with you absent
and all, well, I got approval from Hal to proceed on
that feature idea we discussed at his party, remember?"

Valerie heard little of Denise's speech after opening
the folder. She found herself staring into the eyes of
Judge Edward Martindale.

"I've made appointments with these three judges,"
Denise continued. Eager to inform the staff, she spread
photographs of the jurists on the table. "Valerie already
knows the theme of the feature I've got in mind. The
personal journeys of these three judges are just awesome
and I think our readership will be as blown away by
reading them as I was in researching them. That
includes y'all, too. In running this feature, I believe

we're taking the magazine in the direction that Valerie herself has been pushing for months. It has a . . . well, a high-toned flavor, it's inspirin', it's intelligent." She smiled brightly all around. "In short, it's the kind of feature that could benefit us when they're totalin' up points in the National Magazine Award."

Her blatant conceit caused general discomfort in the group. Nobody looked at anybody else. Eric, doodling on his legal pad, finally said, "Why stop at the NMA, Denise? Let's shoot for a Pulitzer."

Denise shot him a cold look. "Maybe you'd like to read the proposal before trashin' the idea, Eric."

Eric shrugged. "I'm low on the food chain, honey bun. My opinion hardly counts. Besides, what's the point? If Mr. Kurtz is onboard, then who among us can say him nay?"

Eyes narrowed in disgust, Denise turned her attention back to Valerie. "Do you have any questions, Val?"

"A few. About the proposed date to publish, the timing is off, Denise." Her stomach churned as she slapped the folder shut on her stepfather's face. "This appears to be an ambitious project and our schedule is already set for the next four months on major features."

"I've taken that into consideration," Denise countered. "I'll need to personally interview all the major players and some people who know them—coworkers, their law clerks over the years, their wives, their kids. It'll take me quite some time to do that well. In fact, I've already started."

"Eager little beaver that you are," Eric muttered.

"We discussed this feature idea at Hal's party," Valerie said. "You were vague about where the idea originated. You told Jordan Case you received an e-mail, but were unable to follow up on it when you tried later. Is that true?"

Denise looked genuinely perplexed. "What difference does that make, Val? I'm not even sure it was on my e-mail. It might have been when I was surfin' the Internet. Ideas abound there, you know."

Roxanne was back now, pale but composed. "What are you talking about, Denise? A.J. suggested that feature to you weeks ago. She's the one who found it as she was surfing the Internet."

Denise gave a shrug. "Maybe, but I really don't see how it matters. I picked up the *germ* of an idea and I developed it."

No believer in coincidence, Valerie felt a little prickle of alarm. She never believed for a moment that the idea for the feature on three jurists—one of them her stepfather—had been dropped into Denise's lap accidentally. Someone behind the scenes was pulling the strings. But A.J.? Roxanne's lover? For the first time, she wished she'd paid more attention to Roxanne when she'd wanted to talk about A.J., a lost opportunity now that she'd vanished. Had Martindale somehow fed the idea to A.J.? As incredible as it seemed, could her stepfather be her stalker? Surely not, he'd be more direct if he wanted to destroy her. Wouldn't he? And why wait all these years?

Or was she getting so paranoid that she saw danger and betrayal in everyone, friend or enemy?

Most worrisome of all was having no chance to kill the feature since Denise had sold Hal Kurtz on it. Edward Martindale was again entering her life and the terrifying fact was that she was helpless to prevent it.

"Judges are pretty dry people," Roxanne said. "I said that to A.J. when she first mentioned it. What's going to make a reader stay with us beyond the first paragraph?"

"Y'all just didn't look deep enough, sugar. I can see the cover teasers now. There's poverty here, pathos, struggle, triumph over adversity." Denise hitched her chair closer, getting into her pitch. "Take Martindale, for example. Valerie has already heard some of this, so just 'scuse me if it's repetitious, Val. I know how valuable your time is."

"Discussion is the purpose of this meeting, Denise," Valerie said. Rising, she went to the drinks cart to refresh her coffee.

"Martindale's stepdaughter, Caroline, disappeared one night when she only fifteen years old. Nobody knows if she simply ran away or was kidnaped or murdered. Her parents were just devastated, you can imagine. No trace in all these years. His wife died tragically, too. This man has had so much pain in his life and he's just made lemonade out of lemons, y'all. It's a testament to a person's character, that's what it is."

Valerie returned to her chair as Denise was winding down. ". . . so everything's goin' so well on this that I've already arranged to meet with him. He's the first, although the others are just as interestin'."

"Who's first?" Valerie asked sharply.

"Martindale. We've got an appointment already as he's here in New York on business. Tomorrow." She gave another bright, sparkling smile. "He particularly asked to meet you, Val. He says he's been following your career forever."

The rest of the day was as harrowing for Valerie as the staff meeting. A rigidly constrained conversation with Hal Kurtz failed to dim his enthusiasm for the judicial feature. Ted Carpenter's lawyers served her with a notice to appear for a deposition in the actor's last-ditch effort to kill that story. Roxanne had disappeared and was unable to resolve a problem with the photo layout for the feature on Prince William. To end the day on a low note, Wayne Coulter appeared, unannounced, wanting to take her to dinner. It was probably bad timing, but she decided to tell him frankly that she didn't want to see him again. His reaction startled her. He acted as if she'd broken an official engagement. He was possessive and stifling and she didn't know why she hadn't realized just how pompous he was. Jordan wouldn't for a minute—

Oh, the *hell* with Jordan! Why did her thoughts turn to him every time she was pitched a curve? She was still angry with him for tricking her into leaving without him, but there was no denying that it was reassuring to know he was around. Besides, she'd have to tell him everything and she didn't want to—couldn't—unless she was willing to lose everything.

Thank God, the day was almost over and her staff gone. She'd pushed Eric out the door over his protests that she should go home, too. She'd caught him eyeing her intently from time to time after Denise dropped her bomb about Martindale, but he couldn't guess the cause of her distraction. Distraction. A tame word for the dread growing inside her.

She stopped in the act of shoving papers in her brief-case and dropped her face into her hands, trying to calm the fear that had her stomach in a knot while the wheels of her mind spun frantically. Tomorrow, when Denise saw Edward Martindale, she would no doubt accede to his request to meet *Panache*'s editor. What possible reason could she drum up to avoid seeing him?

What could she do? What could she do?

The telephone rang, jolting her out of her paranoia. Hands still unsteady, she fumbled with the receiver, thinking—*hoping*—it would be Jordan. "Hello?"

"Is this Valerie Olivier-Long?"

A woman, not Jordan. She swallowed a disappointed sigh. "Yes, who's calling?"

"I'm a private investigator, Ms. Long."

As an editor, she occasionally got calls from people

wanting to pitch ideas . . . for money. "Let me give you my assistant's number. He's away from his desk right now, but—"

"I don't think you'll want your assistant in on this, Ms. Long. It's pretty personal."

Was it her stalker? No. After three calls, she instantly recognized that voice. "Personal?"

"It's about your past, Ms. Long. Or maybe I should call you Caroline."

Valerie went perfectly still all over. "Who are you?" she asked sharply.

"Before we get into that, I'm honor-bound to tell you that Emilie Trent is my client."

"Emilie Trent?" Valerie's heart was knocking like a jackhammer in her chest.

"You may know her as Amy's mama." When Valerie said nothing, the caller's voice dropped to a silky tone and repeated, "Amy Trent, darlin'. Now is it convenient for us to talk?"

"What is this all about?"

A quick laugh. "What's it all about? How much clearer do I need to be? It's about you and Amy Trent and the pretty incredible scam you perpetrated on the world and that poor woman, Emilie Trent. My client."

"Scam?" Valerie looked around wildly, petrified that someone might hear.

"Okay, I see I've got your full attention at last." There was a sound as if the caller settled back, ready to get down to business. "Now, here's the deal, Valerie. I can call you Valerie, can't I, hon? I mean, how many people know you as well as I know you?"

"What do you want?"

"First of all, I'd like to say up front that I'm not proud. Or loyal. I represent Emilie Trent, but she's a risky client. She coughed up a retainer, but without me producing Amy herself, which we both know is an impossibility, she's not going to be good for much more. You, on the other hand, seem a better prospect, from my point of view."

Valerie rested her forehead on one palm. "Go on."

"I like that, Valerie. A practical woman. But you've been extremely practical all your life, haven't you? Like when you realized there would be no future with Oscar Diaz. So, bam, you were outta there."

"It's no secret that I knew Oscar. But that was a long time ago."

"Actually, it is a secret, Valerie. Only a handful of people know." A pause. "Oscar, Kelly Lott, myself, and of course, your personal private investigator, Ray Bergeron."

"Then it's hardly a secret," Valerie said, getting angry now that her initial shock was fading. "You said you're a private investigator. I know about an investigator who has been active in New Orleans. One Angela LeBlanc. Is that you?"

"Practical and smart." Angela chuckled. "You got me. I am that investigator and not to toot my own horn too much, but I have done some pretty impressive investigative work on this case." Ice rattled in a glass as she drained it. "I heard about your trip to the Big Easy. Sorry we missed each other, hon, but it's been a bitch following all the leads on this."

"You aren't calling from New Orleans?"

"No indeed. I'm right here. In a hotel, and at the rates they charge here, I can't stay long." More noise as she poured more liquid. "But now that we've introduced ourselves, I think we should just be honest about what's what, don't you?"

"What do you know about honesty?" Valerie charged hotly. "You're milking Amy's poor mother for money and now I expect you've got some kind of scheme to do the same to me." Her mouth shaking, Valerie pressed a hand to her lips until she could speak coolly. "I won't be as easily victimized as Emilie Trent."

"Hmm, you're pretty ballsy, too. I'm impressed. Only problem with that approach is . . ." Angela could be heard tapping her nails. "I'm holding all the cards in this game, hon."

"What cards?" Valerie asked in disgust. "If the mistakes I made when I was fifteen come to light, it'll be awkward, but I think I can survive it. A lot of people make mistakes when they're teenagers. A lot of kids run away and then put their lives back on track. I did that. In fact, it's something to be proud of!"

"Are you equally proud of stealing Amy's baby?"

Valerie's heart dropped to her toes. She sat there, stunned, her brain scrambling to find a way out of a nightmare. Here it was, the moment she'd feared for twenty years.

"Still there, Valerie?"

She nodded, idiotically, as if Angela could see her. "I'm here," she managed. "I'm just wondering how you came up with such a preposterous accusation."

"I don't think it's preposterous." Angela clicked a lighter, inhaled, and blew the smoke away. "In fact, I know it's true, thanks to damn good investigative work on my part."

"I suppose you have a birth certificate."

"No. And the funny thing about that is . . . there is no birth certificate at all in the state of Louisiana for one Sara Janine Olivier. So I'm betting the birth certificate you've been using all these years for the kid is as bogus as your claim to be her mama. 'Cause we know you've never had a baby, am I right, Caroline? You've never even been pregnant."

"And you can prove all this," Valerie stated, knowing that, at least, was not possible.

"Maybe not the kind of proof that would hold up in

a court of law, but I can sure as hell build a very believable case with circumstantial evidence."

"And what good would that be?" She heard the rattle as more ice was added to a glass.

"I'll tell you." Angela paused to take a drink. "I think it'll be good enough to generate a million questions from your little Sara."

"You'd go to Sara with this?" Valerie whispered as deep, dark fury burned in her chest. "You'd destroy a young girl's innocence just for spite? Just to torment me?"

"For spite? To torment you?" The surprise in Angela's voice sounded almost genuine. "No, hon. This is about money. Income. My ticket to a nice retirement."

"How much money?"

"Well, I figure you're raking in at least a couple hundred thousand, plus stock options and all the other shit that comes with a cushy position like your spiffy apartment, Sara's tuition to Boston College, not to mention Sister Janine's expenses at Rose Haven, may she rest in peace. So, if you want to keep that cushy position and if you want to keep Sara in the dark, you're just going to have to share some of it with me."

"You know about Janine?"

"I had a helluva time finding her, but when I did—"

"And you've been in my apartment?" Valerie went on red alert, unable to believe what she heard. "Have you been stalking me? Are you the one who's been making those obscene calls?"

"I'm the one who—"

"You killed Janine!" Valerie cried, jumping up from her chair. A kind of wild hysteria bubbled up in her. This miserable, cruel subhuman had intruded into her life leaving disaster in her wake. And now she wanted money to keep quiet? "Why did you have to kill Janine?" Anguish and anger trembled in her voice as she fumbled with the articles on her desk looking for a pen. Exposure meant nothing if she could lead the police to Janine's killer. "Where are you now?"

"Hold on here. I haven't killed anybody!" Angela said, sounding shocked. "I'm no murderer. Not my style, hon. And I haven't made any fuckin' phone calls either."

"How do I know that?" Valerie argued, pulling a notepad from beneath a jumble of files.

"Because I wasn't within a thousand miles of Rose Haven when it happened, for God's sake. You can check with Sister Frank at the convent in New Orleans. I spent the whole morning with her."

"Pumping her for gossip about me," Valerie guessed bitterly.

"Nothing personal, just part of the job. Look, it's a damn shame about Janine, but it doesn't change the fact that you've got secrets. And they're safe with me as long as we can come to some understanding about the money."

Valerie sank back into her chair. "I need to think about this." Playing for time seemed the only option she had at this point.

"Now there's that practical streak showing up again." Angela's lighter snapped as she lit a cigarette. "Tell you what. I'll give you 'til . . . say, noon tomorrow to come up with the cash."

"How much cash?" Valerie asked.

"Twenty thousand to start. I don't want to be too greedy."

After hanging up, Valerie sat for long minutes suspended in a black void of anger, fear, and dread. First the stalker, then Edward Martindale, and now Angela LeBlanc. From how many directions could a person be assaulted? Blackmail was a despicable vice, and in spite of her denials, Angela LeBlanc was shamelessly greedy and immoral. But she was not the stalker. It would be easy to verify her claim that she was in New Orleans on the day Janine died. So she was not the killer. Still, Valerie was unable to shake the fear that something evil lurked, waiting to close in and destroy everything she valued—her career, her reputation, her daughter's respect and devotion. Possibly even Sara herself.

Her gaze settled on a framed picture of Sara. She picked it up, traced her daughter's face with a tender touch. Her worst fear had never been that Sara would find out that Valerie was not her natural child, but that she would discover the sordid circumstances surrounding Amy's death and the way Valerie had taken her. What if Sara resented never having a chance to know the Trents? What if Amy's accusations about her father were untrue? What if, by claiming Sara for herself, she'd been denied two loving grandparents? Would Valerie ever be forgiven? If her relationship with Edward Martindale came to light, Sara would know everything about her. Like dominoes, all her secrets would be revealed, one by one.

Replacing the photo, she stood up and went to the window. It was dark now, although a thousand windows were lit in skyscrapers, testimony to the countless workaholics like herself who, for reasons of their own, resisted wrapping up and going home. Maybe it was the threat of real danger, but after only a few weeks in her dream job, Valerie realized the void in her life as a result of her devotion to her career. Success was a poor substitute for intimacy and loving relationships.

She watched a lone occupant busy at a desk in an office across the street. With Janine gone and someone else occupying first place in Sara's life, and her own fear of sharing her past with Jordan, who was left for her to turn to? Roxanne was distracted by problems of her own. Wayne Coulter was history.

Turning away, she ignored the stacks of work to do in her briefcase and reached for her coat instead. She was tired, exhausted, and scared. She was also in a box. It was left to her alone to face down her enemies, one at a time. Edward Martindale would have to be dealt with. And it was beyond stupid to begin paying a blackmailer, so she would have to meet with Angela LeBlanc to call her bluff. Once they were gone, the only threat to her was the stalker.

CHAPTER
TWENTY-ONE

For the second time in as many weeks, Jordan found himself in a Catholic institution. The elderly nun who admitted him at St. Francis Convent was dressed in the traditional black habit. The only concession she made to the changes brought about in Vatican II was her headdress, a simple lace cap.

She clucked with disapproval that he had not called in advance for an appointment. "It's highly irregular for someone to just walk in off the street and ask for an audience with the Mother Superior," she told him.

"I apologize. And I promise not to impose on her time." He hadn't been sure that an appointment would have been granted. It had seemed better to take his chances in person.

He hadn't wanted to spend another night in New Orleans, but the convent closed its doors to visitors at sundown and it had been dark when he left Oscar Diaz's neighborhood. He'd spent the evening in his hotel room trying to analyze what he'd learned by making a list of what he did know about Valerie and what he didn't. It had been a lopsided list. More questions than answers.

He reached inside his jacket for an envelope. "I have a letter of introduction from the archdiocese in New York, Sister. Father Alphonse, do you know him?"

"Hardly, sir. It's mostly the younger nuns who like to travel."

"Of course." Chastened, he tucked the letter away.

She turned another corner and ushered him into a small room, standing aside while he took the seat she indicated. "I don't know how you got the idea that you could see Mother Mary Abbott. Her calendar is booked weeks in advance. Sister Evelyn will be in to see you soon. There is reading material on that small table."

A Bible and two devotionals, he noted. God willing, Sister Evelyn would not be too long in showing up.

"Wait," he said as the nun began to close the door. "Is Sister Evelyn . . . ah, has she been here a long time?"

"About six months. She's a novice." She folded her hands over her abdomen. "Ordinarily, it's Sister Frank you would see, but she had a gallbladder attack last night and is not up to dealing with visitors today."

A novice would be no help. He needed to talk to someone who had been here when Sister Janine had befriended Valerie. "Are you a native of New Orleans?" he asked, searching for small talk until he could figure out how in heck to get access to Mother Mary Abbot.

"St. Francisville," she said, still standing patiently at the door.

"Is the convent named after your hometown?"

"No. It's named after St. Francis of Assisi."

"Oh. Right. Makes sense." He gave her his best smile. "I'm not a Catholic, you probably guessed that."

"I did."

He rose and stuck out his hand. "I'm Jordan Case, Sister."

Some of her starchiness melted, but she did not shake his hand. "I'm Sister Anne."

"I'm pleased to meet you."

"Thank you. We don't get many visitors like yourself." She adjusted a scarf on the ancient table holding the reading material before casting a look outside. The walls of the convent were high—well above eight feet—and thickly overgrown with ivy. How many years, he wondered, had it taken to cover the wall so completely?

"I did travel to Boston a few years ago," she said rather wistfully. "It was a conference. Such an historic city."

"Like New Orleans."

"Much colder."

Still standing, he gestured to a matching chair on the opposite side of the tiny table. "Keep me company for a while, Sister?"

She looked at the chair, then at him. "Well—"

He smiled, shamelessly charming. It had just dawned on him that he stood a better chance at getting information from a nun who might have known Janine than from an official source like Mother Mary Abbott.

Sister Anne sat primly. "Only for a minute, now."

"A minute." He grinned again. "Maybe two." Hitching at the creases in his Dockers, he sat again. "So how long have you been at St. Francis?"

"Thirty-one years. I came as a novitiate and I never left. Well, I did visit Boston, as I said, but—"

"Boston. There was a nun here years ago from Boston. Sister Janine Livaudais. Did you know her?"

"Yes." She raised a hand to genuflect, murmuring a

prayer. "I knew her very well. Her death was a terrible thing."

"How did you know she died?"

"Her obit came out in our newsletter."

"Ah . . ." He nodded. "Do you recall why she left New Orleans?"

"As if it were yesterday. She didn't only leave New Orleans, she left the order altogether."

"That must have been an extremely difficult decision."

"Just how difficult can only be understood by another nun, believe me. Once she renounced her vows, her life was over. Her soul was damned." Sister Anne's lips trembled as she pulled a lace-trimmed handkerchief from her pocket and pressed it to her mouth. "It was one of the worst things to happen in all the years I've been at St. Francis."

"You were a friend of hers," Jordan guessed.

"Oh, my. Yes. We were" she smiled tearfully—"sisters."

A clock on the table ticked the seconds away. Jordan forced himself to be silent, sensing that to push her might bring the flow of reminiscences to an end.

"It was that girl," Sister Anne said, resuming the conversation after slipping her handkerchief back into a cuff. "I've often wondered what happened to her. I hated her for a long time, God forgive me. It was her fault, I imagined, that Janine made such a foolish decision. But time has a way of putting things in perspective, don't you think? No teenage girl could have influenced me to renounce my vows and it was no different with Janine. She'd been dissatisfied for some time. She'd shared her doubts with me, but I didn't really understand how deeply troubled she was."

"What about the teenage girl? Did Janine tell you anything about her?"

She looked at him then, possibly just realizing how much she'd revealed. "May I see that letter of introduction?" she asked, putting out a hand.

He gave it to her and watched as she read it, holding his breath. Finished, she kept it and asked, "Why all these questions about Janine?"

"You were a friend of Sister Janine's," he said, choosing his words carefully. "I'm a friend of that teenage girl. You wondered what became of her. Thanks to Janine, she was able to turn her life around. She changed her name, she changed her lifestyle, she went back to school, which must have been difficult under the circumstances, even with Janine to help. Now she has a successful career in New York." He took the letter she returned to him. "Janine was the mother she never had."

Sister Anne was once again looking outside. Or was her gaze fixed on some other place without walls? he wondered. "We were so shocked to hear how she died," she murmured.

"Valerie was devastated. Sara, too."

"Valerie? Is that the name she chose, the girl, I mean?"

"Yes. And she named the baby Sara."

Sister Anne frowned. "I don't know anything about a baby."

He hesitated. "Did Janine not mention that the teenage girl was pregnant?"

"No. She wasn't pregnant. So much of the publicity at the time was wrong. She was a runaway, yes. And she had compelling reasons for getting away from that awful man."

"Oscar Diaz."

"Yes. I don't know how many young girls he's ruined, absolutely ruined. But Janine was determined that this one was going to escape if it was in her power to make that happen. She came along just at the time that Janine was searching for a sign. It was God's will, she told me."

"Do you know the girl's name?"

"Yes, Janine told me, although at the time she insisted that for the girl's safety we should keep it in confidence."

"It can hardly matter now," Jordan said.

"Amy Trent. Her name was Amy Trent."

Jordan reached the departure gate just as the final call was made for his flight. The wheels in his mind were spinning like crazy. He'd thought there could hardly be anything more in Valerie's past to shock him, but his visit to the convent had only added another level of mystery.

Was it conceivable that she was the missing Amy Trent? My God, the thought was staggering.

He sank into the seat in first class and absently accepted a copy of the newspaper handed him by the flight attendant. She smiled and asked if he would like a drink. He ordered whiskey and drank it straight up. Then, while waiting for another, he glanced idly at the folded copy of the *Times Picayune* in the empty seat beside him. He read—and then reread—the caption on a small item below the fold. "EX-CONVICT FOUND DEAD. OSCAR DIAZ, 44, PETTY CRIMINAL WITH A LONG RAP SHEET, DIED FROM GUNSHOT WOUNDS YESTERDAY IN HIS RESIDENCE AT . . ."

Jordan dropped his head back against the seat, closed his eyes, and tuned out.

CHAPTER TWENTY-TWO

It was Sara's turn to take Curly outside. There was only one disadvantage to having a dog in an apartment instead of a cat and that was having to having to take him outdoors to do his business. After donning coat, hat, and gloves, she found the Yorkie's leash and paused at the tiny room that served as a home office to tell Charlie. "I'm taking Curly for a walk, Charlie. I think I'll stop at the deli and pick up something for lunch, okay?"

Busy at the computer, he barely looked up. She smiled as he grunted a vague "Hmm."

As soon as Curly spotted the leash, he was hopping with excitement. He loved going outside whether it was frigidly cold or hot as blazes. Sara had almost bought him a little doggie sweater at the start of winter, but Charlie had hooted so that she reluctantly gave up the idea. Rusty had had a sweater that Granny Janine knitted for him even though Curly was one-eighth the size of Rusty. Charlie claimed that Mother Nature had equipped dogs to survive outdoors, that they didn't need sweaters. He said she was an old softie because she'd been reared in an all-female household. Maybe so, she thought, but today it was as cold as a hooker's heart outside and Curly was such a tiny dog.

She giggled at the term she'd picked up from Charlie. He had some really colorful sayings, stuff she'd never heard before she met him. He teased her constantly about her all-female upbringing, saying he had his work cut out trying to reeducate her as to the real world. She had a thing or two to teach him, as well, but she knew enough about the male ego not to tell him so. And she could only imagine her mother's reaction if she'd ever said something like "hooker's heart." Or Granny Janine's. Language, of course, was only one of the drastic differences in hers and Charlie's upbringing, but she didn't care about their differences. There were a thousand and one things that she and Charlie were on the same page about, and the places where they were different never seemed important when she was with him.

She stood at the top of the steps, shivering in a gust of cold wind. Curly, dragging at the leash, didn't seem to notice. He was as eager as if the temperature had been a balmy eighty degrees.

"Goofy dog," she muttered, but she was smiling. Snuggling into the hood of her coat, she was just about to go down the steps when the door burst open and Charlie came flying out. She gave him a startled look. He didn't even have his coat! One sleeve dangled while he struggled to put it on.

"What are you doing, for heaven's sake?" she demanded, reaching to help him. "Where are your gloves? It's freezing out here. Did I forget something?"

He slapped a ball cap on his head. "I decided to go with you. Needed some fresh air."

"Charlie." She gave him a chiding look. "Try another one. You were buried in some research on the Internet."

"Yeah, and I've been at it for hours. A break'll be nice."

"Okay." Whatever. She knew enough not to argue when he got like that. At their feet, Curly yapped and strained at the leash, eager to get going. She tucked her free hand in his arm. "I don't care what your excuse is, it's more fun to walk Curly with you than to do it alone."

He looked down at her with a stern look. "You haven't been out by yourself today, have you?"

She frowned. "What is it with you lately? I'm a big girl. I can find my way home," she said with sarcasm, "even from the park, which is two blocks that way. Or the deli, four blocks the other way. I can even manage going to and from the supermarket as well as my job, which as you know is quite a way from here."

"It's too cold for you to be venturing outside."

"I have a coat. I have gloves. I have a hat." She blew out an exasperated breath. "Charlie, will you please tell me what's going on? For the last two days, you've been worse than a mother with a toddler."

"Consider it a new quirk of mine," he told her, but he was looking at his feet, not meeting her eyes.

She stopped as Curly signaled his readiness to relieve himself and gave her big, burly guy a shrewd once-over. "You know what, Charlie? You can put all that protective energy on hold for now because, speaking for myself, I'll appreciate it a lot more later."

"That's another reason for you to be careful," he said, shifting to block the icy wind from her with his body as she stood waiting for the dog.

"A woman doesn't have to be pampered during a pregnancy."

"I want to pamper you."

"This is going beyond pampering, Charlie. Something else is going on. Please be honest with me. Didn't we promise each other we wouldn't let things grow and fester for lack of communication?"

He reached out and touched her face. Even through his gloves, she felt the warmth of him. He was so alive. So vital and strong. So manly. She loved him with every fiber of her being. "Your mom spent three days in New Orleans this week," he said.

She frowned. "What does that have to do with anything? She's out of town a lot. I'm used to it." She smiled softly, turning to touch her lips to his hand. "Mom's schedule isn't as important to me as it once was. I have much more interesting things to occupy my mind now."

"Yeah, so are you feeling okay?"

"You'd be the first one to know if I weren't, Charlie." Her eyes narrowed suddenly. "Do I sense a deliberate change of subject?"

"Can't a guy ask about his wife's health?"

"Let's go back to my mother. She was in New Orleans—and . . ." She gave him a questioning look.

"I didn't want to bother you with this, but if you won't leave it alone—"

"Bother me with what?"

"Valerie is being . . . ah, harassed by someone, maybe a fan or something. She went down there on her own to check it out, if you can believe that."

"What do you mean, harassed?"

"You know how nutty people can be when you're in the public eye. Being the editor of a major magazine puts her in that category, something I don't have to tell you. But this particular person—Dad wasn't sure whether it's a man or a woman—seems to be like an apple short of a bushel. Anyway, in view of your Granny

Janine's death, it seemed a good idea to try and flush him out."

Curley jerked on the leash, ready to go again. "Wait. Just wait a minute." Shaking her head as if to clear it for straight thinking, Sara caught and held Charlie's arm. "You're saying that someone is stalking my mother? Someone—maybe the guy who murdered Granny Janine—might try to hurt my mother?"

He cupped her face in both his hands. "No, sweetheart. I'm just saying that your mom became concerned that these two things might be linked. There's no way of knowing that until he's identified. But Dad—actually she and Dad—are taking no chances. And that's why we thought—"

"We? You're in on this, too. And you didn't tell me?"

"I didn't want to worry you."

"Worry me? You didn't want to worry me by telling me that the sicko who killed my grandmother might possibly be trying to get to my mother, too?"

"You didn't need the hassle," he said, looking away from her flashing eyes. He didn't like making Sara unhappy. He liked her sweet and easy. There had been enough pain in their relationship.

"I didn't need the hassle." She freed herself and turned, setting off at a brisk pace, letting Curly have his head.

Charlie hesitated, then bolted after her. "We're only trying to protect you, Sara!"

"By keeping me in the dark?" Her pace increased. Now she was almost running, much to Curly's delight.

"You're pregnant, goddamn it!"

There was a dangerous light in her eyes when she stopped and spoke softly. "I think I'm the one who knew that fact first, Charlie. And now that we're on the subject, you'd better be telling me that you haven't told that to your dad . . . or my mother . . . without me being there to share it. You better not, Charlie.''

He was offended. "I wouldn't do that.''

"Then on what basis is all this" waving a hand, she looked about, baffled—"this overprotective shit!''

"You shouldn't talk like that.''

She gave him a look that made him rear back slightly. "Don't tell me how I should talk or shouldn't talk, Charlie Case. I'm your wife now, not some dizzy teenager you're screwing and promising the moon to.''

"We always get back to that, don't we?''

"Well, are you treating me like an adult or like a dizzy teenager? An honest answer, please.''

"I've told you a million times that I was wrong to walk away after the miscarriage, Sara. I'll always feel bad about that. I'm trying to show you every way I know how that I love you. A man wants to protect the woman he loves, is that so hard to understand?''

"How do I need protection, Charlie? I don't get it.''

He pulled the bill of his ball cap down low. Looked away. Studied intently a large truck lumbering toward them on the narrow street. Watched it pass in a cloud of dirty diesel fumes. Looking down at his feet, he knocked packed snow from one of them. Curly, sensing drama, had stopped tugging at the leash and now stood at their feet, watching them.

"What if your mom's stalker and the killer are one and the same, Sara?" he asked quietly. "Stalkers like to torment their victims. Say he murdered Sister Janine for no reason other than to torment your mom. There's nothing else that would hurt her more than for something to happen to you.''

She stared at him, speechless.

He took her hand and held it close to his heart. "I can't let that happen. I would die if something happened to you. It's my place to see that it doesn't happen, that he can't get to you."

She blinked. "I . . . I don't know what to say." She looked at him. "You don't really think—"

"I don't know what to think," he said, taking her arm and guiding her around a U.S. Mail box. "But I'm not taking any chances."

"Okay." She was nodding.

"It could be we're all overreacting. Maybe they'll find out something in New Orleans."

"Did you say your dad went with her?"

"Yeah. She didn't want him to. Didn't ask him to go with her. Actually, she went without telling him and he was royally pissed, I can tell you." He gave a wry shrug. "I guess you got that streak of independence naturally."

"Why? Why should she tell your dad that someone's threatening her? They don't know about us, except that we're living together. They don't know that we're married. That I'm pregnant."

He squeezed her hand. "No. I don't think this has much to do with us, sweetheart. From the way he talks, I think Dad's got a thing for your mom and I don't think he's got a clue yet."

"You're kidding!"

He shrugged. "I know the signs."

Sara was silent, pulling at the leash as Curly tried to dart between two garbage cans where a war-torn tomcat sat in a pale shaft of winter sun calmly grooming himself. "Curly, calm down!"

She was unprepared for the sudden confrontation between the two animals. Instead of making a dash for safety, the tomcat turned and hissed a warning. Curly, eagerly ready for battle, jerked free of the leash. In a flash, the cat was off with Curly following in hot pursuit. Sara called his name, and before Charlie could stop her, she had dashed into the street.

There was little traffic, but a car parked and idling in front of the deli suddenly pulled away from the curb. Bent on rescuing Curly, Sara didn't see the car accelerating.

Nor did she realize she was square in its path.

Charlie was never sure what happened next. His only thought was to get to Sara and save her. With a leap, he cleared the curb. The panicked cat, who had now reversed direction and was heading back across the street, dashed between his legs with Curly close behind, barking furiously. Not as nimble as the animals, Sara stopped in disgust. It was only then that she noticed the car bearing down on her. She froze with horror.

Galvanized by fear, Charlie dove the last few feet and in the nick of time gave her a mighty shove. She went sprawling painfully in the street. The last Charlie remembered thinking was that he'd hurt her after all.

CHAPTER
TWENTY-THREE

Valerie unlocked the door of her apartment, signaled to the doorman who'd accompanied her in the elevator that all appeared well, and went inside. She stood for a moment listening to the silence. The house was so quiet it seemed to be holding its breath. Or maybe that was her. Letting out a sigh, she dropped her briefcase and bag on a chair. Before the violation of her home by a stranger, she'd loved coming into her apartment at the end of a long day. To peace. Quiet. No phone calls. No last-minute glitch in a deadline. No Ted Carpenters spewing obscenities or anonymous callers tormenting her.

Still in her coat, she went to the answer machine and touched the button to play her messages. Half a dozen, with a couple of blank hang-ups. Her stalker? Angela LeBlanc? Edward Martindale? Dear Lord, the possibilities were endless. If it hadn't been so scary, it would be almost farcical.

Nothing from Jordan. She stood for a moment feeling

oddly hurt. She was supposed to be angry with him, but damn it, he could have the decency to call. Had the night they'd spent together meant so little? That was the real source of this strange mood, she admitted, tapping the code to pull up caller ID. Sure enough, the hang-ups were unfamiliar.

She took off her coat and put it away. She'd skipped lunch except for a hurried yogurt that Eric had forced on her at about three in the afternoon. With little enthusiasm, she went into the kitchen, opened the refrigerator, and studied the contents. There was nothing to eat except more yogurt. Everything else had green mold growing on it or was limp from dehydration. She took the yogurt and plunked it on the counter a little too hard. So much for that New Year's resolution to keep a stocked-up cupboard.

"How about Chinese instead?"

She wheeled about with a screech, knocking the yogurt to the floor. Jordan stood at the door holding up two white paper sacks. The yogurt, still sealed, rolled to a stop at his feet. He'd had a long day, too, from the look of his creased khakis and wilted shirt. His leather jacket hung loose on his lean frame and his hair looked finger-combed, as if he hadn't been in front of a mirror since shaving that morning. But the fatigue showed most in the grim look on his face. Just seeing him reminded her how good it felt to be held by him. She resisted the urge to rush over and throw herself into his arms.

"How did you get in here?"

He set the bags on the table and held up a key. "Did you forget I had it?"

Yes. It had seemed a good idea at the time. Multiple break-ins, threatening phone calls, Janine murdered. Peering a little closer, she saw not simply exhaustion. He looked gruff and disgruntled. Like he was up to here with . . . something.

"Did you get the flowers?" he asked.

"Yes."

"Still ticked off, huh?" He stood at the end of her table in shadowy light, overwhelmingly masculine in her decidedly feminine kitchen. Even with exhaustion showing, he always seemed to look so quintessentially male.

Instead of answering, she asked, "Was it worth the effort? Did you find out everything you wanted to know? Do I have any secrets left?"

"Here's a flash. Everything I found out led to more questions." His gaze as he studied her face was uncomfortably keen and overlong, but after a while he shed his jacket and began opening the bags, checking what was inside. "What's your pleasure, shrimp with lobster sauce or triple dragon?"

"Why? What did you find out?"

He went to the cupboard and took two plates out. "I usually eat mine right from the carton, but I bet that's not your style." He set the plates on the table and pulled a drawer open, found utensils, and shoved the drawer closed with one hip. "I'm having beer, Chinese. There's green tea for you, but if you want water or something—"

"Will you answer me, damn it! What have you been doing? Why didn't you answer your cell phone?"

He met her eyes, still holding the utensils in his hands. "I didn't want to."

"Why? Didn't you know I was out of my mind worrying?"

He dropped the utensils with a clatter. "Yeah? Well, how does it feel, Valerie?"

"You're saying you deliberately refused to call me just to punish me?"

"I'm saying you've got me in such a tailspin that I

didn't trust myself to call you. I had Charlie watching out for Sara and Eric as point man for you."

"I'm not talking about your overprotective urge to babysit me, Jordan. I'm talking about you cutting me out of the picture as you go digging into things that don't concern you. Things about my personal life."

"They sure as hell do concern me. I'm up to my ass in concern for you, woman!" In a heartbeat, he skirted the end of the table and his silver-gray eyes were locked with hers. "And here's another flash for you. I've just spent the last two days thinking your real name might be Amy Trent. Amy Trent, did you get that, Val? And that's just a hint of how crazy the last two days have been for me."

A healthy dose of caution made her take a step back, bumping up against the counter. "You thought I was Amy?"

"Janine rescued a teenager with a baby. The girl was running from Oscar Diaz. You admitted Diaz might be Sara's father. No trace of Amy has ever been found. It was possible."

She was shaking her head, her hands braced on the counter behind her. "No, it wasn't—isn't possible. Amy's dead. You heard Kelly call me Caroline. Oscar called me Caroline."

"Maybe." He swung away from her, frustration in every line of his body. "But Emilie Trent had photographs of her daughter everywhere. Even at age fourteen, a blind man could see there was no resemblance."

"You went to see Amy's parents? In Connecticut?"

"Is that something else you didn't want me to do?" He raked a hand over his face and she realized that, along with the anger and frustration in him, he was bone tired. "After I left New Orleans, the Trents had to be my next stop. He's dead, did you know that?"

"Who, Amy's father?"

"Yeah. Not a single picture of him anywhere and Emilie wouldn't have mentioned it if I hadn't asked." He removed the cap from his beer and took a long swallow.

"She said he abused her," Valerie murmured, still trying to take it in that he'd seen Emilie Trent. "Did you tell her that I was with Amy in New Orleans . . . when she disappeared?"

"No, Valerie. Your secrets are safe with me." He took off his jacket and tossed it on a chair, then added with biting cynicism, "What few of them you've shared."

When she remained silent, he shook his head, releasing an ironic half-laugh. "It's funny. It's supposed to be men who keep everything bottled up. We're the ones with the reputation for resisting intimacy in a relationship, but you could give lessons to the best of us in that department, Val."

"I know it must seem odd," Valerie murmured, wishing it were simply stubbornness keeping her silent. It was her fault that he had such a critical opinion of her. If she'd just been able to tell him about Martindale or about Sara's birth or to share her fear of the consequences if everything came to light.

He quit pacing to look at her. "You had a tough time, I grant you that, but keeping people who care about you in the dark is putting more people at risk. I know you don't want to hear that," he said as she opened her mouth to protest. "Before you try to put me off yet again, you ought to know that Oscar Diaz is dead. Murdered."

Valerie pressed four fingers to her mouth.

"Don't ask, because I don't know any details. It must have happened just minutes after I left his place, according to what I read." He dug into his jacket and pulled out an article torn from the newspaper. "Here, read it for yourself. I didn't stick around waiting to be

304

Karen Young

identified as a likely suspect. Two canny kids helped me
get to Diaz. They're probably ID-ing me to the cops as
we speak."

She was still staring at him. "Oscar's dead? You saw
him? What did he say? Did he admit attacking me in
the hotel?"

"Yeah, he made sure I knew he did it and that he
had a gun on him in case I wanted to go *mano a mano*
to defend your honor right then and there."

"Oh my God." She turned away, her hand still
pressed to her mouth.

"He's a lowlife loser who got what he deserved. The
runaways in that picture with you are just five of the
countless innocent kids he's defiled. Only God—and
the devil—know how many there might be. Too bad
somebody didn't kill him years ago."

Valerie wrapped her arms around herself. "Do you
have any idea who did it?"

"Only that I didn't. But it would be useful if we knew
where your stalker was at the time of death."

"Why would he kill Oscar?"

His gaze locked with hers. "I was hoping you would
tell me that, Valerie."

His keen eyes were taking in every aspect of her reaction and probably making judgments that were logical,
but wrong. Not his fault, Valerie thought, unable to
bear more scrutiny. If he looked too closely, he might
see all the way into her soul. But what on earth could
she tell him? Then, to her great relief, the phone rang.

There was no extension in the kitchen and the answering machine kicked in before she reached it.

"Mom, Mom, this is Sara! Are you there?" She
sounded almost hysterical. "Mom, please pick up. Oh,
God, Mom, Charlie's hurt!"

She grabbed the receiver, barely beating Jordan, who

dove to get it when he heard Charlie's name. "Sara, I'm here," she said. "What's wrong?"

A strangled sob. "It's Charlie, Mom. He's in the ER. He's hurt and it was my fault!"

"Hurt? How?" She tilted the receiver to allow Jordan to listen, too.

"A car, a hit-and-run. I'll tell you after you get here." Sara began sobbing. "Just come. I need you right now, Mom. Charlie's dad isn't—"

"He's here. He's with me, Sara. Try to be calm. We'll leave right now."

"Oh!" Sara gave a choked gasp. "I'm so glad. I thought he was in New Orleans. We—"

"Which hospital?" Jordan snapped, taking the receiver from Valerie. Fear had bleached the color from his face, leaving it gray and strained. She watched him anxiously while Sara talked on the other end of the line. She closed her eyes in dread when he said in a hollow tone, "It can't be that bad." She found Jordan's hand and squeezed it.

"Well, can't they do something?" he barked. "They've got high-tech medicine for this, haven't they?" He waited, listened. Then, "Okay, okay. I understand. It'll take us—I don't know how long, but we'll be there as soon as possible." He was nodding at something Sara said, then freeing his hand, he motioned to Valerie for a pen. She snatched one from a small drawer in the table, then gave him a notepad. "Yeah, now what's the doctor's name?"

He scribbled on the paper. "Yeah, is he good? Okay. Okay. And thanks, Sara."

"What, Jordan?" Valerie asked anxiously. "How bad is it?"

"He's not conscious. They're doing a CT scan right now." There was fear in his eyes when he looked at her. "The ER doctor says he's suffered a concussion and the

CT scan will tell how bad it is. He . . . They're concerned about brain damage.''

Jordan was out of the taxi almost before it stopped at the entrance to the hospital emergency room. He tossed money to the driver and hit the doors of the ER at a run. Valerie followed, but it was impossible to keep up with him.

Once inside, the admissions clerk rose, but failed to halt him as he dashed down the corridor leading to nuclear medicine. On the wild ride to the hospital, he'd used his cell phone to try and get more details about Charlie, but the only useful thing he'd been told was exactly where he was at the moment.

"Sir, you can't go in there," another hospital employee said, blocking a door labeled NO ADMITTANCE. AUTHORIZED PERSONNEL ONLY seconds before Jordan pushed it open.

"I want to see my son," he said, fighting off an image of Charlie, white and lifeless and all the energy and quickness that made him who he was fading. He felt a primal need to protect what was his.

The technician referred to a list on a clipboard. "What is your son's name, sir?"

"Charlie. Charles Walker Case." Jordan's gaze flashed to Valerie, who slipped her arm around his waist in a silent show of support. Somewhere inside, he was dimly aware that his terror eased slightly. He found her hand and held it tight.

"He's in a CT scan right now, sir. He should be out any minute now."

"Can I talk to the doctor who saw him in the ER?" Jordan asked.

"That would be Dr. Flynn, senior trauma surgeon.

He's in the x-ray area right now. Your son is getting the best care, Mr. Case. You can wait—''

"Mom! Oh, Mom, you're here!" Sara emerged from a small waiting room and rushed over to Valerie. "It's awful, Mom. He's so white. I was so scared. He wouldn't wake up, and the doctor said they don't have any idea how long it would be before he . . . he . . .''

Valerie opened her arms and Sara threw herself into her mother's embrace. "Shh, it'll be all right, sweetheart." One hand gently rubbed Sara's back while her eyes met Jordan's. "We were just told that he'll be out any minute.''

"Here he comes now," the technician said as a stretcher was wheeled out of the restricted area. "Hey, looks like he's awake.''

Charlie was as pale as the bleached hospital sheets covering him. His arms were in restraints and he was hooked up to an IV drip that beeped his vitals on a portable monitor resting between his legs. Sara's eyes filled and she made a small, strangled sound. Valerie slipped an arm around her. Jordan swallowed hard and kept his gaze locked on his son. Charlie was a man in his own right now, but to Jordan the emotion swamping him was the same as if Charlie were still a toddler.

He looked groggy and confused as the technician spoke to him, trying to pull him fully back into the world. "Talk to me, Charlie. What day is this?''

Jordan's throat was as tight as a drum as Charlie mumbled something.

"C'mon, Charlie. Tell me, who's the president?''

"Clinton," Charlie muttered.

"Close." The technician grinned, looking at Jordan. "Good sign. He's coming around now.''

Coming fully awake, Charlie saw the ring of faces around him. "Hey, what—Let me go, damn it!" Thrashing and tugging against the restraints, he tried to sit up.

"Okay, okay, take it easy, Charlie." The technician quickly subdued him, pressing him down. "You're in a hospital. We're here to help." He glanced over his shoulder at Jordan. "Aggression. It's a classic sign of head trauma. Oxygen deprivation will do that. He's got a couple of fractured ribs, too, so thrashing about is bound to hurt. We'll give him a minute to orient himself."

It didn't take a minute.

"Where's my wife?" Charlie strained to find Sara in the sea of faces around him. "Is Sara okay?"

As Jordan and Valerie stared, Sara touched his hand, stroked it lovingly. "I'm here, Charlie. I'm just fine."

He settled back with a weak groan of relief. "Is the baby okay?"

Jordan and Valerie exchanged a startled look.

Sara smiled and bent to kiss Charlie. "Baby's fine, too. You're the one we're worried about. Be still now. Let these people do what they need to do. You nearly scared your dad and me to death!" The hysteria that had almost overwhelmed her was under control now that she saw that Charlie was awake and seemed lucid.

"Dad's here?" Wrinkling his brow, he found Jordan in the group around the stretcher. Again he tried to get up on one elbow, but his face twisted with pain and he fell back. "Dad. I need to—"

"Don't try to move yet, Charlie." Jordan stepped into his line of vision. "You've got some fractured ribs."

"Yeah, feels like it. But, Dad, you were right to be worried."

Jordan put a hand on Charlie's chest, as much to reassure himself as Charlie. "It'll wait, son. We'll discuss what happened after you feel better."

In obvious pain, Charlie closed his eyes. "The car, it was a dark blue Toyota Camry, new," he managed, stubbornly determined to say what was on his mind. "Tinted windows."

Jordan gave in. "What about the driver?"

"Couldn't see. He pulled out from the deli. Ask in there. Somebody must have seen something. He meant to kill Sara."

This time, it was the doctor who intervened. "It's not a good idea for him to be stressing right now over what happened. Can't this wait?"

Jordan reluctantly stepped back. "We'll talk about it later, Charlie."

At midnight, Valerie was still at the hospital keeping vigil with Sara and Jordan. Charlie objected to an overnight stay, but finally gave in after pressure from the trauma surgeon and Jordan. Next, he refused to settle down until a cot was brought into his room for Sara. He told his dad he didn't intend to let her out of his sight, not even to go home with Valerie.

While he was being treated, a detective from the NYPD had waited for a chance to question him. Now that Charlie was settled and seemed able to talk, the detective insisted on seeing him. Both the doctor and Jordan objected, but Charlie overruled them. "I've got busted ribs and a headache, not amnesia," he grumbled. "Getting a report out there fast might make the difference between finding this dirtbag and giving him time to split. What do you want to know, officer?"

"Everything you can recall." Detective Dan Sorensen was a huge bear of a man, well over six feet and blond, with piercing blue eyes. He looked as if he might have once belonged to the Worldwide Federation of Wrestlers instead of the police department. "Describe the vehicle, the driver, and the circumstances," he told Charlie, "exactly as you observed them."

Charlie repeated what he'd told Jordan as he regained consciousness after the CT scan. "I'm sorry I didn't think fast enough to get a license number. But when I saw him bearing down on Sara, all I thought about was getting her out of the way."

"You thought fast enough to save your wife's life," Sorensen said. "And you actually observed more than most people do in a situation like that. The owner of the deli didn't notice anything until the accident was over. There were several people inside before it happened, some strangers, some regulars. Not much help there, either. Hit-and-run," he continued, "is one of the most difficult types of offenders to trace. They're mostly ordinary folks who accidentally whack some pedestrian and then they flee in panic. Sometimes they show up at the nearest precinct and come clean, but some of them never admit to anything and just go on about their lives as if at that particular point in time they simply had a bad hair day."

"This was no accident, officer," Charlie said emphatically. "This was a deliberate attempt on my wife's life. And I think it has something to do with the fact that her mother is being stalked by a sicko. In my opinion, you should also look for a connection in the murder of Sara's grandmother a couple weeks ago and what happened today."

Valerie stood in the corner of the room listening. She bent her head, pinching the bridge of her nose with two fingers. Now the stuff would hit the fan.

Sorensen turned to look at her. "What's this all about, ma'am?"

It was Jordan who answered. "Check with Homicide. There's an ongoing investigation into the murder of Janine Livaudais at the Rose Haven Care Facility. There may be a connection, but no one seems to be able to figure it out."

"Why would anyone be stalking you, ma'am?"

"Good question, Detective." Again, Jordan replied. He crossed his arms over his chest. "That's exactly what we've been trying to figure out ourselves."

An hour later, Valerie and Jordan were in the hospital snack bar. Each filled a Styrofoam cup from a vending machine, then sat down. Valerie tasted the coffee and pushed it away with a grimace. A full minute passed in silence.

"I can't believe they're married," she said finally.

Jordan scowled at the late-night cleaning crew swabbing the floor nearby. "And pregnant."

Valerie rubbed at both temples with her fingertips. "I don't know what to say. I had no idea. Sara never said a word."

"Which shouldn't surprise you. Keeping secrets seems to be a family trait." He finished his coffee and crushed the cup in his hand.

Stung, Valerie rose, picked up Jordan's mangled cup and her own, and dropped them in a waste receptacle. Guilt was a leaden weight in her chest. Whatever evil was closing in had now touched Charlie and Sara. Jordan clearly blamed her, but in her heart of hearts, she knew she would rather have been in the path of that car herself than have either of their children harmed.

"It takes two, Jordan. Maybe Sara had her own reasons for not telling me, but Charlie was hardly a mute bystander." If Jordan chose to focus on that part of it, then fine. He couldn't deny they both had a lot of work to do to mend fences with their children.

"Yeah, well, I don't know about you, but I got the message. They want us to butt out of their lives, but how in hell we can do that now beats me. I have no doubt the psycho who's stalking you and the driver of the car that hit Charlie are one and the same. Charlie was right on when he told Sorensen that.''

"He's very protective of Sara."

"Yeah."

She managed a tiny smile. "A family trait on your side?"

"It's better than secrecy and deception."

She had no argument for that. She had secrets. She had deceived the whole world. And the guilt had never felt so overwhelming before.

But what bothered her most was knowing in some way she was responsible for everything that had happened. And everything that might yet happen. She'd struggled with guilt over Amy's death all her adult life, but she'd never dreamed Sara—and Charlie and Janine, even Oscar—would be the ones to pay for her mistakes.

She slipped her bag on her shoulder as Jordan stood up. It hurt that Sara hadn't wanted her at her wedding and Jordan's bitterness told her he hadn't missed the implications either. They'd both been denied sharing the single most meaningful event in Charlie and Sara's lives. There was a message in that for both of them. But it could come only after they figured out who was trying to destroy them, one by one.

Jordan shrugged into his jacket. "Are you ready to go home?"

"No, I'm staying." He might not want to look at her after what happened to Charlie, but she was staying as long as Jordan stayed. It was the least she could do.

"I remember how I felt the only time Sara was ever hospitalized," she said. "She suffered a concussion when she fell off her bicycle. Janine was sick with a bout of flu and I was on my own. It was awful."

"How old was she?"

"Eight."

"Charlie's twenty-two and he has his wife to hold his

hand," Jordan said dryly. "Besides, he knows that I have other priorities, now that I know he's okay."

"What other priorities?"

"You." He took her arm and urged her toward the door. "You're the primary target, Val. Janine and Oscar and Sara or Charlie—whoever he meant to harm—were all staged for the final act. He wants you."

CHAPTER
TWENTY-FOUR

Valerie lay alone in her bedroom, miserable and sleepless, while Jordan slept in the guest room. He was here as her bodyguard, nothing more. They'd hardly shed their coats when he'd politely mentioned he'd like to shower. He'd then taken a bottle of Scotch and a glass and retired. To the guest room. He hadn't shown a hint of the emotion they'd shared that night in New Orleans. Or any desire to repeat it. If she'd had no connection to Charlie and Sara, he wouldn't be here at all.

The hit-and-run wouldn't have happened at all, but for you.

She turned restlessly and stared at the shadowy outline of picture frames on her bedside table—Sara and Janine, her whole world until now. It wasn't enough, she realized. And it wasn't enough that Jordan was here out of a sense of duty.

She tossed the covers back and sat up on the side of the bed. Sara's pregnancy was an odd twist of fate that now linked them together for all time. With a rush of deep regret, she realized how much she longed for that link to be one of love, not duty or honor.

Would he ever forgive her?

Jordan lay with his arms crossed above his head, staring at the ceiling. His thoughts were as tangled as Valerie's past. His brain buzzed with a dozen questions. Possibilities sprang up like mushrooms, some as poisonous as the deadliest variety. People and how they fit in Valerie's life danced in his head—Janine Livaudais, Oscar Diaz, Kelly Lott, the Sisters of St. Francis. And even as he tried to hold on to anger and frustration, he couldn't shut out the picture of her lying in the next room. Nor could he deny the way his body stirred at the thought of having her. Or the hope that she would open up, tell him something that might explain everything.

He was a fool living on hope lately. Hope that the attack on Charlie and Sara would yet turn up a clue. Hope that what eventually emerged wouldn't mean the end of a relationship barely begun. Hope that the next time the stalker struck, it would not be to kill again.

He may as well hope to win the lottery.

He went still at a soft sound from down the hall. Then Valerie appeared, moving tentatively into the doorway, backlit in the glow of a small nightlight in the hall. She wore another of those silky kimonos, like the one Oscar Diaz had ripped off her in his assault. Even in his panic, Jordan had been aware of her breasts, the color of cream and the feel of silk. His body went tight now with the memory of what had come afterward when he'd touched and tasted and pleasured every sweet inch of her.

"Did I wake you?" she asked, still hovering at the door.

"No."

"I wanted to—I mean, ah . . . I'd like to talk to you for a minute."

"You'll need to come a little closer." He rose on one elbow and patted the bed beside him. She came into the room, still moving with uncertainty, as if she might yet change her mind. "Just let me get this lamp . . ." He reached to find the switch.

"No." Quick enough on that. "No, this will be easier in the dark, I think." She waited until he settled back, then sat gingerly on the side of the bed, facing him, one leg tucked beneath her.

A small mantel clock in her living room chimed the hour. Three A.M. She rubbed her arms as if chilled. "Are you cold?" he asked, lifting the sheet. "Here, let me—"

She touched his hand. "No, I'm just—nervous."

He nodded. "I'm not surprised. This whole business is enough to rattle anyone's nerves. But if you're worried about Sara, don't be. Charlie's on red alert now. She's in good hands."

"I know." He heard a faint smile in her voice. "You Case men make nice bodyguards."

"What was it you wanted to say, Val?"

"I know you think what happened to Charlie is my fault. I accept that. I—"

"Whoa." He put a hand on her knee. "You never heard me say that."

"No, but it's plain that you believe it. And you're furious. I don't blame you. If the situation were reversed and I thought Sara was nearly killed because of something you did, I'd be furious, too."

"I'm frustrated, Val, not furious. A psycho is out there and we don't know when or where he'll strike again. I'm trying to figure out his next move, but it's like working on a puzzle with a few vital pieces missing. It's . . . frustrating."

"And you think I'm withholding those pieces. I'm not, Jordan. At least, I'm not aware of anything. And that's what I came in here to tell you."

"You've told me that a dozen times."

"But I've left out . . . facts that I'd rather keep to myself."

"Such as . . ."

"Facts about Sara."

Valerie turned away, unable to hold his gaze even in the dim glow coming from the hall nightlight. She stared at her hands, struggled to speak around the tightness in her throat. She sensed Jordan waiting, almost holding his breath.

"Sara is—" She stopped, giving a short, humorless laugh. "This is very difficult."

"Maybe I can help." Jordan shifted, stacked two pillows against the headboard, and kicked the covers aside. Then he reached for Valerie and she came willingly—eagerly—settling in the curve of his shoulder and arm. Only then did she realize he was naked.

"I think I know what you're trying to tell me." He spoke the words gently against her temple.

She was shaking her head. "No, you can't—"

"Sara is Amy Trent's child," he said quietly.

She went absolutely still. Only her heart, dropping to the floor, had movement. Then tears sprang into her eyes. She didn't know whether it was relief or confusion or what. Her mind raced with possibilities. If he knew, why hadn't he said something long ago? But how could he know?

One hand moved slowly up and down her arm. Now his chin rested on the top of her head. He seemed to be waiting for her to say something and she quivered with the need to respond. All she had to do was to open up and she'd be enveloped by his warmth, his strength. He was everything secure and reassuring. And he knew.

She wanted to burst into tears with the sheer relief that someone else knew.

"Wondering how I figured it out, hmm?"

"I . . . Yes." She wiped tears from her eyes with her fingers. "I guess I am."

"It was the only explanation. Everyone we talked to knew about Amy's pregnancy, which was well advanced when she died. No one ever mentioned you being pregnant. I knew Sara was born in New Orleans. She told me that three years ago when we first met. You left New Orleans the same week that Amy died. I think you took her baby rather than allow Oscar to toss her in a Dumpster and leave her to die."

"That's exactly what he meant to do," she whispered fiercely. "He was evil. He had no thought for anyone except himself. Amy's value to him on the street would have been reduced with a baby. So when Amy died, the baby had to go."

"Was Oscar the father?"

She plucked at the sheet with unsteady fingers. "No one knows. Amy said she wasn't sure. You saw him, he has a dark complexion and nearly black eyes. I don't think Sara looks anything like him, do you?" She shifted to give him an anxious look.

"No. She seems very fair. She could be your daughter."

"She is my daughter!"

His hold tightened and he kissed the top of her head. "I know, sweetheart."

"Oscar forced Amy into prostitution. It was most probably one of the johns."

"Probably."

"And I never worked the streets for him," she said fiercely. "He pushed and pushed, but I was never that desperate."

Both his arms went around her, crossing beneath her

breasts. "I think I guessed that, too. It's hard to feign inexperience." He dropped a kiss on her cheekbone. "When we made love, you just didn't act like a lady of the night."

There was a smile in his voice, but she was crying again. "I did things as a runaway that I'm ashamed of, Jordan, but I wouldn't have Sara if I hadn't been there at that moment in time. So I can't regret it." Using the corner of the sheet, she blotted more tears. "Still, it haunts me. And the other thing I needed to say is about Charlie. I'm so sorry, Jordan."

"Do you think you know something that would have prevented the hit-and-run?"

"No!"

"Then no apology is necessary."

"But I feel responsible. I know it's the same person who's calling me and breaking into my house. He's close, Jordan. He might even be an employee at the magazine. How else to explain the acts of sabotage going on there?"

"I think you're right."

She shuddered. "It's so terrifying. I don't know where it's coming from. I don't know who it could be. I don't know where he'll strike next. I don't know anything and I feel so . . . so helpless. So scared!"

Jordan heard the anguish in her voice and his heart swelled painfully. Where was his stubborn, willful, defiant Valerie now? He stroked her hair, rubbed the soft skin at the nape of her neck. "You do know something, sweetheart. You just don't realize it."

He felt her go still. He'd been careful to allay her guilt about Charlie and her checkered past, but he was convinced that she held the key to flushing out the stalker, if only she could find the courage—or trust him enough—to bring it out into the light of day.

"What do I know, Jordan?"

He shifted just enough to tilt her face up and meet her eyes. "That's for you to work out, Val. Sooner or later, you're going to have to dredge the depths of your past, no matter how hard it might be."

She was shaking her head, not looking at him. "I don't know anything. I don't!"

He bent and kissed her temple. "It'll come in time, Val. Trust me."

As she settled back, a corner of his mouth lifted in a bitter half-smile. Trust was a commodity missing in their relationship. It hurt that she still held back, but she'd taken a major step tonight. He wanted to mean more to her than a dependable protector.

"Will you make love to me?" she asked, shifting and placing a hand on his chest.

Or a good lay.

But what he said was, "Just try to stop me."

He thought what she was asking for had little to do with sex, but with her body, warm and giving, pressed to his as close as two people could get, it felt like sex. He wanted to please her. He wanted to allay all her fears, to take her so far out of herself that she would forget her past. The need was basic and fundamental. It shook him to realize what that kind of need meant.

He caught her face in his hands and kissed her softly. It suited him as well as her to lose himself in passion tonight. He was tired of trying to coax confidences from her. Tonight he'd settle for coaxing a mind-blowing climax.

The cynic in him disappeared at the first touch of the feather-soft kisses she was sprinkling across his chest. And when she touched her tongue to one nipple, his restraint fled in a wild gust. He fell back, allowing her full range to explore his body, but soon he was gritting his teeth and fighting his own climax. She reached down and cupped him, smiling as a helpless shudder went through him. She was soft and seductive, her newfound boldness as thrilling as any courtesan. Need pounded in his chest like a jackhammer. If he didn't stop her now—

He groaned and slipped a hand beneath her hair to tilt her face up and kiss her again, this time not so gently. It was hot and hungry, a deep, soul-searching blending of mouths and bodies and mutual need. He pushed the kimono off, baring her breasts and belly and long, long legs. He brought her mouth to his again in a deeply possessive kiss while his hand kneaded her breasts, soft as ripe peaches, the nipples tight and sensitive. She moaned and moved restlessly, then with a soft, strangled sound, she caught his hand and dragged it down.

"Is this what you want, sweetheart?" His fingers moved to the juncture of her thighs. Opening the folds, he found her warm and dewy. She whimpered, pressing her face into his throat, moving against his hand as he probed the bud of her desire. And then she climaxed, coming apart in his hands. His heart gave a leap even as it ached. She wanted him, he would have to be satisfied with that for now. But even as he turned her, mounted her, found his place, and plunged deeply into her, he knew he would not find complete satisfaction. That would happen only when he had her heart.

Long after Jordan slept, Valerie lay awake. Her body still hummed with arousal. Ached in delicious places. She'd wanted this, but couldn't believe what she'd done. Asking outright. For years, self-control had been her mantra. To let go meant ruin. Hadn't that wild abandon once dragged her to the depths? But something stronger than self-restraint had driven her tonight. She couldn't share the ugliness of her past, but she could share her body. Between the two of them, they could share passion and comfort, if only that.

She turned with her cheek resting on her hands and watched Jordan as he slept. Maybe there would be regrets, for he would still demand facts, details, truths pulled from the mists of her memory. But that would be tomorrow. The need that had overwhelmed her tonight had been irresistible.

CHAPTER
TWENTY-FIVE

"What's your schedule like today?" Jordan said, punching the elevator up to the *Panache* offices. While the taxi waited, he'd insisted on accompanying her all the way to her door, where he planned to leave her under Eric's watchful eye until lunchtime.

"You can't keep this up, Jordan," she complained, ignoring the question about her schedule. She stepped into the elevator. "You've got a life, a job. Playing bodyguard is not necessary. I've promised to be careful."

"I'm not playing. And neither is the psycho who's out there getting closer and more daring. Until he makes a mistake and shows his hand, we can't take chances. I hope you'll be careful. Don't go anywhere alone, even if it's to the deli downstairs." He reached for his Palm Pilot and popped it open. "Now, what's on your schedule today?"

"Lots of things. It's packed. We're close to deadline on several features." Hefting her briefcase, she removed a sheaf of papers.

"You didn't forget the appointment with Judge Martindale, did you? Denise set it up for two this afternoon. She knows I'll be going with you."

Avoiding his eyes, Valerie thumbed through several of the pages. "I'm not interrupting a packed schedule just to stroke some judge's ego. If you recall, I never wanted to do the feature in the first place. But since you're so keen on doing it, you can accompany Denise."

"He wants to meet the editor of the magazine," Jordan reminded her.

"When he finds out who you are, he'll forget he ever asked for me."

Now Jordan was watching her carefully. "Okay, what's the deal here?" he said as the elevator doors slid open. "Is it the feature or is it Martindale himself?"

"I think I've made myself clear from the outset about Denise's ideas. They're mediocre. When she comes up with something more original, I'll be the first to applaud."

He stopped her with a hand on her arm, blocking the open doors with the other. "So it's Denise."

She sighed. "Jordan, I have a very trying day in front of me. I'd like to get started."

He studied her intently for a long moment, sensing more in her rejection of the Martindale feature than she revealed. "I haven't overruled you on many things, but I want you at that meeting today, Val." He said it more to gauge her reaction than from any real desire to honor Martindale's request.

"I don't think so," she said, looking at him defiantly.

"We'll discuss it later." The main corridor of the magazine was no place to challenge her. With his hand keeping the elevator in place, he added, "Remember to be on your guard today. I've got a feeling the stalker is spiraling out of control. If he shot Oscar Diaz in New

Orleans, then it was very risky to zip straight back to
New York to hurt Charlie or Sara."

"Did you hear me, Jordan? I'm not going to that
hotel."

He reached out, heedless of anybody watching, and
brought her so close that their lips were within a whisper
of touching. "Don't think because you called the shots
last night you can defy me today, sweetheart." Then he
kissed her, hard. "Be ready at a quarter to two."

Valerie detoured to the powder room to collect herself. She had no intention of accompanying Jordan to
Edward Martindale's hotel because she planned a private visit to the judge before that. It was the only way.
It might be a wasted effort. He might call her bluff, but
she had run out of options. She'd deal with Jordan
afterward. If he was still speaking to her. Or if she still
had a job.

Eric stood up as she entered the office. "You're going
to just have a kitten today, boss," he said, following her
through the inner door. "The shit has hit the fan ten
different ways. Chaos reigns."

Office gossip. *She didn't have time for this!* She dropped
her briefcase on her desk. "Be a little more specific,
Eric."

Eric sat down, eager to comply. "Someone trashed
the coffee room, can you believe that? Sugar in the
watercooler, creamer in the coffeepot, all those little
packets of ketchup, mustard, and mayo squashed on
the floor." He shuddered. "A real mess."

"What kind of joke was that?" she asked with a grimace.

"No joke. It was real vandalism, Val. I think it's the
person who messed up the photo lab a few weeks ago."

She sat down slowly. "Was Security notified?"

"Of course." He rolled his eyes. "For what it's worth." He scooted his chair closer. "Second item: Greg is flipping out."

She frowned. "Greg?"

"He came in early this morning, he found Denise snooping at his computer. They almost came to blows! You know how he guards that thing as if it contains the secrets of the universe. Well, I had to step between them, darling. It was a very nasty scene."

She sighed. "Where is Greg now?"

"He said to tell you he's taking the day off to decide whether he wants to work here anymore."

She sat back in her chair, relieved that it was Denise and not her stalker who'd ticked off Greg. She'd have to try and persuade him not to quit. He'd become vital to the magazine. As for Denise, this was exactly the kind of thing Valerie needed to get rid of her. Hal might resist, but if Jordan went along with it, she'd be rid of Denise, once and for all.

"Any good news?" she asked, expecting none.

"Roxanne is Miss Sunshine once again."

In the act of opening her briefcase, she paused and looked at Eric, who was making kissing noises. "Oh, what's her name is back?" she guessed.

"Her one and only A.J. has returned," he intoned, nodding and lifting his eyebrows meaningfully.

If Roxanne was correct, A.J. had been the one to feed the Martindale feature to Denise. Valerie had hoped for an opportunity to talk to Roxanne's lover about it. She made a mental note to try and arrange lunch or cocktails with the two women. "I've never met A.J.," she reminded Eric. "If she shows up here again, let me know, will you?"

"Oh, she'll show." He stood, brushing a few specks of lint from his pants. "To meddle, if nothing else. That is one irritating bitch."

* * *

In the end, it wasn't difficult for Valerie to slip away without anyone knowing. It was about midmorning when she sent Eric to the photo lab to get a mock-up of a feature, which she knew wasn't ready. She then grabbed her coat and bag, zipped downstairs in the elevator, and hailed a taxi. Within twenty minutes, she was at the registration desk in Martindale's hotel.

Calling him from the house phone, she identified herself as a staff person from *Panache* magazine. He agreed to see her without hesitation and invited her to come straight up.

Her hands were cold and her mouth was dry as she stood outside Martindale's hotel room waiting for a response to her quick knock. There was no peephole, of course, so he would not be able to see her face and thereby refuse to let her in. Or would he even recognize her at all, she wondered, passing the tip of her tongue over dry lips. Nontheless, her nerves were screaming by the time he opened the door.

She wasn't sure what she'd expected. Naturally he was much older, twenty-three years older, but he was still a handsome man. His hair was no longer black, but a distinguished silver-gray. He seemed fit except for a puffiness beneath his eyes, but only someone who knew his corrupt past might see beyond the facade. Smiling with practiced ease, he ushered her inside. Clearly, he did not recognize her.

"I'm Valerie Olivier-Long," she told him, watching his reaction closely.

"Ahh, I'm delighted to meet you," he said, putting out his hand. "You're even more beautiful than you appear in the media."

So he did know what she looked like and had not made the connection with a scared fourteen-year-old

stepdaughter. Valerie pretended not to see his extended
palm and walked quickly past him into the luxurious
suite. When she turned to face him again, he wore a
polite look of puzzlement. "Did I get my wires crossed,
Ms. Long? Weren't we scheduled to meet at two this
afternoon with your journalist—what is her name?"

"Denise Grantham."

"Yes, yes. And Jordan Case, Kurtz-Whitman's second
in command."

"When you hear what I have to say," she told him,
"that meeting might not be necessary."

"What do you mean?" Still frowning, he was studying
her more closely. Without waiting for a reply, he gave
a short, puzzled laugh. "It's funny. You seem somehow
. . . familiar. Have we met?"

"You truly don't recognize me, do you, Edward?"

Something flashed quickly in his eyes. Shaking his
head, he said, "I . . . don't think so."

"Then perhaps you should sit down." Feeling more
confident suddenly, Valerie slipped her bag from her
shoulder and dropped it on an exquisite Sheraton sofa.
Why had she worried about this snake for so many years?
"I'm Caroline Weston."

"Caroline—" For the space of a moment, he seemed
genuinely confused.

"Hannah's daughter," she explained patiently. "The
rebellious teenager who saw you commit murder."

Martindale's heavy brows snapped together as he eyed
her suspiciously. A dull flush appeared on his neck,
then moved up to his face. "This is ridiculous!" he
blustered. "Caroline's been missing for over twenty
years. She . . . we . . . we thought she was dead."

"Don't you mean you hoped I was dead?"

He drew himself up with dignity. "If this is a joke,
madam, I don't find it amusing."

"I wasn't amused to be thrust into the world as a

scared kid either. Or forced to run away and survive on my own after you threatened to kill me. A fourteen-year-old girl is in dire jeopardy under those circumstances."

"I never threatened to kill you!"

"I was the only witness when you murdered that man in cold blood. I don't think you could afford to let me live."

"This is preposterous! I don't know what you're talking about. What man?"

Valerie was feeling stronger now, more confident. This was less harrowing than she'd feared. Martindale was less intimidating than she remembered. "I believe his name was Stephen Parks. Of course, it was only after I finished college and started to work that I was able to do serious research to identify him. There was a businessman in Chicago named Stephen Parks who disappeared in 1976. According to his family, he'd been despondent over financial issues. It was suspected that he might have committed suicide, leaving no means of identification." She saw his Adam's apple bob as he swallowed nervously. "But you and I know he didn't commit suicide, don't we, Judge? Stephen Parks was murdered. By you."

"I didn't murder anybody, missy!"

"Missy . . ." She managed a bitter laugh. "You always called me missy when we argued, but I'm not fourteen years old anymore, Edward. I don't threaten so easily now."

Martindale pulled at his shirt collar, stretching his neck to ease his discomfort, but his reply was still forceful. "If you're thinking of trying to trip me up with silly references to the past, think again. I'm admitting nothing. And as long as we're talking secrets here, I don't see how you can do anything with this tale without damaging your own public image. You'd have to admit you've been masquerading under a false name for more than twenty years. There'd be hell to pay from your superiors."

"And I can't see you surviving the scandal if I reveal what I know." She moved to a desk where he'd been scribbling notes for the upcoming feature. "Even so, I find it isn't as frightening as I thought to reveal my past. I was a scared kid. I believe there would be some sympathy for a fourteen-year-old in my shoes. But you, sir, are a murderer."

Brows beetling, his eyes glittered with hatred. "Then what exactly is the point of this visit?"

"For starters, I want to know if you've been calling me, harassing me personally, and doing acts of vandalism at my home and at the magazine. Were you at Rose Haven and did you kill Janine?"

His jaw dropped. Confusion mixed with the anger on his face. "I don't have the faintest idea what you're talking about. Who is Janine? What is Rose Haven?"

She didn't bother to explain. She hadn't really believed he was her stalker anyway.

"The second point," she continued, "is to force your withdrawal from the feature planned in *Panache.*"

"Why should I do that?"

"Because if you don't, I'm prepared to tell the police that I saw you murder Stephen Parks in cold blood. I'll reveal everything I suspect about your business dealings with him and your connections to the mob in your law practice at the time. I don't think a public relations bonus in a national magazine is as valuable as your entire career, which would go down the drain. Your cushy life has been built on lies, deceit, and murder. A few words from me will destroy everything you value."

"Who're you to talk about living a lie?" he sneered, but he was obviously shaken. Sweat glistened on his forehead. "Who would believe you?"

"Enough people so that your career would be over,

Edward, trust me on that." She swept up her bag from the sofa. Why had she waited all these years to face him down? He was pathetic. At the door, she turned back. "You've escaped punishment for murder, but only because I was young and too terrified to tell what I saw. I'm no longer that frightened kid. And I'm willing to bet you won't jeopardize everything that's important to you for ten minutes of fame in my magazine."

"You won't get away with this!" he raged. "I'll call Hal Kurtz, see what he has to say about you misrepresenting yourself. If you lied about that, you've lied about other things."

Valerie heard the bluster in his tone and recognized it as a last attempt to save face. She'd won. He wouldn't call Hal. He didn't dare. But she was not in a generous mood. She stopped, removed her hand from the doorknob, and faced him again squarely, needing to defeat him utterly. "Does this mean," she asked coldly, "that you refuse to phone Denise and tell her you've decided to forgo the feature in *Panache*?"

Faced with an ultimatum, Martindale's gaze was the first to fall. "The magazine's a piece of shit anyway," he hissed. "Now get the hell out of here!"

Ten minutes later, Valerie settled back in a taxi, closed her eyes, and waited for her shaky insides to calm. One nasty errand done, one more to go, although when she finally connected with Angela LeBlanc, she couldn't expect the outcome to be as gratifying as defeating Edward Martindale.

Revenge, however, left a bitter taste. Many times in years past, she'd imagined the scene with her stepfather taking place, but in her fantasies she was always elated by the outcome. He was a pathetic, dishonorable, despicable man and a disgrace to the exalted position he held. If there had been a way to force him to resign from the bench, she would have demanded that. But any leverage she had over him hinged upon his lust to remain a part of the judicial system. It was some comfort that he knew she had survived and was not powerless, so he would never quite be able to take his position for granted.

Turning her head, she watched pedestrians hurrying by as she neared her office building. Denise would be puzzled over Martindale's abrupt about-face, but Valerie cared less about what she thought than Jordan's reaction. Already he sensed something more in her reluctance to pursue the feature than she let on. But she might be relieved of telling him anything since Denise was bound to go straight to the top—to Hal or to Jordan—when she learned the feature was in jeopardy. Tough.

She remembered she'd turned her cell phone off to prevent Eric or anyone else from distracting her as she faced Martindale. Studying it now, she saw several calls missed—two from Eric, three from Jordan, and one that she didn't recognize, although there was no voice mail message left. As her brow puckered in thought, the phone rang.

"This is Valerie."

"I thought we had an agreement, Valerie," Angela LeBlanc said. "I'd give you some time to think over my proposition and you'd stand by ready for my call. I even gave you a little leeway and then you're nowhere around when I pick up the phone. Am I going to have to come up to your office and we discuss this deal face to face, sugar?"

Valerie pinched the bridge of her nose. Great. The second of two despicable characters in her life back to back within ten minutes. "Sorry to have missed you,

Angela," she said through set teeth. "I had . . . other business that couldn't be delayed."

"Hey, I understand you're a very busy executive person, making big decisions, managing your magazine, controlling all that money. But . . ."

"But what?" Valerie repeated, expecting the worst.

"But I need to be convinced you're taking me as seriously as your career."

"I'm taking you seriously, Angela."

"Because," she went on, "you have a lot on the line here."

Valerie waited in silence.

"For example, there's the small secret we share about your little Sara," she said slyly.

"We've been over this, Angela. More threats aren't necessary. I believe you. And Sara isn't little anymore. Even if she did find out, I think she's strong enough to hear the truth."

"Oooh, getting a little feisty, aren't we? But maybe you aren't so quick to give up this bogus life you've been living. A lot of folks would find it interesting reading. I mean, here you are a woman at the pinnacle of success and"—her voice dropped to add in a theatrical tone—"living a big lie! Hey, it's tabloid stuff, but since it strikes so close to home, I bet somebody at *Panache* would be interested."

"As I said, I understand the threat. You'll destroy my career and my daughter's innocence without a hint of conscience unless I pay up."

"Well, that's putting it in pretty raw language," Angela said, sounding genuinely offended.

"How else should I put it?"

Angela sighed. "This sparring is getting us nowhere, sugar. Look, like I told you before, prices where I'm staying are way out of my league . . . that is, until I've got an extra twenty thousand in my hands. You do have the money, don't you?''

"I certainly haven't forgotten the reason we're meeting, Angela.''

"Good. That's good. Now, there's a Chinese restaurant on the corner of—'' She paused. ''Wait a minute. I've got a map.''

Valerie's stomach was again in a knot. Unlike with Edward Martindale, she had no leverage to control Angela's demands, whatever they turned out to be. Except for money, there was nothing she could offer to appease the PI without entering into a sleazy partnership that could—would—last for years and eventually drain her dry financially. Blackmailers never let a victim off the hook. Damn it, there had to be a way out of this! She was sick of being a victim.

"Get that, sugar?''

The location? While she'd been obsessing, Angela had been talking. Valerie scurried to backtrack mentally. A Chinese restaurant . . . where? Rubbing her forehead now, she asked the location again, then promised to meet Angela as soon as the taxi could get there. She was suddenly anxious to hear the woman's terms.

"How will I know you?'' she asked, wondering when this nightmare would end.

Angela chuckled with real amusement. ''Well, I don't know how I could come up with a red carnation or something like that to wear in my lapel—if I had a lapel—but my purse is an animal print. Zebra. I'll have it propped square in the middle of the table. Can't miss it.''

Angela quickly tossed off the last of her martini, not bothering to muffle a satisfied burp. Ignoring the disgusted irritation emanating her way from the group at

the next table, she caught the eye of the Asian waiter
to order a third drink, glanced blearily at her watch,
then decided she had time to go to the ladies room
before Valerie showed up. Grabbing her purse, she rose
and made her way clumsily through the packed tables.
Her bladder simply wasn't what it used to be, she
thought, pushing into the dimly lit toilet. Gin gave her
a helluva hangover, too, unless she drank a ton of water,
which took the fun off the buzz and made her need to
pee even more often.

As she headed for an empty stall, she caught a glimpse
of herself in the mirror above the sink and shuddered
at the sight. God, she could pack for a week's vacation
with those bags beneath her eyes. Guess it'd been a
mistake to stay so long in the hotel bar last night, but,
hell, she'd felt like celebrating. This time tomorrow,
she'd be on her way back home to New Orleans a rich
woman. Or at least a well-fixed woman. So her bladder
was aging and her capacity for booze was waning, plus—
to be honest—she was looking every day of her forty-
seven years. A steady income and plastic surgery would
go a long way to making it all bearable. She heard
someone else enter and next thing, the light was
snapped off. Grumbling, she rose, thinking the place
was already too dim to see shit and adjusted her clothes,
then flushed, fumbling in the dark for the handle. She
finally found the latch on the stall door and stepped
out.

It was almost pitch dark now except for a sliver of
light coming through a crack in the window mounted
high above eye level. But Angela sensed somebody
nearby. Squinting, she finally made out a shape near
the sink. "This is really crappy, huh?" she said, laughing
at her own joke. "If they wanted to go cheap, they could
have cut out the fortune cookies. Or the toilet paper.
We could drip dry. How much does a lightbulb cost?"

"It wasn't the restaurant," the newcomer said in a cool tone. "I turned out the light."

"Huh?"

"And I've wedged the door shut to keep everybody else out while we talk."

"You—" Her mouth fell open. "What the hell . . ."

The next words were soft and menacing. "You made a big mistake prying into Valerie Olivier's life, Angela."

Though an alcohol fog, Angela could see only a murky silhouette in dark shirt and pants, heavy boots, a baseball cap. "Who the fuck are you?"

A hand came up, quick and emphatic. "Save the bluster for somebody who gives a shit. I'll do the talking now, you'll listen."

"In your dreams, you—" Angela had a only a split-second to move before she saw the knife. She stopped short. "What the hell is going on here? That's a knife!" Then, in a flash, the knife was at Angela's waist. She risked taking a stab in the gut if she dashed for the door.

"Gosh, yeah. This is a knife." Smiling, the stranger swayed from one foot to the other in a macabre dance, the blade moving lazily back and forth through air, catching the tiny glint of light visible at the window.

"Hey, I don't want no trouble." Angela took a cautious step back and bumped against the stall door.

"Valerie belongs to me, you stupid lush!" The knife flashed now as the words were hissed in fury.

"Just tell me what I can do to fix things and I'm outta here." Another step and she'd be inside the stall. Would that be smart, Angela wondered, trying to think her way out of this mess. Or would this nut follow her inside the stall and kill her there? Her voice took on a wheedling tone. "I'll forget I ever heard of Valerie Olivier, honest to God."

"But will you forget Caroline Weston?"

Angela frowned, shook her head, trying to clear it. "Who?"

"Or Amy Trent?"

"Amy Trent?"

Head cocked. "Do I hear an echo?" Cold laugh. "Okay, try this one: Baby Sara."

Oh, shit. How to talk herself out of dying? "Listen, I'm just an innocent bystander in all this. I read about the case in the paper, for Christ sake! I'm a PI. I snoop into people's business. It's what I do. But whoever you are, I can see I'm in over my head here." Angela put her hands out, warding off disaster. "I'll board that plane, I'll forget all I know about this shit."

The knife danced closer. "Oh, you'll forget about this shit, alright." The words came even softer, made more chilling by the brief there-and-then-gone flick of light on the blade. "But there's a price to be paid by all who've had a part in Valerie's treachery. Didn't you learn anything when Oscar died? And Janine? They had to pay and so do you, Angela."

Angela's heart was racing. An urgent need to pee again was on her. She thought of her gun, ordinarily never far from her hand, but now useless back in her apartment in New Orleans. "You killed them all?"

"I killed them all."

The thrust was so quick, she didn't see it coming. Even braced to expect it any second, she was still caught by surprise. Shock froze on her face as pain exploded in her middle, sharp and excruciating. A last, startled gasp was choked off by a gush of blood welling up into her throat. Then she was falling, sliding slowly down the framework of the toilet stall, eyes fixed on the silhouette of her killer.

The knife was slashing now, plunging again and again in frenzied rage, but Angela had slipped into a near-death state where, oddly, her mind still functioned. Why, after her excellent investigative brilliance in this case, she thought bitterly, hadn't she anticipated this? And what was with the stupid disguise? The dark. Turn on the fucking light, she demanded in her head. Have the guts to show me your face. Most galling of all was to die without knowing the name of her killer.

The drive to the restaurant took almost an hour. Lunch accounted for the increased traffic, both from pedestrians and on the street. Then, a block from the restaurant, traffic came to a standstill, blocked by a police car. Craning forward in the taxi, she saw that the whole area was crawling with official vehicles. With a sense of foreboding, she quickly paid the driver and set out on foot, spotting an ambulance, a fire truck, and three additional police cars as she neared the restaurant. A crowd was gathered out front, but held well back from the activity going on by yellow crime-scene tape strung in a semicircle around the restaurant's entrance and the sidewalk approach. Apparently, there had been some kind of incident.

In such a crowd, it was difficult to see much of anything, but she scanned the bystanders anxiously. There was no woman carrying a distinctive zebra purse. Asking no questions, she made her way toward a knot of people closer to the entrance, picking up scraps of conversation as she went.

"A stabbing . . ."

"Happened in the ladies room . . ."

". . . at a table eating and suddenly this woman came out of the bathroom screaming like a banshee."

". . . from the waiter who said blood was everywhere. I used to work in an ER and I can tell you a knife wound, if it's in the right place . . ."

For a long moment, Valerie stood watching the

entrance, where the movements of paramedics and police could be seen. She wanted to leave, but a premonition of disaster rooted her to the spot. Unconsciously, she pressed her fingers to her mouth as a sick feeling roiled her stomach. Now two paramedics emerged carrying someone on a stretcher. The body was draped with a sheet pulled over the victim's head.

"Covered up like that, she's dead for sure," said a twenty-something runner, sitting astride his bicycle.

A cop followed behind the paramedics carrying a clear plastic bag stuffed with bloody towels and other medical waste. A ripple of horror went through the crowd, but Valerie was beyond hearing. Her eyes were riveted on the article the cop carried in his other hand.

"The deceased's effects," someone murmured close to Valerie.

A woman's animal print handbag. Zebra.

CHAPTER
TWENTY-SIX

"You are in trouble, lady," Eric said as Valerie, shaky and queasy in the stomach, walked into the office half an hour later. He gave a nod of his head to the closed inner door and spoke in a confidential tone. "Jordan's inside making phone calls to everybody in your Rolodex trying to find you."

"I had urgent personal business." She avoided Eric's quick, sharp appraisal and picked up the sheaf of pink telephone messages stuck in a wire holder on his desk. But her hands were shaking so she couldn't read them. She quickly stuffed them in her briefcase.

Something about her struck Eric. He rose, circling his desk, to get a better look at her. "What's wrong, Val? You look as if you're ready to fall to pieces." His blue eyes grew wide. "You've had another scare, haven't you?"

"No! I'm fine." What was one more lie in a life of lies? Her heart was still doing a slow drumbeat and she couldn't banish from her mind's eye the sight of that zebra bag in the hand of a cop. Or the draped form of Angela's body on a stretcher.

"It's the stress of all this," Eric stated, studying her anxiously. "Jordan doesn't think you're treating the threat of this stalker seriously enough, but he doesn't know you as well as I do. I think you're terrified. It's enough to send a person round the bend."

"Yes."

"And you're probably worried about Charlie and Sara."

And anybody else who might have the remotest connection with me.

"All well and good," Eric said, noting the strained look on her face, "but why in God's name did you sneak out and not tell anybody? I got my ass chewed out again by Jordan. It's getting old, let me tell you." He gave a quick shrug. "I mean, there are times when I like this real forceful stuff he dishes out, but not when he's looking wild and . . . well, terrified on your behalf."

"I'll try to be a more model prisoner," she said, but the attempt at sarcasm fell flat. She was feeling pretty terrified herself.

"He's mad about you, Val," Eric said, ignoring the sarcasm. "Haven't you ever been mad about anybody?"

"He's mad *at* me, Eric," she said wearily. And he'd be even more incensed when he found out the PI who was blackmailing her had been murdered. "Before I have to face him, are there any more acts of sabotage or other disasters befalling us while I was out?"

"Everything's a disaster, love, but except for Roxanne grilling me quite sternly about all this stuff and a little dust-up regarding the Martindale thing, we're still in business."

"Martindale?"

The door was jerked open and Jordan stood with his

hands on his hips, a picture of outraged male. "Where the hell have you been?"

He looked fierce and frazzled and unlikely to be kind to a hysterical female. And for one wild and crazy moment, she wanted just to throw herself into his arms and burst into tears. She wanted to feel his arms around her, holding her close. That might not shut out the evil that was closing in, but it would be a welcome buffer against it.

"We can talk in here," she said shakily. Avoiding the dark scowl on his face, she ducked past him and scooted into the safety of her office.

"Hold all calls," Jordan snapped to Eric without taking his eyes off Valerie. He closed the door and stood watching as she put her briefcase in a chair, slipped out of her coat, and hung it on a coat tree in the corner of her office, then went around and sat down behind her desk.

"I'm sorry if I worried you," she said quietly, still not meeting his eyes. "It was unavoidable."

He moved away from the door and sat down opposite her. "It wasn't just that I was worried. I got over that when Martindale called and said he was having second thoughts about doing the feature. When Denise questioned him—"

"He called Denise, not you?"

"When Denise questioned him," Jordan continued with only a minute pause, "he told her that upon reconsideration, he decided it would be unseemly for a judge to be profiled in a magazine with the kind of popular appeal that characterized *Panache*. That struck me as odd, so I called him. And in the course of our conversation, he finally admitted that he'd had a little visit from Ms. Olivier-Long, but he declined to give me details. He said he simply decided to avoid what might be questionable publicity."

"I wondered what excuse he would come up with," she murmured.

"You admit you saw him and somehow forced him to back off from the feature?"

"Yes. It turned out to be easier than I thought."

He was staring at her as if he'd never seen her before.

"I want to know what you said to him, Valerie," he said in a dangerously quiet tone. "I want to know why you went to see him privately, before the scheduled appointment this afternoon. I want to know what it is about Martindale personally that made you go to such lengths to kill the feature."

"I've never made a secret of my—"

"Goddamn it!" He surged up out of his chair. "I want the truth, Val. No more of your mysterious little side steps, no more deception and secrecy and sneaking around."

Valerie sat with her hands clasped tightly in front of her on the desk. Otherwise he would see how uncontrollably they were still shaking. "I suppose Denise was crushed. She'll have to go back to Eric or Roxanne or A.J.—" She stopped, recalling that A.J. had fed Denise the original article. And Jordan never was able to find the source of the e-mail that had mysteriously appeared in his mailbox suggesting the Amy Trent feature. Could it have been A.J.? And why was Roxanne grilling Eric about the sabotage in the office? Could she suspect A.J. was involved?

"Is that it? That's all you have to say?"

"What?" She tried to recall what they'd been talking about.

"If I'm boring you—" Jordan stood with his hands on his hips, grim-faced and furious.

"No, I'm sorry. I was just—"

"Then I'd like you to explain a few things, Val. And I'd like a straight answer. I'd like to know what the hell is wrong that you're pale as a sheet and look as if you're ready to fall apart.'' He leaned forward, both hands on her desk, and waited, forcing her to finally look directly at him. It was then that he saw the shattered look in her eyes.

In a heartbeat, his whole demeanor changed. ''What is it? What's wrong?'' he asked sharply.

''Where to start?'' she murmured, shaking her head helplessly.

''My God, what is it, sweetheart?'' His anger fizzled as quickly as a punctured balloon. He quickly skirted the desk, pulling a chair with him, and sat down facing her.

She looked up at him, drew a deep breath, and spread both hands in a gesture of utter despair. ''Angela LeBlanc has been murdered,'' she said.

The private investigator had never crossed his mind as a possibility when trying to think why Valerie had left the building. ''When?'' he asked, his mind buzzing with questions. ''How?'' A thought suddenly struck him. ''Were you involved?''

Her mouth trembled. ''Only in the sense that people who know me and my past are dying and Angela was one of them.''

He sat trying to fit new pieces of the puzzle in the right slots. ''How did you find out?''

''I—She set a time and place to meet me, a Chinese restaurant. When I got there, she was being carried out on a stretcher. Someone said she was stabbed in the bathroom.''

''How do you know she was dead?''

She gave a vague wave of her hand. ''People were talking. Some had been inside the restaurant when it happened. They said . . .'' She shuddered, remembering the bag of soiled articles. ''There was a lot of blood.''

''People survive even if they lose a lot of blood.''

"Her whole body was covered when the stretcher was wheeled out." Valerie wrapped her arms around herself, chilled at the memory. "She was dead, Jordan."

"And you're sure it was Angela LeBlanc?"

"I think so. When we arranged to meet, I asked how I'd recognize her and she told me to look for her purse, a zebra animal print. It was in the effects of the victim being carried out by a policeman."

He sat for a moment imagining how she must have felt arriving for a meeting and finding the PI murdered. "Why were you going to meet Angela?"

Tears sprang into her eyes as she drew a long breath. "She planned to start blackmailing me."

"Blackmail." As she gave a single nod, he sat back. "She found out about Sara?"

"Yes."

A whole host of emotions swirled around inside him. He was stunned to find how much it hurt that she hadn't turned to him when everything she valued was in jeopardy. What about the danger of meeting a blackmailer? What about the risk when leaving the safety of the building?

"You were willing to pay her to keep Sara from knowing she isn't your natural child?" he asked.

"There's so much more than that, Jordan," she said quietly. "You may want to wash your hands of anything remotely connected to me and my life when you hear—"

She was interrupted by sounds of an altercation in the outer office. Eric's voice was raised in an angry exchange with a woman. Muttering an oath, Jordan got up, walked to the door, and jerked it open. "What's going on out here?"

"Nothing I can't handle," Eric said grimly, giving Denise Grantham a dark look. "Denise insists on seeing both you and Val. I told her it wasn't a good time, but she was going to barge in the office anyway!''

"What is it, Denise?" Jordan asked impatiently.

Denise hissed an obscenity at Eric, then pulled at her jacket and adjusted the cuffs of her blouse as she spoke to Jordan. "I just couldn't believe that Judge Martindale was serious when he called, Jordan. I decided to try one more time to persuade him to reconsider.''

"I think it's too late for that, Denise. Let him walk. There are other interesting judges in the country. Find a replacement.''

"It's definitely too late," Denise agreed with a gleam in her eye. " 'Cause the good judge is dead.''

Valerie rose abruptly from her chair, pressing a hand over her heart. Eric's jaw dropped.

"Dead?" Jordan repeated with a fierce scowl.

"Yeah," Denise said, gleefully noting three stunned reactions. "Pretty interestin', huh? I thought something was just too fishy about him decidin' out of the blue to cancel and pack up and get out of Dodge. He was thrilled to be in that feature, Jordan. There's no way he would renege unless something really dire came up.'' She gave a slightly hysterical giggle. "What could be more dire than dyin'? And get this. It was no heart attack. Somebody shot him. He was murdered.''

"Charlie, you're supposed to take it easy for the next forty-eight hours!" Sara rushed over and took a length of shelving from him, stood it on end against the wall, and blocked access to the remaining articles inside the carton with her body.

Charlie straightened up, then chucked his wife playfully under her chin. "Haven't you ever heard that old saying that a quiet wife is a pearl among women?''

She wrinkled her nose at him, fighting a smile. "No,

I haven't, but I've heard the one that says sometimes a husband will try the patience of a saint! Charlie, we don't need those bookshelves hung today. Wait until you're feeling better. You have a concussion."

He caught her by the upper arms and set her aside gently. "I'm feeling fine. I laid up for most of the day, that's enough resting. I'll go stir-crazy if I don't do something."

"Go ahead, then. Be foolish." Her pretty mouth curved down in a pout. "But don't blame me if you toss and turn all night with a headache and can't sleep."

He kissed her on the mouth and smiled wickedly. "I can probably think of something better to do in bed than sleeping."

"Promises, promises . . ." With a sassy smile, she reached for a plastic bag containing hardware for the shelves. "If you're determined, at least let me help."

She was ripping the bag open when the doorbell rang. "I bet that's your dad," she said. Dropping a handful of screws in a cup, she started for the door.

"Wait, sweetheart." Charlie stood up. He'd never admit it, but the aftermath of the concussion had left him with a dull ache behind his eyes, hence he wasn't able to move as quickly as usual. Sara got to the door before him. "Don't open it," he told her.

She was standing on tiptoe looking through the peep-hole. "It's flowers!" she cried, reaching for the lock. "Someone's sending you flowers, Charlie. I bet it's from the parents. You were right about that. Something's happening with those two."

Charlie was at her side as she flipped the deadbolt and opened the door. "Oh, roses. They're gorgeous!"

"Charlie Case?" A smile lifted the corners of the woman's mouth as she peered around the lavish arrangement of red roses.

"That's me," Charlie said, a hand anchored at Sara's waist.

"Shall I just put them on that table?" With a hitch of her chin, the woman indicated the small library table standing in the foyer of the apartment. She stepped smoothly inside and carefully placed the large vase in the center of the table. Stepping back, she turned to look at the young couple. "They'll need water."

"Who sent them?" Sara asked, burying her nose in the blooms.

"There's a card." The woman plucked it from the arrangement and handed it to Sara, who started to open it. Watching, Charlie felt vaguely uneasy. There was something about the way the woman looked at Sara. Thinking to get rid of her, he reached into his pocket for his money clip and peeled off a bill.

"We'll take it from here," he said, offering the tip.

"The card is unsigned," Sara said, looking up in confusion.

The woman ignored the tip. "That's because I didn't sign it, Sara," she said with a smile that gave Charlie a distinct chill.

"Do I know you?" Sara asked, studying her face.

"No, but you will. Charlie," she ordered without looking at him. "Close the door."

"Get the hell out of here," Charlie said.

That smile again. "I don't think so." She sidestepped to avoid him as he lunged to grab her. Sara made a startled sound and he felt a rush of adrenaline with the need to protect his wife. He pushed her behind him as pain exploded in his head. Sudden movement was not a good thing with a recent concussion. Then the woman turned and faced him directly. Her eyes were wild, yet she still smiled that eerie grin. He felt panic like the force of a fist in his gut. And then he was looking down the barrel of a gun.

CHAPTER
TWENTY-SEVEN

As soon as Jordan managed to get rid of Denise, Valerie's fragile hold on her emotions broke. "Oh, my God, Jordan, what's happening? Who's doing this?"

He caught her by her arms, pulled her close, and just held her for a long minute. "I'm as much in the dark as you, sweetheart. But you've got to get hold of yourself and think. You're the link between the killer and the people he's murdered. So far, only you and I are aware of this, but someone may have seen you at Martindale's hotel. And if you were standing in the crowd at the restaurant, there will be photos by the press and television. Someone may recognize you."

Trying to calm herself, she stopped, put a hand on her throat. "You're saying I may be a suspect? They may think *I* killed Edward? Or Angela?"

"You were the last person to see Martindale alive. The reason Angela was at that restaurant was to meet with you. If those facts were ever uncovered, you'd have to explain yourself."

"I wasn't the last person to see either of them alive!" she cried. "The killer was."

But who would believe that? She closed her eyes, wondering if anybody would believe her. Would Jordan believe her? Did he think she wanted her secrets to remain hidden badly enough that she would kill to protect them? With a sinking feeling, she realized how crushing it would be if Jordan did believe that.

"Do you think I killed all those people, Jordan?" she asked quietly.

"Of course not." He walked to her and again folded her into a tight embrace. She was trembling and his palm moved along her spine, although his own unease was quickly turning to fear. "But you know who the killer is, Val. We just have to pry it out of your past." He kept coming back to that, racking his brain to find a link, a glimmer of something—anything—as a starting point.

They stood for a moment, swaying together, minds swirling, hearts fearful and aching. Jordan kissed the top of her head and let her go. "I'd better call Charlie and warn him not to let Sara out of his sight. Except for you personally, Sara is the most logical target in your life."

"Not just Sara," she said, pushing a strand of hair behind one ear. "Charlie, too. And you."

A whisper of a smile touched his mouth. "Yeah."

"Call them now, Jordan."

He pulled his cell phone from his pocket and hit a programmed button. "I'm getting their machine," he told Valerie. Then he left a message cautioning Charlie and Sara about leaving the apartment or, if they stayed in, not to open the door to any strangers.

"I probably should have cautioned them about admitting anybody they didn't know extremely well," Jordan said after breaking the connection, "not just strangers.

If this is the same person who's harassing you and is behind the sabotage going on here at the magazine, then it's somebody you know. Somebody you'd recognize, even if you'd never suspect them."

"Yes . . ." Valerie looked thoughtfully out the window. "I had this crazy notion about Roxanne's friend, A.J." She turned back to Jordan. "Did you ever meet her?"

"Yeah, why?"

"Well, she gave the Martindale feature idea to Denise and I wondered if she might have been the source of that e-mail you received suggesting the Amy Trent feature."

"How are the two features related?" he asked.

"And you know my connection with Amy." She gave Jordan a quick glance, then looked away. Taking a breath, she said, "Edward Martindale was my stepfather."

"Edward Martindale was your stepfather?" Jordan was floored. He'd imagined several scenarios, but never so straightforward a connection.

"There was nothing fatherly about Edward," she said, as she twisted her fingers mercilessly. "So I can't feel any grief that he's dead."

Watching her, Jordan guessed at the bitter details she chose to keep to herself. "You and Amy shared similarities in your upbringing. Both of you were from affluent families, both runaways. Were you both molested as children?"

"There was no sexual abuse from Edward. He simply wanted to kill me."

"You want to explain that?" he said, studying her bleak expression.

She went to her desk and sat down. "It's a pretty sordid story, Jordan."

"I'll try not to be judgmental."

"When I was fourteen, Edward had connections to the mob in Chicago. He conspired with them to cheat another client—an honest man—out of his business. He ruined him. Then one night the man appeared at our house, pulled a gun on Edward, and threatened to kill him. I remember thinking how desperate he seemed," she murmured, seeming to look inward, as if examining the old memory. "I felt sorry for him. They wrestled and Edward managed to take the gun. I thought he would call the police or send the man away with a threat or something. Instead he shot him. In cold blood."

Jordan stared, amazed at her cool explanation of the event that had changed her whole life. And then, looking closer, he saw the dark emotion swimming in her eyes and, again, the way her fingers were almost tied in knots in her lap. No, she wasn't cool, she was desperately trying to contain a memory that had turned her life upside down. "You heard everything? You saw this with your own eyes?"

"Yes. I was a kid, so I was horrified. When you see someone murdered, you're supposed to call the police." She gave him a sardonic smile, but now he knew not to take a smile at face value. The memory of that night had to be vivid. "Instead of calling the cops, he began making plans to dispose of the body. He was going to wipe out all evidence that the man had ever been at our house. I argued with him, as usual. What about the man's family? What about justice? I foolishly said I was going to call the police whether he liked it or not. That was when he let me know in no uncertain terms that I was to keep my mouth shut or else." She looked up, met Jordan's gaze squarely. "I was only fourteen, but I was old enough to know he meant it. He was ruthless, he'd never wanted me in the first place. Although he married my mother, he'd considered me a pain in the neck from day one. I knew he couldn't take a chance that I wouldn't tell. Only by killing me could he be sure I was silenced. So I ran away."

Jordan was silent. He already knew about the months she'd spent as a runaway. He knew she'd taken Sara rather than see her disposed of by Oscar Diaz. He knew she's stolen the identity of another baby. Now he knew the reason she'd set out on that path.

He managed a half-smile. "That's some past you've got there, lady."

One shoulder fell in a shrug too casual to be real. "I never wanted anyone to know."

"But now it's caught up with you."

"Uh-huh."

Jordan felt instant loathing for Edward Matindale, the same kind of disgust he'd felt for Oscar Diaz. Valerie was a remarkable woman. She'd survived incredibly negative odds, raised a lovely daughter and built a fabulous career, but someone wanted to see her punished. Why? A twisted, amoral killer wanted . . . what, revenge? Who, in all the tangled web of her past, wanted to see her punished enough to kill? Over and over again.

"You don't think my theory about A.J. is worth looking into?" she asked.

"I'm not willing to dismiss it until we do a little checking." He picked up the phone to call Roxanne.

"I wonder what the A.J. stands for?" Valerie murmured as Jordan spoke into the receiver.

"Roxanne's not in," Jordan said, hanging up with a frown. Something nagged at the back of his mind, but he couldn't quite grasp it. "She told her assistant that A.J. called saying it was an emergency. Roxanne dropped everything and went to meet her."

Worried, Valerie chewed on her lip and stared out the window. "You said Charlie and Sara weren't home. Do you think he's well enough to be out?"

"No, but have you ever tried to keep a twenty-something tied indoors?" Jordan, too, was distracted, still trying to pin down the thought that kept eluding him.

"I think we should call again," Valerie said and reached for the telephone.

"A.J.," Jordan said suddenly, stopping her with a hand over hers at the phone. "It's probably nothing more than coincidence, but Amy Trent's initials were A.J."

"How did you know that? I never knew what her name was."

"I visited Emilie, remember?"

"And . . ."

"It's Amy Juliana Trent." He tapped the top of the desk with a pencil, still frowning in thought. What he was thinking was a stretch, truly beyond the realm of reason. But they were dealing with someone acting beyond the realm of reason.

"I'm going down to Roxanne's office and have a word with her assistant," he said, as he dropped the pen back into the caddy. "Stay here, Val. I'll be back in a few minutes."

"What are you thinking? You aren't saying that Roxanne—"

The expression on his face stopped her. "Oh, my God, not Roxanne." She was shaking her head, her gaze clinging to Jordan's. "No, no, she would never—"

"Not Roxanne," he said grimly. "Amy Juliana."

It took her a second. "A.J.," she repeated dully. "You think A.J. is impersonating Amy Trent?"

"I know it sounds crazy, but it's a possibility. You said yourself that you've never met her even though everybody else at the magazine has. Could it be she's avoiding you for a reason?"

She pressed a hand to her stomach. "What are you saying, Jordan?"

"I don't know, but just stay put for right now, okay?"

His brows went up, waiting until he had a reluctant nod from her, then he left.

She walked restlessly around the room, stopping at the window, staring at the skyline, turning again and pacing more. She couldn't get beyond the incredible possibility that someone was impersonating Amy. What kind of joke was that? Why would anybody impersonate Amy? And was this woman her stalker? Had she murdered Janine? And Oscar? And Angela? And Edward Martindale?

Shocked and stunned at the killer's boldness, she barely heard the ring of her cell phone. Rounding her desk, she opened the drawer where she stored her handbag and finally pulled the phone out.

Please let it be Sara.

"Valerie here," she said breathlessly.

"It's me again," said a voice in singsong tones.

Valerie sank into her chair. "Who . . ." She cleared her voice and tried again. "Who is this?"

"Better ask where, Caroline. I'm a guest in the home of your daughter."

Valerie's heart pounded inside her chest. Her mouth went dry. "You're with Sara now?"

"That has always been the plan." The voice clearly came from a woman. Any desire to hide her gender was apparently over. That fact alone chilled Valerie to the bone.

"If you're really there," Valerie said, "put Sara on the phone. I want to hear her voice."

"I don't have time to do you any favors, Caroline. I'm at the apartment, and both Charlie and Sara are extremely polite hosts. All that's missing in this little gathering is the guest of honor. That's you, Caroline. How soon can you get here?"

Valerie raked a hand through her hair, while the other held the phone tightly. "Why should I do what you say when I can't be sure you're actually there? I don't even know whether Charlie and Sara are even at their apartment. I'm not going anywhere until I hear my daughter's voice, A.J.''

"Oho, you've figured it out, have you?" She covered the phone as she spoke to someone nearby. "Here's your darling daughter."

"M—mom? Is that really you?"

"Sara." Valerie closed her eyes as her heart turned over. "Sara, are you all right?"

"She has a gun, Mom. Don't come over here. She's—''

"I think you get the picture, Caroline," A.J. said, reclaiming the phone. "So get a taxi and come over here . . . right now. And come alone. Figure out a way to sneak past your bodyguard. I don't need to remind you that I have nothing to lose. Nothing."

"Why are you doing this!" Valerie cried.

"Payback, Caroline. Didn't I tell you that weeks ago?"

"For what? Why?"

"I think I'll save that until I can see you face to face. It'll be a hoot, Caroline."

The phone went dead in Valerie's hand. She stared at the blank readout. And then panic set in. The threat had reached Sara as she'd feared all along. And Charlie. She bit down on hysteria threatening to bubble up. She thought longingly of turning to Jordan, but ruthlessly shut out that possibility. Oh, God, oh, God, what should she do? And how could she get away without Jordan knowing?

Her whole body trembled as she took her coat from the coat tree. If she put it on, Eric would know she planned to go outside. Somehow she had to convince him to let her out of his sight. Grabbing her handbag, she tucked the cell phone back into a side pocket and tried to compose herself. Sara's life depended on it.

* * *

Imogene Dunne, Roxanne's assistant, was a short, plump redhead, homely and shy. Jordan stood at her desk, towering over her. "You don't have a clue where she might have gone?" he asked.

She scurried backward in her chair like a little hedgehog. "No, sir. I—Do you want me to help you find something?"

"Only Roxanne," Jordan said through set teeth. "Just find Roxanne."

"Well—"

Jordan shoved back from the woman's desk, realizing that he was unlikely to get anything useful by intimidating her. "Is she in the habit of walking out in the middle of a workday without leaving word where she'll be? Didn't she say anything?"

"She said she might not be back today."

"Why? What was so important?"

Imogene adjusted her glasses, which had slipped down her snub nose. "The—the call was from A.J. She usually responds, well . . . fast when A.J. calls."

Jordan grunted, then allowed his gaze to drift to the inner office and Roxanne's desk. "Where did she take the call?"

"On her telephone, sir," Imogene replied with a look of wary bewilderment.

He tried again, patiently. "I mean, was she at her desk, in here with you, on her cell phone . . . where?"

"Oh, she was at her desk. I saw her take down the address." Imogene's eyes grew wide as a thought struck. "I just remembered! She wrote something as A.J. talked. She seemed nervous, because she had to write the note twice. She threw the first one away."

Jordan was inside Roxanne's office and heading for Rox's desk before Imogene rose from her chair. He found the trash can, hefted it to the desktop, and began rummaging in the waste paper looking for the discarded note. "What did it look like?"

"Yellow. It was a sticky note." Imogene stood nervously watching. "That's it!" She reached for a yellow scrap that Jordan had tossed out with other unlikely stuff and handed it over. Jordan scanned the scribbled note with a scowl. Numbers were crossed out, then rewritten so that it was almost indecipherable, but it was enough to make his heart drop. He was looking at the address of the apartment where Charlie and Sara lived.

Imogene was on tiptoe trying to read the note. "It looks as if she—"

But Jordan was already out of the office and racing down the hall. There was no good reason for A.J. to be at that apartment, but a whole host of bad ones. And each was worse than the next. A.J. and her mysterious connection to Valerie were the key to everything, to the murders, the stalking, the harassing phone calls, he was convinced of it. And she was impersonating Amy Trent.

He felt chilled at the audacity of the woman—whoever she was—as he strode into Valerie's office. "Call a taxi," he told Eric. "And fast. Tell 'em we'll be down in three minutes."

Eric was on his feet. "Where's Valerie?"

With his hand on the door to the inner office, Jordan stopped cold. "Isn't she in here?"

"She said she was going to Roxanne's office." Eric twisted the pen in his hand. "I didn't go with her because I knew you were there."

For a second both stared hard at each other. "She's done it again," Eric whispered, sitting down abruptly.

"You let her leave? You just sat here and let her leave?"

"She—" Eric waved a hand helplessly. "She said

there was no point in having you come back here to get her."

"Goddamn it!" The oath exploded like the blast of a shotgun. But it was terror, not anger, Jordan felt.

"I knew you were in Roxanne's office," Eric said weakly. "That's why—"

Jordan made an effort to stave off panic. "Did she get a phone call? Did she see anybody after I left? Did you—"

"No. No to all that, Jordan," Eric said, recognizing the dark emotion swirling in the gray eyes. "I don't have a clue."

"She's going to Sara," Jordan said. "I don't know how or what she found out, but she's going to see Sara. Alone."

"What—"

But Jordan was already at the door. "Call down and have that taxi ready for me. It's not likely, but if Val calls, tell her not to go to the kids' apartment, no matter what."

"What's happening, Jordan?"

"I wish to hell I knew."

A stranger rode up with Valerie in the elevator. She wanted to stop him before he stepped out and tell him to call the police because a crazy woman was holding her daughter hostage in her apartment. But she was afraid of what A.J. would do if the police stormed the apartment. Would she kill Sara and Charlie believing she had nothing else to lose?

In the end, she watched the stranger leave and leaned against the wall in despair until the elevator stopped.

Once out, she rushed to Sara's apartment wishing there was a way to turn the tables on this woman, to give her a taste of the terror and intimidation she'd meted out to Valerie and others. But she'd gladly forgo everything just to keep Sara and Charlie safe. Her only hope was that Jordan somehow guessed what happened when she slipped out of the building and would come. But it was a slim hope.

She stopped at the door, knocked briefly, then waited with her heart beating in fear. In a moment, the bolt was shot, the lock turned, and the door opened.

"Sara . . ." Valerie's knees almost buckled in relief. Her daughter was alive. Sara's eyes were red-rimmed and she looked terrified, but she was alive. Maternal instinct brought her arms open for a fierce embrace.

"Be careful, Valerie." Beyond Sara, Charlie sat in a chair, his wrists locked behind him and bound with silver duct tape. With a tilt of his head, he indicated a presence concealed to his left. "She's got a gun and I think she'll use it."

Valerie stepped into the foyer, her hand on the door behind her, but not quite closing it.

"Cute, Caroline." A petite blond stepped from the shadows of the living room into full view. The gun in her hand was leveled at Valerie and Sara. "Sara, lock up," she ordered.

Without a word, Sara shot the chain lock and turned the dead bolt.

"Good girl." Then, with a gleefully terrible smile, she threw her arms wide, looked directly at Valerie, and said, "Surprise!"

It was Amy Trent.

CHAPTER TWENTY-EIGHT

"My God," Valerie whispered in disbelief. "Amy? Is that you? I thought—I never dreamed—"

"Yeah, I didn't die. Sorry." She gave a nonchalant shrug and then the smile vanished and a hard-faced, bitter woman emerged. "Not that you ever bothered to check."

Valerie still struggled to believe her own eyes. Amy Trent had died on the floor of that warehouse over twenty years ago. How could she be here now? Then it dawned on her. "Are you A.J.?"

"No, A.J. is me, you fool!" Using the gun, she waved Valerie to a chair across from Charlie and sat casually between them. "This has been so much fun that I'm almost sorry it has to end. The truth is, Roxanne was getting a little too suspicious."

"What was so much fun, Amy? I'm trying to understand what this is all about." She glanced at Sara, standing anxiously apart, and wished to be able to reassure her. But it was better for Sara to keep her distance as the gun was pointed at Valerie. If it went off, she didn't want Sara to be hurt.

Amy settled back, crossing her legs and resting the gun on her knee as casually as if balancing a cup and saucer at a tea. "Haven't you guessed it yet, Caroline? You've had a cushy life all these years, thanks to me. You tried to kill me so you could steal my baby. And because of you my life was ruined."

A small sound came from Sara. She had her fingertips pressed hard to her mouth and her blue eyes were wide with bewilderment and terror. She looked in anguish at Valerie. "What is she talking about, Mom?"

"Yeah, Mom," Amy said sardonically, "we're all waiting to hear what you tell her."

Valerie longed to get up and put her arms around Sara, to tell her about the night she was born, about the fear and squalor and guilt and pain. But it was too late now. Unless a miracle happened, her daughter's life, as well as Charlie's and her own, might end here at the hands of this madwoman.

"Why are you doing this, Amy? You know I didn't steal your baby. I helped you give birth that night. Your baby would have died if I hadn't been there."

"Helped me? You helped me?" Amy's face twisted into a mask of hatred, but her eyes were bright with tears. "I went to an *institution*, to Mandeville, did you know that, Caroline? I was so miserable after you *helped* me that I turned to drugs. I sold them and I sold myself and when I became a liability instead of a cash cow for that bastard, Oscar, he used his connection to a junky doctor to frame me. That's how you helped me, Caroline."

"I'm so sorry, Amy. I never meant any of this to happen." Mandeville was the state mental hospital north of New Orleans. It would have been hell on earth to be confined there.

"No one would help me," Amy wailed, wiping her eyes with one hand. "I even called my father. I begged him. I promised to do better if he'd send me a ticket to fly home. Because he owed me, Caroline, you know that. He *owed* me. But like you, he wanted me dead and buried. His own daughter." Her lips twisted with bitterness. "I wasn't his sweet little girl anymore."

"If only I'd known—"

"You didn't want to know, Caroline!" Anger flashed, bright and sharp. "It was too convenient to think I was dead, beyond needing anything from you. Well, think about this: How would you feel if you suffered through a difficult birth as I did with Sara, then woke up in a back room of some sleazy abortion mill? That's where Oscar took me when he realized I wasn't dead after all. He couldn't go to a real hospital. First thing they'd ask is where's the baby. This woman has just given birth. So he used his connections—" she made quotation marks with one hand, "and took me to this dirty hole in the wall somewhere in the Quarter that he used when his whores got knocked up or infected with nasty shit. There wasn't even a doctor there, just a nurse who resented having to get up in the middle of the night."

Amy seemed to have forgotten the gun in the flood of memories. "As soon as I had the strength, I asked for my baby, but they kept making excuses, promising I'd see him, lying because they knew I'd never see him. Ever." She stopped, shooting a look of hatred at Valerie. "I thought my baby was a boy for years, did you know that, Caroline? When I finally found out, Oscar laughed, telling me it didn't matter what sex it was since I'd never get my hands on the kid anyway." She stroked the barrel of the gun almost lovingly. "Oscar. Such a sweetheart."

"He was a despicable human being," Valerie murmured.

Amy looked at her. "Do you know what it does to a

woman when she gives birth and is denied her baby? It
screws her all up, Caroline. It makes her crazy. That's
certainly what happened to me. Oscar took me back to
his place after a couple of miserable days and I lay there
in the deepest, darkest misery you can imagine. I don't
remember eating or sleeping or even breathing, I was
so devastated. He got medicine from somewhere when
my temperature went sky high, but after a while he
wanted me back on the streets." Her eyes filled again.
"But I was sick, Caroline. Sick with grief and misery and
with rage, too." Her tone hardened again. "You don't
want to know how mad I was."

"It must have been hellish," Valerie said softly.

"Hellish." Amy considered that. "Yeah, 'cause the
place I wound up in had to be hell. I stayed alive by
focusing on how I intended to find my baby and then
to have my revenge on everybody who had been a part of
stealing her from me. Of course, that kind of obsession is
a road to nowhere. Next thing I knew, Oscar had carted
me off to the funny farm."

Beyond commenting, Valerie made a painful sound.

"Yeah, it was pretty awful," Amy said, sighting Valerie
now down the barrel of the gun. "Being locked away
can really do some damage to a person, you know? But
I survived because I held the image of my baby in my
head and planned my revenge. Everybody was going to
pay for the shit that had been done to me." She seemed
to shake off the darkness. Her spine straightened and
her shoulders squared. "I figure I've got nothing to lose
by just killing everybody in this room except Sara."

"Amy, you had help once before. Don't you think
you might need—" Valerie started to her feet, but in
a heartbeat Amy lifted the gun and pointed it directly
at Valerie again.

"No, you're the one who's going to need help," Amy
said with a harsh laugh. Her story done, the madness

had returned. "You may think you've fooled everyone, but I know who you really are and soon the whole world will know, too. Your golden life will be over when your precious friends—all those professional types—find out everything about you is a lie. Wait'll they find out Judge Martindale was your stepfather and you watched him murder a man in cold blood then lied to keep him out of jail. Oh, he denied everything today when I showed up with my gun, but I knew the truth. After all, I had a firsthand account from the eye witness, namely you, Caroline."

"I don't understand why you had to kill him." Valerie managed not to reveal the horror she felt.

"Because he was there. He's part of an evil justice system and he had a connection to you." She shrugged. "He was an asshole. It's simple."

"And Janine?"

"She had it coming, too."

"How, Amy?" Valerie cried. "What possible reason could you have for murdering an old lady with Alzheimer's?" Valerie fought to control an impulse to fly at her, to bite and scratch and use her fists and make her hurt, to feel pain and fear, to exact some vengeance for the inhuman way she'd murdered Janine. "She saved my life and Sara's, Amy. She took us in when we had nobody. She was a saint! How dare you . . ."

"*I* was the person she should have saved!" Amy screamed, punching her chest with her finger. "*I* was the one who carried that baby for nine months, who put up with Oscar just to get food to eat and a place to sleep when all I wanted to do was die. Where was your precious Sister Janine when I needed all that?"

"She was in the Quarter begging us to let her help us," Valerie said fiercely. "Don't you dare deny that. It was because we were too stupid and stubborn and rebellious to accept help that was offered."

Amy tossed her head and lifted her chin defiantly. "Well, it's too late now. She paid for her sins of omission, and if she's so saintly, she's gone to her reward. Think of it this way, you don't have to make that fuckin' trip to Rose Haven a couple of times a week anymore."

Valerie put a hand on her stomach, which was rolling queasily. "You killed Angela LeBlanc, too?"

Another shrug. "She shouldn't have gotten mixed up in all this. She was in over her head. It was nothing personal. As for you—" She stood up suddenly. "It *is* personal, Caroline. You tossed away your name and your life and you took mine. You think you can do that? You think you can just grab another person's name and baby and assume that person's life and there will be no consequences? You can just run off to New York or Boston or . . . or Timbuktu and everything becomes peachy-keen?"

"Oscar was going to get rid of your body and the baby," Valerie insisted, trying desperately to reason with her. "I thought you were dead, Amy, so I took the baby, and yes, I ran. I ran as far as I could that night because if I hadn't, there would be no baby today. You've got to believe me, Amy."

"Bullshit."

"Stop! Stop it!" Both turned to look at Sara, who stood with both hands over her ears, her face contorted with horror. "Both of you," she said, her tone going quiet as her hands fell to her sides. "Just tell me this: Am I the baby you're both talking about?"

"Sara—" Valerie begun to rise, but Amy swung the gun around, forcing her back in the chair.

"Damn right, you're *my* baby," Amy said, not taking her eyes off Valerie. There was malicious pleasure in her voice as she said, "I'm your real mother and I think after twenty-three years, it's time for Sara and me to be reunited, don't you, Caroline?"

Calm, Valerie told herself. Stay calm. Try to reason with her. Amy had murdered four people in the last few weeks. She was teetering on the edge of a complete breakdown. It wouldn't take much to push her completely over the edge.

"How—" She cleared her dry throat. "How were you planning to be a part of Sara's life?" She darted a glance to Charlie. "You can see she's married now. You want her to be happy, don't you?"

"She'll be happy with me." Almost leisurely, she pointed the gun directly at Charlie, squinted one eye as if getting a good bead. Valerie held her breath.

Sara gasped, "No! Please, don't."

Charlie sat unmoving, holding Amy's gaze. His young features were sternly set.

"Nah, I'm not ready to kill him yet." Amy jerked her head in Charlie's direction. "Go over and keep him company, Sara. He earned it."

Sara rushed over to Charlie, dropping to her knees and slipping her arms around him, chair and all. She turned her face into his side, desperately resisting an urge to burst into hysterical tears. Valerie felt a fierce rush of love and pride. They were so brave and so young, so undeserving of this vicious fate.

Oh, Jordan, Jordan, I'm sorry.

"Speaking of Oscar," Amy said, studying the nails of her left hand, "did you know he was dead?"

It took a moment for Valerie to adjust to the abrupt switch to almost normal conversation. "Yes. I—Jordan read it in the newspaper the day he left New Orleans."

"Yeah, I happened to be with Oscar the day Jordan showed up. He was very impressive, all outraged on your behalf." She glanced at Charlie. "Those are prime genes, kid. You ought to be proud."

Still stonily silent, Charlie simply looked at her.

To draw her attention from Charlie and Sara, Valerie asked, "Did you have anything to do with his death?"

"Of course. It's like you said, he would have dumped my baby and me without a blink. He could only die once, which seems unfair considering the long list of grievances I had against Oscar."

"He victimized all of us, Amy. It wasn't just you."

"Yeah? Well, I didn't notice you spending any time on the street turning tricks or shoplifting for him or kicking drugs in a mental institution."

"How did he manage to have you committed? I can't believe a doctor would have treated you without asking some awkward questions."

She laughed cynically. "Questions like my real name? You're not the only one who knows how to fake an identity. You picked it up from Oscar, didn't you? Well, he made up some bogus shit for me, but as soon as I got out, I—unlike you—resumed my real name."

"Didn't the doctor know you'd given birth recently? Didn't he ask what had happened to the baby?"

Amy shrugged. "Oscar said it died."

Valerie was shocked. "What kind of doctor was he that he just accepted that, no questions asked?"

Amy was shaking her head while the gun bobbed on her knee. "You're still the same naive, bleeding heart you've always been. Some things never change." She leaned forward and said with patience, "The shrink was a junkie himself, Caroline, get it? Oscar was his source for drugs. He was happy to do a favor if it meant an unending supply of nose candy. Same as the dirtbag doctor who treated me the night I gave birth. I only remember the jaded nurse, but she told me I'd almost bled to death and needed a transfusion. Somehow the doctor managed to put his hands on enough to pull me through." She shuddered. "I used to wake up in the middle of the night worrying about that blood.

Where did it come from? Who donated it? What if it
was tainted? Was I going to develop AIDS or become
HIV-positive? Get Hepatitis? How'd you like to live with
that fear for about seven years?" Her face changed as
she spoke, tightening around the mouth, becoming
hard and set. "But we don't have to worry about Oscar
anymore, do we? He won't hurt anybody ever again."

"Did you ever think of getting in touch with your
mother?" Valerie asked, desperate to delay whatever
Amy planned to do.

"Did you ever think of getting in touch with yours?"
Amy shot back.

"She died several years ago," Valerie said. Then a
ghastly thought struck. "According to the newspapers,
it was a carjacking."

A sly smile. "I know. It was my first attempt to square
things. Of course, I didn't know you were still estranged
from her or I might not have bothered."

"You killed my mother?" Valerie asked in disbelief.

Amy shrugged. "No need to thank me."

As Valerie sat in stunned silence, Sara asked, "Who
was my father?"

"It wasn't Oscar." Amy turned and scanned Sara's
face almost clinically. "Just a guy. Not as prime as this
one." She hitched her chin at Charlie. "But he wasn't
dog meat either."

Sara looked at her with disgust, but said nothing.
Valerie, still reeling, managed to say, "You knew who
it was?" She'd always believed it was impossible to know
who'd impregnated Amy considering the number of
Johns she serviced for Oscar.

"Remember Jack?"

"Jack, the artist who did those fabulous impressionist
paintings in Jackson Square?"

"Yeah, that Jack."

"Did he know?" Sara asked, but her interest now was almost clinical. "Did you ever tell him?"

Amy shook her head. "What was the point? He was in no shape to do anything, like take us in. He was only in New Orleans for the summer. He was going to Paris as soon as he scraped together the money for airfare."

"Do you know his last name?" In spite of herself, there was color in Sara's cheeks now. She'd always longed to know her father's identity. Valerie wondered if they survived today, would her relationship with Sara be destroyed by the Pandora's box of secrets and lies that Amy had purposely ripped open.

Amy looked disgusted. "No, I don't know his last name and besides, you don't need him. You'll have me after this is done."

"What are you going to do?" Sara burst out. "You can't kill my mother or Charlie. I can't love you. I don't know you."

Charlie jerked against the tape binding his hands behind him. "Honey, it's okay. Just try to be calm, please. Remember the baby."

"Baby?" Amy stood up abruptly, holding the gun in both hands, pointing it at Valerie. "Nobody said anything about a baby. I—"

She stopped at the sound of a knock on the door. Valerie's heart jumped. If it was Jordan, he would be walking into a deadly situation. She sat frozen as Amy moved into the foyer and stood not in front of the door, but at one side, the gun in both hands raised in a police-like stance.

"Sara? It's Roxanne. Let me in, honey."

"Shit!" Amy lowered the gun and stood for a moment in indecision. Then she motioned to Sara, who stood up and after giving Charlie a loving caress on his cheek, walked slowly to the door.

"You want me to open it?" she asked Amy.

Amy made a sarcastic face, wagging her head and stretching her thin mouth into a grimace-like smile. "Yes, I want you to open it." She then dropped all pretense of sarcasm and humor. "And don't try anything, you hear me?"

"Yes."

Valerie felt another surge of love and pride as Sara calmly dismantled the locks and coolly opened the door.

After a startled moment, Roxanne rushed in. "Sara, thank God, I was afraid—" She stopped, put her hand on her forehead, and took a deep breath. "You'll think I'm crazy, but I had this wild notion that you might be . . . umm, not okay."

She noticed Sara's silence then and quickly darted a glance beyond her to the living room. She blinked in shock when she saw Charlie bound in the chair. She turned back then and gasped as Amy, chuckling, kicked the door closed. Sara slipped back to be near Charlie.

"Now the gang's all here." Amy motioned with the gun. "Join the party, Rox. It's always more fun when you're in a good mood, of course, and I can see by that gloomy look on your face that you're not really up today, am I right?"

"What are you doing, A.J.?" Rox demanded, her tone rising with alarm. "Is that a gun?"

"Looks like a gun," Amy said, lifting it in a mock examination. "Feels like a gun, probably shoots like a gun." Again, she took a bead on Charlie. And again she shifted it away, chuckling as he stared her down.

"Oh, my God, what's happening?" Roxanne looked at Valerie, whose head moved briefly, negatively.

"What took you so long, darling?" Moving close, she lifted herself on tiptoe and kissed Roxanne's cold, unresponsive mouth. The difference in their height made Amy seem almost juvenile. But there was nothing childish in the smile as she stepped back and motioned

Roxanne into the living room with everyone else. "I told you I had something special planned for tonight, didn't I?"

"Mr. Case, I understand your concern, but we can't just go barging into your son's apartment. I want you to wait for me down here and I'll call you as soon as I check everything out."

Detective Sorensen stood inside the elevator holding it open. It was his intent to hold Jordan in the lobby of the building while he checked out the situation in 4C, but once the elevator closed and Sorensen headed up, he suspected Jordan would go charging up the four flights of stairs.

"There's a crazy woman in that apartment," Jordan said. "I can name four people she's murdered, three of them in the last two days! I'm not waiting around while a tangle of red tape gives her time to kill my son or his pregnant wife and the woman I love."

Sorensen sighed. "You haven't produced any proof that she's a killer, Mr. Case. Hell, you don't even know that she's in the apartment."

Jordan shoved his hands in his pockets to keep them from grabbing Sorensen's throat. "My son was released from the hospital with a concussion yesterday. He's not at work. His car is parked there. On the street. So why isn't he answering his phone?"

"Maybe he's got a headache, Mr. Case. Maybe he's not taking any calls."

"From telemarketers, maybe, but not me. Something's going on in there, man!" He swung about, frustrated and terrified. While they argued, three people could be murdered by a psychotic. Why else was nobody—Valerie or Charlie or Sara—answering their phones?

"I'm going to have to insist that you let me handle this my way, Mr. Case." Sorensen had abandoned diplomacy. And he had the power.

"Fine. Do it your way." Jordan's gaze was as cold and implacable now as the detective's. "But I'm holding you personally responsible for what happens."

Without waiting for Sorensen's reply, he stalked off.

Two police vehicles were parked well down the street out of sight of Charlie's windows. Fortunately, Sorensen had agreed with Jordan that by converging on the scene, if A.J. was inside and was somehow a threat to Valerie and the kids, seeing a show of force might push her over the edge.

Jordan reached a narrow alley separating the apartment building and its neighbor. When passing the day he and Valerie had surprised Charlie and Sara, he'd noticed a fire escape. Checking that nobody watched, he turned into the alley.

Looking up, he realized it would be a long climb.

As he stood contemplating four flights and wrestling with a longtime fear of heights, he knew it was the only possible way to get inside the apartment without spooking the psychotic who threatened his family. Stretching both arms out, fingers locked, he flexed his shoulders. Then, dropping hands to his sides, he limbered up and took a deep breath.

He caught the ladder on the first try. Incredibly, none of the cops had checked the side of the building, so no one was around to object as he started up the four flights.

He was sweating by the time he climbed twelve stairs. Midway to the second landing, he made the mistake of looking down. His stomach was in a knot and his hands were cold and clumsy. Already he was aware that most of the windows in the apartments he passed on the way up were shuttered and locked. That was a problem he'd deal with when he got there.

If he got there.

He chanted names in his head: Charlie, Sara, Valerie. People he loved, needed. People who were necessary to give him joy and completeness.

At the third landing, he made a misstep and grabbed frantically at the side rail. Scrambling to find firm footing, he fought panic and a compelling urge to look down, certain disaster. It was too late to abort this plan. All that remained when he reached Charlie's place was to figure how to get inside.

"A.J., you've got to give me that gun." There was a tremor in Roxanne's voice as she put out a shaky hand. "You don't want to hurt these people, do you? These are my friends." She managed a wobbly smile while her eyes were terrified. "Sara's so dear to me, Amy. She's special, almost the daughter I never had, I told you that, remember?"

Amy wagged the forefinger of her left hand and smiled evilly. "But I didn't tell you about my special relationship with Sara, did I? She's almost yours, but since I gave birth to her, she's wholly mine, Rox."

"What?"

"I'm her mother, stupid!"

Roxanne was shaking her head. "You can't—That isn't possible. She—" Again, she sought out Valerie and saw the truth in her eyes. "Oh, my God."

The buzz of the doorbell silenced everyone. Amy stood with her back to the wall, her eyes darting from one to another of her victims. "We aren't answering that," she snapped.

"I'm not feeling very well," Sara said suddenly. Still

on her knees beside Charlie's chair, she pressed both hands to her stomach.

The doorbell buzzed again, followed by an authoritative voice. "Police, Mr. Case. Open up!"

"Do you want me to answer?" Charlie asked quietly.

"How, dickhead?" Amy wagged her head in disgust. "You think I'm going to cut that tape and let you walk over and answer the door?"

"Do something for my wife," Charlie told her.

"Like what? Let her walk out and ask the cops for a ride to the ER? I don't think so."

"Let her go to the window. The nausea passes if she can breathe a little fresh air."

"This is the police! Open up, Mr. Case!"

"I—I'm going to throw up," Sara said, putting the back of her hand to her forehead.

"Oh, for God's sake! Go to the window," Amy said in disgust and immediately refocused her attention on the police at the door. Sara rose and rushed to the window, a long, old-fashioned single-pane style. Cold air rushed in as she pushed it open.

"Last chance, Mr. Case! We're going to bust your door."

The gun wavered as Amy stood trying to decide what to do. She raked an unsteady hand through her hair, then motioned to Valerie, who stood up from the sofa. "Tell them I've got four hostages in here and I'll kill everyone if they don't back off."

Valerie rose slowly. Amy seemed more and more agitated, and the clumsy attempt to force entry by the police was not helping. "Amy, you don't want to hurt anybody else. You're a good person. You need a doctor."

"Go to the door, damn you!" Amy screamed.

Wordlessly, Valerie held up her hands and moved cautiously past her, but before she reached the door, Charlie suddenly came to his feet like a grizzly bear coming awake. The tape binding his wrists was cut jaggedly and hung in bloody strips. With a ferocious yell, he hurled his chair across the room at Amy. Caught off guard, she had no time to think. She went down hard when the chair struck her at the knees. But she still held the gun. Then Jordan charged in through the open window, and when he straightened up, he had a gun in his hand.

He leveled it at Amy, gripping it with both hands. "Give it up, Amy, and nobody will get hurt."

A gasp went up when she suddenly put the gun beneath her own chin. "This was my idea," she said fiercely. Her eyes darted ferally around the room, marking each person. "It's for me to say when it's over."

"Think of Sara," Valerie said in a desperate voice. "You were not able to be near her as a baby, and if you do this, you won't ever get to see your grandchild."

"He won't be my grandchild," Amy said bitterly. "He's yours. Sara's yours. Everything's yours and I've got nothing, nothing . . . nothing . . ." Still on the floor, she threw the gun away and with an anguished wail pitched forward, covering her head with both arms, crying in abject misery. Valerie started forward, but Roxanne stopped her and went to Amy, dropping to her knees beside her. With a soft sound, she wrapped her arms around her and began rocking her, murmuring soothing, meaningless words. Sara, giving them a wide berth, went once more to the door, unlocked it, and admitted the police. Then she turned and stumbled blindly into Charlie's arms, weeping out her shock and terror and relief.

CHAPTER
TWENTY-NINE

Amy Trent was taken by ambulance to a psychiatric hospital. Roxanne asked to accompany her and, after pleading with the officials, was finally allowed to go. Detective Sorensen took preliminary statements from everyone and agreed, when Jordan asked, that they could come in the next day for more complete questioning. But with Martindale dead and Amy in a psychotic state, details of Valerie's past would probably remain a mystery except to those closest to her.

Valerie was still too upset to sit after the police and paramedics left, so she headed to the kitchen to make coffee, although everyone looked as if they could all use something much stronger. Sara followed her.

"I can do it, Mom."

"You just sit, Sara. For the sake of the baby."

Sara smiled, her hand going instinctively to her still-flat tummy. "The baby's fine, Mom. Don't worry."

Instant tears flooded Valerie's eyes, blinding her to the coffee carafe in her hands. She shut off the water

and looked at her daughter. "You must have a million
questions," she said.

"I do, Mom."

For a moment, Valerie simply looked into the blue,
blue eyes so like Amy's. Many times, she'd been struck
by Sara's resemblance to her birth mother and she'd
always felt glad. She'd liked being reminded of her debt
to Amy, had taken pleasure through the years of imagining Amy's pride in Sara if only she could have known
her. How long, she wondered, before she forgot this
hour when she saw that likeness now?

"She was too deeply wounded, Sara," Valerie said,
looking beyond her daughter into the past. "She was
like a kitten taken away from its mother too soon. She
was needy and delicate. Fragile." Shaking her head, she
looked down at her hands. "I just never realized how
fragile."

"I think that was obvious today, Mom," Sara said
gently, touching Valerie's arm. "My questions aren't
about her. I don't know her, and even if you remembered everything about the time you were together as
street kids, it wouldn't mean much in light of all that's
happened since you walked away from that lifestyle,
would it?"

"I suppose not."

Taking the carafe from Valerie, Sara filled it with
water and set about making the coffee. She moved con-
fidently in her tiny kitchen, finally taking a hand-painted
dish towel from a drawer to wipe up a few drops of
water. Pausing suddenly, she studied the art on the towel
and gave a soft laugh. "Well, now we know where my
artistic gene came from, don't we?"

"Do you want to try and find Jack?" Valerie asked.
"It would be possible, I think. He was very talented.
He's certain to have made it in the art world."

"Maybe I will. Later. And I'll save my questions for

later, too, Mom." She leaned over and kissed Valerie's cheek. "But for now, at this particular moment in time, I just want to tell you I love you and to thank you for what you did that night. Unlike many babies born under those circumstances, I luckily fell into your hands."

"You're not shocked by everything you heard tonight?"

"Sure. Who wouldn't be? And impressed, too. Soon we'll get together and I'll ask all those questions. But not tonight."

Valerie touched her daughter's cheek, tucked a blond strand behind her ear, and then pulled her into a loving embrace. "I loved you from the moment I first saw you," she said fiercely. "And I wouldn't change anything, Sara. I'm the lucky one. As frightening and desperate as those days were, I wound up with a precious gift."

"And so did I, Mom."

In spite of the horror of the past hour, Valerie felt a deep gladness. There would be many complications if and when her true identity was known. Whether it would impact upon her career didn't matter to her now. She would deal with the consequences of actions taken when she was fifteen years old when they happened.

For Sara, it was another matter. With so little family, and knowing Sara's hunger as a child for blood relatives, it wouldn't surprise Valerie if she wanted a relationship with both Emilie Trent and Jack, her father. It would be up to Sara to decide. The important thing was that Valerie would always be her mother.

"Hey, what's going on in here?"

"Charlie." Stepping free, Sara blinked back tears and slipped an arm around her husband's waist. "We're making coffee. Want some?"

"After what we've just been through, I think I prefer beer." He kissed the top of Sara's head. "I also want to toast my wife's quick thinking in sawing through the duct tape around my wrists."

"How did you manage that?" Jordan asked, coming up behind Charlie.

"Nail scissors. I was doing my nails when Amy arrived. They were in plain sight on the coffee table. Later, when she was busy venting all that stuff, I slipped them in my pocket. The real problem was getting close enough to Charlie to use them."

"You weren't really sick, were you?" Charlie asked.

She gave him a quick smile. "How did you know?"

"Well, from the moment you started having nausea in this pregnancy, you never had time to do that little act you put on tonight." He rolled his eyes back and threw his hand up to his forehead. "I'm not feeling well," he said in falsetto tones, winking at his dad. "I think I'm going to throw up!"

"Stop it," she said, bumping his shoulder. "I wasn't that bad."

"So how come when you're really ready to hurl, it's so fast you barely make it to the bathroom?"

"I had to think of a way to get to the window," she said primly.

"And I'm eternally grateful to you," Jordan said, rubbing a hand over his face at the memory. "Another minute at that altitude and I would have just kicked in the window."

"Dad, I never knew you were afraid of heights."

"It's not something you tell your kids, Charlie. Are you going to admit to yours that you have a fear of spiders?"

Charlie's expression was comical. "Point taken."

Valerie watched Sara arrange coffee cups and the carafe on a tray, then followed her into the living room. "I just have one question," she said, filling a cup and handing it to Jordan. "Where did you get the gun?"

Jordan paused to let Charlie liberally spike the coffee with whiskey. "From your trusty assistant."

"Eric?" Valerie said in disbelief.

Jordan drained the cup in one swallow, then stood up. "He told me he started carrying after that hostile visit from Ted Carpenter."

"That's amazing," Valerie murmured.

"You can tell him for me that I'm personally guaranteeing him a raise," Jordan said as he reached for Valerie's coat. "Are you ready to go home?"

"Home," Charlie repeated with a gleam in his eye as he surveyed his dad and his mother-in-law. "And where would that be . . . just in case Sara or I decide to drop in?"

"Valerie's place . . . for the moment," Jordan said, nudging her toward the door. "And wish me luck."

"Luck?" Both Charlie and Sara looked curious.

"Yeah," Jordan said, pulling the door open and ushering Valerie out. "One of us will be moving if I can talk Val into marrying me."

"That ought to give them a taste of their own medicine," Jordan muttered as he punched the button in the elevator to the lobby. "Springing marriage and then pregnancy on us like an afterthought. Two can play that game."

Marriage. To Jordan. The light-headed sensation she was feeling had nothing to do with the elevator. "Were you serious?" she asked.

He turned then and looked at her. "As a heart attack." His face changed and he gave a wry smile. "I guess it wasn't a very romantic proposal, was it?" Reaching out, he ran his knuckles lightly along the line of her cheek. "You already know I'm in love with you.

I think I know all your secrets now." He bent slightly at the knees to look her in the eye. "Don't I?"

"Yes."

"Good. So, will you do me the honor of becoming my wife?"

"Jordan—"

"Charlie's not the only man in this family who gets a second chance, is he?"

She stood looking into his eyes, feeling a glorious rush of warmth and delight. The elevator pinged. "Are you sure?"

He slapped a hand over the Close Door button. "I just spent the last few hours being terrified that I might lose the three people who mean most to me in the world," he said. "A man tends to get his priorities straight after that. So, yes, I'm sure. I've never been more sure of anything, Val."

"Neither of us has a very good track record with relationships."

"Neither of us has had the right partner in a relationship, that's why." He waited, studying her face intently as if waiting for something more. The elevator alarm went off.

She ignored it and smiled. "I don't know about you, but lately my taste has improved considerably." She put her arms around his neck and raised her mouth to his. "I love you, Jordan."

He released a huge sigh and the elevator button at the same time, then wrapped both arms around her as the doors slid open. Neither of them noticed.